The Author worked with an insurance broker with Lloyd's of London handling claims worldwide. On retirement he spent nigh on six years with two companies handling their claims.

Masthead Lookout

I dedicate this book to all shipmates who gave their lives escorting the convoys to the U.S.S.R. Also, to the men from *HMS Saumarez* and *HMS Volage* who were killed in the Corfu Channel.

On a happier note, I include in my dedication my dear wife, the beautiful young girl from Lam Lash.

Geoff Shelton

MASTHEAD LOOKOUT

Copyright © Geoff Shelton

The right of Geoff Shelton to be identified as author of this work has been asserted by him in accordance with section 77 and 78 of the Copyright, Designs and Patents Act 1988.

All rights reserved. No part of this publication may be reproduced, stored in a retrieval system, or transmitted in any form or by any means, electronic, mechanical, photocopying, recording, or otherwise, without the prior permission of the publishers.

Any person who commits any unauthorized act in relation to this publication may be liable to criminal prosecution and civil claims for damages.

A CIP catalogue record for this title is available from the British Library.

ISBN 978 184963 368 0

www.austinmacauley.com

First Published (2013)
Austin Macauley Publishers Ltd.
25 Canada Square
Canary Wharf
London
E14 5LB

Printed and Bound in Great Britain

Foreword

Sixty years ago, I wrote a book based on my personal experiences whilst serving in the Royal Navy between 1943 and 1947. I used to spend half an hour a day, five days a week, endeavouring to recall events and times and people. It took me five years to complete.

During the war, all service personnel were instructed not to keep diaries. I complied with that order, but was amazed that the post war period produced a host of biographies by Admirals, Generals and Air Marshals giving such details that could only have come from a well-kept diary, however, the book to which I refer relied on nothing more than memory. I can confirm the accuracy of the general account, it could and may be faulted on specific items. I apologise in advance for this, and though memory or lack of it may contribute to such errors, by far the main cause was because we in the lower deck did not know. We were not told everything, and what little knowledge we did acquire came from mess deck buzzes.

Two years after my retirement, I came across this rough, handwritten document of memories lying in a wooden crate in the loft. As I thumbed through the yellowing pages, so the years rolled away, the joys, the fears, the ships and seas, the wounded and dying, the sorrow and love. It was all there, and in fact would still be there, except that in 1991 I watched a report on television concerning a party of veteran sailors who were going to Murmansk in September to celebrate the fiftieth anniversary of the first convoy to North Russia. A sudden reawakening created a desire in me to attend. A period of my life was being resurrected, and I wanted to be a part of it. The emotional effect this visit had on me is recorded elsewhere, but suddenly I had this desire to share with others my old journal. The first twelve pages were missing, but it only covered my joining up in December 1943 at *HMS Collingwood*, a shore based training establishment at Fareham near Portsmouth. I was an eighteen year old youth who had never been away from home, and though the pangs of homesickness sometimes visited me during the hours of darkness, we were kept very busy on the parade ground, also learning knots and splices, the flag signals, the points of the compass, rifle drill, firing, gunnery quick loading and breech loading, swinging the lead, and ammunition.

We had route marches, physical training and guard duty. A run ashore was generally confined to Fareham, and a visit to any one of numerous taverns. Being eighteen, this was now quite a unique experience and one which allowed you to enjoy all the comforts that a roaring fire, horse hair seats, wallpaper, pictures on the walls and lampshades would provide. The cold inhospitable barracks devoid of heating with rows of double-tiered iron beds was not a place you wanted to stay in. We had a NAAFI canteen that was bright and sociable, and also a cinema, where occasionally ENSA put on live shows. It was said that Flanagan and Allen played there one night because Flanagan's son was one of the trainees.

Three months I spent there among a mixture of men from all walks of life and from all over the country, and yet just one sticks out in my mind. He was a miner from Newcastle, who I believe had recently come out of prison. I found him to be a real character who I was proud to know. The biggest surprise was the authorities allowing him to leave the mines – you see, there was a shortage of miners and Ernest Bevin was taking some lads due for call up down the mines. They were known as the Bevin Boys. I, however, had always wanted to be in in the Royal Navy.

My great grandfather was a sea captain in the previous century, and two of my uncles who I hero worshipped were in the Royal Navy, so to ensure Mr Bevin did not side track me, I joined the 'Y' scheme. It was a scheme where you had to pass certain exams, and once qualifying it meant that not only would you be called up on your eighteenth birthday, but it also meant that you would be considered for training for a commission. The penalty was that your classmates were, after three months, sent home on leave, while you were denied this luxury and were sent to a training ship. The thought of going to sea filled me with joy, and especially so soon after training I had no fears or apprehensions. This, then, covers those twelve missing pages, and we pick up the story by joining *HMS Corinthian.*

Contents

Chapter 1
HMS Corinthian.. 19

Chapter 2
Royal Naval Barracks, Portsmouth 23

Chapter 3
HMS Cabot and HMS Valkyrie 27

Chapter 4
Whale Island 32

Chapter 5
HMS Vindex 38

Chapter 6
Up The Stick 48

Chapter 7
Vaenga Bay 52

Chapter 8
First Love 61

Chapter 9
Shipboard Humour 66

Chapter 10
A Winter Convoy 75

Chapter 11
There Is Always Someone Worse Off 81

Chapter 12
Refit 83

Chapter 13
Post Refit Activities **92**

Chapter 14
Nobby **107**

Chapter 15
Meeting Up With A Convoy **109**

Chapter 16
Going Home **112**

Chapter 17
April 1945 .... **114**

Chapter 18
VE Day **128**

Chapter 19
Hospital **133**

Chapter 20
HMS Croziers **143**

Chapter 21
HMS Mauritius **153**

Chapter 22
Gibraltar **165**

Chapter 23
Malta **174**

Chapter 24
Crete **183**

Chapter 25
Cyprus **190**

Chapter 26
Trieste **197**

Chapter 27
Palestine **215**

Chapter 28
Fleet Exercises **227**

Chapter 29
Corfu **244**

Chapter 30
Minefield **248**

Chapter 31
Fleet Regatta **255**

Chapter 32
Twenty-First Birthday **266**

Chapter 33
Cortina D'ampezzo **274**

Chapter 34
Homeward Bound **294**

Chapter 35
Demobilisation **305**

Chapter 1

HMS Corinthian

With a party of other lads, we made our way from Portsmouth to Edinburgh, and finally to the dockyard at Rosyth. *HMS Corinthian* was an old coal-burning armed merchant cruiser. She was nothing spectacular to look at, but that did not matter. She was going to sea, and I was joining her.

The forward hold had been converted to a mess deck, and after the usual formalities of joining, we took our kitbag and hammock to our new home. I soon realised that while I had used the 'Y' scheme to ensure my entry into the Royal Navy, the Royal Navy had viewed it from a different perspective – namely, the purpose of the 'Y' scheme was to have a pool that could be used for the training of young men to become commissioned Officers. The idea certainly appealed to me, but it was more the glamour of the uniform than the responsibilities that went with it that decreed my enthusiasm. We were referred to as CW (Commission Worthy) candidates, but time would tell as to just how worthy we were.

Discipline was strict, and what little time we had to ourselves was spent in studying. We put to sea, and while steaming down the Firth of Forth I with the other lads were instructed to chip, wire scrub and grease the upper deck. It was a noisy and somewhat smelly task, but even before we had left the land behind, I was hanging over the ship's side feeling ill and sick, thoroughly dispirited and wondering why. Why had I joined? What on earth had possessed me to join the Navy?

The ship was devoid of any degree of privacy. The heads were on the upper deck, running athwart ship. There were no doors to the cubicles and one merely sat there either talking to the one sitting in front of you, or trying to avoid the gaze of a fellow shipmate desperate to occupy your toilet. The embarrassment and the indignity of this experience has never left me.

At six o'clock each morning, in bare feet, we scrubbed the decks. The North Sea in March is a very cold place. There was no escape from the icy winds, and the pumps merely succeeded in gushing the seawater over our already frozen feet.

After breakfast we scrubbed and cleaned the paintwork, and then there was more chipping and wire scrubbing and greasing. I was reminded of the old naval saying:

"If you see anything, pick it up,
If you cannot pick it up, then paint it,
If it moves, then salute it."

This was so very true of *HMS Corinthian.*

We did, of course, have instruction classes, but one day in an exercise to establish initiative and leadership, three smoke floats were thrown overboard. They then filled three 32 foot cutters with oarsmen, and quite out of the blue the boat Officer picked on me to be the coxswain of one of them. I had had experience of boat training in the Sea Scouts, but there is quite a difference between four boys in a gig on the River Thames, and sixteen plus youths on a cutter in the middle of the North Sea. It was blowing hard, the seas were rough and the *Corinthian* was rolling so much that as we were being lowered, we started to swing like a pendulum. I ordered the port oars out and instructed them to use the looms of their oars to bear off from the ship's side. This worked extremely well until some idiot got the loom of his oar stuck in an exit pipe. The boat was in turmoil, and then she swung against the ship's hull and smashed the starboard gunwale from bow to stern. This did not delay our departure, because the next thing was "Out pins" and releasing the disengaging gear. With two lads on each sweep, we pulled away from the ship and headed for the smoke floats. The sea was rough and the troughs were like being at the bottom of a basin. The only time we could see the ship or the smoke floats was when we rose to the crest of a wave. We eventually recovered two of the floats and made our return.

We took part in a night exercise with *HMS Diamede* and *HMS Dauntless*, both of which were also used for training purposes. The sky was illuminated with star shells and they kept us up all night. We were getting experience, so they said.

Once every four weeks, we put into Leith where we went alongside and coaled ship. We were not allowed to wear overalls during this exercise, but had to wear our number threes. The coal was dropped out of railway wagons from a great height, resulting in coal dust going everywhere. The boats, the deck, the winches, the capstans, the guns, the bridge, our clothes, our eyes, our lungs and nostrils – everything was covered in coal dust. No one was allowed ashore until every particle had been removed and all paint work scrubbed down. When this had been accomplished, it was a matter of personal hygiene with a shower and the washing of clothes, but with all our efforts, the smell of coal dust lingered with us.

One weekend, we were given three days leave. This was my first leave in over four months and though I didn't know it at the time, it was going to be the last for many months. I arrived home early one Saturday morning, which was a surprise to my parents because I hadn't told them I was at sea, but the weekend down south passed all too quickly and soon the train from London was speeding back to Edinburgh.

Our skipper was an unusual character. He had come out of retirement to take up this commission, and was often to be seen around ship with a cine camera, taking shots of the crew when they least expected it. On our return from leave, he called the ship's company together and informed us that due to D-Day being not too far away, all leave would be cancelled.

There was a cinema on board, but it was a somewhat Heath Robinson affair. The soundtrack was lacking in quality, but even that which we could hear was drowned by a Scotsman playing the bagpipes every night in the port waist.

We had tests every week and my favourable results endorsed the time and effort I had put into the various subjects.

After two months, the Captain sent for eight of us and told us we were not up to the standard they were looking for. I was absolutely devastated, and my spirits sank to a low ebb. I could not understand. We left the *Corinthian* the following day and I was instructed to lead this draft to *HMS Victory*, the Royal Naval Barracks at Portsmouth.

The train journey seemed to take an age, but all the while my mind was a turmoil of disappointment. I was confident in my ability, but as Robbie Burns said, 'O wad some pow'r the giftie to gie us to see ourselves as others see us.'

As my hopes and aspirations were in ruins around me, I tried to direct my mind into accepting the situation – maybe it was for the best. I finally reconciled my feelings by acknowledging my age; I was only eighteen, and if I had been commissioned I could easily have found myself responsible for battle-hardened veterans, responsible for their very lives, and me still wet behind the ears. How would I stand up to battle? I didn't know, and in any case the time spent in training for a commission means you would have less time at sea, and that is where I wanted to be.

I was possibly fooling myself, but it helped me to get over my disappointment.

Chapter 2

Royal Naval Barracks, Portsmouth

The Royal Naval Barracks at Portsmouth was comprised of huge sombre looking buildings that surrounded the parade ground. Under the parade ground was the Air Raid Shelter.

It has been said that the barracks had been condemned years before as being unfit for human habitation, but war changes authorities' views as to what is deemed to be fit, and so our little band of eight ex-CW candidates were absorbed into barrack life. Each floor of the building must have accommodated about five hundred men. If one arrived in a depressed state then these surroundings could only exacerbate the problem. Hammocks were slung from every available space, and when there was no space left, you slept on the tables or under the tables.

We all decided that the sooner we got out of this place the better, but how? Six of the lads decided that by volunteering for Defensively Armed Merchant Ships they would get out quickly, and another thought a Radar Mechanic would achieve the same object and possibly give him a trade in civilian life. As for myself I had formed the opinion that the discipline on the *Corinthian* was a blueprint used by all His Majesty's warships. Without therefore wishing to offend His Majesty I had no desire to spend my war washing and scrubbing decks in bare feet in the middle of the North Sea. I therefore thought that gunnery controlled radar had an appeal. We all put our names down for the course of our choice, though we did have a carrot dangled before us in that we could have a commission if we joined the Combined Services as Sub-lieutenants on infantry landing craft. I had visions of my head being the only thing visible to a Panzer division on some hostile foreign shore, and politely declined their most generous offer.

Our days in the barracks were varied. One day, a dozen of us were rushed to Hayling Island where a huge concrete caisson had broken adrift and we had been sent out to rescue it. We accomplished this without too much difficulty, but we didn't know what it was or what it was for, and only later did we learn it was part of the Mulberry harbour.

At nighttime, there were fire watching duties on the flat roofs of the barracks. They weren't always flat, but bomb and incendiary damage had been the cause of their current appearance. Many sailors were lost and it has been suggested that half charred pay books were found in the debris, leading the authorities to believe their owners had died, but there are those who say that many went over the wall never to be seen in uniform again.

There were nightly raids on Portsmouth, and when we weren't on duty we had to go to the labyrinth of passages beneath the parade ground. We were wedged in like sardines, while above us we could hear the firing of the anti-aircraft guns, and below the tremors and noise of exploding bombs. The walls of the shelter vibrated, dislodging dust and debris to add to the heat and smell of sweating bodies in such a claustrophobic atmosphere.

It was most noticeable how many local men were stationed in the barracks. Their families lived nearby and some of them had not seen a ship since the war began. It was as though they were all in a self-protective brotherhood, and yet on those rare occasions when one of the barrack room stanchions received a draft, it was as though their world had fallen apart.

The mess decks of a night-time were a hive of activity, the like of which could not be repeated elsewhere. It was constantly changing as the evening progressed. Slowly, the hammocks were slung, looking like huge white bats as every available space was used. The atmosphere became close and sweaty, small groups sat and smoked, played cards or yarned. Suddenly you would hear, "Olly olly olly. Hands down for the Kidley die." This was an indication that a game of Crown and Anchor was about to take place. The game is against King's Rules and Regulations, so for security, paid lookouts were posted at each door.

Throughout the night, men arrived in the mess from shore leave in various states of inebriation. Some were quiet, most were noisy, and some just wanted to vomit. They banged into hammocks, disturbing the occupants and bringing forth muttered oaths and curses. "Get your bloody head down," says one. "Cut the bleeding cackle," says another. It makes no difference to the one causing the disruption; he will probably trip over another sleeping on the deck, and fall into a drunken slumber.

With so many men about, a lot of pilfering took place, but there was little you could do about it.

There was a job going in the gymnasium which entailed being the odd job man and cleaner, so I managed to inveigle my way into it, mainly because you were out of the way and left to your own devices. I must say it was a bit of a come down by comparison with my previous abortive hopes and expectations, but I had already come to terms with that and had learnt to accept the cards destiny had laid down for me.

The gymnasium task only lasted for a few days because I received a draft chit to *HMS Cabot,* which was a land base – commonly known in the Royal Navy as a stone frigate – at Wetherby in Yorkshire. When I was on the *Corinthian*, the canteen frequently sold tins of jam and fruit as well as soap and other commodities not easily available in civvy street. I had bought as much as I could in order to give to my family when I was next on leave.

Unfortunately that leave did not materialise, which left me humping excess baggage around the countryside. As soon as I knew the travel arrangements to *Cabot*, I rang my parents and arranged to meet them at Waterloo Station.

On arrival at Waterloo, my father found a Regulating Petty Officer (RPO) who was most helpful, and he directed both my parents and my two younger brothers to the arrival platform. The Portsmouth train duly came in and all the sailors were immediately put on board lorries to be transported to Kings

Cross. The RPO, however, had not neglected his duties, because my father clambered up the tailboard to join the rest of the draft, while my mother and two brothers joined the driver.

Arriving at Kings Cross and with time to spare, I was able to slip away to a cafe with my family, and transfer the supplies that would help to eke out their meagre rations.

In no time at all we said our farewells and, with a much lighter kitbag, the train made its way north.

Chapter 3

HMS Cabot and HMS Valkyrie

Cabot exceeded all my expectations. There were cabins for two with curtains and wardrobes. This I felt was living in the lap of luxury and could so easily seduce me into abandoning youthful and foolish ideas of going to sea. In the draft with me was Wilf Gough, who was in his early thirties, and Dick Baldwin, who was about the same age as me. Wilf was from Halifax and Dick from London. They too were joining me on the Radar Gunnery Control course which was to be held on the Isle of Man.

Cabot turned out to be a training camp for potential chefs from the Navy and the WRNS. This meant that the food, its preparation and its variety was of the highest standard, and the fact that attractive young WRNS served out the food gave it a semblance of civilisation, a factor most previously noticeable by its absence.

There was, of course, a price to pay, and this was extracted from us by means of constant squad drilling, physical training and assault courses. I must confess I fell down lamentably on the latter.

Alas, our sojourn at *Cabot* lasted but three days. I believe the camp was closing down, so we bought as much of the NAAFI stores as we could afford and went on our way.

The draft was quite a big one and was more than the Chief Petty Officer in charge could handle.

We assembled at Leeds station, and in response to the calling out of our names, we answered in the affirmative and boarded the train. Unfortunately for the Chief, two teenage girls came onto the platform, and caused more chaos than could a Panzer division. With wise cracks passing to and fro intermingled with wolf whistles, the Chief lost all control. He, however, was not the only one to lose control, for suddenly the train doors opened, half a dozen sailors jumped out and picking the girls up bodily they carried them into the carriage. After about ten minutes, two tussled haired young ladies staggered onto the platform. Their clothes were in disarray, their make up was smeared, but nothing could disguise the broad grins that adorned both their faces, and yet somehow I felt it will be a long time before either will attempt to challenge a carriage full of matelots.

The train took us to Fleetwood where we boarded a ferry to Douglas in the Isle of Man and thence to *HMS Valkyrie,* another stone frigate.

All the old Victorian boarding houses that stretched along the front at Douglas had been requisitioned for the purposes of housing sailors taking the various Radar courses available. The parade ground was, in fact, part of the main road which ran between the houses and the sea. The near side lane had been utilised for this purpose, and it was separated from the shore side of the road by a huge fence topped with barbed wire. I shared a room with two other lads on the top floor of our boarding house and facing the sea.

The training establishment was at the top of Douglas Head which necessitated our marching there every morning.

We spent our shore leave in exploring the glens, visiting the huge wheel at Laxey and of course climbing Snez Fell, with Dick and I usually together on these jaunts. Sometime during the lunch period, we might slip out to a small restaurant and indulge ourselves. We also went to the small fishing village of Peel, but parts of the harbour area were sealed off – I believe due to the Irish fishing boats calling in. The Isle of Man gave the impression that it had escaped the rigours of rationing as experienced on the mainland. It was like a little backwater of tranquillity that the war seemed to have passed by.

The WRNS cooked the food and local ladies used to serve it out, but on Sundays we took care of ourselves, each mess taking a turn. When it came to our turn of duty, I was put in charge of the cake and butter. Very studiously I apportioned it according to the number of men, but by the end of Sunday night a mountain of food was left over, so I formed the opinion that the cause must be because so many were on shore leave, whereupon I distributed it to those who weren't ashore.

On Monday morning the ladies arrived but couldn't find the butter – apparently I had used up one week's ration in one day, but at least some of us were fortunate to have cake and butter in our rooms for the next week.

The Captain of the barracks was an odd sort of character. Every Saturday it was his custom to do the rounds, visiting every room. It was of course meant to be an inspection, but in one room he noticed that a piece of paper had been used to wedge a locker door shut. He pulled the paper, and the doors swung wide revealing a bottle of beer in all its glory. A bellow of rage suggested he was much displeased.

We had in our class a fellow who was just plain cussed and awkward. By all accounts, he had not elected to join this course, but had rather been ordered into it. His only means of expressing his views was to constantly fall sleep and to misinterpret the lessons being taught. Needless to say he failed, and we wondered whether his actions were motivated by his reluctance to go to sea.

The seagulls used to come and sit on the windowsill waiting for the lads to feed them. In short bursts they could be tolerated, but you reach the point when enough is enough and, sure enough, that day arrived. We filled a bucket of water and threw the contents over them. A chorus of rage came from below where the liberty men had fallen in for inspection. It was, however, the Officer of the Watch whose sodden uniform suggested he had received more than his ration.

We enjoyed glorious weather but in the mornings before breakfast the Physical Training Instructor had us running along the promenade, following which we had to go swimming. The water was ice cold, and it was most noticeable that our instructor had very carefully avoided the experience he had imposed on us. We soon remedied that.

Whilst on the Isle of Man, D-Day, on the 6th of June 1944, took place. We had all seen the build-up of men and materials in the southern counties, but none of us knew what the reception would be like to the first wave of troops landing. Our thoughts and prayers followed them, but even that didn't seem to be enough. We felt we should have been part of it; we should have been there giving those lads our support.

Our time at *Valkyrie* soon came to an end and while I was happy at my own results, the next stage of our training was the least desirable, for we were due to be drafted to the world-renowned school of gunnery at Whale Island, otherwise known as *HMS Excellent*.

A few days before our departure, word came through of a new German weapon being used on London, namely the Buzz Bomb. We did not pay too much attention to it until we reached London, where the noise from their engines, the cut out, and finally the explosion appeared to be happening all around us. We were due to stay in some Air Force premises near Euston station, but I was so near my home at Staines that the seeds of an idea to get home soon germinated.

I spoke to the Chief in charge of the draft and said, "I hope, Chief, you won't be needing us or making another call in the night."

He said, "As far as I'm concerned, as long as you are at Waterloo Station at 07.45 tomorrow morning, it's alright by me. I don't know anything else."

It was obvious he knew what I was up to – indeed what we were all up to, because Dick had the same idea. There were others, however, who had beaten us to it, to the extent that a procession of sailors were caught by the Military Police and led back to the barracks with the door locked once they were in. I had asked Wilf to look after my gear while Dick and I explored other means of breaking out. By one of those strokes of fate, Dick literally bumped into a WAAF he knew. After a brief exchange, he told her what we wanted to do but couldn't get out.

"Don't worry," she said. "Follow me, I've got the key to a back entrance."

We could hardly believe our good fortune, and so the next thing was Dick and I crept up some iron stairs to stand on the blacked out streets of London, breathing in the smells associated with burning buildings while around us the explosions of Buzz Bombs offended our ears. Dick and I parted and I made my way to Waterloo Station. The last train to Staines had gone, so I caught the underground to Richmond. I had not thought my actions through as to how I was going to reach Staines, so I rang my parents and told them where I was. In the middle of our conversation, I saw a taxi and made a dive for it. When I asked the driver to take me to Staines, he said it was outside his permitted limit and he wasn't allowed to take me. He then said "Come on, Jack, hop in."

A policeman who had been standing near the station observed all this. Whether he could hear the conversation or not, I do not know. Nevertheless, as we pulled away, I saw him flash his torch and the next thing was that we saw a police car on our trail. I warned the driver, who then diverted from his route and managed to give them the slip. I eventually arrived home at around one thirty a.m. The sirens had sounded so Mother and my two brothers were already down the shelter while my Father took up his customary stance outside, scanning the skies for signs of enemy activity. None of us had any sleep that night, and I had to leave at six in the morning, but those few hours were treasured.

I duly arrived at Waterloo at the appointed time and rejoined my draft to catch the train to Portsmouth.

Chapter 4

Whale Island

Whale Island had a fearful reputation for harsh discipline, high standards and cruel punishment. The navies of the world, including the Japanese, were sent there for training, but the most frightening aspect to Whale Island were those who did the training, the Warrant Gunners and the Chief Petty Officers. They ruled with rods of iron and fear. No one questioned their authority; indeed you were not allowed to. There was no appeal, no recourse to justice. The trainees, and this included the commissioned ranks, were the lowest of the low – they had no rights and were expected to go everywhere at the double, the only exception being when you were drilled on the parade ground. Even the name *HMS Excellent* typified the standards to which they aspired – at least we thought they aspired to these standards, but we were soon to find out that excellence was not enough.

It is in the nature of men that we believe the situation could be worse, so we look for a bonus. In this respect we were fortunate because *HMS Excellent* was overcrowded so we were billeted at North Parade School near Cosham. The food was good and the classrooms made quite good messes.

Each morning we marched about a mile and a half to Whale Island, and once through the portals the order was given to 'Double March'. We doubled past old and ancient guns, piles of cannon balls, and figureheads and masts. The parade ground was not of asphalt but of shingle, and around two sides was a lush green embankment. The place was like opening up a time capsule from the Victorian period. We were brought to a halt and allowed to stand easy. Before us, standing on the embankment, was a Warrant Officer Gunner. He wore black, highly polished gaiters, and stood to attention with his thumbs in line with the seams of his trousers.

With a loud voice, he roared across the parade ground.

"My name is Pantlin. The main interest in my life first and foremost is the Royal Navy. The second is myself, and the third is my family. That is going to be the same with you."

He descended from his lofty position and proceeded to inspect the squad. Boots had to be polished and well repaired, caps on straight, uniform correctly ironed and collars clean. Any breaks in clothing had to be remedied, and any deficiencies were to be taken care of by the following morning. This was to be the first and only warning.

He put us through our paces and any slight errors in the squad drill were punished by doubling. Alongside me was a fellow in his mid-thirties. He had come straight from sea service and probably had not been exposed to rifle drill for some years. It was therefore reasonable to believe that such a man was a little rusty and allowances should be made. Dear Mr Pantlin was, however, not a reasonable man. He noted a little slowness in presenting arms and marched briskly to confront the offender. Pantlin stood rigidly to attention, but from the ankles up he bent forward with his face barely six inches from our rusty shipmate. He then verbally lambasted him. The confrontation was literally eyeball to eyeball.

At the end of his tirade he said, "Why do you look at me like that?"

"Sir," came the reply, "When I was in training I was told never to be scared of an Officer and to look him straight in the eye. That is what I'm doing now."

I could see out of the corner of my eye Pantlin getting redder. I could see his face changing into a grotesque mask.

"You what?" he yelled. "You what? Get over to my gun."

Now, running around the parade ground in full kit was an experience. To do it holding a .303 rifle above your head was torture, but Pantlin's gun was a destroyer of men.

The six-inch shell is the heaviest and largest shell used in the Royal Navy that is manoeuvred by hand. Pantlin's gun was a six-inch breech loader without the barrel. The shells had to be inserted, and the breech closed, and the shell fell out onto a tray. The one under punishment had to pick the shell out of the tray and repeat the process. Fifteen minutes of this was bad enough, but two hours found forearms and biceps screaming in agony. Our friend spent the rest of the morning satisfying the sadistic Mr Pantlin.

Divisions were held every morning but they have to be seen to appreciate the precision and smartness of the participants. All who took part were trainees, including the Officers who wore their traditional swords, and the result was an accolade to the instructors. The onlookers were, of course, the Captain and permanent staff of the *HMS Excellent*. It was an unwritten rule that if you dropped your rifle then you should fall down with it as if you had suddenly fainted. One of our squad did not heed this advice, fumbled his drill and found at least six Officers and gunnery instructors standing before him in line of seniority, each of which gave him a dusting down which collectively would have exceeded anything he had previously experienced or, indeed, was likely to.

In my first week at Whale Island, I went through the soles of two pairs of boots.

Our training on the Isle of Man was on the technical side of the radar system. Whale Island was to produce the gunnery side which would work in conjunction with radar and so allow the guns to be fired with the benefit of knowledge obtained by means of radar. We exercised on the four-inch breech and quick firing guns, and also the six-inch, and then entered the huge gun turrets which faced Horsea Island, and which contained the transmitting stations. These activities did allow us some respite from the parade ground.

Eventually the final day of training arrived, and we were still all in one piece. Hemmings, our class leader, took charge and assembled us outside one of the offices. He was quite a stout chap and his uniform almost cried out under the strain. Mr Pantlin passed by, and as he did so, Hemmings produced a salute that would have done credit to any manual of seamanship.

The response was not quite what he expected, for the reason that Pantlin screamed, "Get over to my gun."

We were left wondering what had caused this apoplectic outburst, when suddenly we noticed a telltale piece of clothing showing through a hole under the very arm that had been raised in salute.

We crossed the bridge and went through the large wrought iron gates, not daring to look back but all giving an audible sigh of relief.

Back at the schools we had sentry duty every fourth night, but the thing that occupied most of us was trying to find ways of getting home. The ban on leave still applied, and a line had been drawn across southern and southeast England. No one was allowed out without a pass, and no one was allowed in. The stations were manned by the Military Police and security on the roads had to be seen to be believed. The perimeter of the school had a twenty-four hour guard, but as the guards came from the ranks of the inmates it became relatively easy to arrange for these guards to turn a blind eye, this being a trait of Lord Nelson who would have been proud of them, though I doubt if the authorities would see it that way. In the early hours of Saturday morning, a lorry would be standing about a hundred yards away. As soon as it was full, you would be taken direct to London. On one occasion I walked out to the Cosham Hills and hitchhiked to London, and on another weekend when my family were having a brief break in Cheddar in Somerset, I managed to see them without being stopped.

There was one drawback about the school and that was a programme that came on the wireless at about 7am each morning called 'Bedtime Stories for the Children of Night Watchman'. The theme tune accompanying the programme was 'Holiday for Strings'. It was broadcast over the tannoy so we couldn't turn it off, but our annoyance was not the programme as such, or the music, but merely the fact that it was a constant daily reminder that our presence at *HMS Excellent* was expected. It was as though it was Whale Island reveille just for us.

We left the schools and went to Stamshaw, an accommodation camp just four hundred yards away, and from where we could expect a posting to a ship. We had various duties which embraced gardening, sweeping, guard duties and going to the docks at Portsmouth, where we were put to loading and unloading the ships going to and from Normandy. We frequently worked until gone midnight.

Apart from the guard duties, we also had to watch for the Buzz Bombs coming over. They were a regular every night occurrence as they sped across the skies, spurting flames and falling either in the vicinity or crashing into the Cosham Hills. One night I was sound asleep in my hammock, and the next thing I recall was standing beneath it in vest and pants. Wilf Gough in the next hammock was leaning over the side, laughing his head off.

"That's the fastest bit of work I've ever seen," said Wilf.

Apparently my slumbers had been disturbed by one of these infernal machines exploding.

Soon after we arrived, a circular went round asking all the sailors who had not had a long leave for over eight months to report. I had never had a long leave and was one of the first in the queue. Eight days of leave passed all too quickly and the nightly disruptions at home were as bad as those in the Portsmouth area. I had to walk the last two miles back to the camp, where I arrived after midnight. I slung my hammock, but noticed the spaces that Dick and Wilf usually occupied were empty. Were they on leave, or had they moved on? Some fellows were playing cards so I asked them if they knew where my two pals had gone.

"They went out yesterday," they said. "Had a draft chit."

My spirits fell as I realised my mates had all gone.

The following day, I was still indulging in self-gloom when I was called to the drafting office. Apparently someone on the draft had gone over the wall and I was the replacement. Within the hour I was on my way to the Royal Naval Barracks Portsmouth, and there was Dick and Wilf. When we compared draft chits, we were all down for *HMS Vindex* and now spirits soared.

Then I sobered up a little because everything had happened so quickly, and I thought and indeed said, "I've never heard of *Vindex*. What is she, where is she, and where is she going?"

"Well," said Wilf, "as far as we know she's an escort carrier – you know the carriers they converted from merchant ships – but where she is and where she's going we've not been told."

Although I was excited at the thought of going back to sea and the fact that the three of us were together, there was something about an escort carrier that did not satisfy my idea of what a warship should be. I believed the sleek lines of a destroyer or the magnificent sight of a cruiser with raked funnels and bristling with guns, were what a warship should look like, but beggars cannot be choosers, so there was no alternative but to accept the cards in the manner in which they had fallen.

The following morning, the draft for *Vindex* assembled outside the drafting office all ten of us. We were all gunnery control radar ratings and had all been at *Valkyrie,* so we knew each other.

HMS Vindex was apparently in the Clyde, so we made our way to Glasgow and reported to the Regulating Transport Officer. He informed us that she was no longer at Greenock, and he didn't know where she had gone. While efforts were made to locate her, we wandered around Glasgow, just killing time. Late that evening we were told that *Vindex* was at Scapa Flow so we boarded a train which took us to Perth where we had to change.

Regrettably, there was a four hour wait for our connection, so we went to a local fair. We eventually arrived at Thurso the following morning and were immediately taken to the Town Hall, where we were able to have a wash and brush up and also enjoy a decent breakfast.

From the Town Hall, we were taken out to the harbour where a boat was waiting to take us across the Pentland Firth to a depot ship anchored in Scapa Flow in the Orkneys. We then had to wait for a boat from *Vindex* to come and pick us up.

Chapter 5

HMS Vindex

Scapa Flow is not the most inspiring of places. It is bleak and cold and unfriendly. The waters are unsociable and choppy, and the windy grey sky contaminated everything it touched, and merely endorsed the air of inhospitality that pervaded everything. A variety of warships were scattered over the area while small motor cutters, launches and drifters criss-crossed the waters on various missions.

Ten pair of eyes peered into the dull and grey visibility looking for the *Vindex*, but it was not until we were aboard the motor cutter taking us to our new ship that we caught our first glimpse of her. None of us showed any sign of enthusiasm, but then how can one show enthusiasm for a flat top? The big aircraft carriers had some character about them – they had lines and contours, they exuded strength and power – but this it was a rust-stained floating tin box that didn't inspire confidence or any degree of affection. Time would tell just how wrong first impressions could be.

At long last, we finally boarded *HMS Vindex*. We could see on our approach she had four 20mm twin Oerlikons mounted in electrically controlled cockpits either side of the flight deck. On each quarter were two pounder quadruple pom poms, and in the stern just below the flight deck was a twin four-inch gun. She also carried about six Hurricane aircraft and twelve Swordfish.

Each of us was given a mess number and told to report to the Gunnery Office. I quickly scribbled a short letter home to let my parents know my new address, and though I was on a ship, I didn't know where we were going, and if I did I could not have said so.

On reporting to the Gunnery Office, the Regulating Petty Officer said, "Radar Control ratings. We've no use for you lot on here as none of our sets work in coordination with the guns. In fact, they don't work at all."

As quick as a flash I said, "In that case, you'd better send us off."

"Oh no," he said in an odd but knowing sort of way. "Oh no, we can make use of you."

The following morning I was sent for by the Gunnery Instructor, who said, "Report to 08 Oerlikon as No. 2 guns crew."

Meanwhile, Wilf and Dick and two of the others were sent to fuse the rockets which help the planes to take off. Jock, a fellow near forty, clicked for a cushy number as 'Gunnery Office Writer'.

We had already weighed anchor and were proceeding out of harbour and I made my way to 08 Oerlikon, which was sited on a catwalk adjacent to but just below the flight deck. As I made my way there, I kept turning over in my mind my lack of training on Oerlikons. What the hell would I do? It was just typical of the Royal Navy, all this training and I get stuck on a gun I knew nothing about. I reported to Bob, the number one on the gun. He realised I didn't have any experience and quickly put me through a course of instruction which entailed loading the gun, keeping a lookout, and switching on the current whenever instructed to do so. Bob then sat me in the cockpit and showed me how to train and elevate by means of a joystick. Once the instruction was over, Bob took up his position in the cockpit. In my foolishness I was attired in an overall suit and a seaman's jersey, but this did not stop the cold penetrating.

Looking around, I could see that we were in company with *HMS Striker,* another escort carrier, and also a colony class cruiser, *HMS Jamaica*. Rear Admiral Dalrymple Hamilton was flying his flag in the *Vindex*.

Two hours out of Scapa, the Bosun's Mate piped "Attention," throughout the ship. "This is your Captain speaking. I wish the ship's company to know that tomorrow night we will be meeting up with a convoy. It is our task to take that convoy to the North Russian port of Murmansk."

The rest of the Captain Bayliss's message was lost as the silence of the mess deck was broken with oaths and curses of every conceivable description. All of us had heard of the Russian convoys and the fear it brought to men's hearts. Didn't Winston Churchill describe them as 'The Gateway to Hell'. It was not just the U-Boats and the air attacks, though they were bad enough, but the weather, the cold, the ice that covered the ship to the point of upsetting its stability, and the unceasing chatter on the mess deck as each told tales that bettered the next man of conditions and fear. I listened in silence as each yarn filled me with foreboding.

I had been kitted out with a sheepskin coat, gloves, leather sea boots, thick woollen long johns and a fur hat with flaps that came down over the ears. Self-consciously one dwells on self-preservation, and with this in mind I decided that I would not sling my hammock but sleep on the deck. I was due to keep the morning watch from four until eight in the morning, so I picked a spot furthest away from the ship's side. I inflated my life jacket to use as a pillow – that was my lame excuse – and laid down to offer up my prayers. Suddenly the reality of war hit me – this was the real navy stripped of its glamour. Somewhere the other side of the ship's side were U-Boats awaiting their chance to fire torpedoes into us, or into any other vessel which came within the view of their periscopes. German sailors were out to kill me. They didn't even know me and for that matter I didn't know any Germans, how futile, how ludicrous.

"Please God, if they leave us alone, may we leave them alone."

I lay back my mind in a turmoil until I was disturbed by a noise.

Sitting bolt upright I said, "What's that? What's that?"

The fellow in the hammock above leaned over the side and said, "It's the Oerlikon's gun practice."

His head disappeared from view, leaving me to think and ponder and fear. I lay awake, listening to the gentle throb of the engines and the snores of men able to dismiss their fears and sleep in swaying hammocks above. Suddenly a horrendous roaring noise obliterated every other sound.

"What's that?" I said sitting, bolt upright.

The same head looked down on me. "It's the aircraft taking off. They use rockets to help them."

"Thanks," I said and lay back again.

Why were they taking off? Is there something we should know? A myriad of thoughts and questions criss-crossed my mind, but there were no answers.

The next thing was a series of explosions that shook the ship from stem to stern, that made the emergency lights flicker and brought loose crockery crashing to the deck.

I sat up, but before I could say anything the head above leaned over and said, "Bleedin' depth charges, now get your bloody head down and shut up."

What was going on out there, and why was everyone so calm? Sleep was definitely out of the question, but one thing I did find out as children we often put our tongue across torch battery points – it gave us an unusual feeling and a metallic taste on the tongue. I experienced that feeling that night and knew that the expression 'tasting fear' was in fact a reality.

I went up on deck to relieve my opposite number on the guns. It was bitterly cold and there was no cover for the number two. It was alright for Bob – he was in the cockpit protected from the elements. After a while Bob offered to change places, and I was only too pleased to accept. I put on the headphones which were connected to the bridge and the other guns, but then without realising it my lack of sleep caught up with me and I must have dozed off.

Suddenly I heard, "Switch On."

"Switch On," I called to Bob.

"Is that right?" he said, knowing that if there were an alert it was his trained finger that should be on the trigger.

"Sure," I said. "It was quite clear."

Bob switched on, while I elevated and trained the guns and rotated the cockpit. There was no activity from the other guns, but the Swordfish on the flight deck were having their engines turned over which they did periodically to protect them from the cold. Obviously the "Switch On" I heard related to the aircraft, not the guns. I never ever fell asleep on duty again.

The telephone contact between the guns and the bridge was often the source of amusement, much to the annoyance of the Gunnery Officer for the reason that there were some who tried to imitate his voice. For example:

"Bridge 06 Oerlikon."

"06 Oerlikon Bridge."

"Are you keeping a good lookout, 06?"

"Oh yes, sir."

"Is that Swain speaking?"

"Yes, sir."

"Well go and fry your bloody head."

Scouse would explode, "You great big bald 'eaded son of a bastard wait till I get you down the mess."

The rest of his string of oaths would be drowned with laughter from the other gun crews.

The following evening, I was sitting in the mess awaiting my watch to come round when a messenger from the Gunnery Office came down.

"Anyone named Shelton?" he said.

"Yes," I replied, "that's me."

"Good," he said. "The Master at Arms wants to see you."

I duly went to the Gunnery Office and was confronted by the Regulating Petty Officer, Sandy Lane.

"Shelton," he said. "I'm going to elevate you."

"Me?" I said. "Am I going to be made up to Able Seaman?"

"Higher than that," he said.

My mind raced ahead and I thought blimey, I'll be a bloody Admiral before this trip's over. The Jaunty snapped me out of my dreams.

"I said I was going to elevate you, not promote you. The masthead lookout's gone sick, and you are his replacement."

I was never enamoured with heights, but to be a masthead lookout on a ship that was ducking and diving, weaving and swaying filled me with foreboding. The lads in the mess thought it was one hell of a joke and nagged me accordingly. I only hoped my face did not portray my feelings.

My first duty was in the morning watch at four. Two of us ascended the mast and instead of being up there for four hours, it was an hour up, an hour down, hour up, and an hour down. In the hour we had down, we used to go the galley and get a mess can of Kye cocoa, which we then took round to all the gun crews and lookouts.

We joined up with the convoy during the night. There were thirty-four merchant ships. Apart from the ships already mentioned, there were four sloops, namely *Cygnet, Kite, Mermaid* and *Peacock,* and the frigate *Loch Dunvegan.* The Flower class corvettes were *Bluebell, Camellia, Charlock, Oxlip* and *Honeysuckle.* The destroyers were *Keppel, Whitehall, Caprice, Marne, Meteor, Milne* and *Musketeer.*

As daylight improved, so did our view from the mast, and the lighter it became so the sea area the convoy covered became greater. The merchant ships in lines went at a constant speed. The escort rushing hither and thither like mother hens protecting their chicks, and the panoramic view the like of which I had never seen and could not possibly have conceived. Behind one of the merchant ships, I saw what I thought was a periscope. I called the bridge immediately and was told not to worry because in the convoy were twelve Russian PT boats, but in the heavy swell I could only see their masts. Also in the convoy was the old battleship, *HMS Royal Sovereign.* She had been handed over to the Russians, was renamed *Archangelsk* and had a Russian crew. Occasionally we left the convoy to fly off the Swordfish on their four hour patrols. The view from the crow's nest allowed us to look into the pilot's cockpit as they came in. These old biplanes took off and landed on a deck that was rising or falling ten, twenty, thirty and some times over forty feet, their task demanded a high standard of courage, and these men undoubtedly had that.

Rumour had it that the convoy was being used as bait to encourage the *Tirpitz* to come out and attack us, because her presence in a Norwegian fiord meant that we could not release our capital ships to the Far East theatre of war. The idea of my being part of that bait did not exactly appeal to me, though the rumour for what it was worth did include the fact that some hundred or so miles astern of us a striking force of Battleships, Aircraft Carriers, Cruisers and Destroyers were ready to respond should the *Tirpitz* take up the challenge.

We knew our position was known to the enemy because of the U-Boat activity taking place, and our escorts being kept busy following up and depth charging their Asdic contacts.

At 06:44 on the 21st of August, U344 put two torpedoes into *HMS Kite*. She sank within one minute and only nine men survived out of a crew of over two hundred. The waters now were so cold that life expectancy for anyone falling in was barely four minutes. The sinking of the *Kite* had a profound effect on me. Surprisingly it did not increase my fears, but had the opposite effect. A fearful teenage youth changed overnight to a teenage man seeking retribution with a vengeance. Revenge is a harsh and hard state of mind. It can be a product of a twisted outlook on life. It is bitter, unsociable, and without care or love. It was not compatible with my nightly prayers. Yet, as I fought to analyse my feelings, I knew I was guilty of generating double standards. I could not rationally justify my thoughts or feelings. All I did know was that over two hundred men, fathers, brothers, and sons had died within the space of sixty seconds by some bastard hiding below the waves and looking for more opportunities.

On the following day, our own Swordfish found U-Boat U344 and sank her, and then for good measure our Hurricanes caught one of the huge planes that shadowed us night and day and shot them down. Yes, vengeance had been assuaged, but I did not revert to a frightened youth – a frightened man maybe, but no longer a youth.

The battle fleet astern of us did not escape attention because the escort carrier *HMS Nabob,* which formed part of that fleet was torpedoed by U354. She did not sink, but it was the buzz on the mess deck that *HMS Bickerton* stationed herself between the *Nabob* and U354 and was herself torpedoed and sunk as a result. The *Nabob* limped back to Scapa Flow, but on the 24th of August, Swordfish from our ship, together with *Keppel, Loch*

Dunvegan, Mermaid and Peacock caught U354 and consigned her to the deep.

If we were not keeping a watch in the forenoon we were expected to work about ship. On one such occasion, a party of us were assigned to bringing the bombs up from the magazine. This necessitated going to the bowels of the ship, putting the bombs into canvas bags, and then hoisting them up into a flat where other hands loaded them onto trolleys. These were pushed about ten yards, then individually hoisted up a shaft four feet square and about sixty feet in length. A further winch on the upper deck brought them to the surface. Everything went according to plan, except the final evolution, namely that of hoisting the trolley. Somehow it was not attached correctly and fell down the hatch, hitting one of the fellows below. His head was split open and he was laid unconscious. I rushed off to get the Medical Officer. Meanwhile, one of the lads lifted him bodily and brought him up on deck. From there he was strapped up in a Robinson stretcher and taken to the sick bay. Fortunately he was not as bad as he looked, and resumed duties within twenty-four hours.

The ship's company had been put on four hours on and four hours off, and still had to work in the forenoon if you were not on duty watch. One had very little sleep, and we never fully undressed. Washing and cleanliness ceased to be of prime importance, and it was a matter of sleeping when you could and eating when you could. You felt dirty and unclean, and knew you were dirty and unclean.

It has been said that the speed of a convoy is the speed of the slowest ship, but that is not always the case. Some of these old Merchant Navy skippers have sailed the seven seas and have been answerable to no one except their shipping line. Once out on the ocean they are truly master of all they survey, so it comes as no surprise that some of the stubborn old skippers found it hard to conform to the rigid discipline demanded by the Commodore of the convoy and the Admiral. Occasionally their stubbornness was reflected in their speed. They would slow down and lag behind the convoy expecting the convoy to do likewise, but it never happened. An escort was appointed to look after the straggler while the convoy steamed toward the horizon. It only needed an increase in enemy activity for the straggler to find some energy somehow and soon she was back in the fold.

From the masthead position, we did not just scan the skies and seas for signs of aircraft or U-Boats, but were always conscious of signs we ourselves were making. In the Arctic, smoke hangs around for hours. It does not disperse but could be seen from miles away, even if the ship making it was not to be seen. We would therefore keep an eye on any vessel, endangering the convoy's position by this practice. Discharging oil or dumping garbage was likewise forbidden.

It was light nearly all night long, which was advantageous to lurking U-Boats. One day a Hurricane coming back from patrol bounced along the deck. Its hook missed all the arrester wires and she went straight into the crash barrier and caught fire. From my position above I saw the pilot's head hit objects in front of him knocking him out. Meanwhile the Flight Deck Officer and one of his crew leapt onto the wings, ripped back the canopy and pulled him out. At the same time the fire crew soon had the fire under control.

HMS Striker, the other carrier, had Martlets instead of Hurricanes and I saw them take off one day and chase a huge Blohm and Voss aircraft that used to circle the convoy out of gun range. She was so high that if she saw fighter aircraft taking off, she had more than enough time to get either beyond range, or to take refuge in the clouds. This day she had misjudged it and the Martlets were able to damage her. Whether she got back to Norway or not I didn't know, but *Striker*'s aircraft had to return through lack of fuel.

Archangelsk should have left us two days before we were due to arrive in Murmansk, but increased U-Boat activity decreed she was safer in the convoy. It was also two days from the Kola Inlet when a Russian Catalina paid us a visit. It would seem that a number of U-Boats had converged on the entrance to the inlet necessitating absolute vigilance at all times.

At about 14:00 on the eighth day, the convoy left us with a screen of destroyers to escort it, while we remained outside for a further twenty-four hours to attack the enemy submarines.

Finally the huge cliffs either side of Kola Inlet showed us the way to a haven of peace and tranquillity. Peace and tranquillity be damned, the front line was less than sixty miles to the west, and a state of alertness was maintained throughout our brief stay. It was with some relief that our convoy, coded JW59, was now discharging its cargo to assist our valiant allies, in the struggle and sacrifices they had and indeed were still making. We were however given a warning – be careful, the Russians are trigger happy. The fleet slowly sailed south when a number of Yak fighter aircraft swooped low over the ships. We were apprehensive. Were they about to be trigger happy, or was this just a salute? Fortunately it was the latter.

Chapter 6

Up The Stick

There were always two masthead lookouts on duty at the same time. Normally Eric Hood would share the duties with me.

What were those duties really like? The first thing was to get up there. This necessitated going via the bridge up a vertical ladder. Half way up was a box like construction for use when the weather was foul. I do not know what the authorities used as a yardstick to measure such conditions, but we never used it, and only once did we experience a storm of such intensity that not only were we unable to get up the mast, but none of the guns were manned and no lookouts were posted. In fact, we were all battened below decks with only the Skipper, The Navigating Officer and a signaller being on the upper deck.

Just before we got to the top of the ladder it arced, which brought you to a small square opening leading on to a platform. Astern of this opening were the Radar aerials, while forward and extending about fifteen feet or more from the mast was the lookout position. To reach it one had to walk sideways along a space that was no more than a foot wide. Guard rails came up to your knees in front, while behind you was a steel construction which we were supposed to hide behind in the event we were being strafed by enemy gunfire from the air. In any event, getting to our position was a most precarious evolution and that was especially so in rough weather. Once in our lookout position, we had a canvas baffle about four feet high to protect us from the elements. We now had the steel construction behind us. A voice pipe helped us to maintain contact with the bridge.

Where clothing was concerned, we had a heavy sheepskin coat, sea boot stockings with leather sea boots and a fur-lined hat with ear flaps which you tied under the chin. The fur hat also had peaks behind and in front which you pulled down. A towel was tied around our necks and a pusser issue scarf covered our mouth and nose. We had sheepskin gloves and a heavy set of binoculars which had to be checked in at the Gunnery Office after each watch.

During a four hour watch, we were only allowed to do one hour up and one down, then another hour up and one down. During that hour down Eric and I would go to the galley and get a fanny full of hot kye. We then visited all the other lookouts and gun positions and those lads really used to look forward to our visits.

If it was dark when we were due to go on watch, we had to wear red goggles for half an hour beforehand which enabled our eyes to adapt immediately to the darkness outside. We always felt that it was a damned annoyance when the time could have been spent more profitably in our hammocks.

Having got up the mast, what then? Well, Eric would take one side and me the other. We then swept the skies back and forth in a systematic manner. Then we scanned the seas from the horizon to the nearest vessels and kept an eye on any ship making smoke.

In the spring and autumn, when it was almost perpetual daylight, our binoculars took in a breathtaking panoramic scene of ships in formation stretching for mile after mile after mile. Destroyers, corvettes and frigates screened the perimeter of the convoy, ever alert to the enemy below. Now and again we would observe the frenzied activity, as with high pitched haunting sirens bleeping away, they dug their bows into the cold and unfriendly Arctic Ocean to hunt a U-Boat below. White water cascaded over their bows as they cut intricate patterns in the sea, and then we would see them firing depth charges following which the sea would erupt with explosions which, in turn, reverberated throughout the convoy. Occasionally those faithful old biplanes, the Swordfish, would be seen diving down onto an unsuspecting enemy below, releasing their charge and then away.

The length of the daylight hours caused us the most misgivings as they presented better conditions for enemy aircraft to seek us out, but in the winter months that was something else. In the spring and autumn the temperature was frequently around the zero mark, but in winter it just fell and fell until figures like thirty and forty below became the normal. With a daily ration of less than one hour of daylight, the darkness gave us some semblance of security, but there was a price to pay. It was possible to see a convoy lit up by forked lightning one moment, and the next it was snow and sleet stinging your face with a thousand cuts and forming crusts of ice on your eyebrows – yes, that was just part of the price. You couldn't use your binoculars as they too were rimed with ice, and even if they were serviceable you still couldn't use them because visibility was almost zero. The many storms we experienced prevented flying operations, but up in the crow's nest we'd be pitched back and forth and side to side as our bows dug deep into the turbulent waters shipping huge green ones over the forecastle and even at times soaking those on the bridge with spindrift. The old ship rolled from side to side throwing us with it, sometimes not being able to see the deck but only the angry raging waters. At other times, we appeared to be going faster than the skipper as we dipped again and again with the screws racing as they came out of the water. You couldn't keep watch, so with only our canvas baffle to protect us, we'd crouch down behind it feeling as though we were the only two left aboard. Occasionally we would stand up to stamp our feet and swing our arms in a fruitless attempt to get some life back into them. The rain and sleet had already penetrated our towel and scarf and slowly your inner clothes became wetter and wetter and you knew that with no heating in the mess deck there was no means of drying them off before the next watch. In temperatures way below zero, going on watch in wet clothes is not to be recommended.

Eric and I would talk about our homes and the last run ashore; we talked about girlfriends and the strong desire to get back to the sanctuary of the mess deck, but then, while it was better than the mast it was not welcoming, there being no heat, and water was sloshing back and forth all night long. You could only remove your sea boots once you were in your hammock and then you tied them to the clews so that they would be ready to put on in the morning. As you pulled up your one and only blanket, you looked at the icicles hanging from the deck head and snapped them off in case they dripped over you. We were tired and exhausted but we didn't sleep. We couldn't sleep, and the time was spent in trying to rub life back into our frozen limbs.

We never discussed death and yet even without mentioning it we knew the Grim Reaper in the form of the enemy was always there, waiting for an opportunity. None of us knew whether that opportunity would come from below the seas, on the seas, or from the air. We also knew that the elements, although impartial, had the ability in more ways than one of snuffing out young men.

From our perch up high, we could look down onto the bridge and see what they were up to. The Skipper seemed to be always there, which imbued in us a sense of confidence. He did have his sea cabin nearby where he was able to snatch a few hours' sleep but they were just a few hours. Unlike his crew he did not have a regular watch to keep, and no matter what time of day or night it was, he had to be on or near the bridge. Unlike the other forces where you could lead your men into battle from behind, the Senior Service executive was right there in the front line, shoulder to shoulder with their men, facing the same dangers at the same time with the same possible consequences.

Occasionally a steward would arrive with a tray of food for the Skipper, and then it was that our binoculars were trained on those victuals to see what he was about to enjoy. We soon came to the conclusion that while he shared our dangers shoulder to shoulder, he was able to do so in a rather more refined manner than we enjoyed.

Chapter 7

Vaenga Bay

We didn't go to Murmansk, but anchored in Vaenga Bay, a small village a few miles north of Murmansk. It looked a bleak sort of place; in fact, wherever we looked was bleak. The countryside was rocky and rugged. It looked cold and inhospitable and in many respects reminded me of Scapa Flow. I thought of Scapa Flow and my ungracious and critical comments about her and felt ashamed. I would love to see her now and get to know her, but to do that was to run the gauntlet again with a south bound convoy.

Leave was granted between 13:00 and 18:00, so Dick and I went ashore. On landing at a jetty we found ourselves surrounded by Russian soldiers, sailors and civilians. The women and children stayed in the background. The men, who all carried rifles or revolvers, were of older stock. They weren't members of a Home Guard as we understand the meaning, but rather members of the regular forces who were too old to be in the front lines. Some were injured and others though in uniform, too young to take their place alongside their older brothers at the front.

As we left the jetty children followed us asking for 'ceegerettes' or 'chockelots'. They would not however accept anything without giving a little token in return. We made our way along this unmade road, toward the buildings at the top which formed the village. The road was dusty, full of potholes and broken bricks.

Coming down the hill towards us was a woman in a black coat and wellington boots, with a white scarf round her head. She looked as though she was the village post woman, as she seemed to be carrying letters and papers. I wanted to purchase a newspaper as a souvenir, so I approached her waving some roubles, whereupon she dropped the lot and ran.

Dick's response was "You've bloody screwed it now Joey."

I hastily put the papers together and we departed. I should add that somehow the lads in the mess had started to call me Joe or Joey, hence Dick's referring to me as such. Anyhow, halfway up we came across this large grey brick building. Apparently it was used as a Naval hospital and was about the only brick constructed building we saw. A large quantity of two floored wooden houses made up the village, except for a very imposing wooden building that could have been the Town Hall. In front of it was a huge portrait of Stalin, and another had this large war map showing the frontline movements. Next door was a restaurant which invited our attention, but all they sold was a rough type of bread for which they required ration coupons. Prices were worked out by means of an abacus. We watched the procedure for a short while and found that the customers, having bought the bread, retired to a table which was devoid of plates, knives or butter, tore the bread apart and ate it as it was. Language was a problem but by various signs we knew our continued presence was not welcome. Further along the road was another wooden building with the most exquisite shapes and designs built into the facing boards. On entering, we realised it was the local concert hall. Rows of red plush upholstered seats faced a stage on which stood a piano. Like bees around a honey pot, the lads slowly came in to find out what was going on. Among them was a pianist, which meant that twenty or so sailors were singing their hearts out.

On the way back to the jetty we went into a nearby hut. It was crammed full with Russians wearing thick padded coats and fur hats. In the middle of the room was a potbellied stove, too hot to touch, while around three of the walls men, fully clothed, slept in double tiered bunks. The smell of sweat and dust and grime invaded our nostrils.

We were constantly overtaken by British and American lorries laden with men, moving at great speed down the hill. The drivers must have been maniacs to have exposed their vehicles to the rate they were going on such treacherous roads, but even more surprising was the fact that the passengers in these vehicles were being used to pull out of the water pine logs which had been floated down stream. It never seemed to have occurred to them that the lorries could have performed the task far more quickly and effectively.

In a similar manner, there was an airfield on the other side of the hill, but the workshop repair facilities were on this side of the hill. It was not therefore an uncommon sight to see that the villagers, both men and women, had been engaged to push a Yak fighter plane up and over the hill to be repaired. At no time was a lorry utilised to assist in this operation.

The following day, in spite of it being exceedingly cold, we had boat races between the ships of the fleet, and then in the evening the Russians kindly arranged for a party of musicians and singers from Moscow to entertain us. We had fixed up a stage in the hanger and set out the seating. The Yeoman of Signals had provided flags with which to decorate the stage. Invites were extended to other ships to join us and when we had all assembled one of our own officers addressed us and said that on no account was anyone to whistle as this to Russian people was deemed to be an insult, clapping and cheering was however in order.

The entertainers began ascending the stage. There was a pianist, two violinists, a bass, another male, presumably a singer, dressed in sports coat and flannels, the bottoms of which were at least six inches above well-worn dirty shoes, and last of all came a young lady, an audible gasp of appreciation could be heard from the audience. Her jet black hair was parted in the middle and pulled tightly to the back of her head. Below a pale but beautiful face, a most exquisite and delightful figure was clad in a black tight-fitting dress that left nothing to the imagination. With eyes protruding like organ stops, the onlookers took in every movement of this delightful creature. No one was interested in the pianist or the violinists, no one was interested in the singers, and in fact none could give a toss whether this divine creature could sing or not. To sit and look and drink in the picture, this young lady presented was enough.

It was at least two weeks since the lads had seen a member of the feminine gender and it would be likely that another two weeks would elapse before they saw another. Meanwhile, this vision of loveliness could only invoke fantasies of many varieties in many minds. Safety valves were at breaking point, but the animal instincts and the basic desires of a shipload of frustrated men were restrained under a veneer of respectful appreciation.

The fellow with the short trousers had a shock of curly hair, and the sleeves of his coat were as short as his trousers. He had a comical expression, but the problem was that we did not know whether he was singing a humorous song or a serious one. To look at the man you couldn't help but laugh, and his facial contortions, allied to his voice and appearance, had the whole audience in fits of laughter. When he finished, we still did not know what response he had expected from us, and one can only hope ours was the correct one.

On the 28th of August 1944 at 15:00, we weighed anchor and prepared to escort a convoy of nine merchant ships back home. Rather than return empty, a number of the ships carried a cargo of timber. For the first two days all was reasonably quiet, but the Germans soon became aware of this southbound convoy and directed their U-Boats to intercept us. The escorts took the necessary procedures to ensure that the U-Boats were either sunk or kept below the surface, thereby denying them the opportunity of taking aim. From my masthead position I witnessed the destroyers, the sloops, the frigates and corvettes racing toward their asdic contacts and releasing patterns of depth charges. The Swordfish too scanned the waters and worked in conjunction with the escort. *Keppel, Mermaid, Peacock* and *Whitehall* between them located U394 and consigned her to a watery grave.

On the seventh day, one of the Swordfish crashed into the sea, but a speedy rescue response picked up the crew. Aircraft from both escort carriers put in a record five hundred hours of flying time between them.

We finally left the convoy and headed toward Scapa Flow, where we stayed long enough to pick up over a hundred bags of mail, and then headed south. All that day the mail office was besieged by sailors hungry for news of home and their loved ones. Constantly and at regular intervals hands were piped to the mail office. A man from each mess was appointed to collect and distribute it to his messmates. The suspense was unbearable, and the atmosphere was electric with anticipation and despair. Those fortunate enough to receive mail picked a quiet spot where letters were feverishly ripped open and contents devoured. Those who were not so lucky stood on the periphery with a sad face just hoping, and then would silently creep away to lean over the ship's side and wonder why, why? Were the loved ones alright, had they been killed or hurt in air raids, or had they just not bothered? When all the mail had been sent out, then came the parcels – biscuits, homemade cakes, soap, a variety of useful items – and some came out of the loved one's meagre rations.

We passed through the Hebrides and the little islands forming part of the Western Isles. The sky was a clear blue with not a cloud in sight. The sea was calm, and yet it had a stomach disturbing motion, which was neither a roll nor a pitch or toss, but a mixture of the two like a corkscrew effect. The air was crisp and clean and from my perch up high I could see the little crofters' cottages with wisps of smoke lazily floating skywards. Dry stonewalls surrounded each one, enclosing small well-kept gardens. Sheep dotted the wild and rugged terrain and the crofter's wives and children waved to us as we passed by. It was like a welcome home as the waves sent telepathic signs of warmth and love and care. One drew comfort from their gestures and hoped that as we returned their salute, they too would know the warmth we felt for them. Yes it was great to be going home.

Just before entering the Clyde, the Skipper came over the tannoy and announced that there would be seven days of leave for each watch. The Port Watch to which I belonged was going first. We came up the Clyde, passed the boom ships at Dunoon, and passed all the ships anchored off Gourock, until we finally anchored just off Greenock, the Tail of the Bank. Before the anchor hit the water, my bag was already packed ready for departure. I had already decided that I would not phone nor would I telegraph my parents, in case the receipt of the latter should cause them undue concern. I also thought that, although I had written regularly, my letters which had left the ship at Scapa would probably not reach them until after I arrived home.

The drifter took us ashore, and with all haste we went to Greenock station to catch the first train to Glasgow. From there we caught the night train to London. I must confess I felt dirty, not having had a full shower for four weeks and having had constant sleepless nights for nearly a month, but the train and the rhythmic motion as we sped south sent me into a deep sleep, free from constant calls to action stations, free from the noise of guns and depth charges – just free.

I arrived at my home at 7am on the Saturday morning and rang the bell. It seemed an eternity before I heard any response, and then my mother opened the door. She just said one word, "Son", and burst into tears. My father came rushing down the stairs in his nightshirt followed by my two younger brothers.

Almost in unison they said, "Where have you been? It's been so long we thought you were in the Far East."

Their questions embarrassed me, because the names of ships and their missions should not be revealed.

However, I said, "Please promise you will not let this go further than these four walls, but I've been to Murmansk."

There was a silence as they took the reply in, but I do not think the significance of being on a Russian convoy had sunk in, and I was not prepared to enlighten them and so increase their concern.

My father went to work, and the rest of us agreed to meet him in the High Street.

That afternoon, a young lady from my father's office cycled by and, seeing me, called out "Hello Geoff, I hear you've been to Russia."

I was cross, but my mother, in the middle of a crowded High Street, lambasted my father, the source of the leak. It was as though he had a hot line direct to Adolf Hitler, thereby endangering the life of her son.

Leave passed all too quickly. A train had been put on that would take us all the way to Greenock without having to change, and I was lucky enough to have a whole compartment to myself. The Starboard watch was eager to get on leave and were therefore happy when they saw the drifter full of liberty men from the Port watch arriving.

We were kept busy around the ship, but one night a storm broke out over the Clyde and we dragged on our anchors. Normally this would not have been a problem, but during the night the *SS Queen Mary* had arrived with thousands of American troops. She had anchored just astern of us, which meant that our anchors dragging took on a greater significance.

I went up to the flight deck and found that we were lying at right angles to the *Queen Mary* and very slowly drifting toward her. Her bows towered over us and, as the troops looked down, we had the feeling that we were taking part in a very slow motion movie picture. We could not flash up in time and could only send for a tug to get us out of this predicament. Before the tug arrived the port catwalk was hit by the bows of this 83,000 tonne Leviathan with the result that it just crumpled like tissue paper. Very slowly we bounced off, only to come back again and have the port quarter pom pom sponson destroyed. The significance of what was taking place soon had sailors realising that we could not go back to sea without having the damage repaired, and this realisation brought forth cheers of delight. Time would tell as to just how wrong we would be.

We had shore leave every other night and it was customary for Dick, George and I to go together, though every time we passed a pub we lost George. Before returning to the ship, we would call in at the Church of Scotland canteen which was run by Mr and Mrs Love and a number of voluntary workers. The Loves were a very dear old couple who looked after our welfare and could always be relied on to give us advice and counsel whenever we asked for it. We in turn would sweep the floor and clean the tables before our departure.

Within the area were camps full of Italian prisoners of war. The war in Europe was going well, so the authorities decided to allow some of these POWs to go into town. Coming across some sailors, a gang of these men proceeded to beat them up. The British sailors were outnumbered ten to one, but the news of what had transpired soon got around the fleet. The very next night, the streets of Greenock were busier than usual. It need only be said that no sailor ever had to worry about being on his own in Greenock thereafter.

One night we went to a show in Greenock Town Hall. The audience was made up of sailors, soldiers and airmen from many nationalities, and they had come to witness and hopefully appreciate the individual acts that were being presented to us. The opening number was an old song sung by a very much older lady. Without wishing to be uncharitable, it is doubtful whether this lady, even in her younger days, could sing, but whatever abilities she may or may not have had father time had dissipated it with a vengeance. The next item on the bill was introduced as a surprise item on the programme by an American soldier but "we do not know what he does". Well, the artiste came from the wings with two drumsticks. Without musical accompaniment, he tapped the floor, he tapped the piano, he tapped the footlights and he even tapped the announcer's head. The audience cheered at the relief of his act ending. He misinterpreted it and was only prevented from doing it all again by the jeers and catcalls.

When the Starboard watch returned from leave, we weighed anchor and went to Belfast. Dick, George and I went ashore and proceeded to have one hell of a good time. The Irish Jaunty cabs were a prominent sight. Every few yards we were stopped and invited to go for a ride. We eventually succumbed and asked the driver to take us to a restaurant. He took us for a ride alright, doing all left turns and depositing us a hundred yards from where we first started, and then had the audacity to charge us six shillings. We had a good meal of steak and eggs – a pre-war meal back home – and then went on to a dance which was being held in honour of *HMS Belfast*, a cruiser that had been adopted by the city, and which was also in the harbour.

George had taken aboard more drink than was advisable, and before we could stop him, he grabbed a Commander and tried to dance with him while holding a bottle of beer in one hand and trying to do a jig. We managed to extricate George, though in all fairness the Commander took it in a good spirit. We caught a taxi back to the docks. Now, matelots do not take taxis, Officers take taxis, but seamen walk or in this case roll, but *Vindex* was tied up to the wall, and when the gangway staff saw a taxi draw up they called out the Officer of the Watch. He was not amused when three jack tars exited the cab and tried desperately to disguise the unsteadiness in their gait as they ascended the gangway. The sentry muttered a few choice and well-chosen adjectives to welcome us aboard.

Chapter 8

First Love

We left Belfast and sailed back to Greenock where we ammunitioned and stored ship, and then we went to Scapa Flow. It was almost a foregone conclusion as to where our next mission would be, and those conclusions were further endorsed when Admiral Sir Dalrymple Hamilton arrived on board with his staff. I refer to him as Sir for the reason that the day before we sailed, he had been knighted. The convoy of thirty merchant ships had left Loch Ewe on the 20th of October 1944, with escorts comprising the destroyer *Walker*, sloops *Lapwing* and *Lark*, and corvettes *Camellia, Oxlip* and *Rhododendron.* On the 22nd of October, the main escort joined the convoy comprising the cruiser *Dido*, destroyers *Obedient, Offa, Onslow, Opportune, Oribi* and *Orwell,* frigates *Byron, Conn, Dante, Fitzroy, Inglis, Lawson, Loring, Louis, Mounsey, Narborough, Redmill* and Rupert, and escort carriers *Nairana, Tracker* and *Vindex.*

Winter was still in its infancy but its effect was soon felt. The nights were long, and as a relief to the darkness the Aurora Borealis craved our attention. As we looked up, beautiful shades of pastel greens wafted like swirling smoke above our heads. As the patterns changed, so periodically did the colours into various hues of blue, which seemed to follow us for miles. Visibility was down to a minimum as snow and sleet stung our faces, causing us to get down behind our canvas baffle in our masthead position. It beat down our necks and found every crevice in our clothing. Soon we were shivering as the melting snow trickled down our spines. We changed our clothes two or three times a day, and when we could not get our clothes dry in time, we put the wet ones back on. The weather just made the days long, damp, wet, cold and miserable. Over and above this was, of course, the constant threat of air and submarine attacks. It was reported that eighteen Stukas circled the convoy, but for some reason did not press home an attack. The escorts did a magnificent job in that the U-Boats were kept down, thereby preventing them from getting a chance to fire off their torpedoes. The bad weather reduced the flying activities, and it also made the mess decks inhospitable places to live, with water rushing from one side of the ship to the other, hitting the bulkheads and any other object in its way, breaking into spray and filling ones sea boots at the same time. We did not remove our sea boots until we got into our hammocks, and then tied them together and hung them from the clews. The bad weather and the unpleasant conditions were compensated by the fact that all the convoy and its escorts arrived safely on the 28th of October 1944, but not before we had the usual battle with the U-Boats outside the Kola Inlet.

Dick and I went ashore at Vaenga. The usual crowd of children and soldiers hung about the jetty. One soldier came forward.

"Watch, watch," he said.

I shook my head and said, "No," for the simple reason that while I was wearing a watch they were hard to come by and I had no desire to part with it.

Dick then said, "Geoff he wants a watch," and without further ado he raised my wrist and showed our Russian friend the watch.

His face lit up and he then produced what I can only describe as a stiletto. It was a magnificent weapon, about fifteen inches long, the handle being made of rings of coloured Perspex. Each ring had a small hole drilled into it, and these were then filled with other materials. It was a work of art, so I offered him cigarettes which he declined. I then offered him a jersey, but this too was refused. It was the watch he was seeking.

Eventually, Dick and I ignored him and made our way up the hill. Halfway up, we came across a building which had escaped our attention previously. Inside and leading off a long dark passage was a shop. It was jammed shoulder to shoulder with shoppers, but all that was being sold was American dried egg and children's rag dolls. While observing the transactions taking place, some Russian soldiers approached us and indicated that we should follow them. One of them was, of course, the one who wanted my watch. Thinking that I could still persuade him to take the cigarettes, I followed. At the time, I did not notice Dick was not with me. The passage was unlit and gradually it became darker and darker. The soldier then turned right into a pitch black passage. By now I was decidedly apprehensive, knowing he had the weapon and I had the watch. Suddenly I was conscious of two men, one either side of me. I did not know whether they had stepped out of a side passage or whether they had been waiting in a couple of doorways, but whatever the explanation was, I stopped dead, turned round and beat the hell out of there pretty quick with the sounds of heavy boots and shouting behind me. Reaching the relative security of lights and other people, I saw Dick and suggested we move on.

On our way back, an open topped lorry stopped and invited us to jump aboard. A tall, red-bearded Russian assisted us, and then the lorry took off at high speed down this pot marked and unmade road. We hung on for dear life as the vehicle made a sharp left turn, scattering stones and pebbles in a cloud of dust, then, with screaming brakes, the lorry skidded to a halt. We climbed out with every limb shaking, and thankful to be alive.

Just before the homeward bound convoy left, the escort went forth to attack the U-Boat force that was lying in wait. They succeeded in keeping them below the surface thereby allowing the convoy to steam over them unmolested. Regrettably the frigate *Mounsey* was torpedoed, but managed to get back into the inlet. It was rumoured that the U-Boat U295 that had caused the damage was attacked by other members of the escort and in her effort to get away, ran into a minefield and was blown up.

With so many U-Boats congregating outside the Kola Inlet, it meant that they were few and far between on the journey south. At no time did we allow our vigilance to slacken with the result that we brought convoy RA61 safely home.

We were slowly adapting to a routine procedure – namely returning to Scapa Flow, picking up the mail, and then sailing down through The Minches to the Clyde, where we would anchor in the Tail of the Bank. Seven days leave was granted to each watch, and in between we would restore, refuel and re-ammunition.

When a new squadron joined the ship we would go for trials in the Clyde estuary. If there was no night flying, we would anchor at either Rothesay or Lam Lash in the Isle of Arran. One of our pilots had a very talented but carefree attitude. One of them in particular was a Lieutenant Bennett who had apparently been awarded a gallantry medal but who nevertheless retained an almost boyish and cavalier manner. I had seen him on numerous occasions fly around the ship and give a two fingered victory sign to the officers on the bridge. On one occasion, and contrary to instructions, he took up two of the flight deck crew. On his return, he missed every arrester wire and landed up in the crash barrier. Fortunately there were no injuries, except for the ear bashing the Skipper administered.

One night in Lam Lash we were allowed ashore. There was little to do in this small village apart from a Forces canteen and a dance hall. I decided a visit to the latter would not go amiss. Sitting on the side, I watched the couples dancing by, and then I saw a young lady in a green dress. I don't know what came over me because I just could not take my eyes away. She was beautiful, with long dark curly hair and small bright eyes. Her figure was divine and those beautiful legs – I was smitten. My mind was a kaleidoscope of thoughts, all confused and mixed up. Never had I seen such a pretty and attractive girl, but pretty and attractive were pathetic adjectives to describe such beauty. What was wrong with me? I had never seen a girl who had had such an effect on me. This apparition, and vision of loveliness it couldn't be true, it couldn't be real, and yet it was real; it was happening beneath the corrugated iron roof of a hall in the village of Lam Lash in the Isle of Arran. I plucked up courage to ask her for a dance, and apart from finding out she was called Anne, we had no further conversation. Leave ended at 21:00 and I had the last dance with her. I stepped out into the cold night and made my way back to the small pier. There was a spring in my gait and I knew there was a sparkle in my eye. Of one thing I was sure, and that was that I did not dare to tell the lads in the mess deck. I knew I was the youngest in the mess, but I was also the only one who had never been out with a young lady. A basic shyness where the opposite sex was concerned, plus a fear that a rebuttal would hurt my ego, caused me to adopt a veneer that I couldn't care less. I knew of course it was just that – a veneer, a cover for my emotions – but that night that veneer was shattered, and to think she danced with me not once, but twice.

Wilf noticed, but I think he was the only one, though on the two other occasions I went ashore in Lam Lash the lads probably thought it odd that I preferred my own company. They were not to know that I had fallen in love, and I mean love, with this beautiful girl called Anne, but my two shore leaves were spent unsuccessfully looking for her. Was I destined, was it going to be my fate that my heart overflowing with love was going to be broken in such a short time by a young lady who was probably unimpressed by the young sailor she danced with, and no doubt couldn't even remember him? The joy of love and the pain of love tore my heart asunder.

Chapter 9

Shipboard Humour

Routine aboard ship followed much the same pattern every day, and only varied when we were at sea.

We had a good and lively crowd in our mess.

There was Reg, a tall fair man in his late twenties, regular RN, but probably spent more time in the cells for various misdemeanours. He did a little boxing and would challenge me to a wrestling match, which usually ended with both of us exhausted and me getting the worst of it.

There was Crash, so named for always crashing his swede, or to put it another way, always going to sleep. He was short and stocky, with a large mouth always set in a perpetual grin. He was a born comic and had us all in fits of laughter. The written word does not do justice to the performance because the voice and facial expressions were part of the act. His repartee went something like this.

Deep voice: "Don't come down those steps, they ain't there."

High voice: "I'm half way down."

Another piece was of 'Mary Anna shall carry the banner', which I will not repeat here, or the dialogue between the Stores Officer and rating who wanted a new cap.

"Vot do you vont?"

"I want a cap."

"Ve have not got a cap. Ve have der blue collar, der silk and der lanyard. Vot do you vont?"

Louder, "I want a cap."

Louder, "Ve have not got a cap. Ve have der blue collar, der silk and der lanyard. Vot do you vont?"

Louder still, "I want a bloody cap."

Louder, "Ve have der bloody cap not got. Ve have der bloody blue silk, der collar and der lanyard. Vot do you vont?"

Shouting, "I want a bloody blinding bleeding cap."

Yelling, "Vot for you want der bleeding cap ver, ve have none, when you can 'ave der bloody blue lanyard, der bloody blue collar. Vot are you vonting?"

This dialogue was endless, the language became worse and the yelling and shouting reached a high pitch.

Then there was the Donkey. How he acquired this name I do not know, but Donkey always had trouble getting out of his mick (hammock) in the morning. A Petty Officer would come down the mess to ensure all hands had turned out. He was the type of PO that would rather give you a thump than turn you in.

He was quite good at the thumping anyway, he knew about Donkey's bad habit and as he came into the mess deck he would yell, "Wakey, wakey, rise and shine, the morn is fine, you've had your time, now get out you idle shower of bastards. Where's Donkey?"

"Here I am, Chiefy."

The PO would then make a dire threat as to what he would do with Donkey if Donkey called him Chiefy again, to which he would respond, "Chiefy, Chiefy, Chiefy."

All the time Donkey was crawling from one locker to another whilst the PO was yelling,

"Where's that bugger got to?"

In the next mess to ours was Joe, old Joe; regular RN thick set, stocky with a magnificent beard. He didn't go ashore much, hoarded his cigarette ration and then would cadge off everyone else. If rum was his god, then I would say he was a religious maniac. Once or twice a week he would get paralytically drunk, and then his messmates had the task of trying to conceal his condition from the officers. At 21:00 every night, the Commander would do his rounds of the mess decks and the ship in general to ensure that before lights out everything was ship shape and, where applicable, all watertight doors and hatches were shut. Were he to find Joe in this drunken condition then, without doubt, Joe would be spending some time in the cells. To ensure this did not happen, we would open up one of the hatches and, by using a hoist, lower him down to the deck below and then batten the hatches on him until the coast was clear. Joe was the ship's sail maker and had a cubby hole – the bosun's stores – way up forward where he would spend hours on his own, slowly drinking himself unconscious.

During the last convoy he went missing, and those in the mess not on watch sent out a search party. It did not meet with any success which put us in a dilemma – should we report him missing? If we had reported him and then he had turned up drunk, he would have been put on a charge; on the other hand, if he had gone overboard what could we have done? What could anyone have done? In those waters you wouldn't survive for more than four minutes. We held our peace, and then half an hour later there was an almighty crash. Joe had come down the hatch, missed his footing and bumped all the way down, landing in a heap at the bottom. He had a black eye and above it a lump on the forehead the size of an egg. He was still tipsy, but coherent in a slurred sort of way. He had apparently and obviously got drunk and collapsed. When he came to, he found himself lying outside the spud locker in the working space. It was a wonder he had not been washed overboard, but that did not explain the lump and the black eye – until, that is, someone remembered that in the search they went forward in the dark and tripped over what they thought at the time was a sack of spuds.

In his sober moments, Joe would sit in the mess and have us enthralled with his stories of many years at sea, embracing wine, women and song, and as the lads sat around captivated, they unconsciously handed Joe cigarettes as though it was the oil that kept the stories flowing. Joe was a man devoid of any great ambitions, but was nevertheless looking to the day when he could retire. He was already in the throes of making himself a leather waistcoat, complete with a variety of pockets earmarked for his pension book, his money and his smoking requirements, and then he would walk continually from Land's End to John O'Groats and back again. He would build a couple of huts on the route so that if bad weather or tiredness overcame him then he could recuperate in one of his huts. His locker gave cause for much speculation, for it was always padlocked and no one saw it opened.

Also in Joe's mess was a young fellow known as Yank. He spoke like an American, but whether he was or not was never divulged He was a bit of a keep fit fanatic and believed himself to be the picture of health. He would prance around the mess in leopard skin trunks and was always practising on dumbbells and springs, but in spite of all this so called fitness, he was supposed to be the masthead lookout. When the skipper announced over the tannoy that our first trip was going to Russia, Yank reported sick and I got his job.

The leading hand in our mess was Joe Hool, a damned nice bald headed chap. He was very clever at making models and did in fact make a one inch model of the Queen Mary in a show case, complete in every detail. He also made small Jeeps in tin and a variety of swanee whistles. Wilf, who in civilian life was a commercial artist and had a shop in Halifax, painted the ship's crest for the skipper. For once the Navy recognised someone's ability, and Wilf's job on board was to go round painting the damage control signs on all doors, bulkheads and hatches.

Now and again we would have some semblance of a band. Yank had a guitar which he couldn't play, and Joe had his swanee whistle, while the rest of us armed ourselves with knives, spoons and buckets, plus combs and anything else that would contribute to the noise.

In Dick's mess at the far end was a character they called Swain. He was short and square with big arms, built like a gorilla but with comic capabilities.

He would literally swing down the hatch to the mess deck and yell out, "Swain's the name, and who was the best bastard before I arrived?"

There was another fellow, a great womaniser, but who would never reveal his correct name to the ladies.

"What's your name?" they would ask, after he had had his way with them.

"I'm sorry," he'd say, coming over all shy. "I don't like to say."

"Why not?"

"Well, it's a bit embarrassing."

"What do you mean embarrassing? What's in a name?"

"Well, it sort of can be pronounced the wrong way."

"What on earth is wrong with that? Many people's names can be pronounced the wrong way."

"Yes, but mine is different – it can cause offence."

"Considering what you've just done to me up that dark alley, I can't see how I can be offended by a name."

"Promise you won't laugh."

"Course I won't."

"Well it's Bast Ard."

The young lady went away happy, knowing that if in nine months' time her child needed a father she could soon track him down now she had acquired his name.

Then there was the London Cockney, who spoke a different language to anyone, and his attitude and mode of speech was the same, no matter whether he was speaking to an officer or a shipmate. He was into every racket that went on and was a great leg puller.

There was the Misfit. I refer to him as such because he just used to sit and glare. He was big, broad and muscular, but sullen and morose. I never knew his name but he was quick to oppose any topic brought up in the mess. He gave the appearance of spoiling for a fight all the time. I did hear later that a girlfriend of his had died giving birth, and that the experience had soured his whole outlook on life.

Then there was the Canadian fellow Rogers who could talk about nothing else but sex. He couldn't talk about women or girls, only sex. To go seven days without brought changes of mood and edginess. He had a young lady in Glasgow who lived with her parents. At every opportunity, he would go to Glasgow to seek comfort and satisfaction within the confines of her bedroom. She used to work in a biscuit factory, and he would return to the ship armed with packets of them, which helped to build up his strength during the voyage. I never saw Rogers go ashore with any of his messmates, and I never saw him even offer a biscuit round the mess. A very private man who did not fit into the description of a messmate.

07 Oerlikon was just aft of the engine room vent shaft and this meant that the crew who manned that gun used to come off watch as black as the ace of spades. One night, when visibility was almost nil due to sleet and snow coming down, the crew took refuge in a cubby hole below the flight deck normally used by the flight deck party when the aircraft went up. They of course fell asleep, with the result that when the Gunnery Officer was making his rounds he came across this unmanned gun. He immediately went to the cubbyhole and found our miscreants covered by a tarpaulin.

The first they knew they had been discovered was when a stentorian voice yelled, "What the devil's this?"

Awaking from his slumbers, one of the occupants blustered, "We're not in here, Sir, we're not asleep."

As he was saying this, he kept shoving his partner hoping to stop his snores and wake him up. Fortunately for them, the Officer concerned realised that even though technically they had deserted their post, the weather had denied them from carrying out their duties. He very kindly and understandably gave them a caution and took no further action.

One of the men, a Midlander, was big, crude and uncouth. One shore leave he went up to Paisley, met this girl, spent the night with her and returned to the ship next morning. During the next convoy he found that a trip to the sick bay was necessary and soon his worst fears had been confirmed, for he had caught venereal disease or, as he described it, 'Blue Fever'. During the trip he voiced vengeance on the young lady concerned to such a degree that we had doubts about her safety should either of them have the misfortune to meet again.

It was some three months later that he was in Paisley with his mates, indulging in a pub-crawl, when suddenly who should he see but the young female carrier of 'Blue Fever'.

"That's her," he yelled, "that's the one."

And before his mates could stop him, he sprinted up the road.

He did not return to the ship that night, and it was with some trepidation that his messmates awaited his arrival the next morning. In unison they wanted to know what had transpired.

"That girl," they said. "What did you do to her?"

"Do?" he said in a manner that suggested they were mad to make such an enquiry. "Do?" he said. "Why, I slept with her, of course – what do you think I was going to do?"

Christmas was drawing near and we were anchored off Greenock. The Commander thought it would be a nice idea to invite some young ladies aboard and the men could entertain them, and so on Christmas Eve boat loads of girls arrived. We had decorated the messes with flags and balloons, and a hand from each mess was appointed to go to the gangway and bring back six girls. They were given a tour of the ship, taken to a film show in the hanger and then brought back to the mess for a festive tea. The thing that amazed me was the respect that was shown to these young ladies. You will have already gathered that we had a few over-sexed and reprehensible sailors aboard, but they too showed moderation in their language and their actions. There were of course exceptions, but they were few in number.

At 18:30 a drifter came alongside to take the girls ashore, but twenty six were missing. The Regulating Petty Officer searched the ship, but without success. The drifter pulled away, and as it did so another one arrived carrying young ladies for the officers' party. As they came aboard, so officers could be seen peeping out of their cabins in a furtive manner. When the coast was clear they emerged with a lady in hand. Yes, the twenty six missing females had been shanghaied by the officers and kept hidden in their cabins until the appropriate moment. We now had a different set of standards and the routine became to take them to the wardroom, get them well liquored and then retire to your cabin. At first privacy was a requirement, but that soon went by the board, for I recall passing one cabin where the sub-lieutenant was sitting on his bunk scratching his head, his hair askew and his tie half undone, while lying on the deck was a prostrate drink sodden female. At 22:00 they were supposed to go ashore, but the duty PO had to search every cabin, and in some cases literally had to pull the girls out of the bunks. In fact the drifter did not leave until 23:30.

The following morning the party detailed to clean up aft found broken bottles, bits of ladies' underwear and even some of the cabin doors were broken.

Christmas Day, I was detailed as one of the six duty hands which could be called on at any time to do minor tasks that may crop up around the ship. This saves calling the whole watch out. We had a magnificent lunch, but suddenly at 13:00 we were piped to muster on the forecastle. We did so and found Lieutenant Reed was looking over the bows. We followed his gaze and noted that the anchor cables had been twisted. It would seem that with both anchors out and the change of tide, they had twisted around one another. Lieutenant Reed decided to weigh one anchor and then by releasing it, it might shake itself loose. We tried this, but on bringing it up again he found the situation had been exacerbated by the cable now being wrapped around one of the flukes of the anchor. He tried the same evolution again only to find it now wrapped around the other fluke. Midnight came, by which time we had the cable wrapped three times round the shank and twice round each fluke. The Skipper was made aware of the problem, so in the early hours of the morning he arrived on the scene. All this time we, the duty hands, had to wash and scrub the cable every time it came in. The water was freezing and the hosepipes leaked like sieves to the extent that we were constantly working in a spray of water, and to make matters worse we had been on duty for over thirteen hours without so much as a cup of tea. The Chippy (shipwright) who worked the capstan hauling the cable and letting out the cable as directed, was getting a little dithery. I guess, like us, he was tired too. Anyway, the Skipper and the Lieutenant were looking over the side, as indeed we all were. It was pitch black and not a sound penetrated the darkness. Suddenly the cable ran out when it shouldn't have done. Now, standing next to cable being let out is an awesome experience; the noise is frightening and this frightened the hell out of all of us, to the extent we all hit the deck, the lieutenant included. On looking up, there was only one man standing. It was the Skipper, and our fright was caused by none other than Chippy who had lost concentration. The Skipper was cross and got the

Chief Shipwright out of his bunk to come and operate the capstan. Eventually the conclusion was reached that we could not resolve the problem ourselves, so the Captain sent for a boom defence vessel in order that we might lower the anchor to the foredeck where they would unshackle it, disconnect all the offending links and rejoin them. At 09:30 we were relieved, having completed over twenty hours of duty.

We soon found out why the Captain was eager to resolve the problem for, no sooner had the boom defence vessel finished its task, than we weighed anchor and once again sailed through the Western Isles and the Minches in the direction of Scapa Flow. Nobody said anything; we just knew and accepted what the gods and the Admiralty had in store for us.

Chapter 10

A Winter Convoy

To my surprise, I was relieved of my duties up the mast and transferred to the port forward pom pom.

The gun was on a sponson, which jutted out over the ship's side just below the flight deck.

There were four of us in the crew, but being in such an exposed position we were constantly being drenched with spindrift and waves coming over the bows, so we decided that if we left one man on watch together with the earphones he could maintain contact with the bridge. As far as keeping a look out was concerned, we had almost twenty-four hours of darkness which cut out airplane attacks, and the rough seas reduced U-Boat attention so there was really nothing to look for. The three lads not keeping watch had gathered wooden crates from around the ship – nothing was allowed to be thrown overboard – built them up and covered them with a tarpaulin off the guns. By this means, they were protected from the bitterly cold Arctic winds and the freezing spray. Every hour one of them left the caboosh to relieve the man on watch. The caboosh only allowed you to lie down. There was no such luxury as being able to sit up, and though we covered the steel deck with cardboard, the cold penetrated our sheepskin coats, so that we still shivered even with this protection. It was a real Heath Robinson affair and nearly caused our downfall. I say ours, but in fact it was the other watch that were in danger. One day in heavy seas, as the bows dug deep into the green ocean waters, waves came over the top, caught the shelter and swept it along the deck, including the occupants, and then slammed it against a bulkhead. The crew crawled out, bruised and battered, swearing they would never do it again, but they did. It is hard to imagine that this was allowed on a ship of the Royal Navy, but in true Nelson tradition, a blind eye was a necessary requirement in these conditions. There was of course the snow and ice, which had to be chipped away constantly to avoid making the ship top heavy. The flight deck crew were always busy keeping the flight deck clear.

The ships in the convoy were barely visible but the sea itself was always a source of interest. As the ship's bows ploughed through the water so it threw up huge pieces of phosphorous that danced a thousand steps as it passed beneath us. We would go off watch wet and frozen, our fingers and feet devoid of life. We would go down to the mess deck which, by comparison, was warm and hospitable, yet all the signs suggested the contrary was true. There was no heating and the deck head was thick with ice. We would sit up in our hammocks trying to bring the life back into frozen limbs. Our heads would knock against the icicles and send them crashing to the deck below, after which we would try and make the one and only blanket do the service of four. There was no sleep, just an uncomfortable rest with the only prospect being to get up within four hours and to put on wet clothes for another turn of duty. We did have heating once. Somehow, the Engineer was able to divert the heat from the engine room through the fan pipes to the mess decks. It was so hot, and while it helped to dry our clothes we were all in danger of getting pneumonia once we stepped out on to the upper deck, so it was never used again.

There were thirty-eight merchant ships in the convoy, and the escort was comprised of the destroyers *Keppel, Walker* and *Westcott,* sloops *Cygnet, Lapwing* and *Lark,* corvettes *Allington Castle, Alnwick Castle* and *Bamborough Castle,* the cruiser *Diadem,* and ourselves, *Vindex,* as the only escort carrier.

The outer escort was made up of the destroyers *Myngs, Savage, Scourge, Serapis, Zambesi* and *Zebra*, the Canadian destroyers *Algonquin* and *Sioux* and the Norwegian *Stord*.

The long dark nights and the cold and inclement weather all contributed to the fact that we were not detected by the enemy, which allowed us to arrive in the Kola Inlet on the 8th of January 1945 without losing a ship.

The countryside had a thick blanket of snow which disguised the craggy rocks with gentle waves of undulating snow.

Going ashore was treacherous, especially if one went off the beaten track or indeed slipped off the high flight of wooden steps that went up the hill.

There was nothing inviting to keep you ashore, but you went nevertheless just to get the feel of solid earth beneath your feet. Back aboard, however cold you were, at least you were out of the wind that cut you like a knife and in the mess deck huddled in jumpers and coats you read or wrote letters, played cards or talked. They talked of wives and families, of parents and children. They talked of other ships and mainly their last ship which, without exception, was always better than this one. They talked of ports and girls, but rarely politics and hardly ever religion, and yet the majority of sailors recognise their own weakness when compared to the sea and without making a big issue of it, they believe alright – they believe there is a Deity. They don't necessarily understand him, but with simplistic belief they know he is there. For my part, I was still mooning about this fabulous, beautiful girl from Lam Lash. Will I ever see her again; how can I possibly see her again? The ship may never go back to the Isle of Arran. Should I just forget her and merely treasure the moment? The lads in the mess still didn't know. I guess they would have laughed at me, but from my point of view she was on a pedestal, and I would never allow her name to be spoken of in a sailors' mess deck. Wilf knew – well, I think he knew. I didn't say anything apart from that first night I met her, but he would give me a knowing look now and again as though he knew the lovesick turmoil that was racing through my head.

On the 11th of January 1945, convoy RA63 set sail from the Kola Inlet. There were thirty one merchant ships, the weather was about thirty seven below and we knew that for a short period it would get worse before it got better. We didn't know at the time just how much worse. We didn't realise that weather-wise there can be far more dangerous elements than ice and cold. We came round North Cape homeward bound, and all seemed well, but I was sitting in the mess one day just before lunch. A tray of mince pies had been put at the end of the mess table, when suddenly it slid down toward me and just as suddenly went back and landed on the deck. As the ship rolled back, one of the lads could not stop himself running. With hands held out before him, he placed them on the table, did a somersault and landed up in the scuppers. Another lad in a similar predicament could not stop his onward rush, with the result that his head smashed into a plywood bulkhead from which he had to be sawn free. As for myself, I was still wedged in a corner with cups, pots and pans raining down upon me. We had been hit by a seventy mile an hour gale, and such was its severity that none of the guns were manned as no one could reach them. The only people on the upper deck were the Skipper on the bridge with his Navigator, bunting tosser and a lookout. The rest of us were battened down below decks. The Skipper had to change his clothes three times as the waves not only came across the bows and flight deck but drenched the bridge as well. There were twenty six casualties. The water was nearly two feet deep in the mess, which necessitated one keeping his sea boots on and only removing them once he was in his hammock. During the night the hammocks swung violently from side to side, banging into each other and disturbing the occupants. Meanwhile, the water, with a rhythm of its own, sloshed from side to side hitting bulkheads and other obstructions with a mighty thwack and then bursting into spray.

In the early hours of the morning, the barrels of rum in the rum locker aft broke loose, the timbers gave way and soon this golden liquid was swilling about. The Officer of the Watch ordered the rum to be pumped overboard as it presented a fire hazard. News of this disaster percolated into the mess deck, and soon a number of figures could be seen making their way aft with deck swabs, bottles, cups and tins. As long as it could contain liquid, they took it, and then down on hands and knees they mopped up the rum with the filthy dirty deck swabs and wrung them into the receptacles. Years of dirt and grease plus a mixture of flakes of grey paint and red lead all went into the concoction.

Back on the mess decks, the liquid gold was strained through clean handkerchiefs and then bottled for future consumption. *Vindex* was a happy ship, but for some time after this occurrence we were a very happy ship.

Tins and buckets floated back and forth throughout the night, bringing with them their own distinctive irregular melody. Wading through the water you kicked obstructions or ground down the already broken china, while portions of food floated tantalisingly back and forth. The galley was out of action, but fortunately the previous day's bread was intact and that, with tins of bully beef, constituted our food.

As far as the convoy was concerned, there was no way they could keep station and whilst it was bad enough for us, our fears went out to the smaller ships and in particular the mostly empty Liberty ships wallowing in the gale with the screw racing as their sterns came out of the water and taking turn about with the bows. One of the merchant ships, named *Fort Highland,* suffered collision damage, but who she hit and how the other vessel fared I know not.

We were north east of the Faroes so the Admiral sent out instructions for all ships to make for the Faroes and regroup. He then called up *HMS Westcott* and ordered her to join us, but the answer came back that she had suffered considerable damage, was steaming north into the storm and was in danger of breaking up or capsizing were she to turn broadside on.

All things come to an end and as the storm blew itself out so the ships of the convoy straggled in. We made the Faroes in a day and a half, but it was still two more days before they had all arrived. By God's grace, all the ships arrived safely though not necessarily in one piece.

We spent the next two days cleaning up the wreckage, and on inspecting our gun we found our shelter, our protection from the elements had been washed overboard. It was as well that we were not closed up at the gun, for had we been then most assuredly three men would have been swept overboard.

We finally left the Faroes and resumed our orderly sail back home. This weather did however prove that in an odd sort of way it was our protector. For different reasons, convoy PQ 17 scattered and lost over two thirds of the merchant ships, twenty one of them in five days. We scattered under the umbrella of this foul weather and didn't lose one, and yet if one U-Boat had gotten lucky and seen us at a time when we were all battened below decks, there would have been no survivors.

Having called in at Scapa Flow, we then sailed south to Greenock, but surprise surprise, we didn't stop but carried on up the Clyde to Meadowside Wharf where we were due for a refit.

Chapter 11

There Is Always Someone Worse Off

It was close to forty below zero as we stood our watch. There were still three hours to go before our relief took over, and already we were shaking from the wicked penetrating cold. Our clothes and jumpers were still wet from our previous watch, as there were no means of drying below decks. The Arctic winds swept across the angry seas littered with hundreds of small growlers, the guard rails and everything around us was coated with a thick layer of ice. We stamped our feet and swung our arms, but it did very little to restore life and circulation into cold limbs. We cleaned the ice off our binoculars in order to sweep the seas for danger, and when we came to remove them, we found them welded to our eyelashes with ice. We wallowed in self-pity and envied our mates tucked up in their hammocks. There was never any heating in the mess deck and the deckheads were all rimed with ice, but at least the lucky devils were out of the biting wind. Our minds strayed and we wondered if there could be any part of our planet that was as Godforsaken as this. Our thoughts were constantly changing and slowly we forgot our self-pity when we realised that at that precise period we were passing over the graves of other shipmates killed in previous convoys. They no longer felt the cold, they had no fears nor pain, but were at peace.

It was only a short step to the realisation that there were others who were worse off. Somewhere out there in the darkness of an Arctic night, beyond our vision and over the horizon, were other shipmates in a leaking open boat, struggling for life. Their ship had been torpedoed and as she went down so this small gathering of men scrambled into the lifeboat. Their clothes were wet through. Some were covered in oil, others had no shoes and they all sat with water up to their ankles. They shivered and shook far worse than we were experiencing, and they could not look for a relief in three hours' time – in fact they would be lucky to be relieved in three days' time if they lasted that long. With matted hair and oil-grimed faces, they tried to bale the water out of the boat. Some were young teenagers and some were old. Some were noisy and some were quiet. Some were optimists and others were pessimists. Some swore, some sang with croaked voices and some who had never prayed before and didn't know how quietly kept repeating the Lord's Prayer, something they had learnt at their Mother's knee and never forgotten. Another lad had his rosary beads a gift from his parents and he took comfort in the memories of home, the very feel of them invoked a feeling of trust and hope. Some were injured but the cold had numbed the pain and congealed the blood. Inevitably someone took charge – they didn't have to have rank or authority, just the desire to live and the ability to motivate the others to share one's own optimism and lift their spirits, to encourage them to row the boat or to bale out and help the less fortunate shipmates.

As night wore on, the boat became quieter with just the noise of the oars in the rowlocks and the constant baling. The groans of an injured man ceased. He would not need his coat anymore so it was removed and his body slipped over the side. His companions barely had the strength to wish him farewell as his body floated away amid the ice-strewn sea. The freezing cold can easily weaken a man's resolution and cause him to lose the will to live. They all knew that time was not on their side and that if rescue did not come soon they would all drift into unconsciousness.

As all these thoughts flitted through one's mind, we forgot our own discomfort, we forgot our coldness and misery and instead offered up a prayer for those unknown shipmates who were far worse off than we were.

Chapter 12

Refit

There was something appealing about a refit. For a brief period you knew you weren't going anywhere, we knew other convoys, other tasks lay in the future, but it was the present that needed to be savoured and appreciated.

We had of course taken all of the ammunition off the ship at Greenock and sent one watch on leave. Meanwhile, the ship was cleaned and scrubbed. She was painted inside and out, and then there were the dockyard mateys who swarmed over the ship like flies. Alterations were being made and repairs carried out following the bumps with the *Queen Mary*. Riveting, drilling and banging was deafening and went on all day. A huge hole was made in the flight deck through which they lowered a new self-contained radar unit. The lads found being alongside very comforting with easy access to the entertainments Glasgow had to offer, and such was their comfort that they were able to divert the work force to other interests, and so the dockyard mateys were invited down the mess to partake of cups of tea and anything else that was on offer. After tea, the workers promptly found themselves a comfortable spot and went to sleep, propped up against the lockers. It was not long however before the foreman came looking for his men and kicked up hell, but it did not stop them.

One day the radar boys wanted an aerial, that projected over fifteen foot from the top of the mast, taken down. They were reluctant to do it, so I offered to do it for them. The aerial was at the end of two inch angle irons in the shape of a 'Y' so it was necessary to lay alongside this projection and unbolt the aerial. However, that is just an aside, because the end of the story is that I came down the mast and suddenly found myself hanging in mid air. The dockyard workers had only chopped off the bottom eight foot of the ladder while I was up there.

A large dome made of Perspex which contained radar material was taken down and left on the jetty. Now, Perspex was a product much used by the lads in their spare time to make a variety of objects, such as bracelets, brooches and many other things, and many a covetous eye was cast in the direction of this dome. Unable to contain themselves one night, they broke the dome and, like vultures, descended on the shattered fragments.

Being alongside the wall, it was necessary to have gangway sentries. One of these sentries was Taffy, who had the amazing ability to do everything wrong and get away with it. One night, whilst on duty and feeling cold, Taffy drew his bayonet and scoured the dockside for wood. Having acquired the wood, he returned to the gangway and used his bayonet as an axe to chop the wood, after which in spite of the blackout he lit a fire.

At the same time, the Commander whose cabin was at the top of the gangway was entertaining his wife, also the Padre. Throughout their conversation all they could hear was 'chip chip chip – chip chip chip'.

The Commander called a messenger and said, "I don't know what that infernal noise is but have it stopped."

It had however already stopped because Taffy, having abandoned his rifle and sheathed his bayonet, was now roasting chestnuts. The fire died down, leaving Taffy nothing to do – nothing, that is, apart from guarding the gangway and checking boarders. He happened to look in the water between the ship and the wall when he espied hundreds of light bulbs popping up and down. Taffy could never resist temptation so, armed with a selection of pebbles, he proceeded to take aim – pop, pop, bang, splash, pop.

The Commander was now quite cross. "Officer of the Watch," he yelled. "Have that dammed noise stopped immediately."

Taffy was quiet for five minutes and then he saw an old empty oil drum. With a piece of stick, his bayonet and an unmelodious voice, he succeeded in sending the Commander wild.

Old Joe never went ashore much, but one day he took a notion and in a pair of overalls he passed over the gangway and out of the dockyard. No one stopped him; in fact I don't think anybody gave it much thought, as sailors were off and on the ship all day long. Anyway, half an hour later, Joe came ambling back, clutching a bundle of fish and chips. The Officer of the Watch happened to be on the gangway at the time and charged Joe with desertion and breaking ship. He went before the Commander, but the charge was so serious that he was referred to the Skipper. When the day arrived for the Captain's defaulters to be seen, it happened to be the same day that Joe got drunk. When the Regulating Petty Officer came down the mess to get him, old Joe was lying under the table, completely sozzled. We dragged him out and walked him up and down, gave him a cold shower, we then walked him up and down again. The RPO was as much involved as we were in sobering him up. Joe blinked and swore and cussed in no polite manner but he could just stand as he was led before the Skipper.

The Skipper gave Joe seven days in the cells, and as the warrant was read out Joe swayed from side to side and then fell against the bulkhead. The Skipper suggested Joe was drunk, but the two guards swore that he had not even had a sniff of lime juice, but they weren't very convincing liars, and the Skipper remained silent, but he knew.

The bleary, cross-eyed babbling old veteran was half carried down to the cells to start his sentence, but he always had plenty of cigarettes and food and never lacked in alcoholic sustenance. The story of Joe is really a story of the true meaning of shipmates.

As soon as the seven days were up, Joe applied for leave and, to our amazement, it was granted; and yet on second thoughts not even the executive could be hard on Joe for long for he was a lovable old character. The day he went on leave, we saw his uniform for the first time, and as he rolled along the dockside with his steaming bag slung over one shoulder, the lads lined the rails and gave him a real send off.

One day we had an invite from some people ashore for twenty five sailors to go as guests to a party which was being held to raise funds for our lads with the British Expeditionary Forces. Well, we made up the required numbers and I must say they gave us all a wonderful time. Halfway through the evening, an old lady came round and tapped each sailor on the shoulder, asking him to go into an annexe off the main hall. When we gathered in there, they produced a pint of beer for each man, which was not only a thoughtful gesture but an appreciated one. We had not been in the room long when the door burst open and a bevy of young ladies swarmed into the room shouting, "Where are all the sailors?"

A few nights later, Crash and I decided to go dancing at a place in Patrick called the F & F, or Effs for short. We had a good time, so much so that it prompted us to go again. I had not been in the hall more than half an hour when my heart leaped and my pulse raced. Sitting on her own in the shadows was this astoundingly beautiful young girl, the epitome of all I dreamed and yearned for. My deep love for the young lady in Lam Lash was not being usurped by this gorgeous wondrous female because it was her; it was Anne from the Isle of Arran; it was the one whose vision I had carried for so long. Nervously I approached her and she accepted my request for a dance. The warmth of her small hand in mine and the fact that I had my arm around her waist, was so unreal – it was as though I was going to wake up and find it was just a dream, but a very beautiful dream.

I spoke her name which intrigued her as to how I knew it. I spoke of the dance in Lam Lash where I had first seen her. She in turn told me that she lived in Arran with her grandmother and was home in Ibrox for a short while, visiting her parents.

We sat out the next dance – I think she was relieved to get from under my feet – and I ordered tea and cakes. Anne drank weak tea with no milk or sugar and she didn't eat the cakes, but I was famished and even at the expense of her thinking me gluttonous, I finished them off. I studied her beautiful face hoping she did not see me staring at her long dark curly hair and such beautiful small eyes. To say she was pretty would be to do her an injustice. Never had I seen such beauty. I studied her profile; it was exquisite, with the loveliest of small noses. Anne was quiet, she didn't say much and I don't think she was even aware that I was drinking in all this beauty. I'm sure she was in ignorance of the heart that was beating so loudly just two feet away from her.

Anne had to be home by ten and I asked if I could accompany her. She wasn't too keen, but with a little persuasion she agreed I could walk her to the underground station. I didn't like the idea of her travelling alone, so accompanied her to Copland Road.

I desperately wanted to see her again, but was embarrassed as to what I should say. I had never asked a girl to go out before and feared rejection. The thought that I might never see this adorable creature again filled me with foreboding, but if I didn't ask I would regret it for the rest of my life. In a confused manner and stuttering over my words I managed to ask for a date. There were no lights just the blackness of the night. There were no stars nor moon, yet as I looked into those beautiful innocent eyes they seemed to sparkle and she said "Yes". My heart jumped for joy and I vowed I would never lose her again.

We had agreed to meet at St. Enoch's underground station, and in the meantime I was dancing on air. I bought some hair oil, ironed and pressed my suit and carefully shaved.

I was early but the minutes passed so slowly. Eventually the time came round but she was not there. Five minutes passed and then ten; my self-esteem was going downhill fast. Had she forgotten? Was this the right place and the right time? Maybe one of us got it wrong, but I knew it wasn't me. It was far too important an occasion for me to get any aspect of it wrong. Half an hour later I was swearing at myself – what a fool, what a blasted idiot. What girl would give you a second look? What a sucker I was to be so much in love with someone I hardly knew, and who had probably forgotten what I even look like. I sank into the depths of despair, the miserable look on my face pictured the feeling in my soul, and yet I still waited, hanging onto that fine thread of hope and then, and then coming up the steps of St. Enoch's was this dazzling apparition of beauty. How could I have doubted her? How could harsh thoughts have invaded my lovesick mind? In a trice I was transformed. How proud I was as she took my arm; how I wished the lads could see the confirmed bachelor with this beautiful young lady, and yet on the other hand I had no desire to share this knowledge. Her very name could not be spoken in the mess deck for I would not have been able to contain myself if a derogatory remark had been made, the sort of remark that one associates with a mess deck. Anne was very special and above all this.

I told Wilf, but then he had already worked it out for himself, and I also told Mrs Love in the Church of Scotland canteen at Greenock the next time we were down there. She was understanding and shared my happiness. Dick, of course knew, though he had not met her.

Both watches were given leave and Dick and I travelled to London together, but my last train to Staines had gone so Dick invited me to stay the night at his home in Woolwich.

We set out being forced to take devious routes to his home, but at 02:00 we arrived. Mrs Baldwin, Dick's mother, came down and gave us a lovely meal of bacon and eggs. I certainly did not realise at the time, not having ration books on board ship, but that meal must have come out of their meagre rations – such was the heart of gold of these London folk. We were interrupted by a loud explosion, the curtains blew and the boards across the windows rattled, the glass having already been blown out in a previous air raid. We found out the following morning that a rocket had fallen just a few streets away.

We came back off leave to find the refit almost finished and so within a few days we were once again anchored at the Tail of the Bank. I was made Corporal of the gangway which was purely a harbour job and necessitated the checking of everybody coming aboard or leaving the ship. This was on the port side of the ship and from my position by looking aft I could see Taffy. Now Taffy was the keyboard sentry and obviously responsible for all the keys. The keyboard was also right outside the Captain's cabin.

One night, catching sight of me, he came up and said, "Joey I've got the keys to the stores. I'm going to ask the Officer of

The Watch for permission to go to the heads, so will you keep an eye on the key board for me?"

"Yes, that's okay," I replied.

"Is there anything you want?" he asked.

"Anything I want?" I replied in a questioning manner.

"Yes, I'm going to kit myself out," he said.

Now I knew Taffy was mad, but this was really dicing with trouble.

"No Taffy, nothing for me," I responded, and away he went.

Ten minutes later Taffy came back. "Joey I'm in a bloody fix."

"What's the matter?"

"It's that bleeding door. One key unlocked it, but it takes two to lock it up again."

Taffy went down to the keyboard to look for the missing key, and then went missing for another five minutes. He came back all smiles and tossed me a pair of gloves.

"Did you get what you wanted?" I asked

"Yes," he said. "I've got a new oil skin, sea boots and a full kit."

On duty with me was the Quartermaster, a leading hand.

One night the Officer of the Watch, a young Sub-lieutenant said to the Quartermaster, "Quartermaster, how about you wetting some tea?"

"Sir," replied the QM, "if I don't want to wet the tea I won't. That tea happens to be part of the mess allocation."

"Right," said the subby. "If I don't get any, I'll sure as hell see you don't."

"Don't worry sir," said the QM, "it'll hurt you more than it will me."

"That's what you think," said the subby. "I can soon go down to the engine room and get a cup of tea from the stokers."

For a brief moment the QM was stumped, and then he looked up and said, "Right sir, you've got me on the tea situation, but I'll give you fair warning. If I ever catch you asleep in the wardroom, which you do on every watch, I'll wake up the Officer of the Day."

The subby was dumbfounded. It had been looked upon as a privilege to have a nap in the wardroom whilst on duty, provided the Commander didn't know.

Geordie was being drafted and the appointed time to leave the ship was 13:00. Now at 12:00 every day, they piped 'Up Spirits', so a hand from each mess collected the rum allocation. Geordie was a very popular shipmate and spent the time between 12:00 and 13:00 saying goodbye to his mates, and this meant that a sailor's generosity and expressions of goodbye could be measured through the amount of liquor he would allow his parting chum. It was therefore the number of 'sippers', or if he was lucky 'gulpers', he could sink in the period available. Rum, as we know acts, very quickly in its ability to numb the brain and weaken the limbs.

His messmates carried his hammock and kit bag to the embarkation space. Meanwhile the drifter had come alongside. The seas were quite heavy, necessitating the drifter keeping just that much further away from the ship. Geordie was oblivious to this and from the embarkation space he threw his hammock overboard. No one in their right mind would do that – you would at least have gone to the bottom of the gangway – but not Geordie, for more by luck than judgement the hammock landed on the deck of the drifter, and he followed this with his kit bag. Very unsteadily, he descended the gangway and, arriving at the bottom, he faced the drifter with knees bent and his arms swinging to and fro. If it was right for there to be an appropriate time to jump, only Geordie knew. He landed on the deck, slipped, hit his head on the gunwale, stood up and rolled overboard. The danger now was being crushed between the drifter and the carrier. A cry went up.

The Skipper of the drifter was yelling, "That man was drunk before he came aboard."

The gangway staff rushed below. The crew of the drifter ran to the side and between them they hauled him out. Obviously he had to come back on board to be examined in the sick bay. Meanwhile, both the Regulating Petty Officer and Lieutenant Reed, the Officer of the Watch, refuted the allegations made by the skipper of the drifter. What they said and what they believed were, of course, very much different.

Later, the RPO came down the mess and said, "Lieutenant Reed has instructed me to find out if Geordie was drunk. You know what to say."

Eventually, the mess was told to fall in in the embarkation space where we were to be interrogated one by one. As I was the youngest, my messmates were a little apprehensive that I might say the wrong thing. Lieutenant Reed questioned each man but left me to last, then he said:

"Was Geordie drunk?"

"No, Sir."

"Did you see anybody give him rum?"

"No, Sir."

He leaned forward and without looking at me but speaking softly he said, "You are a bloody liar."

As he turned away he was hardly able to conceal the grin that came over him.

The next day, Geordie went on draft at 11:00 and the Commander issued an order that in future all drafts must leave the ship by noon.

One night while anchored off Greenock, the last liberty boat made its way back to the ship containing the usual crowd of well-oiled sailors. This particular night it was fairly rough, and three such tanked up sailors were standing in the port waist of the drifter, when one of them staggered, threw his arms out to catch himself, and only succeeded in knocking his two mates overboard as well as himself. The offender couldn't swim, but his mates could. The offender was saved but his mates drowned. It was a very sad and tragic accident, but the astounding thing was the way it quickly sobered up the other men. One of the lads who died had only been married a week.

Chapter 13

Post Refit Activities

The routine in the mess decks had been considerably interrupted with a constant flow of dockyard mateys invading our quarters, plus the two watches enjoying some leave. It was therefore necessary to settle back into some form of pattern where each man followed his own activities without interfering with his messmates. Obviously a game of cards or someone wetting a brew made it more a communal pastime.

Bill Fallows, a broad and well-built young lad and I used to indulge in wrestling matches nearly every lunch time. Why goodness only knows, but after half an hour we were dirty, dishevelled and exhausted. In a way it was a substitute for exercise, though at the time we did not look at it that way.

At times the close confinement of a crowd of men together in a limited space created tensions, though they were few and far between, and of a short lived nature.

An example of this was Crash. I've already said he was quite a comedian and very popular in the mess, but he had one habit that I found annoying. Every lunchtime as we were sitting down to a meal, Crash would fetch for himself a cup of cold water, and every time he used to press the wet, cold cup against the back of my neck. It was an inoffensive action but day after day it ceased to be funny and became a source of irritation. I was not the only one singled out for this treatment, for the other lads also found that after a while it just became irksome. We told him to pack it in, but Crash just grinned with that huge mouth of his and ignored everybody. One day I exploded and sprang upon him. Poor old Crash didn't know what had happened as I wrestled him to the deck. The next thing was the lads left their meals and formed a ring around the two writhing figures on the deck. We rolled into saucepans and knocked over mess stools, buckets, pots and pans. For nigh on half an hour the battle went on until at length I had him lying over the mess stool. Suddenly Crash went limp, and as I saw him with that perpetual grin I knew the match was over.

Our little scrap paid dividends for the other lads knew they could never take advantage of me, and as for Crash – well, I never received a cold cup again, and my respect for him as a damned good messmate never wavered.

Every opportunity I could, I travelled to Glasgow to see Anne. She will never know the eager anticipation that filled my breast as the train rattled its way from Greenock. I was running short of money and had to resort to hitchhiking, usually by lorry. Then there was the problem of getting accommodation in Glasgow. The Sailors Society did not have many beds but they were clean with white sheets and cost a shilling a night. If you couldn't get in there, then you went to the YMCA, which was only sixpence a night, but they slept about five hundred in one room on iron double tiered bunks, with one blanket that had not seen the cleaners since the outbreak of war. There was a motley collection of men from all walks of life. The three services were represented plus merchant seamen from nearly every country in the world, and also some old tramps, whose hygiene was little better than the blankets. You didn't undress and even kept your boots on in case someone stole them, and any money was kept in your money belt. Sleep was out of the question for the bed was merely something for you to lie on, and the fleas to take advantage of. In the dim light everyone was a potential thief or murderer, so with one eye open for security you lay awake and scratched.

They had a canteen to which I would go about 23:00, having left Anne at 22:00. It was like a League of Nations with so many different uniforms and different shades of skin.

One night I was sitting at a table and a Palestine policeman joined me.

"I say, Jack," he said. "This place ain't nice to know."

"How do you mean?" I replied.

"Glasgow," he said. "I was sitting in a cafe under the bridge near St. Enoch's station not ten minutes ago. I was talking with these civvies when one of them brought out a large pair of barber's scissors with a cork on the end. The next one brought out a razor – you know the cutthroat type? – and another a bicycle chain. Not realising the significance of these items I said, 'What's this in aid of?'

"'We're on a raid tonight,' said one.

"'How do you mean?'

"The guy with the razor just passed his left hand across his throat and with an evil grin said, 'You ain't seen nuttin yet.' At this another fellow, built like a tank, takes out of his inside pocket a carving knife as sharp as a razor. I'm telling you Jack, I ain't never seen such an evil band of brigands and got the hell out of it pretty damn quick. Give me Palestine any day."

With that, he got up and went to the dormitory.

Another night, I was talking to a Canadian soldier and the conversation got around to morals.

"I consider," he said, "that I have a very high moral standard. Take for example the other night. I went to a dance, met this dame and walked her home. Now, you can tell when a dame wants more than a good night kiss – they sort of send out signals. Well, I'm telling you Jack, these signals were coming over strong. We were outside her front door and I says, 'Lady are you married?'

"'Sure,' she says, 'husband in the Navy.'

"Now Jack, this bird, she's desperate, she's just pleading for it and I'm ready to accommodate her and I says, 'Husband overseas is he?'

"'No,' she says, 'he's down in Portsmouth.'

"Jack, you could have knocked me down with a feather and this is what I mean by morality; if he'd have been overseas I'd have taken her to bed, but if he's still in the same country and she's desperate, she can go and visit him. I was disgusted with her and walked off."

Waiting for Anne one night outside St. Enoch's subway, an old man came up to me.

"Good evening Jack," he said. "Got the price of a cup of tea for an old sailor?"

It so happened that I recognised him from a few months earlier when he had stopped me outside Euston station.

"Old sailor?" I said. "Old sailor? Why, three months ago you were an old soldier."

"Not me, Jack, never been a soldier in me life. Anyway, three months ago I was in London."

"I know," I replied. "I saw you there, and if you can afford to go to London, you can afford the price of a cup of tea."

He turned away, and out of curiosity I followed him. He stopped two soldiers and I heard him say, "Good evening, Tommy, have you got the price of a cup of tea for a down and out old soldier?"

I went my way, silently contented my memory had not let me down.

Another evening, whilst waiting for a train at Central Station, I went down to the toilets.

As I was going down the steps, an old boy came up to me and said, "Say Jack, like to buy a gold bracelet for ten bob?"

It looked good value to me, but then I had visions of him having stolen it, and with the police on his trail he was trying to palm it off on me. I declined his offer.

At the YMCA, they always asked at what time in the morning you wanted a shake. At the appointed time they would come round and hit the iron bed supports with a chunk of timber. This meant that no matter what time you wanted to get up, everybody was awake from the noise made to rouse the earliest risers.

The first train to Greenock left at 06:30. It was always full of bleary-eyed sailors, many nursing mammoth hangovers. On a cold morning the train built up a hot sweaty fug until it reached its destination, where it disgorged its occupants onto the drab and wet cobbled streets of Greenock. I would often meet some of my shipmates on the train and we'd go into the canteen for a cup of tea before going down to the harbour.

The drifters were tied up alongside each other and you might get a dozen or more together. Each one was designated to take their passengers to one or two specified ships moored in the stream, so you would get the early morning scene, usually wet and grey, of hundreds of sailors clambering from drifter to drifter until they found the right one. You then looked for a position in the lee of the smoke stack and waited for the innermost boat to cast off first. This prevented last minute pier head jumpers. Once the first boat had cast off, then each drifter cast off its neighbour, and so the transition was made from a world of entertainment and gaiety to the reality of a ship at war.

On arriving alongside, it was the custom for the Officers to ascend first and the other ranks afterwards. On one occasion the Commander was standing in the embarkation area as his officers arrived.

When they had mustered, he said, "Gentlemen, the drifter is for the men. The Officers have their own launch for returning to the ship. Now, just go back aboard that drifter and wait until the men are aboard before you follow them."

The men appreciated that gesture and the Commander who was already held in high esteem went up a little further.

Our Commander, Williams, by name was strict Royal Navy. When he first joined us he was astonished at the lack of discipline and the state of disrepair into which our damage control system had fallen. He rectified this and introduced further rules and orders which, although we kicked against them at first, we realised on second thoughts that they were for our own benefit. Further, when he did anything new, he told us his reasons. There was a rest room aboard, but it was rarely used, for the simple reason we were usually too busy. On the convoys all we wanted to do between watches was eat and try and get some sleep, and of course in harbour, half the watch were ashore, so there was more room in the mess and less need to use the restroom. Another factor was that it was frequently taken over to be used to house survivors from other ships or, as on one trip, it was used for a party of Norwegian soldiers trained in Arctic warfare. Dressed all in white and carrying skis, the object was to land them in Russia and for them to make their way into Norway. Anyway, the Commander had it redecorated and endeavoured to encourage the men to partake in spare time activities, such as model making or painting or writing. I don't think it was too successful because the Commander's ideas of spare time activities differed somewhat to that of the men. As far as they were concerned, spare time was to be spent thinking of the theory, and shore time was meant for putting theory into practice.

I've mentioned the cells on board earlier – well they were situated up for'ard near the Petty Officers' ablutions. There was usually at least one man incarcerated, and that meant you needed someone to keep guard, namely a cell sentry. Part of the prisoner's punishment was to pick about 7lbs of oakum. A pound would roughly represent a foot of tarred hemp, so there were seven pieces. You then had to tease each strand using just your fingers. It is a tiring and time consuming task which left you with tar stained and sore and painful fingers. The cell sentry would assist the prisoner to meet his quota and would also turn a blind eye when other shipmates ensured that the one under punishment never went short of liquor or food.

The cell door was usually left open – after all, where can you escape to with the ship anchored over half a mile off shore, and in cold inhospitable waters? With help and a little determination it can be done; in fact it was done. A prisoner went missing and was most certainly not on the ship, but how did he get away? Well, I don't really know, but let us look at it this way. The prisoner was a stoker, who we referred to as clinker knockers. His best mate was also a stoker, but his harbour duties were as a stoker on the motor cutter. Now, the motor cutter was always tied up to the stern boom, and the prisoner's departure coincided with his mate's turn of duty. We now have a situation where the sentry is asleep at his post. The prisoner slips out and goes over the stern boom and hides beneath a tarpaulin. Under that tarpaulin was his overcoat, uniform and all other basic needs. The crew of a motor cutter are usually a tight knit bunch – well, there are only four of them – and the three seamen in the crew are certainly not going to welch on a shipmate, so the very first trip in the morning has our prisoner stepping ashore. It was some time later that we heard that the police were holding him at Perth Police Station on a house breaking charge. Apparently they couldn't make it stick, and a Naval Patrol brought him back to the ship. The cell sentry received fourteen days of number elevens.

One day a new fellow arrived on board and was put in Dick's mess. There was nothing unusual about this, because crew members were often drafted ashore, maybe for courses or promotion, and by the same manner, the vacancy caused by their going had to be filled – but this fellow was different. He was quiet and reserved, and as soon as he had settled in he sat down to read the Bible. Sailors in general have a deep and abiding faith. Their respect for the strength of the sea probably accounts for it, but they do not talk about it. If anything they will talk against it, but that is just a veneer they use to cloud what they perceive as a weakness in themselves. This attitude means that you just do not see a Bible in a seamans' mess deck. It is like oil and water. Well, our Bible reading friend soon acquired the name of Moses. It was not long before Laker, our London cockney, and Scouse arrived from the upper deck.

"Who was the best bastard' afore I arrived?" yelled Scouse as he swung down the hatchway in his customary style.

Quickly he and Laker noticed the new man, and just as quickly they saw what he was reading. In unison the two let forth a string of oaths which, were one to interpret, meant, "Gentlemen, what have we got here?"

Scouse and Laker verbally attacked Moses with a string of questions which usually started with the words, "Well, wot abaht this?" Moses remained quiet and unruffled, and he gave satisfactory answers to every argument that was put forward which only had the effect of making Laker and Scouse madder. Moses was not trying to convert them, and I think even at this early stage of their acquaintance he soon realised he would have had greater success with the Devil himself. Back and forth it went with the mess deck looking on as Laker and Scouse became more and more exasperated.

They realised they were getting the worst of the argument, and in desperation Laker suddenly exploded, "Before you come here bloody preaching, you convert the Padre. That bloke's never been down to see the lads since the bleeding ship commissioned."

"Yes," interrupted Scouse. "And another thing, 'e's got a store of warm clothing and comforts and 'ave we seen any of it? Like 'ell we 'aven't. Bloody Russian convoys. D'you 'ear that? That's where we been, an 'e ain't seen fit to give us nuttin'. Bleeding Officers, they gets kitted out, but not the likes of us."

Laker could see they had taken the initiative and was determined to capitalise on it.

"An' another thing, Moses," says our cockney, "'e stands on the gangway at nighttime, an' if any o' the boys come back a bit seven sheets to the wind 'e'll run 'em in, and then to cap it he goes down the wardroom and probably gets pissed."

With broad grins on their faces Scouse and Laker rested their case.

Moses very quietly and calmly closed his Bible and said, "Tomorrow I will see the Padre."

True to his word, Moses did see the Padre with the result that the warm clothing locker was opened and a distribution made. The fact that such warm clothing was later sold to the Russians is just by the way.

There was another by-product resulting from Moses's visit, and that was shortly after when one night the mess was surprisingly quiet when footsteps were heard coming down the hatch way. Looking up we saw officer's shoes followed by officer's trousers, and by the time the visitor had his foot on the bottom step we saw the dog collar. The lads sat with open mouths, but before he could say anything, Scouse let forth.

"What's 'e come for chaps? Mind your cups, keep your lockers shut and watch your arses."

The Padre withdrew, never to be seen on the mess deck again.

Moses was never afraid to pursue the cause of justice. He was not a barrack room lawyer, but take for example the food. It really was atrocious and was a constant source of complaint, but only between the mess deck bulkheads. No one took it further – at least not until Moses arrived. I don't know who he spoke to or who he saw, but the complaint reached the Captain's ears, who then called upon the Commander to convene a meeting and find out what the trouble was.

The meeting was comprised of the Commander, the Paymaster, Chief Purser and the Canteen Manager, as well as representatives from the lower deck, one of whom was Laker. During the course of the meeting, one aspect that was disclosed was the fact that meals arrived cold from the galley. The allegation was refuted, when Laker stood up.

"Sir," he said, "the galley is dishing out the grub now. I'll go and get a plate."

So saying, he disappeared. On leaving the galley he thought it prudent to make his way back to the meeting by going over the flight deck. Opening the door Laker showed the meal.

"This," he said, "this is todays dinner. The fat is congealed, the gravy is dry on the plate, an' look at this."

At that moment he took a roast potato off the plate and slapped it into the Paymaster's hand.

"Feel that," says Laker. "Feel it. Does it feel warm? Now stick yer thumb in it, its 'ard, bloody 'ard, I tell you it ain't cooked proper."

The Paymaster passed the object of Laker's passionate dialogue to the Commander. Laker however was in full flow – he'd got the bit between his teeth and wasn't going to let an opportunity like this slip by. That is, until the Commander interrupted him.

"That's enough, Laker," said the Commander. "Sufficient has been said to lend strength to the men's allegations."

The Officer of the Watch was instructed to visit the mess each lunchtime and ask for any complaints. Further, the victualing allowance, which by custom is higher for officers than the other ranks, had all been lumped together with the apparent result that the men were not getting as much as they were entitled to. This was then apportioned correctly, and thereafter the food improved no end. The Chief Purser, following their meeting, decided to give the lads a special treat. In his cold store he had some oxtail, so it was duly extracted and served up. The Officer of the Watch came round.

"Any complaints?" said he.

"Yes, Sir," speaks up one bright spark. "The rabbits off."

The Chief couldn't win.

Aboard ship, everyone is constantly on the lookout for perks. It may be currants and sultanas that have been written off as 'contaminated' by seawater. Unallocated soap or maybe a little too much water gets into the rum barrels, thereby having a surplus when everyone has had their tot. Such surplus is thrown overboard – those are the rules. The Officer who presides over the distribution of rum quietly turns his back, knowing he can trust his men to do that which is correct. Such courtesy and faith is later rewarded when one of the men slips a flask into the Officer's cabin. Rum is probably the most prized possession in the lower deck. It opens doors, it acquires favours, it carries with it the means to receive favourable treatment from those who have something that you require. It can be used to get an extra run ashore or to change watches. Rum is like liquid gold dust that men covet; it's like a fever, an addiction, and it bestows on the owner a power that they normally would not have.

In our mess deck was an office used by one of the Chief Petty Officers. I will not say what service he performed for the ship, but suffice to say that when we were in the Tail of the Bank he was accustomed to receiving visitors from ashore. One day, a most attractive young WRNS called upon him and, after ushering her into his office, he closed the door. The young lady had not escaped the notice of those sitting in the mess deck, and as she passed through this gauntlet of staring eyes, all took in that part of her anatomy to which that person was particularly attracted. Having feasted their eyes on this piece of feminine beauty, they realised that she was entering the lair of a well-known and practised womaniser. This invoked a desire to listen in to his technique, so the motors to the fresh air ducts were turned off. Those ducts not only went through the mess deck, but also the office where our Chief and the lady were confined. With the motor off and by standing on the tables with an ear to the vents, everything that was being said in the cabin was being channelled to the listeners. Absolute quiet was necessary to get the best reception, but of course there is always one, there always is. It was Donkey; he waited until a delicate part of their relationship had been reached and putting his mouth to the vent he yelled, "You dirty bastard, shagging a dame on duty."

The air was filled with uncontrollable laughter, and then some minutes later, a red faced WRNS emerged, adjusting her clothing, followed by an equally embarrassed Chief.

There is, in the Royal Navy, quite a gulf between commissioned officers and the other ranks. There is an ingrained disrespect that one holds for the other. One should however not generalise on this, for the reason that our Skipper, Captain Bayliss, and Commander Williams were respected by the crew. They did not demand respect, nor did they expect it, but they earned it by the way they treated their subordinates. Regrettably, you always have one man who believes his gold stripes make him superior to the other ranks, and causes him to treat them as morons. We had one such person aboard who had spent an evening in the wardroom drinking to excess. Feeling a bit unsteady on his feet, he left the wardroom and staggered down the port passage, only to bump into the Corporal of the gangway.

Pushing him aside, our inebriated officer said, "Get out of my way, you ignorant bastard."

Unbeknown to him, a very popular Lieutenant was about twenty paces behind. Now, this particular officer had made the transition from the mess deck to the wardroom. He understood the men and knew how to treat them and get the right response, and when he witnessed the behaviour of his brother officer, he was consumed with rage. He sprinted the short distance and administered a thrashing that hopefully would result in a lesson having being learnt the hard way.

I've mentioned the Paymaster before, a very quiet and reserved sort of man, bordering on the eccentric. Well, one day, he nearly had the ship's company on his head. It came about through a cat. There were three of them, but we were never blessed with a happy event until one day the buzz went around the ship that our numbers were to be increased. We had reconciled ourselves to the fact that they were all tomcats, so the news was received with gladness. Spies were used to report any sightings of the prospective mother and report back as to her condition and expectant date. Now, sailors do not know things like the gestation period of cats – nevertheless, they were sure that by looking at her size, a pretty good guess could be made, and so the day was awaited with eager anticipation.

Then the news came back, "She's had them."

"How many?"

"I don't know."

"Why?"

"Well, she's thinner, but I don't know where the kittens are."

Everybody was instructed that whoever saw the mother should follow her and find out her place of confinement.

Two or three days later, the mystery was solved. Now when I say solved, I should say they were speculations based on rumour and the rumour was that our Paymaster had paid a visit to the wardroom and with a suitably lubricated tongue he allegedly confessed that returning to his cabin one night he found the cat had given birth on his bunk and promptly gathered up the kittens and the mess and pushed it out of the porthole. The men were angry and disappointed, and such anger was directed at the Paymaster. The truth may never be known.

By now it was the busy time as we took aboard ammunition and generally restored ship. Storing ship had a dual purpose, one of which was illegal, for it was a time when men kept a constant look out in order to seize the opportunity to replenish the mess deck coffers. Knowing this, the officer responsible for the stores had his men keeping careful vigilance, but even he could not stop accidents happening, such as crates of tinned food falling down the hatch and bursting as they hit the steel decks, scattering the contents into the hands of eager helpers below. The tinned produce was quickly hidden behind fan shafts and the myriad of pipes that run through a ship. They would then be collected late at night and taken down the mess.

When this had been accomplished, we weighed anchor and steamed out of the Clyde. A new squadron was then landed, but we noticed that while the faithful old Swordfish was still the mainstay, the Hurricanes had been replaced by the American

Wildcats, a small, snub-nosed aeroplane with a narrow wheel base and claiming to be faster than the Hurricanes. The new squadrons had to get acclimatised, so we sailed round and round Ailsa Craig with the aircraft constantly taking off and landing. Ailsa Craig is a huge round rock in the mouth of the Clyde. Its top is almost flat and the rock itself is a sanctuary for tens of thousands of birds of all descriptions. In the winter, a thick layer of snow covers the surface, giving it the appearance of a huge Christmas cake.

When the trials and exercises had been completed, we returned to Greenock, where I took the opportunity to go and see Anne. These were trying times because I did not know from one day to the next what the ship was doing, and therefore what I was doing. I could not even tell her where I had been and that maybe we would be going back. All I could do was to make arrangements to see her, but at the same time warn her that if I couldn't make it then I was away and it may be some weeks before I saw her again. Anne was very good; she never asked questions about the ship or what I did aboard, and I never enlightened her. On my part it was a question of security, but I don't think the same could apply to Anne. There was a certain naivety about her, but it wasn't that; I just think this erratic coming and going was an accepted part of our courting and that she wasn't particularly interested. My love and passion for this unique and wonderful girl had grown with such intensity that I could hardly bring myself to say good night.

I know one night about two months after I had met Anne for the second time, I said to her, "One day I'm going to marry you."

She looked at me with the light shining in those beautiful eyes and said, "I don't think so. I'll never get married."

At the time it staggered me, punctured my ego as I struggled to understand the emotional attachment I had for this lovely girl. I loved her, I adored her and I could not see me going through life without her. If I felt that way, then why did she not feel the same way about me? Unless, of course, her love was not as strong as mine. The possibility tortured my soul and tore at my very heartstrings. I was aware I did not understand women, but it seemed the more I found out, the less I knew.

I suppose most ships have their share of homosexuals and we were no exception. Fortunately there were not many, and the lads would refer to them as 'Brown Hatters'. My first awareness was when one of the fellows in the next mess offered me a chocolate bar, but when I went to pay for it he withdrew the offer. I thought it strange and mentioned it to the other lads in the mess.

"Blimey Joey," said one, "he's a bleeding Brown Hatter, so bloody watch yourself."

Thereafter I always steered a wide course, until one day I was tipping some gash down the gash chute in the starboard whaler space, when he suddenly came up behind me. I turned round and smashed my right fist into his face, knocking him backwards. As he fell, his head hit the bulkhead, and knocked him unconscious. I then fled down to the mess deck. It was over half an hour later before he put in an appearance, nursing a bruised face. I never had any bother from him again.

One of the seamen in the other mess was a short dark and stocky fellow we called Smiler. As far as the lads were concerned, Smiler was heterosexual, only they did not use words like that – they would say "'e ain't one of them."

One morning, he came back off shore leave and, as is customary for men coming off shore leave, they loved to embroider the facts relating to their run ashore, and tell their messmates of the number of women they had been with, or the number of pints they had sunk, or the result of a fist fight. So with this background in mind we listened to Smiler's story.

"You know what?" said Smiler. "I was standing on the steps of Central Station not knowing where I was going to sleep – the Church Army was full, the Sally Ally full and the YMCA. I missed the last train to Greenock so here's me stuck, then this little Scots fellow sidles up.

"'What's a matter, Jack? Looking for a shake down for the night?'

"Well, you didn't have to be a bloody idiot to know what he was, so I said, 'Yes all the places are full.'

"'Well,' says this wee fella, 'I can fix you up – that is, if you don't mind sharing a bed with me. You see I've only got the one.'

"Well, what could I do? So I agreed to accompany him. Anyway, he took me back to this little one room flat in a dark grey stone tenement. He then makes supper which we washed down with a couple of pints of beer and so we went to bed. I obliged him during the night and in the morning he gives me breakfast in bed, and as I go out of the door he gives me a ten bob note. Now, I asks you what happens when you meet a dame – you're paying out all the time and you still ain't got no guarantee she'll come on afterwards. Make no kidding, my little Scots pal, he's got the right idea."

The conclusion of his dialogue was met with some pretty ribald comments, not least of which was, "You dirty bastard."

Chapter 14

Nobby

I had heard that one of the deck party had fallen overboard. Some weeks later, I ran into one of his shipmates Charlie and asked him what had happened. Charlie was never one to give a direct answer but he said,
"It were Nobby Clark, my oppo. I never knew 'is first name but then Clarks was always called Nobby. I liked Nobby – 'e was a good mate, nuttin' special mind you, 'e were always dead quiet. You'd 'ardly know 'e was there, 'e was that sort o' guy."
"Yes Charlie, but what happened?" I said, interrupting his flow.
"I was coming to that," said Charlie. "'E was on the upper deck, chipping the ice off the stanchions when suddenly 'e's up and over. I reckon 'e must have slipped on some ice. There was nuttin' anyone could do what with 'im 'aving on a duffel coat and wearing sea boots, 'e didn't stand a chance. Straight down 'e went like dropping the anchor. 'E was only twenty an' that ain't no age. Afterwards I went down the mess and the Rum Bosun was putting out the issue. There was one left over, an' it was Nobbys. When we 'ad ours, we just stood around and looked at the cup. We was stood there staring at it and thinking of Nobby, and in our minds wondering what to do with it. Jock suggested we should give it to Nobby by chucking it overboard, but in the end we decided we should in memory of Nobby all 'ave sippers until it were gone, so that is what we did and that was nigh on four weeks ago. It some'ow gets you in the guts when you think that the last time we left The Clyde we 'ad Nobby with us, now 'e ain't. Somewhere in the bottom of the 'oggin is my oppo Nobby. 'E ain't got no marked grave. It's as

if 'e never was, an' now we're back in The Clyde without 'im. When we dropped the hook, Jimmy the One came over the tannoy and said each watch would get seven days leave. Usually the lads would cheer that news, but we didn't cos it didn't apply to Nobby.

"We went ashore in Greenock and spent all evening in the boozer. We was all quiet thinking of Nobby. Somebody said, 'Come on Nobby, it's about time you bought a round.' It was meant to cheer us up, but we didn't feel cheerful. I reckon we all 'ad a skinful that night but strange thing, none of us were drunk. We went back to the ship in silence and got into our micks. Losing a shipmate is like losing a brother, only worse. I miss old Nobby."

Charlie's eyes welled up with tears and he broke off the conversation and turned away.

Like Charlie, we also must never forget the Nobbys we lost in our seafaring days.

Chapter 15

Meeting Up With A Convoy

Scapa Flow in August is not the most appealing of places; in fact it mattered not what time of year it was – it lacked attraction. The surrounding hills were devoid of trees and the wild and windswept terrain was only appreciated by the hundreds of sheep that fed on its grassy slopes. It was, however, a sanctuary for the Fleet, though the crew of *HMS Royal Oak* would have had decidedly contrary views. In fact, the only thing that could have encouraged a man to go ashore was the Naval canteen.

Anchored in the Flo was the old battleship *HMS Royal Sovereign*, which had been transferred to the Russian Navy and was renamed *Archangelsk*. The anchorage also contained the cruiser *Jamaica*, and the escort carriers *Striker* and *Vindex* as well as a host of sloops, frigates, corvettes and destroyers. Launches, motorboats and drifters criss-crossed the turbulent waters, carrying messages, provisions and newer replacement shipmates.

Aboard *Vindex*, Captain Bayliss prepared to move to his sea cabin just below the bridge. Meanwhile, Rear Admiral Dalrymple Hamilton and his staff were welcomed aboard, the Admiral occupying the Skipper's day quarters. Immediately after lunch the cable party and the sea duty men were piped to their stations.

Looking out over the grey waters one could see other ships preparing for sea, and the sound of many cables being hauled through the hawse pipes heralded the news that another operation was about to begin, though why so many ships. This suggested that something bigger than a hunt for U-Boats in the Atlantic was about to take place.

Down in the mess deck the lads occupied their time with cards or writing letters. Tea was always on the brew and then, of course, the constant chatter about their last ship or their last run ashore and inevitably the girlfriends. This all changed to speculation as to what sort of operation we were going to be involved in. Everyone had decided ideas and many had definite knowledge acquired direct from the Skipper himself, which all sounded plausible and would have been believable had not the destinations all been different.

I turned in early as I was due to keep the first watch at 04:00, but I didn't sleep much and just lay there thinking what the lads had been saying and dwelling on what may might lay ahead. Occasionally one's thoughts were interrupted by a rat running along the deck head girders just above their hammock. I guess survival was a mutual interest we both shared.

Just before 04:00, my hammock was shaken and a voice in a loud whisper said, "Come on Joey, time to turn out."

I don't know why they all called me Joey, but somehow the name stuck. I swung down to the deck and quickly put on all my new gear. The mess deck was quiet except for a cacophony of snores coming from within many hammocks. The emergency lights were dim, but it nevertheless showed the chrysalis shaped micks swinging in gentle unison as the old ship rolled from side to side.

I reported to the Gunnery office to pick up some binoculars, and then made my way to the upper deck. The sky was a collection of angry black clouds forever changing shape as strong winds scattered them over the ocean.

We were only allowed to do one hour up and one down, and then in a four hour watch we would do the second hour. In the winter in the Arctic, one hour was more than enough. In our one hour off we would go to the galley and get a fanny full of Kye, which we would then distribute to all the lookouts and gunnery crews.

Visibility was bad, and except on a moonlit night you could rarely see the other ships, but we knew that we would be meeting up with the merchant ships in the middle of the night, but up the stick we, unlike those who had the benefit of radar, did not know if the meeting had taken place, but then as the dawn was breaking we could identify ghostly shapes running parallel to us on either side, and when it became lighter we could see the entire convoy. There were thirty four merchant ships within a circle of destroyers, corvettes and frigates which, like protective sheepdogs, were constantly scurrying to and fro.

From my perch up top, it looked as though the entire ocean was covered in ships. I had such a panoramic view that it nearly took my breath away. Then suddenly, astern of one of the merchant ships, I saw a periscope, and then another and another. I yelled down the voice pipe to the bridge only to be assured that what I could see was the masts of twelve Russian PT boats that were manned by Russian sailors, had come over from the USA and were being delivered under our escort to Murmansk.

The above account was the procedure used for most of the Russian convoys in bringing escort and merchant ships together.

Chapter 16

Going Home

I was standing on the forecastle, viewing the snow-capped bleak and desolate land before me. We were anchored off Vaenga Bay in the Kola Inlet. Arctic winds swept up the river, forcing me to wrap my sheepskin coat even tighter around me. My thoughts turned to Scapa Flo and the islands of the Orkneys that hitherto I had so maligned as Godforsaken treeless land, but now from north of the Arctic Circle, it took on a different meaning. One almost felt guilty of harbouring an affection for it, to the extent that we yearned to run the U-Boat gauntlet for home. Yes, I called it home, because once we had discharged our duties to escorting a convoy, Scapa was the place we headed for, being our first sighting of the old country for nigh on two months. It is true we only stopped off long enough to pick up the mail and then sailed southward through the Hebridean Islands off the west coast of Scotland. They were a joy to behold – the green fields and jagged peaks, the sheep grazing in the meadows and wisps of smoke coming from the chimneys of the little white crofters' cottages, each of which was surrounded by a dry stone wall. Then, like a bushfire, word got around that a bevy of warships were passing and the children and their parents ran out of homes and school to vigorously wave to us. It was such a touching and moving welcome home, and as we waved to each other it somehow conveyed a telepathic thought of mutual love and respect.

Whilst in my perch up the mast, feverish hands below deck tore at letters and parcels from their dear ones, and then the Skipper would come on the tannoy to announce seven days' leave for each watch, and with nearly two months pay in their pockets, the immediate future was one of hope and expectations. But our happiness was tinged with guilt. Yes, we were going home, but what about the shipmates we had left behind, to lie for eternity in the depth of freezing Arctic waters? There would be letters down below, unopened letters. The writers would not know their loved ones would never read them; they would just lie on the mess deck table as a reminder of our own mortality, and this guilty feeling that we had survived.

We must never betray the memory of the lads we did not bring back. They made the ultimate sacrifice, and we can only offer up a silent prayer that Almighty God will forever keep them in his memory.

Chapter 17

April 1945

The night I was due to meet Anne, we sailed and there was no way I could let her know. I went up to the stern and peered in the direction of Glasgow, imagining her waiting for me and hoping she would be as disappointed as I was.

Rear Admiral Cunningham-Graham and his staff joined us, so it was a foregone conclusion as to where we were going. My initial fears and apprehensions over these trips no longer applied and apart from not seeing Anne, my attitude now was relief at the opportunity being presented to save up some money. It was almost becoming a bus run as we ploughed through the corkscrew waters of the Minches and the Western Isles and made our way to Scapa Flow.

Somehow the war seemed so far away from us. It was almost as though the convoys to Russia were isolated from what was happening in the rest of the world. We had our own war going that was unrelated to the events in Europe and the Far East. We were not seeking to subjugate land or people, there was no front line, and the enemy for the main part could not be seen, and yet he was everywhere. Our successes could not be measured in terms of areas of land being liberated. If we could complete our voyage with the same number of ships that we started with, then that was a success. There was no going back, there was no retreat, and whatever ships may be lost you ponderously went on your way. There were no wireless sets in the mess decks, but we did have loudspeakers through which the Skipper spoke to us. They were also used for announcements and calls to action stations, and then gramophone records were played, with the crew being able to make requests. Occasionally the news was carried and this together with papers picked up in Scapa Flow or Greenock kept us abreast of the news. We knew the European theatre of operations was going well, but although our mutual object was the same, our methods of achieving it were different. Indirectly one complimented the other, but collectively we were a team, though at the time it was hard to appreciate it.

I was taken off the pom poms and, together with Wilf Gough, put in the Radar direction room. For the first time I was relieved to get a duty out of the elements and between decks. We sat before this huge Perspex screen. On it was like a large spider's web, the centre of which was meant to be our ship. The object was that Wilf and I sat with earphones on, which were connected to the radar office. They would plot the course of our own aircraft, also enemy planes or vessels. This information originated with the revolving radar aerials at the top of the mast that constantly swept through 360 degrees. Every time an echo was received so it was relayed to us and we marked the range and direction on the screen and altitude for an aircraft if known. We wrote backwards in order that it should be easily read from the other side of the screen. By means of this constant flow of information we could tell by its speed whether it was a surface vessel or an aircraft, whether it was approaching or going away or even circling the convoy.

One did not break wireless transmission in case it gave away our position, but we were fortunate in being able to identify our own aircraft as opposed to the enemy planes as ours contained a small bakelite disc through which our radar pulses went. The disc was capable of sending about ten prearranged coded messages – for example, if one of our pilots saw a submarine on the surface, he need only turn the disc to the correct code number, which in turn would then appear on our screens, and we could find out what was going on without having broken transmission. Even if Jerry did know our position and wireless transmission was in order, it still did not prevent the use of this gadget to convey coded messages by radar.

Convoy JW 66 was made up of twenty-seven ships and had left the Clyde on the 17th of April 1945. We had made our usual brief call into Scapa Flow, but departed in time to meet up with the convoy on the 18th of April.

The warships covering this convoy were the sloop *Cygnet*, the corvettes *Alnwick Castle, Bamborough Castle, Farnham Castle, Honeysuckle, Lotus, Oxlip* and *Rhododendron*, plus the frigates *Loch Insh, Loch Shin, Cotton, Goodall* and *Anguilla*, the cruiser *Bellona*, the escort carriers *Premier* and Vindex, the destroyers *Offa, Zealous, Zephyr, Zest* and *Zodiac*, the Canadian ships *Haida, Huron* and *Iroquois*, and the Norwegian ship *Stord*.

The vessels took up their prearranged positions in the convoy and we set forth. It was customary to have some gunnery practice at the start of each convoy, and this was no exception. The usual drill was to depress your guns and fire off a few bursts into the water. The evolution in and of itself is quite simple; nevertheless, no man should be in charge of a gun unless he also has common sense. One of our gun layers was George, and George did not have common sense. It stands to reason that a vessel rolling in heavy seas is going to affect the angle of the gun in conjunction with the water. In a heavy sea you can one moment be pointing your gun at a 45 degree angle to the water, but when the ship rolls the other way your trajectory is now parallel to the water. Obviously a prudent gun layer takes the former angle, but then George was not a prudent gun layer, and before we knew what was happening George was raking one of the merchant ships with 20mm Oerlikon shells. By means of the aldis lamp, the Skipper of the merchant ship made his views known with a most eloquent choice of words, but still for all that unrepeatable.

When the enemy found out that a convoy was on its way, they would send a huge Blohm and Voss aircraft to shadow it and report back to base. Once you knew you were being watched all day long, there was no point in maintaining radio silence, so another duty Wilf and I had was to listen in constantly on the B28 receivers. These were tuned in to the frequency being used by our aircraft. Any dialogue between ship and aircraft was written down; usually it was just hours of silence, but one day when everyone was becoming a little tired of this shadowing aircraft it was decided to give him a run for his money. To have any chance of success, there were certain basic requirements that had to fall into place – for example, if the enemy saw us leave the convoy, he knew we were going to fly off aircraft and he would therefore take evasive action by dropping back out of range and hiding in the clouds. It was therefore necessary to choose a day when we were heading directly into the wind, and also a day with low cloud base so that our aircraft would not have to expend excessive fuel making the high altitude, and further if we flew off while he was in the clouds it would give us a greater advantage.

The day arrived when all the factors fitted into place. Two Wildcats were scrambled while Jerry was in the clouds, and before he knew what had happened they were on his tail. Suddenly, coming into our B28s, we heard the excited voices of our two pilots.

"There it is," yelled one. "I'm going in, I've got the bugger, I've blown his bloody tail off." There was a brief pause and then, "Where is he, where's he gone?"

The other pilot came on. "I can see him, I'm coming down on top." There was a few seconds of silence, then, 'I'm sure we've got the bloody kite. I've shot half his top gun cupola off."

There was no sound of gunfire over the voices and all went dead. A few brief exciting seconds that was listened to in silence. Everyone except the Admiral carried broad grins on their faces, but declined to allow their feelings to erupt into cheers of appreciation in case there was more to come. The Admiral's sombre brooding countenance gave no indication as to what he thought or felt.

Fuel shortage forced our planes to return and as soon as they had landed they were brought in for interview. Neither pilot could categorically state that the plane had been shot down. Visibility was extremely poor, and whilst they believed they had inflicted mortal damage, they could not vouch for what may have resulted from their actions.

While Wilf and I may have had long periods of inactivity, we often played chess or wrote silly poems. One of Wilf's efforts went like this:

"This is the tale of Geoffrey Shelton
Who went ashore without his belt on,
Jauntily sauntering down the street
His lovely Anne he went to meet.
Whilst stepping from behind a car
Her welcome form he spied afar,
And waving wildly on the spot
He quickly broke into a trot.
Now as you know when a fellow races
It's always wise to wear some braces,
Or at least a belt around one's waist
To counteract the jolts of haste.
Alas, poor Joey, thoughtless chap,
Gave not one thought to this mishap,
And as he dashed on pass the houses,
Something happened to his trousers.
First a looseness around his tummy
Made him think, "There's something funny",
Feeling a coolness round his rump
He pulled up sharp, then gave a jump,
For suddenly stopping in the street
Caused his pants to fall at his feet.
Grabbing wildly as they fell,
He muttered, "Gosh! Oh, what the hell?"
And glancing frenziedly at Anne,
Pull 'em up he then began.
She looking disdainfully under her hat,
Said, "Geoff, I take a poor view of that".
And turning round she left poor Geoff
And stalked off into the F and F,
The moral of this story friend
Is if you have no belt then bend
A piece of rope around your breeches;
It's going to save you many hitches."

Another of Wilfs efforts was entitled 'L'Affaire Arran', or 'Slowly but Surely'.

"Out in the wilds of old Lam Lash,
Where the firelights flicker and lamplights flash,
They tell a tale of a matelot bold,
Who swore that his love would never grow cold.
He came with a crowd from the ship *Vindex*.
They were all spruced up, even washed their necks.
Their collars were clean and their suits well pressed.
In fact, they were dressed in their Sunday best.
Now Joey – the bloke that our story's about
Had made up his mind he was going out.
And fling a loose leg at a dance held ashore.
Because life on the ship was a frightful bore,
So he coughed up his tanner or was it a bob?
That entitled him shortly to join in the mob.
And jogging around like a young camel can,
He soon came aware of the lovely Anne.
Now Anne, you must know, is the pride of the Isle
With dark sparkling eyes and a marvellous style.
Her cohorts were gleaming in purple – oh dear,
I'm mixed up with "Unter den Linden" I fear.
Now, demands on Anne were fast and hot,
Which irked poor Joey an awful lot
Who simply found himself one of a few
And obliged to join in the ruddy queue.
Undaunted though he took his place,
The will to conquer on his face,
And flinging his number elevens around
Into the melee he went with a bound.
His blood was up, his passion roused caution to the gods,
For how can any man die better than facing fearful odds?
For the ashes of his father and temples of – good gracious,
   Isn't that a bit crept in somehow from Tennyson's poem "Horatious"?
However, he hadn't been long in the fray
Before he had cunningly worked his way
To a strategic position upon her port bow,
And said to himself, "Here's my ruddy chance now."

He boldly approached her and said "Please may I?"
And whisked her away in the blink of an eye
And there in the ballroom he whirled her around
Whilst his rivals all called him a dirty young hound.
Now Joey, he made up his mind not to lose
The prize he had won by the use of a ruse.
(I know that the last line's a bit of a twister
But the fellows thought Joey a bit of a blister)
So, mentally counting the coppers he had
He suggested some supper, the artful young lad,
And leaving his rivals all sadly confused,
He escorted her off – feeling highly amused.
Whilst contentedly scoffing their coffee and cake
A hit with the maid our young hero did make,
And told her strange tales of a fierceness to hush her
Of how he took convoys by sea to Russia.
They still tell the tale in the wilds of Lam Lash
Where the firelights flicker and the lamplights flash,
Of the matelot bold who came one day
And stole their fairest maiden away.
But now this stirring tale, dear friend,
Is slowly coming to an end.
Dear Anne has joined the King's Land Army
Half a league, half a league, half-isn't it barmy?
I can't think what it was that made,
Me think of "The Charge of the Light Brigade",
But perhaps it's because she's living in Busby,
Yes I really think that's what it must be.
And now our poor hero gets many hard knocks
When he places his cash in a telephone box
And a voice at the end says "I can't bring her now,"
"She's out in the mistle a milking a cow."

Wilf was a past master at this, but all I could manage in return was:

"I'm looking now o'er our ship's side
I'm looking for a mermaid

But all I see is my inside
So very neat and wind sprayed."

That was an ode to my sea sickness.

To get back to our convoy, one would imagine that with Wilf and I indulging in writing poetry all was peace and quiet outside but regrettably that was not so, for the reason that the enemy knowing our destination tended to congregate their U-Boats in force just outside Kola Inlet while continuing to harass us night and day. This meant that when not at action stations, we did four hours on and four hours off. The escorts' prime task was to defend the merchant ships, and though opportunities to sink U-Boats were seized, the main object was to prevent them firing their torpedoes, and if this could be achieved by keeping them below, then all well and good. No U-Boats were sunk on the outward journey, but then no merchant ships were sunk either, which clearly endorsed the policy. This however was not achieved without the constant explosions of depth charges from both ship and planes as an ever-vigilant watch was maintained. In these northern waters, the ASDIC method of locating U-Boats does not perform as well as it should – something to do with the thermal currents in the waters. Anyway, on the day we left with the convoy, a mine-laying force left Scapa Flow to carry out operation Trammel. The object of this operation was to lay mines outside Kola Inlet, at a depth that would allow ships to pass over them without harm, but would nevertheless threaten any submarine that was forced when evading our ships to dive deep.

On the fifth night after leaving Scapa Flow I was on duty as the forward port look out. I cannot recall the circumstances as to why I was not in the plot room, but it was probably due to the fact that our post for action stations could differ from when we were doing four hours on four off. However, be that as it may, this particular night was pitch black and cold. We were near enough to Murmansk to have received air cover from shore-based Russian aircraft, but for some reason we did not have it. It is logical that shore based aircraft are safer for the aircrew than for the crew of the old Swordfish biplanes landing and taking off from over ten thousand tons of steel rising and falling and rolling.

A Swordfish returning from patrol could be seen approaching the stern of the ship, while one of the deck officers with his illuminated bats prepared to guide him in. This task required the complete confidence and trust of the aircrew to obey the signals. 'Bats' indicated the aircraft's angle of approach by the angle of his bats by comparison with both the flight deck and the plane. Coming in in the pitch dark, they are literally landing blind. This particular night the Swordfish made a three-point landing in the sea and parallel to the ship. We have already spoken of the time span of anyone falling into these Arctic waters – four minutes. We were now about to see for ourselves whether this statement was true. The plane sank immediately, taking with it the pilot. The observer was able to escape and get into a rubber dinghy. It must be remembered that we were less than a day away from Kola Inlet. We were therefore in U-Boat infested waters. Ships were blacked out for the obvious reason that to be otherwise is merely to offer the enemy a target at which to aim. Our Skipper, Captain Bayliss, had a blue searchlight directed onto the unfortunate observer. By this very action, he was putting at risk his ship and the lives of the six hundred men aboard, and yet if his crew had been asked every one of them would have supported and stood by their Captain. Some may say it was foolish and irresponsible, and while I concede such views have some merit, I believe it was the action of a very courageous man who cared for those under his command.

The commander called away the sea boats crew. Our sea boat was a twenty-seven foot whaler which hung from falls on the starboard side. The usual drill is to lower the whaler to a position just above the water, extract a metal pin under each fall and then at the appropriate moment the boat officer above will call "release". The coxswain of the whaler will then move the lever of the Robinson disengaging gear and the boat would literally drop onto the crest of a wave. Regrettably, the officer forgot to give the command to "remove pins", with the result that when the disengaging gear was released the boat literally hung on the pins making it impossible to get away. All we could do now was to call up one of the escort to pick up the observer. While this was going on I watched the dinghy and its occupant through my binoculars. I watched him wave and I heard his cries for help; my thoughts went to his home, his parents, brothers or sisters. Was he married? I didn't know. Did he have a young lady? Probably. No doubt all those who loved him were asleep in their beds, not knowing that I was watching their fit and healthy young son or brother slowly die. The waving hand got lower and lower the voice got weaker and weaker. The hand stopped waving and the cries ceased to be heard, and even though this young man was in a dinghy he did not last the four minutes. One of the escort boats brought the stiff and lifeless body back to their own ship. From ditching to rescue had taken fifteen minutes, but even that was not the end of the drama, because when the escort raised the rescue boat to the davits the crew disembarked with the corpse, leaving two men in the sea boat to lash the falls. I don't know what the cause was, but that boat fell, pitching its two occupants into the merciless waters of the Barents Sea. You couldn't see them but everyone knew the score. They had just four more minutes to live, but after thirty seconds they would not have known that.

We and the convoy and escort carried on as though nothing had happened. All that could be heard was the rhythmic beat of the engines combined with bow waves as we carved our way through these harsh and hostile waters. The watch continued with the scanning of the sea for signs of enemy activity, and yet even as all those who had witnessed this tragic event resumed their duties, their minds were preoccupied with the needless loss of a shipmate. In retrospect, the crew who did pick up the body were in great danger themselves. We nearly ran them down, and to be rowing a boat in the middle of a convoy of this size, none of which were showing any lights, was almost inviting trouble. I believe the Coxswain of the whaler eventually received a gallantry medal for his bravery.

In accordance with the now customary practice, the convoy went ahead into Kola Inlet and we followed later eventually anchoring in Vaenga Bay. The vast contrast in the seasons was most noticeable for now the deep snow was in the process of melting, which made conditions underfoot treacherous. I indulged in the usual swapping of cigarettes, and with the proceeds I was able to buy a doll for my young cousin.

When the Admiral walked around the ship, it was customary for him to be preceded by the Bosun's Mate who piped those in the vicinity to attention. However, the Admiral was now quite at home on *Vindex* and ceased to bother about these formalities, and though this was a nice gesture it meant that he could easily be in your area without you being aware of it. Such was the case when a young lad new to the ship saw his mate down the port passage and yelled out, "Oi, mate, what's the time?"

To his astonishment, a rather refined voice from behind said, "It's just a quarter to ten." Yes, it was the Admiral.

We invited some Russians sailors to join us at a party aboard ship. One was sent to each mess, and the fellow we had spoke excellent English, so conversation was made easy. He lived in Leningrad and had been educated at Leningrad University. He was also a very good artist and kept us entertained with caricatures of well-known personalities, including Mr Winston Churchill. Joe, the Killick of our mess, was as bald as a bladder of lard, and he said to our Russian shipmate, "Draw us a picture of old Joe Stalin."

"Old Joe," said our guest, laughing. "You say old," and he put the emphasis on the old. "You say old, but you have no hair."

Whereupon he patted him on the head, much to the amusement of the whole mess.

It was during our period at Vaenga that it was decided to hold a ships party, the crew providing the entertainment. A stage was rigged up in the hanger, and throughout the ship hurried rehearsals were taking place. The great day arrived. The Admiral and his staff, the Captain, Commander and all the officers occupied the front few rows with the lads filling up behind.

Considering the speed with which this had been put on, the turns were very good. One fellow gave an expert exhibition of tap dancing, another did conjuring, and so on. One of the wardroom stewards came on. He was a very small comedian and soon had us all in fits of laughter as he pretended to be drunk. He rolled round the stage, and at one time his rambling voice was incoherent. He stepped off the stage to address those sitting in the front rows and then collapsed on the Commander's lap. The Commander soon realised that this was no act, and the 'artiste' spent the next week sobering up in the cells.

They called for volunteers from the audience to do impromptu turns. Some of the lads endeavoured to impersonate various characters from the ship such as the Commander and the Master at Arms. They had a third person acting as a defaulter and being brought before the Commander. The exercise proved amusing and encouraged the participants to acquire more volunteers. Then someone suggested that the Commander should take the part of the defaulter. For any other Commander being a participant in this charade, and being at the mercy of his subordinates could only invite trouble, but Commander Williams was too much respected by the men to be taken advantage of. He came on stage and Crash took the part of the Commander. I do not recall the substance of the charge, but Crash gave the 'defaulter' a severe dressing down and finished it by saying, "I order this man sixty days in the cells."

To everyone's surprise, the Commander who had played his part well cheered out loud and said, "Thank you sir, that means I won't have to do another Russian convoy." This brought the house down.

The next turn brought on Laker complete with a swanee whistle and a song. The song, or least the words to it, were mainly for the Padre's ears, but alas he was not present, so Laker continued without him. The lyrics were about a vicar and his curate, who stationed themselves outside the church with the object of looking and passing comment on the young ladies passing by. The comments were to be confined to the personal conquest each may have had with the ladies, and to this end the vicar was expected to say "Ping" when a conquest of his passed by and in a similar vein the curate had to say "Pong" when one of his successes came into view. Unfortunately as the vicar's wife came along the curate said "Pong", where upon a furious argument broke out, with Laker taking both parts.

Our departure from Murmansk was imminent, but when the Admiral found the date fell on a Friday he duly delayed sailing for twenty-four hours. While his superstition led him to this course of action, they apparently did not apply to the escort, who departed on the Friday in order that they may carry out their customary sweep of the entrance to Kola Inlet.

We had twenty-seven merchant ships to escort back home. Meanwhile, the Germans had anticipated and prepared for our departure with the result that at least ten U-Boats were lying in wait for us. The weather was cold and crisp with a beautiful blue sky. The carriers and their escorts sailed due north up the Inlet, and with snow covered craggy rocks acting as a backdrop and glistening in the sunshine, it looked most impressive. The enemy took a different viewpoint to ours, to the extent that I was sitting quietly in the mess when suddenly the ship went hard a starboard. Every loose article went flying and, as pots and pans went cluttering around the deck, we instinctively knew the Skipper had taken emergency evasive action. A U-Boat lying off the rocky coastline had got us in his sight and had fired off two torpedoes. They passed no more than ten yards astern of us thanks to our Captain.

On the same day, *Loch Shin* sank U-307, and then in reply U-968 managed to torpedo the frigate *Goodall*. *HMS Honeysuckle* went alongside her to take off survivors, but in doing so suffered damage as the *Goodall* blew up.

We took some of the *Goodall* survivors with us and headed further north than we usually did; in fact we were in sight of Bear Island which I thought was a bit risky, but no harm was done. The war in Europe was fast coming to a conclusion and it seemed that Jerry was intent on a last desperate fling, for the following five days found the waters alive with U-Boats. They were constantly dive-bombed and depth charged, and therefore never allowed to get their periscopes trained on any of the ships. They were in fact rendered useless. With each passing day, so the enemy activity decreased. Two days before arriving in Scapa Flow, the cruisers and a couple of destroyers departed the convoy in a hurry. It was rumoured they were going to Denmark.

On the 8th of May 1945, we arrived in Scapa Flow where we dropped the hook and prepared for the Admiral and his staff to go ashore. It was apparent that this convoy was going to be the last wartime convoy to arrive in home waters, and the Admiral thought it fitting to address the crew. We were formed up on the flight deck to hear what he had to say. He did of course express his thanks to the crew for all their efforts and cooperation, but the aspect of his speech which stuck in my mind was the part he got wrong.

Our Gunnery Officer used to keep a cockerel on the quarterdeck. Yes, a real, live but cold and emaciated cockerel. Now why a Gunnery Officer, or indeed anybody else should want to keep a cockerel on board ship defies understanding, but we on the lower deck never did understand the executive. The Admiral knew of the existence of this poor creature and one day he heard one of the pilots coming through the transmitter saying, "Is my cockerel crowing?"

In his speech, the Admiral made a jocular reference to this episode by saying, "And here we are in the middle of a war, sailing on a Russian convoy with all the problems that that entails, and here is one of the pilots with time to think about his bloody chicken."

There were, of course, roars of laughter, but what the Admiral did not know and probably still doesn't, was that the pilot was not referring to the cockerel but merely enquiring in coded parlance as to whether the disc that reflects messages via the radar beams was working. Come to think of it, the cockerel disappeared one day – I wonder where.

The Skipper followed the Admiral with his own comments. He did however reveal that he had seen a copy of a letter that the Admiral had sent to the Admiralty. In it he said, "For God's sake take me off these Russian convoys before my balls freeze off."

Chapter 18

VE Day

With the unconditional surrender of Germany very close, the conversation on the mess deck turned to demobilisation and home. There was an undercurrent of excitement, and yet it was controlled as an insurance against anything going wrong, but what could go wrong? Well, the first thing was we didn't go back to Greenock but stayed in Scapa, then from a personal viewpoint there was only one letter from my Anne.

I went ashore in Flotta merely to get away from the ship for a while. There was very little to do – a canteen, a rest room with an occasional film show. The countryside was wild, wet and rugged with not a tree in sight. Sheep were scattered over the hillside and an old lady sold bibles outside the NAAFI.

The walls of the canteen were covered in murals painted by a talented young sailor. While sitting there a Chief walked in all very cheery.

"Come on, you lucky lads, time's up. Victory in Europe to be announced soon."

The response was utter silence as we pulled up our collars and headed toward the windy and wet jetty. This should have been a joyous moment, and yet everyone was morose and miserable.

That very day when we were still in Scapa, they announced VE Day. Why had the ship been prevented from going to Greenock? Were the 'powers that be' fearful that with the European war over the lads would desert in droves? They certainly wouldn't in Flotta but Greenock and its close proximity to Glasgow could present temptations. No one said much in the mess deck – in fact, most of us slung our hammocks and turned in early. The radio was coming through loud and clear with cheering crowds celebrating in Trafalgar Square and outside Buckingham Palace. They took you to some principal towns, and the same feeling of exultation applied. Servicemen and women dancing in the street laughing, shouting, kissing, hugging, and here were we, stuck up here as miserable as sin.

By the time the announcer got to Glasgow, we had all had enough.

"Turn the bastard off," yelled someone and so it was, leaving us to wallow in our own melancholy mood of frustration and self-imposed misery.

To add to our sorrow, we had that night for the first time in Scapa Flow to keep an anti-aircraft guard. No wonder we were cheesed off or to choose a Naval colloquialism, we were 'two blocks'.

It was a week before we left this inhospitable outpost of the Empire and made our way south. The Aircraft Direction Room was now no longer needed so I was once again given lookout duties.

Some of the lads in the Radar Office had made themselves an electric ring on which they made tea, coffee and toast, so a small band of us would gather there together with Laker and his swanee whistle, and also Crash with his mouth organ, and there we kicked up a noise until the small hours of the morning.

Coming down through the Western Isles, we would see the U-boats flying black flags and cruising on the surface coming in to surrender. Some were escorted by aircraft or smaller boats, but as we sailed past their bows with the torpedo exits quite visible, I sensed a most uneasy feeling. What a target we would have made. Would some treacherous Captain not be able to contain himself and fire off a couple of tubes for the last time? Some of the boats had painted out their numbers, but why? Had they perpetrated acts of war which ran contrary to the Geneva Conventions and so, by obliterating their numbers, they hoped to escape retribution?

We sailed up the Clyde and dropped the hook in the Tail of the Bank just after 18:00. I was due to be relieved at 18:00, but it was hardly worthwhile. The order to stand down was not given so I resorted to singing to draw the attention of the bridge to the fact I was still there.

The response from the bridge was, "Port lookout shut up that infernal row."

I stood there wrapped in thought I was due ashore and was looking forward eagerly to seeing Anne, but it was now 19:00. What the hell was I supposed to be looking out for? We were at anchor, we weren't going anywhere, and my resentment grew.

I called up to the bridge, "Did you say secure sir?"

"No," came a sharp reply.

What the devil were they doing? Of what possible use could I be to them now? I started to whistle and then sing again.

"Port lookout for the last time. Stop that row."

I sank into gloom. The ship's bell rang at 20:00. I was two hours over my time. At 20:30, still no orders to secure, so I left my post and went over to the bridge, climbed up the side and put my head over the top. The bridge was empty. The bastards, the inconsiderate bastards. I was furious. I stormed down below to the officer of the watch, my binoculars still slung around my neck.

"I've been on watch three hours over my time, may I secure?"

"Oh yes", he said. "Carry on."

No apology, nothing; my run ashore ruined, I missed the evening meal, and all for what?

The Officer's Wine Steward expected a consignment of spirits and beer for the wardroom to arrive as soon as the ship got to Greenock, and sure enough, the following day it arrived. A party was detailed to bring it aboard, but unfortunately more time was needed which ran into the afternoon, and that afternoon was a "make and mend" where we had the rest of the day off to do just that, "make and mend".

To our amazement the Commander did not ask us to turn out but instead said to the junior Officers, "It's your beer so you get it on board."

It is no wonder the men held him in such high esteem.

The last time I saw Anne, the Ministry of Labour had notified her that she had to join either the ATS or the Land

Army. I had encouraged her to join the latter. My motives for suggesting this were purely selfish in that I thought that with the ATS she could be posted anywhere, whereas with the Land Army wherever they went they usually stayed in the vicinity and so it came about that Anne landed up on a farm in Busby, just south of Glasgow. On my first run ashore I quickly made my way to Glasgow and caught a bus to Busby. It would be impossible to describe the pent up excitement, the expectation. It seemed an eternity and then there she was, a vision of loveliness, wearing jodhpurs which looked so becoming on her.

It was raining hard so I took her to the back row of the cinema. I know not what picture was showing for I could not take my eyes away from her. She looked so pale and fragile as I watched her sleeping – yes, she was sleeping, which was either an indictment of me as a Romeo or the Land Army work was too much for her.

Before we parted I told Anne again, "One day I'm going to marry you." She just smiled and made no reply.

Back on board it came about that *Vindex* was going to be sent to the Far East. Wilf, Dick and I, as well as the seven other gunnery control ratings had to leave the ship, but the rest of the crew were given the option of staying aboard or going ashore. The Skipper was leaving, but the Commander was to take over as the new Captain. We all had to have a medical examination whether we stayed or left. When the M.O. saw my leg, he said I would have to leave the ship anyway for an operation. Apparently the combination of the weight of warm clothing, climbing the mast, and standing for long hours in freezing conditions, all contributed to a weakness in the veins. There were plenty of volunteers to stay aboard, because *Vindex* was a happy ship.

We were all to be sent on leave and then to report to the Royal Naval Barracks in Portsmouth. We bade our farewells to *Vindex* and were reminded how wrong our first impressions were. Whoever said that a ship was an inanimate object was so wrong; she is alive, she has spirit, she has warmth, and those she protects reward her with love and affection. *HMS Vindex*, we shall miss you, the Captain, the Commander, the crew, all shipmates together – yes, we will miss you.

Just prior to leaving the ship it was announced that some campaign medals and stars had been instituted for the various theatres of war. Brightly coloured posters went up showing the medal concerned and what qualifications were required to receive one.

Of course the cry went up, "What's the use of bloody medals? Give us the cash," or, "I wouldn't waste my time collecting 'em."

It became apparent that anyone indicating the slightest interest in medals was a "show off", but their talk was all a veneer, and when you talked on a one to one basis you received an entirely different message.

Chapter 19

Hospital

Leave passed all too quickly and I made my way back to Portsmouth. The badly bombed town hall was near the station and as I passed by I noticed the two stone lions either side of the steps and recalled my father's advice on the day I joined up.

"My son," he said, "outside Portsmouth Town Hall stand two lions. Every time a virgin passes, they stand up and roar."

"Yes Dad," I replied, realising that this piece of advice was the first and only time he drew near to telling me about the birds and the bees. I was eighteen.

From the barracks we were sent to *HMS Collingwood* at Fareham where I received my initial training, and the thought of it and the memories it brought to mind merely filled me with foreboding. However, we found conditions had vastly improved since our training days. It had now been converted to a vast Radar training establishment and as a result we were forced to sleep in the gymnasium.

One day Dick, Wilf and I received draft chits to *HMS Golden Hind* a shore-based place in Australia. The contrast between Russia and Australia was appealing but when we went before the Medical Officer he found my medical report from the *Vindex* and cancelled the draft.

I was saddened to see Dick and Wilf go without me, but I guess it had to be. I was sent to the R.N. Hospital at Haslar, which overlooks the Solent. Whilst there I teamed up with Smiler, who was also there for the same operation on his legs. After two days they sent us to another Naval hospital at Sherborne in Dorset.

Sherborne Hospital turned out to be a very nice place, being on the outskirts of a lovely old town. The hospital comprised all ground floor wards and it was surrounded by fields and hills. There were no perimeter walls, or police or customs on the gates, and to arrive at such a place on a glorious summer day suggested that the quality of life was about to change for the better. I learnt later that had a wall been built the cost to staff it would have been over £5,000 per annum, whereas the anticipated cash loss by way of sheets and equipment was £2,500, so economics had deemed that we would not be restricted.

Most of the fellows in my ward were in for varicose veins or hernias, but there were a few exceptions, namely a fractured pelvis. Another lad a New Zealand boy never ever spoke, but received sunray treatment, as well as leg massage. He looked pale and thin as though he had lost the will to live. One day his brother who was in the New Zealand expeditionary force visited him, but even then he gave no sign of improvement.

Although we were patients, it did not mean that we could expect to be treated in the same manner as a civilian hospital. There was no fear of that because certain duties were expected from us. The floor of the ward had to be polished and meals distributed to bed ridden patients and then, of course, there was the washing up. There was nothing arduous and there was a good spirit among the lads.

We had a free supply of cigarettes that came around every week. Pipe tobacco which I preferred was a little harder to come by, but I managed. I duly had the operation and was confined to my bed, though on the third day I got up early and went for a long walk outside the hospital. That didn't do me any good, with the result I had to stay in bed. There was of course plenty of spare time which we spent in making cloth toys, string belts and duchy sets.

When eventually I was allowed up, I would walk over the hills and down the country lanes. The contrast in smells from a ship to the aroma of the countryside, the sounds of various varieties of birds, the delightful sweetness of the wild hedgerow blooms, the huge cobwebs wet with dew and glistening in the morning sunshine, the new mown hay and the smell of cattle. Everything was so far removed from the mess deck of a fighting ship, the war was so far away, as indeed it was with just the Japanese now to beat.

I was moved to another ward for convalescence purposes, and as the other occupants were there for the same reason it meant we were all walking patients.

In the next bed to me was Nobby, a London cockney. He was tall and round-shouldered, with a big nose and an ambling roll as he walked along. Nobby idolised his wife and never lost an opportunity to extol her praises. One day he received a letter from her to say she was going to spend her holiday in Sherborne and would Nobby fix accommodation for her. Nobby and I immediately went ashore, and together we looked for a suitable place for her to stay. Nobby then sent her a telegram to confirm it and at the same time requested authority to sleep ashore.

The big day arrived with Nobby putting on his best suit – we normally wore blue suits to identify us as being hospitalised. He met her at the main gate and then brought her into the ward. She was a very nice, plain sort of girl, devoid of make up but sadly lame in one leg. Nobby was so proud of her as he introduced her to each of us. They went back together to the boarding house, but Nobby's empty bed prompted a few ribald comments from the lads. The next morning, a party of us met him at the main gate with an invalid chair. Nobby protested but it didn't do him much good. A sick bay tiffie stopped us.

"What's wrong with Nobby?" we said.

"His wife is down here and he slept ashore last night," came the reply. No further explanation was necessary.

On the other side of me was a Scots fellow, a Petty Officer. Jock was a nice sort, very fond of his beer and not so less fond of the women. He was always on at me about mixed marriages – Anne is a Catholic.

"Take a tip from me," he would say. "They don't work, break it off now, and don't wait until later when it'll hurt more."

His advice did, of course, fall on deaf ears. A young man in love wants no advice that would run contrary to his emotions.

A number of the lads, including Jock, took a run ashore to Yeovil. We toured a sample of the local taverns and enjoyed the beautiful weather that nature had bestowed on us. Unfortunately all the seats and park benches were occupied with locals enjoying the sun. Jock, however, knew how to acquire a seat.

"See those two dames over there and the chap sitting alongside them? Well, just stare at 'em."

Along with the stares, Jock pointed toward the occupiers of the bench and made comments, "Look at that", or "Have you ever seen anything like that before?"

Very soon, passers-by stopped to see the object of our interest. It soon had its effect, for all three were so embarrassed that they made a hurried departure.

In a similar manner he would suddenly stop walking and pointing in the air would say, "Look." Very soon, the pavement became blocked with people looking skywards, at which lime Jock would disappear.

We organised cricket matches in the fields adjoining the hospital. Organised is probably not the correct word to use as we only had one wicket and about twenty fielders. None of us were physically fit due to lack of exercise following enforced bed resting, but this was brought home much harder to me when one of the lads who was a boxer asked me to spar with him. I received three times as many punches as I gave, and after four rounds decided there were better and less hurtful things to do.

A number of the patients were expecting to be demobilised on health grounds, but there was always someone that would screw it up. All of us were accustomed to sending parcels home of the things we had made. They called it occupational therapy. I have already mentioned the lack of security; well, one day they decided to check the contents of one of the parcels and found it contained sheets, pillowslips and towels. The sender duly received sixty days of punishment, though what happened to his demob I never did find out.

Lights out was at 21:00, but some of the lads could not resist the temptation to slip out of the ward, over the fields and visit a lovely little public house, getting back about 22:30.

The matron was doing her rounds one night and spotted the two empty beds.

"Where are the occupants of these beds?" she demanded fiercely.

"Probably in the heads," replied the Tiffy.

"Check," she snapped.

The Tiffy knew they weren't there, and of course had to say so.

The matron was no fool, because immediately she sent a party of sick bay attendants to the pub. The men were cautioned, and there the matter should have ended, but it takes more than a matron to come between a matelot and his pint. One of them was very near to being demobilised, but even that did not stop him, for the next night he was in the pub. Again, he was brought back and went before the Surgeon Captain, who told him that as it was so near his demob he would let him off with a caution. This irresponsible behaviour acquired for him the title of Skate of the Ward. Well, Skate's misdemeanours were not yet over. In each ward there were loudspeakers, through which music from the radio could be heard nearly all day long. It emanated from a central control position, so we could neither turn it off, nor reduce the sound. The day following Skate's skirmish with the Surgeon Captain was the day our eardrums were abused with the vilest so-called musical sounds. It was unbearable, but only Skate could think of the remedy and that was to rip all the connecting wires out. Skate's reward was to have his name put down for another meeting with the Surgeon Captain, but that very same night he went to the pub and again was brought back to the hospital. Skate had used up all his chances, and the following day he was discharged from the hospital and returned to barracks.

The up patients were allowed shore leave between 13:00 and 17:00, but when the victory over Japan was announced, this was extended to 22:00. On that particular day we had thirteen bed patients, but miraculously by 13:00 there was only one. I went ashore and attended the service in the Abbey, but there didn't seem much to do so I went back to the hospital. There was only this one fellow left on his own who I felt sorry for.

Anyway, I looked in the galley, and while no staff were present, and for that matter no nurses either, there was enough food there to fill the ward so the two of us made the most of it.

I went ashore again, but Sherborne was most subdued. There was no singing and dancing in the streets as there was on VE Day, but the public houses were full to capacity and the singing and shouting permeated into the surrounding streets. I got back to the ward at midnight and found there were only two others. Throughout the night they drifted in and fell fully clothed into their beds. Jock came in about 04:00 and said that a number of them had been to Yeovil, where they all had a good time. They missed the last bus and thought, "What the hell, let's enjoy ourselves," and they did. The next move was to hitch a lift back to Sherborne. A car stopped to pick them up, but on climbing in they found the driver was one of the hospital's medical officers. I don't know who was the more surprised, but he was very charitable and said to the lads that if any of them should be put on a charge to let him know and he would get them off. Fortunately the matter didn't arise, for the possible reason that those who should have been on duty and could have pressed charges were also in the pubs.

I received a letter from Anne's sister to say that a hay cart had tipped over on top of her and that she was very ill. The news devastated me to the extent I persuaded the Medical Officer to discharge me earlier. To my immense surprise and relief he agreed and soon I was on the train to Glasgow.

Three months had passed since I had last seen her, but now, even though she was thin and pale, she was still as lovely and as beautiful as ever. Anne tried to make me forget about her as the nature of her illness brought about by a nervous breakdown necessitated a series of X-rays, and the future did not look too promising. Her words fell on deaf ears, for I had no intention of ever losing this dear and precious girl. She was only just out of bed and was therefore very weak, so we went for short walks or to the cinema. We spent three days together, but not once would she allow me to kiss her lips. I confess the tears welled up in my eyes as I vowed my everlasting love as I said goodbye.

On the train to London I shared a compartment with an old lady and her son who was an Army Sergeant. They were both returning from Edinburgh, where the son had just been presented with the Military Medal. They were so happy and spoke to me throughout the journey. I tried to put on a bold face, but my heart was aching for my beloved Anne.

I reported back to *HMS Collingwood*, but this time there were none of my old shipmates they had all gone to distant shores long since. I was put into what they referred to as a Foreign Pool. The idea is that they give you fourteen days leave, then on your return you can expect at any time a draft overseas, so three days after returning from leave I am sent on another one.

The leave passed all too quickly but I was glad to get back. They put me in a hut on the perimeter of the camp which looked as though it was full to capacity. I took the last empty bed and then looked for a locker to stow my gear. The Killick of the mess said, "There is a locker over there you can have. The guy who had it before has been demobbed and left some junk in it, so I should chuck it out and use that."

When I opened the locker door I found a couple of odd items of old clothing, a tin hatbox, and a ditty box. When I opened the hatbox I found some fairly new but empty jewel cases. From their size and shape it suggested they had contained watches or necklaces or maybe other trinkets, and then I found some cheap items of paste jewellery and thought this was a most odd selection of items for a sailor to be carrying around. Inside the ditty box was a bundle of letters, a few old buttons and a cutting from one of the national papers. It said "On Saturday Lady Charrington, wife of Major Charrington left five suitcases in a train at Euston Station while she went to get her ticket. During her absence one of her cases was broken into and £1,500 of jewellery is missing. Station detectives were on the scene immediately. No one was noticed getting in or out of this particular compartment. Further, how did the thief know which bag it was in? A firm of assessors is offering £150 reward for information leading to the recovery of the stolen property."

Putting two and two together I guessed the previous occupier of the locker had more than a passing interest in this theft. The letters were all addressed to one named able seaman. I thought long and hard about that £150 and how much it would help Anne get through her illness, I thought how much it would benefit us both if ever we did get married. £150 was a lot of money, especially to a lowly able seaman.

I thought about our alleged thief. Had he been on the convoys to Russia, had he risked life and limb for his country only to find that so soon after being demobilised he was or may be arrested? I thought of the Charrington family, the well-known brewers, whose product was so much enjoyed by seamen, and by their indulgence so they had contributed to the coffers of this rich family. I decided in favour of my unknown and unseen shipmate. The hatbox I gave to one of the other lads, the ditty box I kept and everything else I threw away.

A week later, a fellow walked in and went straight to my locker. It was locked.

"What happened to all the stuff that was in here?" he said.

"Thought you were demobbed," said the Killick, "so we ditched it."

"You're sure it was ditched?"

"Yes," said the Killick, "I'm sure"

"There were some letters there that I wanted as evidence in a divorce".

"Sorry mate," said the Killick. "They're all gone."

Our friend departed and we never saw him again, but I've often wondered.

Surrounding the camp were numerous farms, and as it was potato lifting time, the farmers had asked if any of the sailors could or would help with the work. It made a change, so I volunteered, and with twenty others a lorry arrived to take us to the fields. It was only about four miles away, but on arrival the farmer told us that he would operate the tractor which would turn over the potatoes and all we had to do was to put them in sacks.

Now discipline on a farm which decrees that you work until the task is completed, differs to Royal Naval discipline which is broken down into watches and stand easies and lunch breaks and all the other breaks. It also differs from rural life with its smell of the rich earth and the wild flowers, and the only sound is that of the birds and a rough sounding tractor engine. What a contrast with the throb of a ship's engine going twenty four hours a day, where the smells are that of diesel oil, cordite and sweating bodies and the sounds punctuated with the explosions of depth charges and guns and the occasional screams of a man in the throes of death.

Before work started, it was obvious that farmers and sailors are incompatible. The farmer was no doubt up at dawn. We left the camp at 09:00, and we started picking at 09:45. At 10:15, the Killick said, "Stand easy boys."

The farmer scratched his head and looked at us in disbelief. "Is this the usual practice?" he said.

"Oh yes," replied the leading Seaman in charge, "Half an hour stand easy morning and afternoon."

Officially, stand easy was fifteen minutes, but in reality we took forty five minutes. We set to again, but it didn't seem long before the leading hand called time for lunch. Once again, the farmer stopped his tractor and looked quizzical. We had brought sandwiches with us and the farmer suggested that if we went to the farmhouse, tea would be provided. Whilst his hospitality was appreciated, the nearby tavern had greater appeal.

The farmer was waiting as one or two of the lads drifted back. You could see he was annoyed, but he kept his thoughts to himself. 14:00 came, then 14:15, but no further sign. At 14:30, two of the lads staggered down the road, entered the field, lay down on the grass and went to sleep. In the next half hour, the remainder arrived in a similar state. By now the farmer had lost all control.

"I'll see your Commanding Officer when we get back," he yelled.

This prompted a few to get up off their backsides to start work when the Killick called out, "Stand easy."

The farmer had a ruddy complexion to start with, but now it was purple. When stand easy had finished, the leading hand said to the farmer, "Okay, you can take us back now."

"You what?" yelled the farmer in disbelief.

"Take us back some of the lads are ashore tonight and they're got to have time to get ready."

The farmer must have thought to himself, "How the hell did we win this bloody war?"

The fact that the sailors had served in theatres of war all over the world was of no concern to him. All he wanted was spud pickers and Land Army girls could have done a better job. He drove us over a rough ploughed field, cursing and muttering all the time. He never asked for us to go back, and we never went spud picking again.

Chapter 20

HMS Croziers

It was not long before I received another draft chit. It was to a new destroyer called *Croziers* and we were to commission her in Glasgow. GLASGOW! My heart jumped with joy. I could not get on that draft quick enough.

Our party arrived in Glasgow in the early hours of the morning and they sent us to a barracks for breakfast which was only a mile from Anne's home. I managed to slip out and head toward her address. I half ran and half walked the distance, but that was not the cause of my thumping heart, for I could scarcely contain my excitement at the prospects of seeing her again. She was surprised to see me but quickly she accompanied me back to the barracks both of us hoping I had not been missed. I promised I would come to see her again as soon as I knew where the ship was and when I would be allowed ashore.

I soon found out that the *Croziers* was lying in Princes Dock, and alongside her was the *Chiefton*. They both looked beautiful. They were sleek and painted a pale pastel green, which seemed to glisten in the afternoon sunshine. They were the epitome of what I thought a warship should look like.

The First Lieutenant, Lieutenant Blain, addressed the assembled crew and from the start I thought he was going to be a disciplinarian. The Captain, a two and half ringer, then spoke to us. I got the impression that he was going to be a likeable sort of skipper. His speech basically followed the same pattern that all skippers use when they commission a ship. It is repetitious almost like a prayer that has been ordained by King's Rules and Regulations.

"I want this ship to be a happy ship, and to have a happy ship we must have an efficient ship. If you will play the game with me, I'll be fair with you, but I would advise you that the one thing I cannot tolerate and that is being adrift off leave. I've never sent anyone to the cells yet, and I sincerely trust the occasion will not arise."

We were then allocated our messes and left the dockside to board our new home. I was up in the forecastle mess two decks down. Immediately I slung my hammock in a favourable position near the porthole on the starboard side. This action is primitive in a way, in that like many animals it is a sign to others that the slung hammock marks your territory and is a warning to others not to use that particular billet. Access to the mess was a small round hatch, about three feet in diameter, which didn't help those of a claustrophobic nature, and from a personal point of view I was thankful the war was over because that mess could have been a death trap.

Unlike the larger ships, each mess did its own catering. There was a daily victualling allowance and the caterer of the mess would decide what it would be spent on. The caterer was elected by his messmates, and he would delegate on a per diem basis the person or persons responsible for the menu. Provisions would be ordered from either the Purser's Store or the NAAFI manager. They in turn would submit their bill to the paymaster and he would at the end of the month balance the bills against the victualling allowance and would then charge each mess for any excess or give the mess a credit in the event you had underspent.

My watch was granted shore leave on the day we joined ship, so obviously I made ready to go and see Anne. It is customary for men going ashore to be inspected by the Officer of the Watch, but after he had performed these duties, he took it upon himself to warn us that we were in a particularly rough part of Glasgow, namely the razor slashing and chain wielding gang area. We should therefore go ashore in numbers and not alone. It was alright for me to go ashore, but coming back alone after seeing Anne was another matter. I used to walk down the middle of the ill-lit cobbled streets, with the dark shapes of cranes and warehouses outlined against the sky on the one side, while on the other were big blocks of dirty tenements. Every now and again you'd hear muffled movements followed by a girlish giggle, but you would never see anyone. I would remove my belt, wrap it around my right fist with the buckle on the outside just in case anybody jumped me. It was always a relief to see the police on the gates to the docks, but even then one had the gauntlet of the docks themselves. Either side were the warehouses and granaries, and there were cranes and other machinery scattered around. A furtive figure could sometimes be observed scuttling away in the shadows. Here and there, an Oriental seaman could be seen lounging against a wall. You passed by feeling his eyes were boring holes in your back. It was an uncanny and not very pleasant experience, but then you saw the ship's gangway and knew the warmth of your hammock would soon dispel your fears.

I had my twentieth birthday in Glasgow but I never told Anne, for the simple reason it fell on a Sunday and she would never go anywhere on a Sunday except to fulfil her obligation to go to church, so I wandered around from canteen to pub to canteen. A wet November day in Glasgow is not the most pleasant of experiences, so I returned to the ship.

We weren't in Glasgow long before we sailed down the Clyde to Greenock, stored and ammunitioned the ship, and then departed for speed trials in the vicinity of Ailsa Craig.

We also had gunnery exercises. Our armaments consisted of four 4.7" guns, two sets of quadruple pom poms, two single bofors and one twin bofors, and also four torpedo tubes. Our speed was around the 34 knot mark and the gunnery exercises were deemed to be a success, so we returned to Greenock, where we started to paint the ship. Why she had to be painted when she was brand spanking new I will never know, but one assumes that the Lords of the Admiralty knew what they were doing and who were we lowly creatures to doubt them? There was, of course, the timing, namely December. Now the world and his mother knows what Scotland is like in December, but could we be sure their Lordships knew? In between the rain showers we managed to paint one side of the ship, but before we could tackle the other side orders were received to go south to Portland. It was at this stage I began to feel sorry for the skipper. *Croziers* was probably his first command and here he was taking his ship to Portland where the Home Fleet was anchored, and one side of his ship was pastel green and the other side a light blue. We would be the laughing stock of the fleet. Meanwhile, Jimmy the One worked us like the devil incarnate. He wouldn't allow us to work in overalls as is customary in destroyers, but had us toiling away in full uniform all the time, apart from this two lads deserted before we left Glasgow, and the Buffer (Bosun's Mate) was as much a disciplinarian as the First Lieutenant. The *Croziers* was not turning out to be a happy ship.

It was rough travelling through the Irish Sea. We saw a number of mines that had obviously broken loose and seized the opportunity to use them as targets for the gunners but they were not very successful. We arrived in Portland and hoped the fleet had not seen our multi-coloured hull, meanwhile I had received a change of mess. I left the forecastle mess deck and went to number nine mess which was situated just abaft the smoke stack and below the galley. One advantage this mess had was that the chef and the NAAFI boy were both in it. This meant that our food would be cooked correctly and our choice of supplies was assured.

The following week saw the completion of the painting and the lads who had deserted in Glasgow had been caught and returned to the ship, where the Skipper read out a warrant and gave them each sixty days in the cells. You could see the sadness in the Skipper's face as he read the warrant and we knew he was thinking, just as we were, of his speech at our commissioning where he said that he had never sent anyone to the cells.

A few days later, the Skipper stood on the self same spot and read out another warrant for a lad who had not only broken into WRNS quarters, but had been found lying in bed with one of the occupants.

We continued to carry out gunnery exercises, also the firing of torpedoes, and the testing of radar and submarine devices.

I was terribly disappointed at not receiving many letters from Anne, and with an imagination running riot I feared I was losing her. One of the other lads was experiencing the same shortage so we endeavoured to console one another, though I fear without much success.

Apart from we two there was yet another fellow in the mess who had met a girl from Glasgow and almost immediately had put her in the family way. He of course did receive a letter which merely caused him a worry and fear of a different nature.

I have mentioned the nature of victualling on a destroyer, and as it was left to each mess to decide their own daily menu, we slowly developed into a pattern whereby certain lads were experts on specific dishes, so the work was split up to allow the mess to enjoy their daily expertise. Breakfast was only ever toast with lashings of butter. This allowed all of us time to lie in a little longer and each was responsible to make his own toast, but for lunch we all helped to peel the potatoes and the appointed cook of the day prepared whatever other vegetables we needed. I imagine pot mess was the most popular. We would buy three pounds of beef, cut it into cubes and chuck it in a pot with all the vegetables and a few doughboys. As the chef was also in our mess, we could always be sure that he would give our meal special care. For sweets the lads often enjoyed Manchester tart. Now whether our recipe complied with that attributed to real Manchester tart I know not, but we would line a dish with pastry, spread jam over the bottom and then prepare custard by using sugar and syrup, pour this over the jam and allow to set. Lunch was the main meal of the day, and provided that was up to expectation we didn't bother too much about breakfast or tea.

Following Anne's discharge from the Land Army, she had recovered sufficiently enough to take a job in Biggar just outside Glasgow, so I decided to visit her on my next leave.

Carstairs appeared to be the nearest station so I made my way there, arriving late on the Saturday night. I saw an old boy and enquired from him as to the next train tonight to Biggar.

"B'aint no train tonight son," he said.

"What about a bus?"

"No son b'aint no buses either; best wait till morning."

I went down the street until I saw a policeman's house, so knocked on the door. He wasn't too pleased but couldn't help anyway, so I wandered back to the station and lay down on a bench. I didn't get much sleep, but in the morning when I asked about the train I was informed there weren't any and the earliest bus did not arrive until 11am.

"And," said my informant, "by the time you got there, the last one would have already left for here."

Just as my spirits were at a very low ebb, he informed me that the people of Biggar had provided for servicemen a free private car to pick them up from Carstairs, and that it was due to leave shortly. They made room for me but I confess to my shame that I was so excited at the thought of seeing Anne again I didn't offer the driver a tip.

The hotel where Anne was working was in beautiful grounds, surrounded by lovely trees and bushes. Regrettably she was on duty, but I spent a mere fifteen minutes with her before she had to go. While I could not disguise my disappointment I did at least see her and note the improvement in her health. It is impossible to describe one's racing heart and the eager anticipation I felt at seeing her again, but this brief meeting, while satisfying one aspect, filled me with doubts as to whether I was chasing rainbows. There were no outward signs by Anne of the intensity of love that I had for her – was this all an illusion? It was nearly Christmas and I sadly returned to my parents' home to spend it with them, but I wondered if they knew their son had such an aching heart.

After Christmas I returned to the ship while the other watch went on New Year's Eve leave. When they returned we settled down to normal routine before, as we thought, going overseas, but the next thing was the Skipper calling the crew together and telling us that contrary to our expectations *Croziers* was going into 'A' reserve. This meant that she would be stuck on the mud at Porchester Creek with just a care and maintenance crew aboard. A sailor gets a feeling for his ship, but we had not been aboard long enough to acquire such feelings of affection; but the Skipper, that was a different matter. This was, I believe, his first command and to lose *Croziers* could only have been a major disappointment.

We duly sailed for Porchester in a strong gale where we were due to moor up to a buoy fore and aft. Normally this operation should have taken no longer than half an hour, but fate still had a few tricks up her sleeve, because it took us two hours to tie up to the foremost buoy The usual drill is to disconnect the anchor from the cable and lower the cable chains to the buoy. Meanwhile, the whaler had been called away carrying two buoy jumpers and the shipwright whose task it was to get on the buoy and shackle the cable to the ring on the buoy. A buoy jumper and the shipwright clambered onto the foremost buoy to receive the ship, but as she steamed in, a gale force gust of wind threw us off course and forced us to go round again. On the second attempt we had too much weigh on us so that the buoy passed down our starboard side, causing the buoy to rotate with ever gathering speed. The two men on the buoy looked like a couple of flies on a gramophone record, until that is they were thrown off into the sea. Two more buoy jumpers were delegated to the whaler after the first two had been rescued and were brought inboard. Another attempt brought the same result with two more men having to be rescued. The Skipper must have wondered if we were ever going to get moored, but then he had not allowed for the astuteness of the Forecastle Petty Officer. He tied a heaving line to a stanchion and at the appropriate moment slid down it onto the buoy. The heaving line was attached to a wire hawser, and when this had been lowered he quickly made fast as a temporary measure until such times as the weather allowed us to shackle onto the buoy.

Our difficulties had not gone by unnoticed because a tug was sent out to render assistance, but by the time she arrived the only assistance we needed was to bring the Petty Officer back inboard. This they did, but not before the PO had managed to crush his foot between the tug and the buoy.

This was not the end of the saga because it was the Skipper's intention to use the cable to moor fore and aft, but as there was no cable aft, we had to break the cable and carry one shackle at a time to the quarterdeck, where they then had to be joined up again.

The ship was full of rumours as to who would leave the ship and who would stay. For my part, I had no desire to stay, but even if the contrary were true there was little likelihood of it happening. Apparently the men who made such decisions were all Pompey (Portsmouth) men, and as such they would favour Pompey men for the care and maintenance party.

We carried on normal routine, but one Saturday morning the Captain was undertaking his usual rounds. Just before he entered our quarters, the Killick of the mess found some waste materials stowed under one of the lockers.

"Lofty," said the Killick to me, "take this out of the way quick and ditch it where you like."

I raced up top, thinking that if no one was watching I would throw it over the side. Now, the Skipper had given specific instructions that while in Porchester Creek nothing was to be ditched over the side. On reaching the upper deck, the Chief Buffer saw me.

"What are you doing with that?" he said.

"Killick told me to ditch it somewhere Chief. Alright for me to throw it over the side?"

"Do what you like as far as I'm concerned," said the Chief.

"Fair enough," I replied, and promptly threw it over the side.

Barely had it left my hand before the Buffer yelled with rage.

"But you said…"

"Doesn't matter a damn what I said. You've seen the First Lieutenant's orders about ditching things overboard."

"But Buffer," I went on, but he wasn't listening.

"The First Lieutenant's orders override mine. Report to me tonight and I'll see you work." I turned away, muttering and cursing inwardly.

Having the NAAFI lad in our mess, I decided I would take advantage of it, and so he agreed to sell me the ship's total supply of Capstan medium pipe tobacco. They worked out at one shilling and tuppence for a two ounce tin. My object in doing this was hopefully to build up a store at home for when I was eventually demobilised. Getting it home was a problem because you were only allowed a two ounce tin for a week, and further, the Customs at Portsmouth Dockyard know all there is to know about sailors exceeding their quota.

One weekend I put a tin under each armpit and I also had a prick of tobacco. Now, this prick of tobacco had been treated with rum, lemon and molasses and was all tied up with tarred spun yarn. I had no desire for my clothes to reek of this vile concoction so I wrapped it all in a towel. Well, I must have had a guilty look that day because Customs called me in and, on searching my bag, focused in on the prick of tobacco. I must confess it looked as though I had two pounds of tobacco, so I then for their benefit had to go through the ritual of explaining how one made up a prick of tobacco, by taking the stalks out of the leaf tobacco and soaking it in the other ingredients, then rolling it in canvas and finally tying it up with tarred spun yarn. I hoped he was not telepathic because the tins under my arms appeared to be growing in size and that is all I could think about, but he sent me on my way with a smile.

The funniest story I heard was the sailor who went ashore in Portsmouth with a suitcase. He went straight up to a Customs Officer and furtively took him to one side.

"Officer," he said, "tomorrow night I'm going on leave. I'll be having a few fags aboard, you understand."

He gave a knowing wink and said, "I'll see you're okay."

The Custom Officer agreed and Jack went on his way. The following night Jack went on leave, and surprise surprise, an army of Customs men were waiting for him, but they never found a thing. Yes, Jack had taken his cigarettes through the night before.

At last the day of the draft arrived, and the ship's company had to fall in with all their kit and march through the Dockyard to the barracks, so my supply of tobacco had to be dispersed. Kitbags and hammocks were going by lorry so I distributed a number of tins between them, stuck a tin under each armpit, and tried to look innocent. Every now and again the Customs man would tap a sailor's shoulder and he would go off to be searched. Straight away I thought I was crazy to risk this for a few tins of duty free tobacco, but it was too late now so I would just have to sweat it out.

With a sigh of relief I came through the gates unscathed, only to find that my shipmates were not only guilty but were bragging about the quantities they had smuggled through.

Once more we were taken to *HMS Collingwood* at Fareham and soon became adapted to the usual routine of painting, scrubbing, sweeping, digging and last but not least dodging. The longer we stayed in the Navy so our skills at dodging improved. Our arrival in the camp coincided with the preparation of a reading and information room. By some stroke of good fortune, another lad and I were given the task of preparing and organising the layout. This was a nice cushy number which kept us out of the cold and meant that once the room had been opened, all we had to do was keep it clean, but it did not give me the satisfaction I was seeking. I was restless and uneasy and eventually realised that this state of mind could be linked to the lack of letters from Anne. My feelings had never wavered and the depth of love I had for her was immeasurable, and yet I believed that letters between us were the bonds that cemented our relationship, and though I could have written daily I felt Anne's feeling for me were not as strong as mine for her, hence the lack of correspondence to me. I therefore decided that the only way I could snap out of this depressing state of mind was to volunteer for a foreign assignment.

This came sooner than I had expected for within two weeks of being in the camp I was sent on another fourteen days leave after which we were due to commission *HMS Mauritius,* a colony class cruiser lying in dock in Liverpool.

A number of lads from the same mess as mine had also received draft chits to the same ship.

Chapter 21

HMS Mauritius

Along with a number of other lads we reported to Portsmouth Barracks and there joined a larger contingent. A special train had been laid on to take us on a circuitous route to Liverpool. In fact, it went through my hometown of Staines. I was only four hundred yards from my home and family, and yet they had no idea I was so near. Under normal circumstances it would have been hard to resist the temptation of paying them an unexpected visit, but these were not normal circumstances. I had volunteered for this draft and was looking forward to whatever fate had in store for me.

When we eventually got to the docks in Liverpool, we were mustered in one of the large granaries and allocated our various messes and watches. Again the Skipper spoke to his new crew.

"I want this to be a happy ship, and to be a happy ship, we must have an efficient ship."

They must have had a gramophone record of these words as part of their training.

My mess was on the starboard side up forward so I quickly found a billet and slung my hammock, and then it was a matter of getting a locker to stow my gear.

Already established in the mess was leading hand Ginger Kelly. He was a short, wiry individual with a perpetual grin showing a mouthful of large brown uneven teeth. Ginger was not an H.O. (hostilities only) sailor as the majority of us were. With him was another seaman called Mixter, also R.N. Mixter was a broad-shouldered, thick set character, a little morose and not given to an easy smile. They had joined the ship some time before as an advance party preparing the way for the rest of the crew to arrive.

Joining with me were Alan Emsley, a tall, lanky lad who was also on the *Croziers*. There was Paddy Slavin, a lofty great square-headed fellow from Belfast. Paddy was built like a tank and you could see the seams of his uniform straining every time he flexed his arms. By contrast, a very small lad speaking with a college accent and going by the name of Gwint joined the mess. Paddy very soon started to take the rise out of him, but Gwint ignored it in rather an aloof manner.

The mess deck was beginning to fill as more arrived in ones and twos, and then I heard a familiar voice.

"Why, if it isn't old Joey."

Turning around, I found the speaker was none other than Bill Fallows off the *Vindex*. It was a delight to see him. There were a number of lads off the *Croziers,* including one of my old pals Dudley Light and Smithy from Collingwood who was now a leading seaman, and Froggy French, a stout chap who was also with me in Collingwood.

After settling in, I decided to have a look around. She was certainly a beautiful ship, having been repainted inside and out. Her armament consisted of three triple 6 inch turrets, situated two forward and one aft. There were four twin 4 inch guns, two either side of the ship just aft of the boat deck and abreast the aft smoke stack. There were five quadruple pom poms. In the waist aft of the two whalers and placed either side were a set of triple 22 inch torpedo tubes. On the quarterdeck by the Quarter Master's position was the name Mauritius in huge chromium plated letters.

There is no doubt in my mind that *Mauritius* fulfilled my idea of what a warship should be like.

Our divisional officer was Lieutenant Gutteridge, who was nicknamed Gutts. He came over as a dammed nice chap and was always willing to help. He wasn't a forceful type and was inclined to say little nevertheless the men soon came to respect him.

The Petty Officer in charge of the Quarterdeck Division of which we were part was a huge hefty stout character with a flowing black beard. He was also very quiet, but his intimidating size was his authority, and he got things done for the simple reason no one was prepared to challenge it.

Within two days of joining, Lieutenant Ryan the boat officer came down to the mess-seeking volunteers to man the 32 foot motor cutter as a permanent job. It was an assignment I wanted but I was not prepared to volunteer my services. He then approached me and asked if I had any experience of small craft. Fortunately I had, and was then made bowman of the motor cutter. He then picked Leading Seaman Charlton who lived in Newcastle, so of course he became Geordie, and Scouse, a short, thickset fellow, who was the stern sheets man. He gave us instructions to completely overhaul the boat, which meant repainting the outside and scrubbing all the woodwork as well as polishing the brass. In the meantime he went in search of another crew, the object being that each crew would alternate doing twenty-four hours on and twenty-four hours off. The change over time would be a half hour after noon each day. On our twenty-four hours off, we were expected to work from 09:00 to 11:30 in the forenoon.

Those first few weeks meant we were kept on the move the whole time. The ship had first of all to be cleaned throughout, then we had to restock the provisions and ammunition the ship. We were fully occupied right through the dogwatches, and after a day of humping sacks of flour and carrying six inch shells, we were glad to get into our hammocks.

The local establishments soon became aware of our presence as the nightly takings of the inns and taverns dramatically increased. One of the leading hands we called Blondey was an uncouth, hard drinking character, whose runs ashore were literally wine, women and not so much of the song. He was slight of build but loved to be seen with two of the chiefs, both of whom were built like heavyweight boxers. Invariably the period of heavy drinking resulted in a brawl between the three of them and anybody else who chose to cross their path. About midnight they staggered up the gangway and made their way back to their respective messes. When Blondey arrived in his mess he would button hole anybody that was still up, and give a lurid account of the amount of liquid drunk, the number of adversaries they had knocked out and the manner in which it was done.

"Chiefy picks this guy up and hold's 'im in a full Nelson while I hit 'im in the guts, then another I gives 'im a 'ead butt and knocks 'im out. I tell you between us we cleared the bloody pub."

Blondey would then slide under the table fully dressed, vomit, and fall into a drunken stupor.

The following morning a scruffy blonde mop with eyes looking like burnt holes in a blanket poked his face between the mess stool and table.

"Oh my bleeding 'ead, it's fit to burst. I'm never going drinking again." His pathetic pleas were ignored as one of the watchman came down the mess.

"See the police have come aboard about that trouble in the pub last night."

Blondey was conscious that everyone was looking at him but he could not disguise the fear in his voice when he said, "Don't look at me, I don't know nothin' abaht it. I weren't in no pub."

I often went ashore with Dudley Light, which meant a visit to the cinema, and once we even tried ice-skating. We would book a bed in the YMCA, but like its Glasgow counterpart we never got much sleep. Every nationality and every colour slept there, but we slept with one eye open just in case.

Scouse and I worked on the cutter until the woodwork was almost white. Her hull was a light blue, the interior was painted white and the benches untreated wood. We cleaned the brass work, and the rubbing strake, which was made up of six inch manila rope covered in canvas, which we painted white. We sewed canvas sleeves about eighteen inches in length onto two boat hooks and made Turks heads at either end. We then painted the canvas and rope trimmings in white. Lieutenant Ryan had by now picked the other crew which was comprised of Paddy the Irishman, and his big pal John. Leading Seaman Charlton our coxswain he transferred to the other crew and in his place we got Ginger Kelly. There was also a fourth member of the crew who had to come from the stokers' mess deck, and it was his task to operate and be responsible for the engine. His name was Dennis Davenport. Now, Dennis was a damned nice fellow, but he did have a rather high-pitched voice that gave certain characters the wrong idea, and the idea was most certainly wrong. Dennis would often have to shrug off suggestive comments and ask why it always happened to him.

Scouse was always a source of amusement; he had no respect for rank and his language was peppered with a string of oaths. The index finger on his left hand was missing, and he told me that he had been ashore drinking some time ago, fallen on a broken bottle and was forced to have the finger amputated. Ginger would often disappear in the afternoon and get his head down in some secluded spot, but Scouse and I weren't too concerned because we were very much left to ourselves and could therefore take turn and turn about getting our own heads down under a tarpaulin in the cutter.

It is a well-known fact that sailors can pitch a yarn, they can embroider and embellish a story, they can, with sincerity, tell a downright lie, so I relate the following for the reader to choose.

A fellow in his early twenties joined the ship, and the following evening sitting in the mess, he started to speak.

"A funny thing 'appened to me the other night. I was standing outside this 'ere cinema in Liverpool when along comes a dame; she was just the job, she 'ad everything, blonde good looking and a smashing figure – boy what I could have done to that – bird ain't worth mentioning. I turned round to look at the pictures, you know the ones in the frame, and I was conscious that this bird was standing be'ind me, I mean, 'er perfume was enough to set you off. I turns round and looked into these beautiful blue eyes. Me 'eart misses a beat, me tongue goes dry, I could not speak, and then, all posh like, she says, 'Well, aren't you going to take me in?' You could 'ave knocked me down with a feather, she didn't look that sort but me mind was working overtime. She was just asking for what I wanted to give 'er. Anyway, I says, 'Sorry lady I ain't got a dime.' She didn't say anything but slips a quid into my mitt – well, I was right puzzled. Anyway, I takes this rummy dame into the back row but I couldn't concentrate on the film with her beside me. I slipped me arm around 'er shoulders and she didn't object, so with a bit of encouragement I gets the other hand to work, but she raps me across the knuckles bloody 'ard. When the picture finished I walks 'er 'ome to a flat in a posh area, real classy it was. I made a move to say good night when she says, 'Come in and stay the night if you like.' Well, I was all for that, but thinks there something fishy going on 'ere, but for the life of me I couldn't figure it out. I thinks she don't want my money 'cos I ain't got any, she don't want me mucking abaht so what the hell does she want? She gave me something to eat and then says, 'Why don't you go to bed now? Use that room and you'll find some pyjamas on the bed and I'll bring you in a cup of coffee.' I says 'thanks very much 'cos its getting' late and a bit of shut eye would do me good. Well, I gets in the room and there on the bed is a pair of pale blue ladies' pyjamas and they were real silk. By now the 'airs on me 'ead is standing out like bristles – I mean, I ain't worn nothing like this before. Anyway, I gets into bed, a big un with silk sheets and initials on the pillows. Imagine me, a bloody able seaman lying in between silk sheets in ladies' silk pyjamas I 'adn't been there long afore there's a light knock on the door and she came in. Bloody hell I says to myself, bloody hell, I'm bleeding dreaming, there's this bird in the flimsiest of night dresses. I could see everything through it. I sat bolt upright hoping she wouldn't notice me eyes sticking out like organ stops. She got this tray with a mug of coffee on it. Me 'ands were trembling as she gave it to me. It's not a mug of coffee I want to get my hands around, I scream inwardly, but I controls myself, see. I says, 'now, Charlie boy, take it steady, you're in decent company and the lady don't want no mucking abaht, so 'ave a bit of respect.' She sat on the bed until I had finished. She didn't say owt, we just looked at each other, but I'm telling you I was aching for that bird. When I finished she sort of glided out and said, 'Goodnight.' She turned out the light and I heard the door shut. I'm lying there thinking to meself what might 'ave been, but I'd 'ad a good night so what the hell, and then just as I'm in the middle of all these fantasies I felt someone sliding between the sheets. I nearly jumped out of me skin. She didn't look that type, and yet here she was, sharing the same bed as me. Now, I took that as an open invitation, so once again I starts sort of mucking abaht, but she gets right upset – no sir she ain't 'aving none of it – but she don't get up so I keeps on trying and ain't a kidding when I say it took me till three in the morning before I bring that wench round to my way o' thinking. She got up early and gave me breakfast in bed and then says, 'When you go, will you lock the front door after you and put the key through the letterbox?' I promised I would, and then she says I was free to visit her any time I wished."

As he finished his story, one became conscious of the silence from the listeners. All eyes were fixed with glassy stares upon the narrator, but all minds were dwelling on this beautiful silk-clad blonde in a flat in Liverpool.

At long last the ship was ready to depart with her new crew. Sailors lined the forecastle boat deck and quarterdeck. Also on the quarterdeck was the ship's band and aft of them were the Royal Marines looking just that much more smarter and disciplined than the seamen. Sailors are not imbued with a great deal of respect for any branch of His Majesty's Armed Forces, but the Marines are an exception. A seaman would never convey to a Royal Marine these innermost feelings, but when he sees them on parade marching, drilling or playing in the band, a lump comes to his throat, and when these Marines are off your own ship and when you see them strike the colours, then it takes a tough man to withhold outward feelings of pride, but don't tell it to the Marines.

The caissons opened and we passed out of Gladstone dock. Relatives and friends of the officers and crew stood on the jetty waving, the band was playing, and as our speed increased so Liverpool slowly receded from view.

Our first trip was down south to Portland, but what a noticeable difference to wartime. All the brass work that for many years had been hidden under many coats of paint now glistened in the midday sun. The ugly camouflage that detracted from the sleek lines of a cruiser had gone, and in its place there was a beautiful shade of light green. None of the guns were manned and there were no other laborious duties except for a couple of look outs and a duty sea crew.

As each part of watch went on duty they reported to the PO near the starboard whaler in the waist just forward of the galley. After muster, he appointed lookouts and sea boats crew. The remainder were released to follow their own interests, whether it be writing, washing, sleeping or any other occupation of personal interest. By some quirk of fate my name was never called, so I never worked a single watch all the way to Portland. One does not advertise good fortune of this nature. The weather in the Irish Sea was quite rough and the *Mauritius* rolled in a somewhat exaggerated manner. We had been warned that being a little top heavy she was prone to this behaviour. Once we had turned the Lizard and changed to an easterly course, the weather brightened considerably, so that by the time we arrived at Portland the sun was shining and there was hardly a cloud in the sky.

Our arrival was so different to that which I had experienced on the *Croziers* some months before. *Mauritius* literally glistened, with her new paintwork and shining brass reflecting the sunshine. The ship's crew lined the side as is customary and just as a girl who knows she is good looking cannot hide her conceit, so we too knew we looked good and were conceited enough to be proud of our ship.

As soon as we dropped the hook in the harbour so the booms and gangways were put in position, followed by the lowering of the boats into the water. The Boat Officer congratulated us on the condition of the cutter, and I must say with the benches and gratings scrubbed white, the clean paintwork and shining brass fittings she really did look grand. There were two other launches namely the Captain's boat and the Officers' boat, both of which had twin screws and cabins. We were single screwed with no cabins, though in rough weather we erected a spray hood. There was only one other working boat which was the skimming dish. She was very fast but could only accommodate the driver and one passenger. She was used to collect mail or take urgent messages to shore or to the other ships, but she was terribly unreliable and was always breaking down. The period at Portland was also a resting time for the ship's boats, and the cutter proved to be the most reliable as the others were constantly breaking down. Regrettably this increased our volume of work.

When the liberty men went ashore we would go out of the harbour and head for the pier at Weymouth. I used to enjoy these trips sitting in the bows by myself. The nights were dark but I would keep a look out for the buoys and tried not to let the hundreds of lights from the shoreline confuse me. We did of course have a compass, and while we could appreciate the splendour of the stars in the night sky, none of us were capable of steering by them. The trips were so peaceful, and to approach an illuminated coastline all combined to make one appreciative of the fact that the war was over. The only sounds were the gentle throb of the engine combined with the bows cutting through the waves, and yet even they did not stop this period of peace and quietness where one's thoughts were of home and Anne. An occasional shower from spindrift would bring me out of my dreams, but they were very happy trips.

By contrast, the return journey could not have been more different. The cutter would be full of lads catching the last boat back to the ship. Half of them were drunk, which meant that liquor made some men happy and carefree, whilst in others it introduced a degree of belligerence which invariably ended up in a fight. Those not taking part in the scrap would either be lounging back blotto with eyes wide open and silly grins on their faces, while others were spewing their insides up over the side of the boat and sometimes in it.

A careless clout with a boat hook either brought the protagonists to their senses or knocked them out; either way, we would wedge their heads under the benches and ensure they had a snug fit with a well-placed boot in the backside. Occasionally I would have the worst cases up in the bows with me. The cold spindrift often helped to sober them up quickly.

It is impossible to control a boatload of drunken seamen and Ginger knew this, so very wisely he would allow them to sing and curse and shout until we were a couple of cables away from the ship, when he'd usually say, "Okay. lads, you've had your fun. We're coming alongside shortly, so cut the cackle."

Generally speaking they usually cooperated, which was good, seeing that the safety and good conduct of the cutter was Ginger's responsibility.

The gangway staff always kept a look out for approaching vessels and would hail them. At nighttime they could only see our navigation lights and so when we were within shouting distance they would yell out, "Ship Ahoy."

My response would indicate to the ship the nature of our passengers – for example if I called, "No no," it meant all aboard were below Wardroom rank. If I replied "Aye aye," then they were above. If however we had a ship's Captain aboard, then we would yell out the name of the ship he was Skipper of. However, there was usually little chance of that happening, as they would use the other launches.

On our twenty four-hours off duty, we had watch keepers leave. I would therefore often go ashore at 13:00, and book a bed at the White Ensign Club or at one of the boarding houses that did bed and breakfast. This meant that I did not have to get back to the ship until 11:30 the following day. The joy of sleeping between sheets followed by a decent breakfast and then sunbathing on the glorious sandy beach – this was indeed the ideal life.

There would be a liberty boat at 11:30 to take me back to the ship, and this allowed me time to change, have lunch and then report for duty at 12:30.

One day when the ship was going out for torpedo trials, the Skipper told all the boats crew to take their craft inshore and work on them until the ship returned. It was a glorious sunny day, and it did not take us long to scrub out and generally make clean ,so we encouraged Ginger to move away from the eyes of land-based Naval Authorities to a more secluded area where we would not be noticed. We motored off and tied up alongside some barges near a bridge, and then in pairs we took it in turn to pay a visit to the pub and the NAAFI canteen. We could see that Ginger was nervous and irritable, for if we were caught he covered the woodwork and stained it like rust marks. We scrubbed and scrubbed, we used chemicals and sharkskin but we could not, and in fact never did, erase those marks. It was very disappointing after all our hard work.

The ship's crew were inoculated against various diseases common to the Mediterranean. On the second day we sighted the Spanish coastline, and on the third day we changed from blue caps to white and we replaced our jerseys with white fronts.

We passed three whales on our starboard side and then a school of porpoises followed us.

We espied Cape St. Vincent and then through the night hugged the coastline.

would have to take the can back for it, but very selfishly we did not allow such mood to mar our enjoyment.

Geordie Charlton, the Leading Seaman of our opposite crew, was a tough character. He had in the war been presented with the DSO, but I do not know what for. Anyway, Geordie was always talking about 'Filling someone in', but when he was given Paddy and John as his crew he was a little more subdued. In fairness, Geordie did suffer from a degree of shell shock, to the extent that when the guns fired he would go into the bowels of the ship to get away from them, but another side to Geordie was his wife and home. If you could get the conversation around to that topic, Geordie would talk about his wife with tenderness and compassion.

Both watches were given a weekend leave and then it was a matter of weighing the anchor and departing from Portland. I was quite excited at the thoughts of going abroad, and so Monday morning the day set for our sailing could not arrive soon enough. The day itself was bright and sunny with a beautiful blue sky and not a cloud in sight. I went up top and watched the English countryside disappear below the horizon. As soon as there was nothing to view but endless seas I went below. One sensed a strange feeling, not only one's self but the others too. We were leaving the country of our birth, we were collectively leaving wives, sweethearts, children and parents, and none of us knew when next we would see them again.

The mess deck was quieter than usual and you became aware that nearly all of them were in the process of writing to those loved ones. Ginger and Mixter were playing cards with an air of indifference. They had seen this many times before, so their emotions were on a different level to the rest of us.

Stories of the Bay of Biscay and what it can do to a man's stomach made me a little apprehensive, but I had no need to fear because it treated us very kindly, with a surface that was really nothing more than a long lazy roll. Yes, the ship did roll more than one thought she should, but then we had already been warned about that.

Two days after leaving Portland, we checked out the cutter and found that small flakes of diesel soot from the funnels had

Chapter 22

Gibraltar

As the ship turned to port on an easterly course, so we entered the Mediterranean. In front of us like a huge grey sentinel superimposed against a beautiful blue sky stood the Rock of Gibraltar. Very soon the cable party were piped to muster on the forecastle and the special sea duty men to their stations. The rest of the seamen were kept busy preparing to go alongside.

At 08:00 we lined the ship's side, and with the band on the quarterdeck they played us into harbour. Slowly and gracefully we made our way while the Rock got bigger and bigger. Originally it was just a mass, and then it was massive, but with our closer proximity we could identify rocks and colours, trees and bushes. We could see houses and hotels and vehicles moving, and the array of colours no longer merged one into the other, but stood out with clear definition that transformed the view into a galaxy of colour that took the breath away.

By 09:00 we had tied up alongside the mole, and by midday there was a queue at the Paymaster's office to change sterling into Gibraltar currency.

I was duty watch on the day of our arrival so could not go ashore, but we had all heard how cheap the goods were in Gibraltar so I had made up my mind to buy Anne a wristwatch. The fact I could not go ashore on the first day was a blessing, due to the fact that I could profit from the experience of the lads who were allowed ashore. That evening saw the mess deck looking like some Eastern bazaar, for my messmates laid out the products of their shopping spree on the tables. Silken tapestries, carpets, watches, bangles and chains – everything was there to see, which had the effect of whetting my appetite. Ginger, however, was pessimistic.

"You're a load of bloody fools," he said. "In Malta you can get the same thing for half the price." His words of advice fell on deaf ears for the prices were much cheaper than in the UK, and that is supposing you could have found the goods in any case.

The following day I went ashore with Allan Wheeler, and one of the first things we saw was a barrow load of bananas. We hadn't seen a banana in seven years and here were hundreds of them. Allan just could not resist the temptation, and was soon gorging them one after the other. We approached the North Gate which was of solid brick construction and entered Main Street. The shops were dazzlingly brilliant as they displayed a variety of wares. The windows were full to capacity, without a spare inch of space.

Over the busy and noisy street we could hear the strains of music, and pushing our way through crowds of Spaniards and other unknown nationalities we found ourselves standing before the Tracadero. Curiosity got the better of us so we went through the swinging half doors and found ourselves in a room full of sailors sitting at tables and drinking beer.

Suddenly a voice called out, "Joey, what are you doing here?" It was Bill Fallows.

"I might ask the same of you," I said, and sat at the next table with Allan.

At the time I did not appreciate the implication in Bill's comments, for as far as I was concerned, this was nothing more than a bar with live music.

We sat on wickerwork chairs and at the far end was a small orchestra – well not exactly an orchestra but three men, each playing an instrument one of which was a piano. Nearer to us was a small stage about a foot high. Allan and I ordered a couple of beers and relaxed. The band struck up and a Spanish girl came on stage. Her jet black hair shone and was brushed right back into a bun. Her frock was tight fitting down to the waist and below that it flared out down to the ankles. The material was bright red with large white spots, and in her hands she held castanets which she played in time with the music. Slowly she began to dance but as the tempo increased so did her movements, faster and faster she cavorted around the stage. Her dress spun out higher and higher as she twirled around and then the onlookers realised she was not wearing underclothes.

The various acts that followed were all of a similar nature, although I did not see any of the lads paying the ten shillings that one of the girls was asking to make a bottle of beer disappear. The girls were well proportioned – or to put it another way, they were obese. This was made evident when one of them came on in what was supposed to represent a naval uniform. In reality, rolls of fat could be seen protesting at the tightness of the uniform and at the same time the seams were screaming out at the strains being imposed on them.

With all the doors shut the heat became stifling and the air reeked of the smell of smoke, beer and perspiring bodies. As soon as the show was over we hurriedly got out into the fresher air and resumed our quest.

A shop at the top end of the street had a watch to which I had taken a fancy.

"How much?" I said.

"Thirteen pounds, sir," he replied.

"Sorry, too dear," I responded, and made to walk out.

"It ees very good watch. For you, I charge twelve pounds."

"No good," I said. "Not at that price."

"Eleven pounds ten shillings, sir, and I geeves it away."

"No thanks," I retorted and walked out.

This sort of dialogue took place at every shop we entered, though the price did come down somewhat.

Eventually I found what I thought was a promising shop.

"Have you any watches?" I enquired.

"Just a minute sir," he replied, and went off to the back of the shop which was divided from the front by these large hanging tapestries. I thought I was supposed to follow him but was surprised to see another counter, behind which two officers were being served. The man I was following called out to the other assistant.

"Give me one of the twenty pound watches."

I cringed when I heard him say that. I could not afford twenty quid. When he saw me behind him he quickly ushered me out and I realised then that there were two prices, one being for the officers and the other for the lower ranks.

Returning to the front of the shop he laid the watch on the counter.

"Well, sir," he said. "This watch is twelve pounds."

"What?" I exclaimed. "I can't afford that."

"How much?" he asked.

"I'll give you seven pounds ten."

He went blue in the face. "How can I make money at that price? But for you I make it eight pounds ten."

"If you take eight pounds you've got a deal."

"No, I can't do eight," he said.

"Okay, let's toss a coin for it," I said.

He agreed and I lost the toss and ended up with quite a nice ladies' watch for eight pounds ten shillings.

Allan and I decided to explore the area so we went as far the Spanish frontier, where thick set heavily clad and burly looking guards stood in the boiling sun. Crowds of Spaniards who worked in Gibraltar but lived in Spain travelled back and forth morning and night. The first bullfight of the season was shortly to take place in La Linea, but one needed a pass to get through the barrier, and time was not on our side.

On returning to the ship, a number of the lads expressed the view that I had wasted my money and that I would soon be able to find out myself when we arrived in Malta. For the life of me I could not see how anybody could manufacture a Swiss watch for less than I had paid, and irrespective of the prices in Malta, I thought I had a fair bargain.

On the Sunday I was chosen to be part of a patrol ashore to support the regular Naval policemen. Military Policemen and Naval Patrols are an anathema to sailors for the reason that they represent authority in its meanest form. Jack ashore is out to enjoy himself, and is relatively harmless. Yes he does sometimes drink too much, and yes he is often boisterous and noisy and is quick to lose any respect he may have had for authority, but careful handling and guidance can often keep a man out of making trouble for himself, bearing in mind that Naval Patrols do not carry boat hooks with which to give the offender a quick crack across the skull, but the regular shore based patrolman appear to acquire a belligerent streak in them which destroys any trace of humanity, however we were kitted out with white belt and gaiters.

We were picked up from the ship by the maddest Spanish driver it was my misfortune to experience. He drove down Main Street like a bat out of hell. People fled and dived for the protection of the pavements. His horn never stopped and his speed did not decrease. All corners were taken on two wheels and he never knew the meaning of slowing down. There were only two forms of action he knew, driving fast and an emergency stop at your destination. We skidded to a halt in a shower of dust outside a large stone building. Our legs were still shaking as we hurriedly disembarked and made our way inside where we found the rooms were cool and welcoming, even though they were devoid of any degree of comfort.

The lads off the ship were duly split up and seconded to each of the regular patrols. In my patrol was a leading seaman and one regular, plus myself. We would walk very slowly up and down Main Street. It was at first very quiet and the only trouble we had was with two stokers off *Mauritius*. One of them was a small chap who was trying to help his mate who, in turn, was seven sheets to the wind. The leading seaman gave them a warning but it fell on deaf ears. If they had had any sense they would have disappeared, but with the drink in the wit went out and the leading seaman took them in charge. The boys were off my ship so I urged the leading hand not to make a charge, but these regulars can be bastards when they choose to.

The little fellow with his head in his hands kept on saying, "I'm only trying to help me mate."

Whether this got on the nerves of the regular patrolman or not I've no idea, but the next thing is he picked up the little guy and slammed him against the wall. Immediately I yelled at this burly bastard to lay off. They called for a jeep to take them back to the ship and as I accompanied them I had the opportunity to have a quiet word to the effect that if the Shore Patrol pressed charges I would refute them. Fortunately it didn't happen and they were merely confined to the ship for the rest of the day.

We returned to our patrol, though by now it was quite dark. We turned off Main Street and went up one of the back streets until we came to a large grey stone house with green shutters at the windows and a large brown iron studded door. Pushing a door open we found ourselves in a large open courtyard which we duly crossed until we came to an open door. Inside a small greasy Spaniard was preparing food accompanied by his wife. Apparently we were in the kitchen of a cafe. The couple barely acknowledged us but twittered away between themselves in Spanish. The lady then set before us a delightful meal. The old boy however started yelling at his wife and every time she came near us it reached a crescendo. I never did find out what it was all about and the meal was not paid for so I guess the regulars must have been indulging in some arrangement.

We resumed our patrol and as we passed the various clubs and places of entertainment so the noises became louder. The liquor was certainly having its effect. A yell from down the street sent us running in that direction. A fight had started and tables were being upturned, chairs broken, and bottles and glasses were flying about. We cleared the place out, and while the lads staggered back to the ship we were invited by the proprietor to go behind the stage and have a glass of port.

As turning out time came so I was recognised by a number of my shipmates.

"Well, well," they said, waving bottles and tankards in the air. "If it isn't old Joey. And who are those silly buggers you're with?" Remarks like this did not endear me to the regular patrolmen, but it was passed over.

When the lads had all disappeared back to their ships, then large black limousines arrived outside the clubs and to my utter amazement the entertainers, the dancing girls came out of the clubs dressed in beautiful fur coats, every inch the lady, and got into the cars. We rounded off the night when one of the entertainment managers invited us to join him below stage, where he opened three bottles of spirits for us. I was slowly coming to the conclusion that these fringe benefits somehow purchased for the owner some guarantee that the patrol would ensure that his club and premises would receive favourable attention.

At least our nightcap allowed me to think that the driver who took us back to the ship was indeed a very fine driver.

One can always be certain of a wide experience in the Royal Navy, for you never know from one day to the next what is to be expected of you. Being alongside, the cutter was of course in board, hence the need for authority to extend my horizons.

"Shelton," they said, "here is a scrubber, some soap and a cloth. Get over the ship's side and start scrubbing."

It was a boiling hot day as I diligently carried out my task, but as I was standing on the stage and bending slightly backwards to get a better view of my work, it suddenly shot from under me and I fell in. I would not have minded had I fallen in the other side of ship, but this side was different. It was the shore side, and therefore full of filth and muck. There was oil and potato peelings and cabbage and waste food of every description. I shudder to think what else was there; all I do know is that when I fell in, my hat stayed on the surface of the water and when I came up my head was right under the hat. Trapped between the top of my head and the inside of my cap was a collection of more unspeakable filth. Falling overboard, especially in a warm climate, can attract a charge of breaking ship, for the simple reason that an accident can be devised to ensure a nice cool swim. However, the Commander had been witness to this little scene and even Commanders have sufficient sense to know that even the most idiotic matelot would find a better spot than that to cool off.

I made my bedraggled way up the gangplank looking a very sorry sight, but when the Duty Petty Officer saw oil and filthy water and carrot tops falling off me he screamed, "GET OFF MY QUARTERDECK."

That same afternoon, I went ashore and climbed two thirds of the way up the Rock, passing some of the most brightly coloured foliage I had ever seen. Small white houses appeared to be located in haphazard fashion and the ships in the harbour were just mere specks. The Spanish coast was clearly visible, also the town of La Linea just across the border. The distant hills were covered in a light haze, but apart from that the view was astonishingly magnificent. Coming back down I stopped to admire the Barbary apes. The climb combined with the heat of the day made me hot and uncomfortable, so when I reached the bottom I made my way round the Rock to the east side and went swimming. In the early evening it was much cooler on the east side, and the beautiful clear cooling water was so different to that I had experienced earlier in the day. The sands were warm and fine so that your feet sank to the ankles. Some of the lads off the ship were already bathing in the sea when I arrived, so after we had all dried off we started to walk around the Rock in a clockwise direction. Huge concrete slabs covered a vast and high area on the east side. These were catchments where the rainwater ran down to huge pipes which in turn channelled it off to a reservoir. We followed the beach until suddenly and without warning we found ourselves overlooking the beautiful little Spanish style village in Catalan Bay. The houses sparkled white in the hot Mediterranean sunshine, and the red roofs and green shutters over the windows made it appear like a brightly coloured picture from a child's storybook. Drawn up on the beach were various types of fishing boats and all were covered in nets as they lay out to dry. On the balconies of each cottage were flowers of every imaginable colour and in the court yards and dusty cobbled streets villagers sat and smoked or mended their nets. All were dressed in a wild assortment of clothes. After leaving Catalan we continued south until we saw a huge doorway leading to a cave. On entering, we found it was big enough to accommodate a double decker bus; however we carried on walking, getting deeper and deeper into the rock. The ceiling was dripping with water and underfoot the ground was wet. A dank smell prevailed and the tunnel and our voices became magnified in intensity as they echoed back and forth. A pinpoint of light in the distance indicated that we were nearing the end of our passage through the middle of the Rock of Gibraltar. Very soon we emerged with eyes blinking in the bright evening sunshine, and found ourselves in the dockyard.

The following day we cast off our mooring lines to leave Gibraltar. The local bum boats milled around the ship in a last desperate attempts to sell watches, trinkets or silks. To us leaving port was a little theatrical. We were proud of our ship and its appearance, we were proud of the sailors lining the decks and we were proud of the Royal Marine band playing on the quarterdeck. It would never have occurred to us that others saw our departure in a different light. The inhabitants saw their liquor takings dropping, they saw falling receipts in cafes and shops, they somehow missed the spectacle taking place in their midst.

Chapter 23

Malta

We steamed east, running parallel to the Algerian and Tunisian coastline. Full scale speed trials were carried out, also gun practice. We were heading for Malta, which meant the motor cutter would be needed. Scouse and I spent more time trying to erase the stains from the diesel chippings, but to no avail. We continued to use sharkskin, sandpaper, wire scrubbers and basalt, but nothing shifted those wretched marks. Lieutenant Ryan was none too happy, but then neither were we. The night before arriving in Malta we ran into a heavy storm but it did not slow our progress, for at 09:00 the following morning we steamed into the Grand Harbour in Valletta. My first impressions were the huge battlements of St. Angelo on our port side, the high walls of Valetta on our starboard side, and the noticeable yellow sandstone from which most of the buildings were constructed. The harbour itself which is reputed to be the world's most natural harbour was full of naval and merchant ships, whilst paddling around them were small brightly painted boats being propelled by men who stood up to row these vessels. The boats were called dghaises, but the lads came to know them as dhisos.

We tied up between two buoys being moored fore and aft, lowered the gangways, the booms and the motorboats. Hardly were the gangways in position when a swarm of Maltese men came aboard. These were the laundry men commonly known as Dhobey Wallers, 'official' photographers, tailors to fit you out in blue and white uniforms, and then came the men accompanied by two or three children. They came round to empty the gash containers and could frequently be seen with arms immersed to the armpits feeling around for articles of food. They might find a potato or tomato covered in tealeaves and stale soup. These they would put into large tins and take them ashore. What they did with this I knew not, but lads who had had previous experience of the island said the food ashore was very good. Many of them bought duty free tobacco as a sideline. It was a good job the officer of the watch was blissfully ignorant as to what they were taking down the gangway.

Looking down at the cutter swinging from the boom made our work worthwhile, because she really did look a treat.

One of the first things that came aboard was the mail and I was delighted to get some letters, both from Anne and my parents.

Mauritius had at one time carried an aircraft, so naturally there was a hangar to keep it in, but the aircraft had been dispensed with so the hangar had been converted to a mess deck, a library, an information room, and it also could be used for a film show. By comparison with *Vindex,* this was a floating hotel though the heat in the mess deck was unbearably hot, and with so many men sleeping in such a confined area the smell of sweaty bodies became almost overpowering.

My first spell of duty in the cutter took us around all the ships and in and out of creeks, of which there are quite a number. It soon became apparent that the water in the harbour was most unclean and our waterline was quickly covered in oil and grease.

We had on board Indian stewards for the officers and an English canteen staff. For some reason known only to the Lords of the Admiralty, they were all replaced by Maltese, who promptly opened the Goffer bar and started to sell ices and soft drinks.

At the first opportunity Allan and I went ashore. We landed near the Customs Offices and at the bottom of a two hundred foot high city wall, where a lift took us to the top. We emerged into some flower gardens, then passed the NAAFI, and down some steps into Kingsway the main street. The beautiful old Opera House was but a shell, having been bombed during the siege. Turning away from Kingsway, we passed through narrow dusty streets with houses either side that almost touched. Children ran barefoot, their bodies bronzed and gleaming in the sunshine. We walked from the east side of Valletta to the west side, coming out opposite Sliema, where we took the ferry to Sliema, a much quieter place and not so commercialised as Valetta. The seashore looked as though it had at one time been molten rock into which small rectangles had been carved. In each square was a number which was supposed to represent a Turkish soldier who had died in battle when they tried to invade the island.

We both went for a swim and found the water calm and inviting. The only problem was the heat coming off the rocks, for when you endeavoured to sunbathe, one soon found yourself lying in a pool of perspiration.

That same night, Allan and I went to the east side of Grand Harbour where after getting out of the dockyard we found a delightful little place called Kalkara. The bay was surrounded by small houses and shops, while in the bay itself dozens of those brightly coloured dhisos were moored in the gentle waters. All were spotlessly clean with fresh paintwork, though the latter looked suspiciously like some we used on board. No doubt some enterprising sailor was even now knocking back a few beers bought with the proceeds of such a sale. We found a small bar, ordered a couple of beers, lit our pipes and just relaxed in the cool of the evening.

Our walk back led us between some huge battlement-like walls being more relics of a bygone day. It also came home to us that the Maltese people were also experiencing a housing problem, for they had burrowed into the foot of these walls by chipping away at the sandstone and even removing blocks of it to produce for themselves a cave which they had turned into a home, even including a neat and well-kept front garden.

Malta just reeked of history and I hoped that I would have the pleasure of discovering more, but as always there were diversions. Whether a sailor has been to Malta or not, they all knew 'The Gut'. It is a haunt for sailors, and it caters for sailors, so who were we to have been to Malta and not paid a visit to The Gut? We were not prepared to have that stigma labelled on us, so immediately we went down there. Now, the first thing to remember is that although sailors may call it The Gut, it is in fact Strait Street which in itself is a bit of a misnomer. It is a cobbled street that has quite an incline. It is narrow and does not see much of the sun, but the terraced houses on either side embrace small eating places, lodging houses, wine bars and places of entertainment. There were some young ladies who offer their wares, but for such an area there were surprisingly few. In one of the places that sold beer were two entertainers known as Sugar and Bobby. Both of them were men, but they wore feminine clothes and danced with the sailors – for example we saw Bobby wearing a bright red silk blouse open to the waist and black satin flared trousers that went down to his ankles. It would be very easy to have thought that both these fellows, to use a naval colloquialism were brown hatters, but I've heard many a time that any sailor putting such thoughts into action were swiftly given a bunch of fives and laid out on the deck. Anyway, it is just not natural to see men dancing with men, so Allan and I drank our beers and moved on.

The ship after a few days slipped her moorings and went to sea, where we spent some time carrying out various trials and then dropping the anchor each night at Marsashlok, a small village on the east side of the island.

After a week we went back to the Grand Harbour, and when it was our watch ashore Allan and I would delight in swimming at Sliema during the day and spending the cool of the evening at Kalkara.

The cutter was brought inboard and in its place we were given the use of this huge 45 foot pinnace. Apparently the authorities ashore thought it would accommodate us better and they were right, but the trouble was you could hardly see over the gunwales, and then there were the bilges. She leaked like a sieve, and with being in the sun all day the bilges stank. Added to this was the fact we could carry more matelots, and more matelots meant there was more vomit to mix into the bilge water, so although there were benefits, there was also a down side.

Ginger, of course, enjoyed the bigger boat because she was just like a huge black monster, and if he saw a crowd of dhisos hanging around awaiting fares, he would delight in charging through the middle causing panic, the shaking of fists and strings of expletives coming from all points of the compass.

At night-time I would use an aldis lamp because there were many small boats in the harbour milling about without lights. The last trip at night was always a heap of trouble. Half the boys were drunk, so getting into a deeper boat caused all sorts of problems as they staggered or fell or trod on others then all hell broke loose as they swore at one another, then there would be a scrap between two men and sure as hell their mates would join in, and the boat would roll from side to side as fists and arms and legs were flying in all directions. Amidst all this, lads were hanging over the side being sick and there were lads all hunched up being sick inboard, then those who were prostrate and oblivious to all that was going on around them, and then there were the singers who thought they could teach Caruso a thing or two, and then of course the worst of the lot, the inevitable youngster with half a pint who wanted to fight everybody. There was and always will be the fellow desperately in need of a pee, but what about what the boat's crew what were we doing? Well, the short answer was, that we swung our boat hooks around in an intimidating manner and swore harder than any of the passengers.

There is a gulf between our last trip at night and the first in the morning. We would get to the boat about 06:00. The morning air would be sweet and fresh, and there would be no noise, no shouting, no cussing; it was so peaceful. We did of course have to scrub the boat and remove all foul traces of the previous night's occupants. We would then go inshore to pick up those lads who had spent the night in the YMCA or wherever.

Those early morning trips had an added interest because they coincided with the brightly painted boats arriving from the island of Gozo, each of them carrying a variety of wares. Some were loaded to the gunwales with vegetables, others with fruit and eggs. Some had live chickens and even goats. The traders lining the harbour walls would be pushing and jostling for position, and when the boats were within earshot so the trading and bargaining began. Arms would be waving and eyes flashing as the voices got louder and louder, and I'm sure that before those boats had actually tied up they had already sold their produce.

That afternoon we paid another visit to The Gut. There was so much of a historic nature to see in Malta and yet here we were being drawn like a magnet to the sordid atmosphere of The Gut. The incline down the street was broken every few yards by half a dozen steps and the strains of music was only overridden by men and boys standing outside the bars and places of entertainment trying to out shout their neighbours by yelling, "Lovely eats boys, eggs and steaks, nice girls and Blues." Blues was the popular beer and the girls referred to as hostesses encouraged the sailors to buy them drinks. Of course, Jack thought that by filling these girls up with liquor would make them receptive to suggestions of a more personal nature. In reality, whatever Jack ordered for himself he got, and no matter what he ordered for the girl he paid for but didn't get, for she was always given aniseed water. Obviously management and the young lady make between them a nice profit, while our jolly Jack is getting jollier and his young lady stays stone sober, so that by the end of the evening any nefarious ideas he may have had have been forgotten, and even if he could remember such hopes and aspirations, he was in no condition to carry them out. I think The Gut had two things to be answerable for, namely it unknowingly was the cause of giving Malta the reputation for having the greatest percentage of virgins, and secondly they caused us to have to scrub the bloody boat out every day.

A few days later we slipped our moorings in the Grand Harbour and sailed round to St. Paul's Bay, just west of Sliema. When we arrived there they lowered the cutter and told us to go inshore and clean her up, while the ship went out on trials. We could hardly believe our luck as we made our way inshore. The fact that this bay had historical importance attached to it went over our heads. St. Paul was allegedly shipwrecked while on his way to Rome in this very bay, but his yearning for survival was on a different plain to ours, for while he sought spiritual salvation, we saw salvation in the shape of a wine bar. We tied up alongside a small jetty, then hurriedly scrubbed and cleaned. While Scouse and I were so occupied, Ginger and Dennis the stoker went up to the village that bordered the bay. They came back half an hour later to find Scouse and I chasing lizards among the rocks. We then went to the village and found a bar. It only consisted of a small room, the entrance to which had a beaded curtain. The walls were covered in a mass of old sepia photographs. On closer inspection we found that the majority were of Sugar and Bobby and their fame extended to Spain and London, hence their claim to international stardom. I mentioned the fact we had seen them both down The Gut and the young lady serving us said in a coyish manner, "Oh yes, I know Bobby quite awfully well, he often comes down here to see me." I looked at Scouse and from behind his glass of beer, I saw him give an artful wink.

In the evening the ship picked us up and the following day we went on firing practice and what a noise and what a mess those guns made. When the 6 inch went off, they caused cups, plates and lamps to break. They shook all the dust and dirt from behind the pipes and bulkheads and one could hardly see their messmates in the fog-like cloud of dust. Poor old Geordie, being shell shocked, went as far down the ship to get away from the noise. That night we anchored in Marsashlok.

When next we went to Grand Harbour instead of mooring to a buoy we went down to Dockyard Creek and tied up alongside the wall. Being boats crew this suited us admirably, for the simple reason that, moored in the harbour, the Officer of the Watch could, if he so chose, keep his telescope trained on us. We always felt under surveillance, but here against the wall it was a different matter for the arc of his watchfulness was limited, which meant we could sail round the harbour at our leisure and even pay a visit to the various dockside taverns.

The ship's crew had quite quickly become acclimatised to the Mediterranean but the Physical Training Officer thought we could all do with a bit of exercise so he organised PT and boxing classes on the quarterdeck during the dogwatches.

During my twenty-four hours off, I decided to join in the fun. Fun, did I say? Paddy Slavin was there and hell, that man could pack a punch, but I learnt a lesson; I learnt I couldn't box, I learnt I didn't like Paddy hitting me and I learnt that being unfit was a joyous feeling. I never went back.

Rumour had it that we were going to Crete. Immediately this brought to mind a comment that had been made some time ago by an uncle of mine. He had been in charge of an anti-aircraft battery around Suda Bay at the time of the German invasion. In the hurried evacuation he had left some items of a personal nature with a young lady who lived in a village high up in the mountains overlooking the bay. I therefore wrote to him with the news of our proposed visit, and requested that if he provided me with the details I would attempt to retrieve the articles.

Allen and I continued our jaunts ashore but mainly it was for the purpose of having a swim. We would go to Sliema, but the problem there was where the rocks met the sea it was jagged like coral, and if you weren't careful you gashed your legs on it. Another thing we noticed about the front at Sliema were the salt pits. They were twelve foot square, cut about a foot into the rock. The sea would fill them and the sun would cause the water to evaporate, leaving behind patches of brown crystal salt.

Another place we enjoyed was Bighi Bay and it was probably about the best. Bighi Bay was sited on the port side as you came into Grand Harbour. A natural diving board had been cut out of the rock and we weren't troubled by the inhabitants, for it was in a secluded part of the harbour being accessible only by boat. Not far off the shore was the sunken wreck of the famous tanker *Ohio* which took part in the epic Malta convoys. She rested on the bottom with her back broken and most of her deck awash. We would race each other to the *Ohio* and back, and then endeavour to reach her by swimming underwater all the way. Now and again an old man in a boat would stop by to sell us grapes and pomegranates, but on the whole we stayed there until the cutter came along to pick us up.

With all our activities, never a day passed by without my thoughts being with Anne. Her photograph occupied a prominent position in my locker, but I would never allow any of the lads to catch a glimpse of it. I think if anyone had seen it and made a disrespectful comment I would have flattened them. I wrote most days and though I did not mention it in my letters, my mind was seriously thinking of marriage. I could not understand my reluctance when so long ago I told Anne I was going to one day marry her. At the time the possibility seemed very remote and the chances would have exceeded my wildest dreams. It is of course possible that a refusal lay at the back of my subconscious mind, and I had no desire to hear it. I wrapped Anne's watch in cotton wool and handkerchiefs and sewed it up with waterproof canvas, then mailed it to her.

The rumours about visiting Crete had now been extended to Cyprus, but there was more credibility about the Cyprus trip as it was decided that the Royal Navy was going to put on quite a flag waving show in Nicosia, the capital. We were to provide a large party of blue jackets and marines and unfortunately I was one of those picked out. After a few days we found ourselves with the marines doing rifle and squad drill at Corodina on the east side of Grand Harbour. Our Gunnery Officer was a strict disciplinarian, very smart, erect and alert. In fact he gave the impression he had been manufactured in Whale Island. His every move was a definite action, and his head went round in a series of jerks. He kept us at drill morning and afternoon in the blazing sun, and what was more, even in my twenty four hours off. I was sure I would have had it easier in the Foreign Legion.

It was about this time that *HMS Orion* and *HMS Superb* arrived in Malta. They had come down the Adriatic and sailed through the channel between Albania and Corfu. Regrettably the Albanians objected to the invasion of their waters and promptly fired on both vessels. Their gunners had not been trained at Whale Island so they missed, which was just as well, seeing that the *Orion* carried the Admiral's flag, and it was intended that once we arrived off Famagusta in Cyprus we should inherit that flag.

Chapter 24

Crete

In the early hours we slipped our moorings in Grand Harbour and proceeded to sea. The following day was very rough, but it did not prevent us carrying out various evolutions until two days later when we dropped the hook in the calm and beautiful waters of Suda Bay in Crete.

I had already received a reply from my uncle who informed me that the personal items he had been forced to abandon had been left with a young lady called Nicky, who ran a wine bar in the village of Malaxa. I checked the ship's chart but they gave no indication of a village of that name. They did however show that on the eastern side of the bay was the Malaxa Range of mountains. I scanned the range with the binoculars, but there was no sign of any habitation, but then I saw what looked like the corners of some manmade construction. Its square angle stood out in contrast to the graceful curves and shapes of nature. I therefore decided that I would make for that spot which lay at the top of the range. I had already told some of my shipmates what I proposed to do, and almost immediately Alan Wheeler, Allan Emsley and Dudley Light volunteered to come with me.

On Saturday the 1st of June, the four of us put our feet on Cretan soil for the very first time. None of us knew the language, but by the repetitious use of the word Malaxa, a gnarled finger directed us to a path which led through some olive groves. Two young barefooted boys in clothes which had seen better days took it upon themselves to accompany us. We had not gone far before we met an old shepherd and his wife. The young lads made him aware of our destination, and since they too were going to the same place our party now swelled to eight. The shepherd was very talkative, though we understood very little of what he was saying. It was an exceedingly hot day, but whereas the party off the ship were in white fronts and shorts, the shepherd and his wife were attired head to toe in black. On his head he wore a black silk sweat rag. His walnut coloured face was partially hidden by a black Van Dyke beard. Thick leather gaiters protected his legs from the wild bracken and snakes. A black jacket with trousers to match, holding a sack in one hand and a crook in the other, and there we have the shepherd. His wife was small and chunky. A scarf covered her head and was tied beneath the chin. Thick black stockings were barely visible below her heavy long coat.

Passing through the olive grove, we came across an old man making pottery. A kiln and a fire stood to one side with many examples of his fine work on the other. He had a small hut, and attached to it he had built a shelter from the sun with branches and leaves. While we stood there, the old lady drew from her bag an enamel mug, also some green fruit the size of plums which I believe were large olives. She soaked them in the mug for a few minutes and then gave us one each. They were quite tasty and sustaining.

We picked up the trail again over rocks and bracken. The path rose steeply and soon we were out of breath and perspiring freely, but it was difficult to keep up with the old man, for although he was probably in his late sixties, he was fit and agile, leaping from rock to rock like a young gazelle. His wife was somewhat slower so we would wait for her to catch us up – at least that was the excuse. In reality we were taking a rest. Halfway up we came to a small plateau. The old lady, bending over, pushed her way through the bushes and olive trees which were growing in abundance and there, hidden from view, was a mountain spring, half-covered in green vegetation. We sat down beneath the shade of a large tree while the two old folk filled some tins with sparkling clear water. We all partook and made ready to tackle the rest of the mountain.

As we reached the top, so the concrete promontory came into view, the one we had seen from the ship. Someone must have seen us coming because as we got to the top, so we were met by a number of lads dressed in an assortment of old German uniforms. The main street, if one can call it such, was roughly hewn rock, with a few houses either side, the whole barely a hundred yards in length. By now the adult villagers and their children had turned out, lining both sides of this rough track; meanwhile the shepherd took the lead, a broad grin on his face exposing flashing pearl white teeth. Whether it was luck or design, intuition or coincidence I don't know, but he took us to a door of a wine bar. It was Nicky's Wine Bar, the very place I had been seeking. The old man tapped on the door with his crozier and called out something, and after a few moments, a feminine voice responded in perfect English. "I won't be long. I'm having a bath." Meanwhile, we were all invited inside. We entered a large whitewashed room, and apart from a worn settee, a table and two chairs, it was empty. We did not have to wait long before a slim girl with straight blonde hair joined us and introduced herself as Anthula Vamrunaki, the lady having the bath. She provided drinks for us, and over a glass of wine I made known who I was, and the reason for my visit. The following is the account, in the words of our hostess, of the gap we had been trying to bridge.

"I well remember the day your uncle was here. He gave me some letters and photographs and a very old cup, but I am sorry I have not got them here, but in my mother's house in Canea. When the Germans came, the people fled to the hills. I had to stay. I look after a soldier who is injured. There were two men 'caput' – as how you say in English 'dead'. I bury them and each night I visit their graves with a light and some flowers, but the Germans say I must not and they dig them up and take them to a military cemetery to stop me. They took the injured boy to a hospital in Canea. As for the things your uncle left, I am sorry but the letters I destroy. Every day they searched our homes and we were afraid they find them. I keep the photographs but all the words I rub out as they wanted to know who it was. I will write a letter to my mother; she will be pleased to see you."

Anthula then took us to the cemetery. There we were shown two empty graves. A tin hat with its crown dented by shrapnel lay rusting at the bottom of one. It was half covered by dead leaves shed the previous year by a tree whose branches overhung both graves. We turned away with sadness and a sickening feeling in our stomachs.

We returned to the wine bar and went out on the balcony which overlooked the small white square homes that nestled in crest of the range. Cretan lads put on a display of dancing and guitar playing, while our hostess plied us with wine and coarse brown bread. On the bread was spread a thick layer of butter made of goat's milk and which looked much like rice.

The time passed all too quickly, and when at last we reluctantly said goodbye, it was with a deep impression of Cretan hospitality and kindness. With the aid of one of the villagers, our journey back to Suda was made far more quickly. The two young lads that followed us up were still with us, jumping nimbly from rock to rock. We said goodbye to them and caught a rickety old bus to Canea.

Alighting from the bus, we passed down many streets and turnings until at last we stood outside a very large house. Our guide pulled a string which resulted in a bell echoing and re-echoing from within. The door slowly opened but no one was there until at last, looking up a spiral staircase we noticed a rather attractive girl manipulating a number of strings and wires to perform this unusual feat.

We were invited upstairs and taken into a most beautiful room, the floor being mosaic and the high ceilings being picked out in blue and gilt. A very fine and stately old lady awaited us. The guide told her who we were and what our mission was. She smiled and in fractured English introduced herself as Anthula's mother. As I handed her daughter's letter to her so she plied us with wine and pastries.

She remembered the articles well and soon gave into my care photographs of my uncle's wife and son, and also a cup that was over two thousand years old. I realised as I held them in my hand that a gap had really been bridged, and that my mission had come to a successful conclusion.

After saying goodbye to Anthula's mother, our guide took us into the centre of Canea. A paved square was surrounded by small shops, and our guide suggested that I should leave the articles I had just recovered on a bench in a wine bar. I felt most reluctant to comply with his suggestion, and yet at the same time I had no wish to insult him by declining. Eventually I followed his wishes, and Dudley and I followed him on a conducted tour through the markets and along the water front. It was unfortunate that we did not have a common language between us; nevertheless, hand signs have a universal meaning of their own.

Back in the main square we came across Bill embroiled in a fight with another sailor. We duly parted them, and while Dudley took the opponent in one direction, I took a struggling, cursing, drunken Bill in the other.

By now it was dark and our guide took us back to the wine bar where, to my relief, the goods were still intact.

Dudley and I boarded a lorry to take us back to the bay. There were quite a lot of lads off the ship waiting for the cutter to ferry them back aboard. Bill and his sparring partner had their arms around each other's shoulders. Both were still pretty drink sodden, and stood on the edge of the jetty as the boat began to fill.

Suddenly Bill's pal, swaying on his feet, said, "Let the bastard who took a swipe at my mate step out."

Now already in the boat was a huge Royal Marine sergeant and a Corporal, the latter being quite a useful character when using the fists. Although both were innocent of the allegation, they did in unison say, "I did it." They then clambered out of the cutter, not bothering with whose head or body they trod on in their anxiousness to get ashore.

The Corporal immediately stepped up to the challenger and hit him with a full-blooded right to the jaw.

"You can hit me again, and I won't land a finger on you," said the challenger, holding his jaw tenderly.

The Corporal complied with his request. Meanwhile the Sergeant was having a set to with one of his own men, and finished up throwing the poor chap through the air over the side of the jetty. With size nine boots he landed on the occupants below, causing a unified eruption of oaths and curses.

The Sergeant wiped his hands, threw out his chest, and with a grin on his face said, "Any more of you bastards feel like a fight tonight?"

There were no takers, just the silence of men sobering up rather quickly intermingled with the less conscious spewing over the side.

The following day the ship was opened to visitors, so we were kept busy taking them back and forth. One small boy brought a chicken aboard as a present to the Chaplain. The Padre looked a little bewildered by this gesture; nevertheless, when the lad left the ship, he was not carrying a chicken.

When a ship is open to visitors, the sailors aboard have very little privacy for people are constantly climbing up and down gangways, and in and out of doors. The ship's crew were kind to the children, giving them sweets and old sailor hats to wear, but I was angered to see that once these children arrived ashore the Greek sailors relieved them of their trophies.

During the war, a boom had been placed across Suda Bay, but when we reoccupied the island it was missing. The Admiralty wanted to know what had happened to it, so the Navigating Officer, acting on these instructions, took the cutter and crew to find out. We put ropes, grappling hooks, and a lead line into the boat and set forth. We knew where on land the boom had been secured and merely had to drag the grappling hook in a zigzag fashion between those two points.

Traces of rusting wires were found anchored on one side of the bay, which gave us a good idea of what we were looking for. We did in fact lift those wires over the bow, but it became too heavy and cumbersome, so we then went to the other side of the bay. Our activities came to the attention of some villagers who came down to the seashore and silently watched us from a respectful distance. Being the bowman, I had to jump over the side and pull the boat up the shingle, and in a similar fashion pushed it out later. We found further traces of the boom, and then proceeded to drag the grappling iron to and fro between the two points. Midway, the grappling iron snagged on an underwater obstruction. We tried lifting it, but even with all of us pulling we could only take in a couple of fathoms. We were pretty sure it was the boom, but the Navigating Officer wanted facts not conjecture, and said, "Someone will have to dive down and find out." No one volunteered, so he began to strip off. Meanwhile, I tied a bowline to the lead line and around the rope holding the grappling iron and lowered the lead until I could feel it had reached the obstruction below. It read seven fathoms and by deducting two feet for the bowline I calculated the depth as forty feet.

While the Navigating Officer stripped off to the buff, the rest of the lads were engaged in peeling oranges we had brought with us. They were quite refreshing in the heat of the day, but as the Officer dived, his somewhat corpulent frame presented a fine target for a barrage of orange peel, and so with Ginger yelling, "Bottoms up," a salvo of missiles was thrown. It seemed an eternity before he reappeared and when he did so he was almost unconscious. Looking like a half dead old walrus, we managed to get him inboard. Within five minutes he was apart from a headache and painful eardrums quite alright, and was able to confirm that he had indeed seen the boom. To dive that depth without any aid was indeed a remarkable feat. After releasing the drag, we motored over to a beautiful lagoon. We were surrounded by small cliffs which were covered in a brilliant array of foliage. The blue green water was as clear as crystal, and the seabed was a profusion of weeds and sea plants, giving the impression of an aerial view of a miniature pine forest.

We all stripped off and went swimming.

On our return to the ship, the cutter was hoisted inboard, the anchors were weighed and we said goodbye to Suda Bay, taking with us some happy memories and interesting times.

Chapter 25

Cyprus

Two days after leaving Crete we, in company with *HMS Orion,* arrived at Larnaka in Cyprus where we dropped the hook.

The Gunnery Officer was anxious to get ashore in order to make the final arrangements for the Victory Parade due to take place in Nicosia the following Saturday. He therefore called for the services of the motor cutter to take him to the pier. Now, I should add here that the boats crew were not exactly to his pleasing, for the reason that the Boat Officer had protested at his crews being used in the parade as their service was needed elsewhere. The Boat officer's protest had been upheld, much to our relief.

The boat was duly brought round to the gangway and the Lieutenant Commander Gunnery Officer looked immaculate; dressed in white and with his cap set at a jaunty angle, he made his descent. He did not sit down but stood in the cockpit, with both hands resting on a silver topped ebony stick. His square jaw stuck out proudly in a Mussolini style. He looked a very smart and very imposing figure.

Gathered on the pier were a number of local inhabitants anxious to see who this dignitary was. Unfortunately the steering jammed and we hit the pier. The Gunnery Officer was projected forward over the stoker and landed on top of the engine cover, his hat went in one direction and his stick another. I had seen the collision coming but even then my legs were bashed against the thwarts. Above us the locals could hardly contain themselves, but below in the boat the air was blue. The Gunnery Officer, now stripped of all his dignity, got to his feet and berated poor old Ginger. Once he was out of sight we too just broke into uncontrollable laughter, with Ginger yelling to the people above "The bloody British Navy's here."

That very same day, an invite from the Mayor of Kornos was received on board. He was inviting twenty of the lads to visit his village in the heart of Cyprus. Wheeler, Emsley and I put our names down, and that very afternoon saw us being transported by two trucks to Kornos. The Master at Arms was in charge of the party.

We travelled through open country with hills either side. Orange groves flanked the road amid a profusion of colour. After two hours the driver turned off the main road and drove down deep rutted lanes hardened in the sun. The springs of the truck were tested to their utmost. Ahead of us, we saw this small village of little houses made of mud and straw, but painted white and glistening in the sun. The lane was barely wide enough for the truck, but as we neared the centre of the village so hens flew out of our way and dogs barked and snapped at the wheels of the vehicle.

The inhabitants watched us disembark, chattering vigorously to each other. A bronzed old man with tufts of white hair approached me and said, "I was in the American Navy in 1910 and have lived here for a long time." I would have liked to carry on the conversation but we were ushered away into a large wine bar. We were given drinks which we quickly drank while the locals gathered at the doors and silently watched us.

The Mayor spoke to us through the medium of an interpreter. He said how pleased they all were to welcome us, and that as soon as we had finished our drinks we should all retire for something to eat and then he would take us round the village.

After leaving the wine bar, we made our way through the dusty streets and up the stairs of a house. Here we found a huge table which went the length of the room, and which was groaning under the weight of food. There were tomatoes, cucumbers, lettuces, bread, eggs, cakes, potatoes and numerous other delicacies, the like of which we had not seen for some years. To this was added a variety of wines and spirits that would satisfy an army.

The Mayor gave us another short speech and said that he expected us to clear the table of food and drink, so go for it. The Master at Arms replied on our behalf and as soon as he had finished the boys went to work, and believe me it was hard work because as soon as we finished one load of eggs and chips so another arrived, and the same applied to all the other foods and drinks.

When we eventually got up from the table, we were all feeling a little giddy and bleary eyed.

We were taken on a tour of the village, whose main occupation apart from farming was pottery. The earthenware was all made by hand, and one old lady was seen to be making an urn nearly four feet high. The clay, which had already been mixed, was gathered in her hands and moulded into a snake like shape. This was then placed round the top of the vase so that it grew in a spiral fashion. With constant wet fingers she moulded the clay back and forth until she had the correct shape and thickness required.

Where the old lady used her hands, others worked in white clay and used a spinning wheel. We visited the ovens where the articles were baked, and the Mayor gave me a small brown glazed bowl.

The hospitality we received was unbelievable but the time came for us to depart and make our way back to Larnaka. We were all well lubricated and sang throughout the journey. The Master at Arms was the butt end of some of the songs, but he took it all in good part. Most of us went back to the ship but certain characters decided to stay ashore and top up with ouzo. Before we arrived in Larnaka the Padre had warned us against drinking ouzo, but all his warnings only acted as an advertisement for the product and was the first drink 'Jack' ordered when away from the ship. Such was the effect of ouzo that within half an hour, those lads who had been with us in Kornos and who we had left ashore were being carried aboard unconscious. Ouzo has a very sudden and dramatic effect. A man could be standing at the bar with a clear head, and the next second could find him unconscious on the floor. Their mates usually carried them back to the ship where, for their own protection, they were put in strait jackets and left on the deck of the capstan flat. The following morning found them somewhat more sober, but with a throat as dry as an ash can, but to allow them to assuage their thirst was fatal for the effects were identical to that they had experienced the night before.

Larnaka was quite an attractive place, the front being about a mile long and studded with palm trees. Bamboo tables and chairs stood in the shadow of the trees. On the other side of the road wine bars kept the occupants of those tables supplied with drinks and salted peanuts. The peanuts were of course free, and their salty nature was meant to induce the customers to drink more. Halfway along the front, a small area had been set aside for a cabaret. A low level fence indicated the boundaries. For the want of a better word, the attractions were ladies in two-piece costumes, dancing. Had the ladies been much younger and slimmer then the word attractions would have been accurate, but alas excessive bulges could be seen wobbling up and down like jellies below a series of brightly coloured net skirts.

Some of the sailors were entranced as they sat watching with glazed eyes, but then these men's thoughts were clouded by the ouzo. The more sober men tended to view it as a comic act, they laughed and passed on.

Just as the pages of a book change so does the front at Larnaka, for the next section revealed the fishermens' boats drawn up on the beach. They were covered in an assortment of fishing nets lying out to dry, while around them smoking hookah pipes were the fishermen themselves, attired in red and black jerseys and coloured trousers.

Moving away from the twinkling lights of the sea front Allan Wheeler and I made our way to the doors of a mosque. We passed through the silence of the graveyard and up some white stones steps. An open doorway presented itself, outside of which were rows of sandals and shoes. We watched quietly as the congregation knelt on richly carpeted floors. Before them was an alcove bathed in the only bright light observable. The room was large and seemly, all male occupants bent forward as they knelt and touched the floor with their turbaned heads; meanwhile they chanted in a slow monotonous tone in a strange tongue. We felt we were intruders of their privacy and silently withdrew to the brighter lights of the sea front.

On our way back, we took it in turns to play on one of the pinball machines and I won a walking stick, though what you do with a walking stick on a naval vessel has yet to be discovered.

We had a meal and a few drinks and pondered over these new experiences and old cultures.

The following day I was of course on duty in the cutter. This coincided with the Skipper going for a run ashore. Now, what skippers do when they go ashore I have no idea, but interestingly when he came back to the jetty he expected a boat to be there to meet him. He was disappointed so he climbed up a lamppost. Now, when a sailor climbs up a lamppost he is deemed to be drunk, but when a Skipper climbs a lamp post, he does so for the purposes of sending messages to the ship. He removed his cap and, by passing it to and fro over the light, a message in Morse could be read by the ship. I say could – but rather, it should have been read – but alas, against a background of twinkling lights, another flashing light would not have been seen even if those on duty were in fact alert to such a possibility.

We in the motor cutter happened to be the first ship's boat to arrive and to receive expressions of the Skipper's wrath. Now, the Skipper does not normally ride in the motor cutter when he has his own launch, and so the side party on duty were in for a surprise.

Our navigation lights could be seen from the quarterdeck and they knew it could only be the cutter, so a half-hearted voice came over the water, "Ship ahoy."

I replied "Mauritius", which should have been an indication to them that we had the Captain aboard.

Obviously they did not believe that answer, so over the water again came the challenge, "Ship ahoy."

Again I yelled, "Mauritius". Well, this had an electrifying effect on the Officer of the Watch and the gangway staff, as in a panic they endeavoured to get together all those who should man the side and pipe the Skipper aboard. All ended well, though I never did hear what was said to the signal ratings on the bridge.

It was about this time that ailments began to manifest themselves among the men who had in Crete found young ladies who could satisfy their desires. With every passing day, the sick bay queue got bigger and bigger. At first a separate mess had been allocated to accommodate these men, but when the mess was not large enough to cater for the numbers, it was decided to have them in the mess of origin. Now, Blondey was one such member of this growing band suffering from blue fever, but he exhibited no signs of remorse, was thankful his wife and family were far away, and gave a running account of his daily visit to the sick bay for his shots of penicillin.

I very carefully kept my cup and eating irons in my locker. On Monday the 10th of June 1946, we weighed anchor early in the morning and sailed for Famagusta. Here we met *HMS Orion* and Rear Admiral Kinahan CB, CBE who transferred his flag from the *Orion* to ourselves, thereby conferring on us the honour of becoming the Flagship of the 15th Cruiser Squadron.

For the second time that day we weighed anchor and, with the Rear Admiral's flag flying, we headed for Mersin in southern Turkey, where we arrived the following morning.

I took the opportunity of going ashore but was not terribly impressed by what I saw. Mersin is very dusty and sandy. The most impressive building was possibly the Naval College, built in white stone which gave it an air of elegance and brightness in the brilliant sunshine. None of the streets were made up, and the local population seemed quite poor. The Turkish sailors were friendly and very smart, but all of them carried a pistol in a holster around the waist.

High up in the gallery of a minaret, a muezzin could be heard mournfully calling the people to prayer.

It was whilst I was walking around that I was suddenly consumed by a terrible weakness. I started to perspire profusely and could barely stand up. I saw one of our boats coming inshore and somehow managed to reach the jetty.

Back on board, I went to the rest room to lay down and promptly fell asleep. I awoke in the early hours and went below to sling my hammock, but the exertion just left me exhausted.

The following day I saw the Medical Officer, who said I was exhausted from overwork. In retrospect I had only been carrying out my normal duties, but in analysing these duties I realised that in the eastern Mediterranean, at about 16:00 each day, the sea gets exceedingly rough and this lasts until midnight. The ship was anchored well offshore, which meant that the cutter would rise and fall twenty feet or more, and trying to hold her alongside in those conditions is indeed a very exhausting job. Another possibility was that my symptoms were similar to that shown by someone suffering from malaria, and as we had been given mepachrine to protect us from malaria, it could have been the body's reaction to those tablets.

By the time we left Turkey, I was back to fitness and found we were making for Haifa in Palestine, but during the night a signal was received that we were to proceed directly to Malta to restore and ammunition the ship, as we were required elsewhere in a hurry.

What place demanded our attention we knew not, but we increased speed, and for two days the throbbing, beating engines shook the ship constantly.

We arrived in Malta at 18:00 on Sunday evening. Ammunition boats, stores and water (Join up following text to here) boats awaited our arrival and then the whole ship's company set to work. By 01:00 on Monday morning, we had accomplished our task, slipped our moorings and left Malta as quickly and as quietly as we had arrived.

Our destination was Trieste in the Adriatic.

Chapter 26

Trieste

Italy and Yugoslavia were embroiled in a controversy as to which country Trieste should belong. The United Nations were on the point of coming to a decision, which meant that the population of both countries were tense. One could almost feel the underlying atmosphere being as taut as elastic and needing a spark to ignite the flames of passion.

We arrived in Trieste the following evening, having sailed at full steam up the Adriatic, and tied up alongside the Mola Bersagliera.

I had imagined a city of small buildings and shacks, but nothing could be further from the truth. Trieste is a magnificent and beautiful place with good solid buildings having character and appeal. She is, of course, the most important port in the Adriatic controlling much of the produce from the Balkans. The town had many modern buildings, but they blended in with the old architecture, and the whole place was clean and tidy.

The mole we were tied to was fairly wide, though not very long. The centre was a Royal Naval barracks, also a dance hall.

There were sentry boxes at the entrance to the pier and it was the ship's job to provide the sentries.

Our bows were facing inshore opposite some large hotels on the seafront. It did not take the lads long to find out that by sitting in the gun's predictor and training the glasses on the hotel windows, some rare sights could be seen and especially was that so regarding the hotel frequented by the commissioned ranks. No doubt an enterprising spiv aboard could have made a fortune.

On the Sunday I went ashore and was surprised at the quantity and range of goods in the shop windows. I went sightseeing by climbing up to the old castle and temple which overlooked the town and harbour. The temple ruins were reputed to be over two thousand years old. There was a wonderful view from the top, and the large hoardings which we could only just see from the ship now showed up clearly, bearing the brief painted message 'VIVE TITO'. In many unexpected places you found a crucifix. They may be nailed to fences or posts or screwed to a wall. Frequently a pot of flowers stood nearby. I entered a small church. Its walls were whitewashed, and a rectangular piece of tin had the face of Christ beaten into it, and rested in a wooden frame on the altar.

I descended to investigate some of Trieste's fine service canteens. They all sold food the like of which one would not expect in the UK; ice cream and pineapple, melons and a variety of fruits. The YMCA was set in beautiful gardens and young waitresses came out to serve you as a three piece orchestra played beneath the trees. The Toc H also had a string orchestra and singers, but their food was not as varied as the YMCA's.

One day in the NAAFI I could only afford a cup of tea, but as I was sitting at the table, one of my shipmates came along with a plate of cakes and a pot of tea and sat with me. I don't think he noticed my envious glances, and he was certainly unaware of my financial status; anyway he departed leaving a cake on the tray. I looked round furtively to see if anyone was watching and promptly hijacked it. At that precise moment I noticed one of the waitresses looking at me with what I thought was pity in her eyes. My embarrassment was further increased when she came to my table with a tray of cakes and tea. The fact she was young, blonde and beautiful added to my discomfort. Though I appreciated the kind and thoughtful deed.

As the ship was alongside, the cutter was not required, so we were directed to work in the other parts of the ship which could embrace scrubbing decks, paintwork or even cleaning brass. Our duty hours were somewhat different to those we were used to as boat crew, but they allowed reasonable runs ashore.

We swam a lot, and then there was a water polo competition between various parts of the ship. Mixter from our mess was the star and probably the best player on the ship, but he did not have the support from the rest of the team, and although we lost the final, we were lucky to get that far.

The Admiral used to do a lot of aquaplaning, and when he was finished he allowed us the use of his barge and the equipment. Its use was confined to the boats crew so I was one of the lucky ones. We tried our skills at many water sports and the beautiful weather and warm waters added to our pleasures.

The nightlife was beginning to take its toll and sap the strength of many of the ship's company. Skeeter, a nickname given to one of the lads, though we never found out why, went ashore the first night after payday. A few drinks at a dance nearby and Trieste just swallowed him up. Leave expired at midnight but there was no sign of him. His messmates began to make enquiries, but only one could remember seeing him giving away handfuls of lira to the local youngsters.

We slung his hammock for him but it was never slept in, and our concern changed to worry and fear for his safety.

The following morning, the Master at Arms started to make enquiries but there was little anyone could tell him.

At 09:00, when we were up top scrubbing the decks, a small, squat, untidy figure came rolling through the dockyard gates. His hair was tousled, and the top part of his uniform was missing. His white trousers and white front looked as though he had been rolling in the gutter. A grin stretched from ear to ear as the lads on the upper deck let out a resounding cheer.

The Officer of the Watch and the Master grilled him, and the Commander spoke to him, but to our surprise, Skeeter came down to the mess deck a free man. No charges were made against him.

"Come on, Skeeter," said one of his messmates. "You must have spun them a good yarn aft. What was it?"

"Well," said Skeeter, "I told 'em I'd 'ad a few drinks then I met this dame who took me down a side street, where some blokes set about me. Until I woke up this morning I didn't know what 'ad 'appened. My wallet 'ad gone, they cleaned me out."

At an opportune moment I took him to one side and said, "Skeeter, what really happened? What was the true story?"

A guilty looking grin spread across his face and then in a low tone he said, "Parts of it were true. I did 'ave a few drinks an' I did meet this dame, and she was bloody wonderful. I went back to 'er place where she lashed me up with some liquor then we shared this large feather bed – blimey, it was right posh. Yeah, she fleeced me of all me money, but I'm tellin' you I've 'ad one 'elluva bloody good time."

For the next month we kept Skeeter in cigarettes which he sold ashore, bought some more with the proceeds and then sold them, thereby allowing him a few runs ashore until the next payday.

They had a swap round of messes and, along with Ginger Kelly, Paddy Slavin, Allan Wheeler, John Grint and Mixter, we landed up in Mess 3. Already in that mess was Scouse, Nobby Clark the 'Killick', and Mac, with two others.

Mac was an amazing character. He didn't smoke and he wasn't interested in women, but he drank and drank and drank.

On the night of the day we were paid, Mac would go ashore. If he was not on watch ashore, he would get a substitute and then he set out to get drunk. When he got to the incapable stage, his shipmates would drag him back to the ship. If the Officer of the Watch was about, Mac usually had his leave stopped for a month. If he could be smuggled aboard then that was his good fortune, and whether he went ashore again or not depended on his financial position. On those occasions when he was confined to the ship, then his shipmates ensured he always had a supply of liquor.

The lads would tease him not about his drinking but his celibacy, and one day Paddy came straight out with it.

"Mac," he said, "tell me honestly – have you ever been with a dame?"

"Well," replied Mac, "in my younger days when the lads kept on about it I thought I'd have a bash. I was in Alex at the time so I took myself off to a local bag shanty in one of the back streets behind the bazaars. Well, I paid me ackers but this dame

– talk about slack Alice. I never went back. I couldn't see any reason."

Another Scot we had on board was Jock MacMillan, an older Able Seaman, who also liked his liquor. I noticed he'd lost the tips of three of his fingers and he told me it had happened while they had been surging wire hawsers around a capstan. Apparently the capstan slipped and he caught the tips under the wire. He was sent to hospital ashore, but after three weeks he rejoined his ship with the wounds still open. He was given duties on the upper deck which was unfortunate, as the ship was detailed to join a convoy to Murmansk. The intense cold caused him considerable pain, but even worse was the fact that he hadn't received any money for over six weeks. Jock went below to see the Paymaster, who appeared to be against the idea of granting some pay, but at length the Pay Bob took five shillings out of the safe and gave it to Jock. Jock could not believe he was seeing right. What could he do with five bob? It was an insult to his drinking capacity. The Pay Bob told Jock to sign the form stating that he was in receipt of five shillings, but Jock just looked at the two half crowns lying in the palm of his still bandaged and painful hand.

"What the hell d'you think I drink?" said Jock.

"Bloody lemon juice." And so saying, he slung the money at the Paymaster's head.

Jock spent the next week in the cells, but he was never without a drink and moreover, because of his disability, the lads picked all his oakum for him. Picking oakum was part of the punishment, necessitating taking a foot of tarred rope or hemp and pulling it apart. Not only is it a tedious task, but it breaks the fingernails and makes the fingertips sore. With Jock's problem, it would have been agony.

After ten days alongside the mole we moved the ship into the stream. This was good for the likes of Nobby, Scouse, Dennis and me because the cutter was now back in commission. It is true that shore leave was not quite as good, for the cutters' departure time from shore and ship was laid down, and liberty men did not have the freedom to return to the ship at a time of their own choosing.

There was also another problem, and that was cigarettes. Ashore, duty free cigarettes fetched a handsome price so smuggling activities took on a variety of ways.

Normally I would take a packet or two of cigarettes ashore and sell them in small wine bars or the back streets, but then I thought that if I could sell them in packets of five hundred it reduced the number of risks I was taking. We did not know how much longer we would be in Trieste, so getting rid of my stock and capitalising on the high prices ashore became of paramount importance. I've already mentioned that we had to provide the sentries on the mole. One of them was on our mess deck, namely John. Now, John had a good business going in that a woman used to visit him in the middle watch and buy cigarettes from him at the current price, added to which she allowed him to take liberties with her free of charge. The going rate that Tickler Lil paid was 135 lira (three shillings) for a packet of twenty, which cost us about seven pence. I had arranged with John for a price of 125 lira and anything he negotiated above that was his to keep. We always knew when Tickler Lil had been there because John would arrive on board with his pockets full of lira, a deadly white face and absolutely knackered.

The only risk I ran was getting the cigarettes down the gangway and into the sentry box.

This feverish anxiety to make some money was brought on by the fact that it would not be too long before one's demobilisation, and therefore the need to buy some presents for Anne and the family. I would therefore take cartons of cigarettes ashore in the middle hours when the Officer of the Watch had his head down.

The fruits of these enterprises became apparent when Allan Wheeler and I went ashore on a shopping spree. Unfortunately the reason for us being in Trieste made itself manifest with rioting that had broken out between the Italians and the Yugoslavs. Apparently the United Nations had decided that Trieste should belong to Italy, and now the Yugoslavs – or Jugs, as we called them – thought this was most inconsiderate. Was not Italy the former enemy? Was not Yugoslavia a patriotic enemy of the Axis powers? Did they, the Jugs, not hope for some favourable treatment or reward for their wartime efforts? As servicemen our sentiments were with the Jugs. It was not up to us to know the reasoning behind the decision, but we were expected to follow our country's lead, and they had apparently endorsed the decision. Anyway, Allan and I were suddenly caught up between the two rioting sides. We were near the American Red Cross but they had locked and bolted their doors. American sailors had taken refuge inside, and indeed some of them viewed the riots from the roof. The crowds became hysterical as they yelled and screamed and threw missiles. They pulled down any military signs they could find and generally made a nuisance of themselves. Mounted civil police tried to keep the warring factions apart, but every now and again a mob would appear from a side street, having by passed the police, and then all hell was let loose. Allan had his camera with him, so while I held the presents, he tried to get some action shots. An English Major was in charge of the civil police and he suddenly appeared on the scene in a Jeep, driving wildly in all directions and throwing teargas bombs to break up the mob. One Italian in a blue and white hooped jersey started to yell out derisive comments about the Major, but he soon regretted it, for the Jeep screeched to a halt, the Major sprang out and chased the offender, who promptly ran for his life. The Major in the midst of this man's compatriots caught him, hit him around the head and then pinned his arms behind his back and tried to push him through the screaming mob. The crowds in a seething, menacing manner surged round to prevent the arrest, but the mounted police forced their way into the crowd, swinging steel tipped batons against any head that got in the way. Having cleared a path, the Major literally carried his victim kicking and shouting back to the Jeep.

Allan and I had been so absorbed by the Major's activities that we had become oblivious to our own safety, because we were in the midst of flying stones and bricks, not to mention teargas bombs and Ities and Jugs knocking seven bells out of each other. We gradually eased our way to the back of the crowd and headed for the jetty.

During the next week, all leave was stopped, so the only recreation we got was swimming off the pier and even here we couldn't find peace, for a bomb exploded in the bathing pool not a hundred yards from the pier.

The atmosphere ashore was very tense; it was like a coiled spring waiting for a spark to unleash the hatred and venom.

Although the ban on shore leave still applied, the regular Royal Navy police asked the ship for additional support. A Petty Officer, three other lads and myself were deputed. An open military police Jeep met us at the pier and we set off for the Provost Marshal's Headquarters. As we entered one street, we met crowds of people intent on mob violence. Shop windows were being broken and buildings set alight. Typewriters, desks, chairs, anything moveable was thrown out of the windows, and then they saw us. I do not believe they were anti-British, but we represented authority, and that was sufficient for them to turn their attention on us. The mob surrounded the Jeep, trying to pull us out and capture the vehicle. We had been armed with metal-tipped axe handles, and it was a matter of self-preservation to bring them into contact with the heads of our attackers. Our driver managed to turn around and we made a quick getaway through the channel carved out by our batons.

At the end of the street a number of men chased us, uttering what were probably obscenities. With the odds now pretty even we screeched to a halt and jumped out. Our verbal abusers disappeared with an amazing turn of speed.

Arriving at the Provost Headquarters, we were told to stay put in case our services were required. We had not been there long before a small squat swarthy Italian came in shouting, "Please come, they breaka my shop, please to hurry."

The lads off the ship dived into a Jeep, while the regular shore patrol appeared to be taking their time in following us in another vehicle.

The man's cafe and wine bar was only four hundred yards away, but as we neared it you could hear the yelling and shouting intermingled with the sounds of broken glass and furniture being smashed. The place was frequented by British and American soldiers. and with plenty of liquor aboard they were fighting hell for leather.

As our driver braked hard we leaped from the jeep and suddenly I realised that I was in the front, I was the first man in. Immediately I thought, 'Bloody fool, you get carried away.' But it was too late to do anything about it. With batons being used like whirling dervishes, we took them by surprise and soon cleared the place out, but then the Regular Patrol arrived on the scene. They thought they were being clever by letting the lads off the ship go in first. In reality, they came off worst, because as soon as the combatants saw us come in they ran out only to run into the arms of the regulars. In fact the lads off the ship did not suffer so much as a bruise, while every member of the Regular Patrol was injured.

The place was just a wreck, with full-length mirrors broken together with tankards and bottles, chairs and tables and all stained with blood. In the midst of all this debris an American soldier lay in a drunken stupor across one of the tables. He was oblivious to everything that had taken place around him.

Two men were arrested, their faces badly slashed with broken bottles.

Although shore leave was stopped for the sailors, it did not apply to the other forces, hence they were well represented at a dance hall. Now the Italian men did not like their women frequenting dance halls and associating with Allied servicemen so they would wait for the dance to end, catch the girls and disrobe them. Two of these girls had been rescued by a couple of marines, taken back to the headquarters and were promised an escort home. Both these girls were fur-clad prostitutes and, from the conversation taking place between the Marines and the girls, this was not the first time they had met. The girls were tanked to the gills with liquor, which made them somewhat talkative, cheerful and willing. It was past midnight when they pleaded for the protection of the patrol so we, with the Marines, were instructed to escort them home. This meant that we had to leave the Italian part of the city and go to the Jugoslav quarter or, as we knew it, 'Jug Land'. To reach Jug Land, one had to go through a long curved white tiled tunnel with electric light bulbs the full length. The previous evening shots had been ricocheting off the walls, so we did not feel entirely comfortable with the idea, and especially was this so when on two occasions the lights went off.

The Marines took their protective duties most seriously and held the girls tightly as they protected them with their bodies. The girls thought it all very funny, and the Marines thought it was a good investment.

We eventually arrived at a small block of flats, and as the two girls alighted with their escorts, the Marines said to our driver, "Give us fifteen minutes with these dames."

But our driver replied, "Sorry mate, but I've got to get these lads back to the ship."

"Don't worry," said Sir Galahad, "we'll spend the night here."

Geordie, the cutters coxswain in the other watch, had a tough crew in Paddy and John, and at times it appeared they were too much for him to handle. Whether this was true or not we didn't know, but nevertheless it came as a surprise when Geordie put in a request to be downgraded from Leading Seaman to Able Seaman. His request was granted, but he still retained his position as coxswain. This unusual event affected our watch, because it meant that Ginger, our coxswain, and being a Leading Seaman held the higher rank of both watches, thereby allowing him to throw his weight around.

Scouse and I were the first to feel the effects, for he had us in the boat all hours of the day scrubbing and cleaning it three or four times a day, while he found a cosy place to have a sleep in the mess deck. We put up with it until he tried to reduce our time off for breakfast and shaving to half an hour. We didn't say anything, but the following morning we turned out of our hammocks at the usual time and went down to the boat, scrubbed her out, cleaned the brasswork, then went inshore to collect the lads coming back from overnight leave and returned to the ship by 07:30, in time for breakfast.

"Be back down here at 08:00," said Ginger.

Scouse and I ignored him and went on board, returning to the boat deck at 08:15, but there was no sign of Ginger.

Lieutenant Ryan, the boat deck Officer, came by, and Scouse asked him how long we were allowed for breakfast. Now, Lieutenant Ryan was no fool, and the very nature of the question had undertones that suggested to him that he was being used.

"If you have any complaints," he said, "make them through your coxswain."

It was a clever answer but not the one we wanted, and in no way could we go through Ginger. Obviously other tactics were required. At 08:30 we saw Ginger standing in the waist, looking at us. He was unshaven and wearing just his under vest and trousers. It is true we had disobeyed his instructions, but we also knew that in his state of unpreparedness there was no way he could touch us.

"I'll have you on the quarterdeck," yelled Ginger, and quickly went below deck to get washed, shaved and dressed.

We quickly went into the cutter to make sure all was shipshape, and returned to the boat deck, where we waited for him to take us aft and charge us. He duly arrived and said, "Why aren't you in the boat working?"

"Waiting for you to take us aft," we said.

"Is the boat clean?"

"Of course it is," said Scouse.

We could sense Ginger was uneasy.

"Why were you standing in your shift at 08:30 when you expected us to be in the boat at 08:00?" I asked.

Ginger was clearly embarrassed and said, "I ask the questions and give the orders round here, and I'll have them obeyed."

"That's okay by us," we responded, "but we've already seen Ryan, and he wouldn't like it if he knew what you got up to while we were expected to be in the boat."

Kelly didn't know how much Ryan knew, and he didn't know that for the most part we were bluffing, but he dare not take a chance, but at the same time he was looking for a face saver.

Suddenly he said, "I'm not satisfied with that brasswork – do it again."

We did as instructed and again fell in on the boat deck to be taken aft. Ginger was by now really worried, but luck was on his side for the tannoy came to life. "Away motor cutter crew." We saw a wry grin on Ginger's face; he was off the hook. We were away from the ship for most of the morning, and though relations were strained, nothing more was said.

While Kelly tried to enforce a strict code of discipline he was himself the most undisciplined person imaginable. If we had performed extra duties, Lieutenant Ryan would often say to the coxswain, "Tell the crew to take a make and mend."

Ginger, however, would not tell us, but instead said, "You lads have worked hard. I'm going to see Ryan and demand a make and mend for you." He would disappear for half an hour and then come back all smiles, saying, "I've got you fellows that make and mend. You don't know what a good coxswain you have looking after your interests."

Not only did he hope we believed him, but he also hoped the least he could expect from us was sippers from our rum ration. His expectations did not bear fruit.

On another occasion he shouted at us with the threat, "I'll have you buggers working in the dogs tonight."

I made a few furtive enquiries, and when he ordered us on the upper deck I said, "Ginger, you can make us work in the dogs, but I hope you realise that if you do you've got to be there all the time in charge. If you are not there, we don't work. Oh yes, have you forgotten tombola is being played tonight?"

Needless to say we didn't have to do those extra duties.

The Commander had laid on a lorry to take any of the lads who felt so inclined to have a sightseeing day in Venice. Having had our shore leave restricted, the opportunity was too good to miss. Early on the Monday morning, Allan Wheeler and I with a number of other lads climbed into our transport. We had heard that the going rate for cigarettes in Venice was 160 lira for twenty, so we duly took a liberal supply. The journey took about four hours and we passed through some beautiful countryside arriving at our destination a little before noon. The lorry was parked at the Piazzale Roma and from there you either walked or went by gondola.

Venice is made up of numerous islands all connected by a variety of bridges. The largest waterway is the Grand Canal which is in the shape of an 'S' and splits Venice in two. Allan and I set off, hugging the bank of the Grand Canal. We followed it until we came to a bridge which we crossed, but this time we took the street that ran parallel with the canal. The buildings here lay between us and the canal, hence our taking this route. We passed the Ca D'Oro (Golden House) on our right and carried on, until at length we came to the Rialto Bridge. Shops lined each side of the bridge so that you were denied a view of the water as you crossed over. At this stage we were lost, though we remembered passing the Campo Dei Frari (Church of Friars) and then, more by luck than judgement, we found ourselves in St. Mark's Square. It was not a slow approach we made to the square, but more as if we burst into it and then became staggered by the brilliance and beauty of St. Mark's itself, which exceeded all my expectations. We walked toward the church with its wonderful mosaic front principally of blue and gold.

As we entered the massive portals, a man started to show us around. Believing him to be guide we duly followed, but before we had been in the place five minutes he said, "Come this way plees. I show you something very interesting."

Like sheep, we followed him out of the church, through the narrow winding passages and over wonderful little bridges. Every now and again he would look behind to make sure we were following. He then stopped by a small shop and invited us to enter. We responded to his wishes, went through the shop and out the back, only to find a workshop busily making mosaic pictures of the sights of Venice. They were not cheap, but the price did not have to be in lira because cigarettes were more acceptable. I must confess to some annoyance that we had wasted our time, so without making a purchase Allan and I walked out.

The YMCA Victory Club was a magnificent building sited at the edge of the canal. It contained rest rooms and recreation rooms in fact all a serviceman's requirements could be satisfied. We had a small snack and then set out on the serious business of finding a buyer for our duty free cigarettes. We met some of our shipmates who informed us that a shop selling filigree jewellery in St. Mark's Square were buying cigarettes at 150 lira a packet. I went in, and no sooner had I started to negotiate when Allan came in and said, "Geoff there's a guy out here offering 160." I quickly retreated and was met by this young Italian lad. He had black curly hair, khaki shorts and a white shirt and sandals. We followed him through the narrow streets until at length he stopped in this quiet narrow passage in the corner of a small building. Allan kept watch while I passed over the cigarettes. They were all in packets of ten, and as they were given to this young lad so he stuffed them in his shirt. Suddenly, in a flash, he was away. I yelled at Allan, "Stop him," but everything happened so quickly, and though we gave chase, the boy and my cigarettes disappeared among the throng of people and were lost in the maze of streets. I had seen a scarf I wanted to buy Anne out of the proceeds of this transaction, but my greed for that extra ten lira was my undoing. The cigarettes had only cost me five shillings and I stood to sell them for ten, but alas it was not to be. Allan looked pretty downcast but was soon shaken out of it when he saw me burst into laughter. What a bloody fool I'd been to allow myself to be played as a sucker by a teenage Italian boy. That lad's face will be forever etched on my mind.

I was now without the resources to buy that scarf, so Allan and I strolled along the Molo Riva which is the promenade facing the Isle and Church of St. George. We passed the Bridge of Sighs and found it dull and unimpressive by comparison with the colourful paintings we had seen, but then that may be just a reflection of the mood we were in. We strolled back and forth between the Palace of the Doge's and the three hundred foot high campanile in St. Mark's Square. By now the time was getting on, so we slowly made our way back to the car park where we met the other lads. The lorry picked us up, and apart from one or two stops on the way, we headed back to Trieste.

Things appeared to have settled down ashore, and soon the time arrived for us to leave. Trieste had probably given us the best run ashore of all the places we had visited, and so we were reluctant to go. Some of the lads had formed liaisons with young ladies ashore, so their parting was even sadder. Turnip 'Ead was a young, damn nice fellow. I don't know why we called him Turnip 'Ead, but I never knew his real name. He told me he'd got this girl ashore. He showered her with sweets and chocolates every time he saw her. Now, Turnip fell deeply in love with every girl he met and the only one who had never let him down was his mother, of whom he spoke with love and tenderness.

"Turnip 'Ead," I said. "She's playing you for a sucker."

He turned on me, "Joey, you know nothing about women."

I smarted about that because I knew he was right, but I didn't want him to be hurt or believe she would wait forever. There were times when he was puffed up with arrogance about this Italian girl, but you only had to say, "Turnip, what would your mother think?" and he'd be in tears.

"For God's sake, Joey, don't talk like that. I'll never touch another dame in my life." I knew he couldn't keep such a vow and he didn't, but to get back to our departure. In the forenoon watch of Friday the 19th of July 1946 we weighed anchor and sailed for Malta.

My ruse for escaping sea-going duties had been rumbled so that I was no longer able to keep a watch in my hammock. In lieu of this I had the job of lookout, and in my time off sleeping on my oilskins in the galley flat. I spent many an uncomfortable night there, though there were other nights when the lure of the hammock overcame sleeping on the deck.

During the trip south in the Adriatic, the Skipper stopped the ship to allow us to have a swim. The water was wonderfully cool and blue but it is somewhat disconcerting to realise how much water there is below you.

We arrived in the Grand Harbour at Malta on Sunday evening. This is always an interesting time to watch the priorities of one's shipmates. Some cannot wait to get ashore to order blues or wine and women. Others went swimming in Bighi Bay, while others were content to stay on board and wait for the mail to be sorted. This last category can be split into three types. Those that get mail from loved ones, those that don't, and those who get mail with news not to their liking. The last two types generally go ashore and drown their sorrows.

There were times when as boat crew we got in more swimming than we bargained for. Grand Harbour is notoriously dirty, and it was not uncommon for us to get rope or some other substance caught around the screw. This necessitated in one of us diving under the boat with an open clasp knife and cutting away the offending material. It was usually Scouse or myself who had to do the job. Environmental pollution was not a term we were familiar with, and it never occurred to us the problems a mouthful of water could cause internally, but our main concern was to get back inboard and have a shower.

The authorities, then put the ship in dry dock and this caused a lot of inconvenience. They couldn't allow a dockyard matey to get a deluge of sewage over him, so no waste was allowed to exit the boat, and all washing and toilet facilities had to be executed ashore. All garbage had to be taken ashore and the ship's boats had to be made fast to the caisson outside the dry dock, and then a twenty four hour guard mounted to prevent pilfering. Some of the locals could make use of anything, whether it was a short piece of cordage or a tin of paint. They were masters at the art of disguising any article they had acquired, and if one were unfortunate enough to have a boat stolen, it would be so altered that within an hour the owner would not recognise his own property. This pilfering was not always one sided, because many of the lads were not averse to doing some bartering with the natives concerning property being the responsibility of the High Lords of the Admiralty.

The hull was scraped and painted, and by the time this was done there was quite a pile of barnacles at the bottom of the dry dock. A few minor alterations were made inside the ship, and for almost a week the sound of hammering and riveting was deafening.

It was of course handy for going ashore, and by the same token it was handy for the local people to come aboard. Our mess decks were full of them seeking food or cigarettes or anything else that had a selling value. There were huge drums on the upper deck in which we put our gash, and it was nothing to see a local with his arm immersed to the shoulder fishing around among the tealeaves, cabbage stalks, potato peelings, cigarette ends or whatever. If they found a whole potato or tomato it was put into a bucket. Sometimes we offered them the leftovers in the mess if they did the washing up. I never saw one refuse. They said they took the food for the large number of chickens and goats they kept ashore, though any tasty morsel was put to one side for the family.

Allan and I went down The Gut one night and had a very tasteful and well cooked meal. It was only when we went to pay that we recognised the proprietor as being one of those dipping into the gash bin. We never went back.

The cutter was always in use about the harbour, and it was about this time that Geordie came off as coxswain of the cutter and was replaced by a small fellow with dark wavy hair. He had just been made up to Leading Seaman. How Leading Seaman Rose would handle his tough crew would only be known with the passage of time. At the same time, Ginger was replaced by Leading Seaman Nobby Clark, the Killick of our mess. Now Nobby was quite a decent chap, though like most of us he had off days and tried to work it off on the crew, much to his cost. Leading Seaman Rose who, against his wishes we promptly called Rosy, was still feeling his way. During that first week he smashed the cutter's rubbing strake as well as a few other mishaps, but he quickly learnt how to control it.

One night when I came off watch I found alongside the head of my hammock a line of wet dhobying. Now if there is one thing sailors do not like, it is wet washing hanging up in the mess deck. I too share an intense dislike of the habit. It was unhealthy and was the cause of more tuberculosis in the Royal Navy than anything else. It is, in fact, against the regulations. I promptly removed and folded the clothes and put them on top of a locker. The next thing I heard was:

"Whose taken down my dhobying?" It was Rosy.

"I did," I replied.

"What for? You've no right to touch it."

"I touch any wet washing I like, including yours, and if you shove it up again, I'll rip it down," I said.

"I'll have you on the quarterdeck for this," yelled Rosy.

"You do that," I replied. "You haven't a leg to stand on."

At that moment the Boat Petty Officer came down the mess deck. I stopped him and enquired the official view.

"It's not allowed," he said. "And you are in your rights to remove it."

"Thanks a lot," I replied, and proceeded to remove the washing Rosy had rehung.

I threw it in his face.

"I'll get you for this," he said. "One way or another, I'll get you."

Ginger Kelly was a silent witness to all that had transpired.

I turned to him. "If Rosy ever runs me in, will you testify to the threat he's just made?"

"Yes," said Ginger.

In a way, I felt sorry for Rosy. He was a nice enough chap and a Leading Seaman's role in a warship is probably the hardest to carry out where discipline is concerned because he is living, eating, relaxing and sleeping in the same place as the men he is responsible for. Even his hammock has to be slung in a billet where he can find room. Therefore Rosy and I had our differences, but in the main we rubbed along alright.

The following Saturday we sailed from Malta. Our next port of call was to Haifa in Palestine.

Chapter 27

Palestine

The old League of Nations had given the British Government a mandate regarding the land of Palestine. Although the Jewish people claimed the land as theirs, limits were imposed as to the number of people of Jewish persuasion that would annually be allowed into the country. The whole world had been shattered and disgusted at the wholesale destruction of the Jewish people as perpetrated by Germany. The word genocide crept into our vocabulary, the extermination of a race. The Jewish people referred to it as the Holocaust, meaning wholesale sacrifice or destruction, whole burnt offerings. When you think of those descriptions and the ovens of Belsen and the other concentration camps, the mind becomes numb. It is hard to conceive that man could be so vile, so wicked, so contemptuous, but he was. Why, even in Trieste we witnessed the emaciated bodies, the living skeletons of some of those who had survived the concentration camps. The hearts of the free world went out to these people.

It is with this background that *HMS Mauritius* ploughed through the Mediterranean waters, knowing that the mandate was soon to expire and knowing that the Jewish people could not wait, indeed would not wait, to get to the Holy Land, the Promised Land. Land they believed was theirs, land they believed they had a right to, not in the future, but now.

The British Government's obligations were to the new United Nations Organisation, but the hearts of her people were with the Jews.

On the ship, we had to obey the instructions of the British Government acting on behalf of UNO, but the hearts of the crew were with those persecuted people, but then our feelings waivered. Three British Sergeants were taken by the Jewish gangs in Palestine and strung up in an orange grove. Like us, they too were doing their duty. Like us, they too, no doubt, had sympathies for the Jewish people, but some of that sympathy goes out of the window when it's your own compatriots that are being killed.

We arrived in Haifa Bay on Monday evening and ran into trouble immediately. The Royal Navy had been scouring the eastern Mediterranean for the illegal immigration ships. Under the terms of the mandate, Britain had to regulate and contain the flow of people seeking refuge and there were many ship owners out to capitalise on those unfortunate people by promising them a passage to the Promised Land. The price was £5 per head for taking them, and a further £5 for everyone that landed. This meant the trickle of people allowed in became a flood and it was our duty to stop it. The night we arrived, one of our destroyers escorted this old sailing ship into the bay. You could see she was overcrowded, but the passengers only had eyes for the Promised Land.

There, just a few hundred yards away, was Haifa, its buildings and beaches bathed in the setting sun. Only those aboard knew what that picture presented, a realisation of dreams and hopes nurtured behind the brutality of the barbed wired concentration camps, and yet still they were not on that hallowed shore.

The authorities ashore wanted to put two Palestine policemen aboard, but the passengers would not allow them onto the boat. We, the motor cutters crew and the two motorboats were called into service. Sailors and marines armed with wooden batons and tin hats climbed into the boats, and this small flotilla set forth with the object of boarding and seizing the ship. The vessel was named *The Four Freedoms*. As we drew near, we were met by a barrage of missiles, tins, bottles, milk churns – anything they could throw, they did. Watching the action was like a film of piracy on the high seas. Lieutenant Davidson, leading the boarding party from one of the motorboats, led his men into action. They scaled the high sides of the vessel, and with Lieutenant Davidson yelling "Charge", they endeavoured to get a foot hold on deck. One spirited old lady saw the Officer's face appear over the gunwale so she promptly hit him with a bottle down the side of the face, and then gave him a shove so that he lost his footing and fell into the water. A bedraggled Lieutenant was fished out but still undaunted he clambered up again, still yelling "Charge." The same woman with the same bottle hit him again and cut his face, with the same wet result. Able Seaman Strickland, with shoulders like an ox, had managed to get on board and was last seen yelling his head off, for the reason that one of the immigrants was holding him in a very delicate place.

It did not take long to overpower the passengers and control the ship. When this had been accomplished, one of the senior Officers went aboard. With the aid of an interpreter, the immigrants vowed to behave themselves if we promised they would not be sent from Palestine.

The senior Officer said, "I give you my word as an Englishman – you will not leave Haifa."

I am sure that this promise was not an expedient. I am sure that the Officer concerned did really mean what he said. The result was a cooling of passions. Two Palestine policemen were put aboard, the boarding party returned to the ship and a police motorboat was left to circle the ship throughout the night. The ship was so overloaded that hammocks were slung between the rigging and the mast because there was no room between decks. All appeared to be very scantily dressed, and some only had bathing costumes or short trousers, and the smell was horrendous.

Prior to our visit, frogmen had attempted to attach limpet mines to the hulls of the Royal Navy ships. Obviously the intent was to disable or sink the vessels and so reduce the numbers on patrol. To counteract this, guards were posted all round every ship, and lamps were hung over the side so that each ship was wrapped in a cocoon of light. In addition to these precautions, we in the motor cutter were called out at various times during the hours of darkness to drop three-quarter pound depth charges.

This went on for two days until the early hours of Wednesday morning, when the police launch hurriedly came alongside calling for a boarding party. Apparently the immigrants had waited for a favourable wind and then let both anchors go and allowed the wind and current to take them onshore, close to Tel Aviv. The cutter full of men was soon in hot pursuit, and then they were joined by a tug coming out of the harbour. The tug was a better vessel to operate from, so our boarding party was transferred to her.

Drag hooks and grappling irons were then thrown over the bowsprit of *The Four Freedoms*, and soon she was taken in tow. We were none too soon, for when we arrested her progress, she was only half a mile from the shore. It is true that a few immigrants had slipped overboard during the night, but whether they managed to swim ashore or not we will never know. It is also true that with emaciated bodies and constitutions ravaged by years of hunger, half a mile must have appeared more like a hundred.

As *The Four Freedoms* was now without anchors, it was decided to tie her up astern of *Mauritius*, but there was still nothing to prevent the ropes making her fast from being cut, so a party of soldiers came from ashore and put barbed wire across the forecastle, in other words between the ropes and the passengers. The soldiers were in the charge of a young subaltern; however when they finished their task they were isolated on the forecastle, so in order to take them off we had to manoeuvre the cutter under the bowsprit so that they could descend down a rope ladder. I have already mentioned the large swell that inflicts the Eastern Mediterranean of an evening – well, it was operating that night with a vengeance. The soldiers came down and dropped into the cutter. Meanwhile, our coxswain Rosie was struggling to control the boat, bearing in mind we were near the stern of *Mauritius* and right under the bows of the immigrant ship, and rising and falling ten to fifteen feet or more. The subaltern was the last to leave, but he had the disadvantage of having a machine gun strapped to his back, with the result that the gun was caught in the standing rigging attached to the bowsprit and the rope ladder, and then the next thing I knew was him hanging by his neck caught in the strap of his gun. He literally could not say or do anything, which left me as bowman to do what I could. There were no choices, no alternatives. As the boat rose in the water, I grabbed him round the waist and lifted him with the continued rise of the cutter and prayed it would unsnag itself. Fortunately it did, and as the boat sank into the next trough, I was able to hold him. He was in a semi-conscious state but was still almost instinctively able to murmur "Save me, save me." I had one arm wrapped around the small mast that held our navigation lights, and with the other I was able to swing him round into the boat, where his men quickly supported him. He regained his composure, and on returning to the ship the soldiers all went inboard. The men were all given a can of beer, and their Officer was entertained in the wardroom.

Much to our surprise, the Lieutenant of the Marines sent a messenger down to the cutter with a can of beer for each member of the crew.

Later on we collected them all in order to take them ashore. One sat next to me but was very quiet, so I opened up the conversation by saying, "That's the first time those buggers in the wardroom have given the men a drop of beer."

To which my until now silent passenger said in an accent that was certainly not lower deck, "Really, is that so?"

I then realised that it was the young Officer that had been strung up. He was obviously not conversant with Naval procedure, which decrees he should have been sitting aft.

The following day a merchant ship came in and tied up with her stern toward the pier and her bows seaward. That very same day, news came through that no more immigrants were to be allowed into Palestine, but were intended to be transported to a camp in Cyprus. The authorities decided that the immigrants should be taken off *The Four Freedoms* at 22:30 the same night and put aboard the *Empire Rival*, the merchant ship we had seen arrive. A curfew had been imposed in Haifa and all shore leave stopped. The harbour and piers were bathed in light and there were soldiers stationed every few yards.

Twenty sailors from the *Mauritius* boarded *The Four Freedoms* to maintain order while a tug took her in tow. We in the motor cutter kept close, ready to pick up anybody who went overboard and tried to swim ashore.

The immigrants were quiet and restrained as the tug slowly took them nearer to the shores of the Promised Land, but as they rounded the pier head and saw what they instinctively knew to be a prison ship, pandemonium broke out. *The Four Freedoms* tied up to some pontoons, parallel with the *Empire Rival*. On the pontoons, tents had been erected and staffed by doctors and nurses. At this stage the army took over and the sailors prepared to leave. Gangways were put in place and the immigrants were expected to descend and pass through the tents, where they were disinfected and then they were to ascend the gangway of the *Empire Rival*.

The atmosphere became charged with rebellion and emotion, emotion that they were so near the Promised Land and rebellion against any authority that should deny them entry. Some old people, bewildered, thin and emaciated, clutched bundles containing their worldly possessions. The bright arc lights blinded and dazzled them as they slowly walked or stumbled down the gangway. Their thin, flimsy and ragged clothing offered no protection against the cold of the late night air.

Old men came out of one tent holding up their trousers, while out of the other old ladies, with open garments revealing flat breasts and wrinkled bodies, staggered under the bright lights, not knowing what was happening to them.

Aboard *The Four Freedoms*, the younger element, seeing what was happening, took refuge in the hold and refused to come out. The soldiers fetched hoses and these were then turned on full blast into the bilges. The night air was torn asunder with screaming and yelling. Sergeants were barking out orders, while both sides swore with venom at each other. Children were crying, old ladies silently weeping. The soldiers endeavoured to help the old ladies and were even more considerate with the young ones. Any bundles of worldly goods were thrown onto the pontoons, but many were seen floating in the water. Young men showing signs of dissent were knocked down, and others came down the gangplank head over heels. The hoses were not very successful, so teargas bombs were thrown into the hold, resulting in more screams and yells and oaths, but it succeeded in getting the people out as they desperately fought to get away from the obnoxious gas. The Army had turned an orderly boatload of immigrants into a seething mass of hysterical anti-British Jews. A British Officer's vows stood for nothing amid this mass of pathetic tragic people. The soldiers were oblivious to the sufferings of these poor people. All they could see was the memory of their three compatriots hanging by their necks in an orange grove, and put there by the very Jewish people they helped to liberate from the Nazi concentration camps.

We were silent onlookers to this terrible scene, and witnessed the shaking of fists and the oaths that accompanied it. They had been cramped for over forty five days aboard *The Four Freedoms*, so walking was difficult, especially among the elderly. And then there was the smell. Never in all my life have my nostrils been invaded by such an awful, revolting, disgusting smell. The hoses had disturbed the filth and muck accrued by all these people being cramped like sardines for over forty five days. The sewage, the vomit, the urine all mixed up to give off a pungent stench that penetrated every fibre of clothing. It was surprising that there was only one case of typhoid aboard, but there were numerous other contagious diseases and over half the ship was suffering from venereal disease.

I glanced at our Coxswain Rose, Rosie of Jewish persuasion. We had been so absorbed in what was going on we had forgotten about him. How did he feel, what did he think? These were his people. Poor old Rosie – he kept his thoughts and feelings to himself. Why was life so complicated? We felt for the Jewish people, but we also felt for our own soldiers. Did Rosie feel that way? We never knew because we never asked. We respected that his thoughts were private to him alone.

Dawn was breaking when we got back to the ship. We tied the cutter up to the boom and went inboard, being careful to keep away from the mess because we just stank. I stripped off everything I was wearing and soaked the clothes in disinfectant. I then scrubbed myself from top to toe again and again, but still I could not rid myself of that terrible smell. It was some time before I felt clean.

The following day the newspapers were full of the trouble, including one which said we had been firing at the immigrants with machine guns. It was of course absolutely false, but why do people print such falsehoods which only succeed in dividing people? The only firing that took place was by members of our crew who fired into the water whilst being trained with the machine guns in preparation for night guard duty against frogmen. If only journalists would check before making these mischief making assertions.

The following day, another immigrant ship was brought in but she did not give us the same trouble as the *The Four Freedoms*.

During the day we would often use the cutter to fetch stores ordered by the canteen manager. He and two of his staff would accompany us as we went ashore to meet the supplies. It usually consisted of oranges, apples, melons and other assorted goods including cakes. I had always had a great respect for the business acumen of the Jewish people. In Malta I saw the impressive way they conducted their business, and now with our Maltese Canteen Manager I was about to witness the two cultures in action. First the oranges. Four hundred were ordered and every one was counted. There were only three hundred and sixty. Every apple and every egg, everything was checked for quality and quantity. Credits were obtained for shortages and I formed the opinion that the Maltese had won. It is true to say that by the time we got back to the ship there was even more of a shortage, but that could not be called business acumen.

We didn't get much sleep in Haifa. When we were on duty we were up all night dropping the charges around the ship, and when we were off duty, we were kept awake by the exploding charges dropped by the other crew.

We had shore leave, but the powers that be did not trust Jack to go ashore armed, as indeed the other forces were armed. In retrospect, it was probably a wise decision.

I bought a new briar and wandered up the main street, Kingsway, which is flanked by large modern buildings. The back streets by contrast were low squat flat-topped buildings, inhabited by the Arabs. For some unknown reason sailors do not pronounce Arab as 'Arab' but rather 'A-rab'.

As bowman of the cutter, I had been given a Lanchester machine gun, but no ammunition. What I was expected to do with a gun without bullets only my superiors could say, and they were strangely quiet. One night, around 23:00, we picked up the liberty men and started our trip back to the ship. Needless to say, the majority were liquored up to the gills. The boat was noisy with singing and yelling, cussing and swearing. I was standing in the bows, keeping a lookout, when suddenly machine gun fire raked the waters on our port bow. It was coming from the destroyer <u>Saumarez</u> and was directed to an unknown boat that was coming toward us. I bent down to pick up the gun but it wasn't there. Three or four of the lads were fighting over it.

"Give the bloody thing 'ere," said one.

"You don't know 'ow to work the bastard," said another.

And yet another said, "I – hic – things yous got a little teeny bit too much – hic – drink to shoot straight."

I joined in the tug of war until with fighting, shoving and cursing I eventually acquired possession, but now what would I do with it? I haven't got any ammunition. With tracers flying over our heads I turned round and saw a drunken bunting tosser holding a very unsteady aldis lamp and flashing messages around the fleet. Someone had pulled his cap over his eyes so he couldn't see.

"Who the hell are you?" I yelled at him.

"I'm a signaller," he slurred.

"And what the bloody hell do you think you are doing?"

"I haven't the remotest idea," he said.

"Well, put the blasted thing down."

"Not me," he said, "I'm sending messages."

He eventually dropped the lamp, fell down and went to sleep.

In the meantime, the other lads thought they knew how to send messages by aldis lamp and proceeded to fight over it. By that time, I had become a little careless in wielding my machine gun and managed to relieve them of the lamp, which was now in a very sorry state.

The next thing we saw was one of our own launches in hot pursuit of this unknown vessel which they managed to capture and take inshore to the civil police.

The following night, Mac and I went ashore and, as I have already mentioned, Mac's sole intent in life was liquor. I realised before we went the sort of evening I could expect, but at the same time vowed that I would not endeavour to compete with him. Mac had years of training, and I hadn't, so I decreed to myself I would exercise a certain self-control and retain my mental faculties.

As soon as we landed, Mac stuck his nose in the air like a sniffer dog and then followed this unseen trail. He never said anything but ambled out of the dockyard, across Kingsway, through the Arab quarter, until at length we stopped outside a modern type of cafe. We entered, sat at a table and then surveyed rows and rows of bottles, all carrying various brightly coloured labels. These labels appeared only in the Med, for I had not seen them anywhere else. The trade name for the beer in Haifa was 'Gold Star' and very good stuff it was. Two quart bottles were put on the table, and very soon Mac and I were able to sit back and feel very contented with life.

In the cafe were some civilians involved in a deep and animated conversation. They were speaking in a foreign tongue and appeared to be from central Europe. I could only catch snatches of what was being said, but Mac, who was nearer to them, was listening intently.

"They're German," he said, rolling his R's as only a Scotsman can. "They're discussing the immigrant ships."

I was suddenly seeing a new side to Mac. I thought his intelligence revolved around the cubic capacity of a bottle in relation to his stomach, but here he was following a conversation conducted in German, word for word.

His interest did not go by unnoticed and as they left they said, "Goodnight."

By this time I was feeling a little light headed, but I was determined to do nothing that would reveal this to Mac. I watched his every move and decided I would emulate it. If he became a little talkative, then so would I. If he became noisy, then so would I. It was vital to my self-esteem that I gave no sign that would indicate my dizzy head. The time came for me to unship some cargo. I dreaded this moment, thinking I would either collapse or steer a zigzag course. I rose slowly from the table and said, "I shan't be long, Mac." The floor was covered in black and white tiles which helped me to go in a straight line. I wanted to turn round to see if Mac was watching but decided not to. I wanted to act naturally, but the effort was indicative of the fact that in and of itself, I was not acting naturally.

The heads were pitch black, and it took some time to focus on where the porcelain was situated. I emerged into the light of the cafe, and found to my utter amazement that my head was clear, my eyes did not send blurred pictures back to my brain, and I did not have to think about the manner in which I walked. I was stone cold sober.

Mac was now getting talkative and his speech was interspersed with short giggles of laughter. Somehow something was wrong, for it should be me with the nervous giggles, not Mac. At 23:00 we rose and left the table full of empty bottles, said "Goodnight" to the proprietor and his wife, and stepped over the threshold into the cold night air. We had to go through the Arab quarter, and I was pleased I had a clear head, even though I could offer no explanation for it.

I was conscious of dark cloaked figures standing in dimly lit doorways, watching our every movement, but not so Mac – when he is out on the beer, he hasn't an enemy in the world, for he would buy a drink for anyone.

There is no doubt that Haifa was not a healthy place to be out on the beer late at night. I say at night but the danger was there twenty-four hours a day and, as has already been mentioned we, unlike our colleagues in the other services, were not armed.

Suddenly Mac said, "Joey, I'm not going back yet. There is still time and room to imbibe some more, and we must not waste time."

We turned left at Kingsway and headed in the direction of Mount Carmel. We found a place which was about to close but Mac, in a very persuasive manner, managed to gain access. We ordered some more drink and then Mac sat down at a piano and, to my utter amazement, played the music from Tchaikovsky's violin concerto.

Mac looked over the piano to the proprietors and said with a glint in his eye and a smile on his lips, "If you give me a wee nip I'll play for you any time."

They did not take up his offer, and soon we were being ushered into the street, where we joined the other lads as with exaggerated rolls they made their way back to the cutter.

The *Empire Rival*, after depositing the immigrants in Cyprus, had returned to Haifa. Unfortunately frogmen blew a hole in the hull, which necessitated the cutter being loaded with pumping gear and standing by until 02:00.

On the Friday, we were happy to dust off the experiences ashore and sail for Limassol in Cyprus.

Chapter 28

Fleet Exercises

Limassol had nothing special to commend itself. It was a port but without a harbour, though it did have quite a long pier.

There were a number of cargo ships in the bay, unloading timber into boats alongside. These boats were similar in style to the immigrant ships. When they were loaded down to the gunwales, they headed inshore to the pier to discharge their cargo.

Mauritius was anchored nearly a mile offshore, and the cutter would bring the liberty men inshore and land them at the front of the pier which, coincidentally, was within vision of the Custom House.

I managed to get ashore on the first day of the ship's arrival and found that before I was even off the pier, I was besieged by men on foot and on bikes, thrusting cards into my hand and jacket. The cards, which were crudely printed, invited the recipient to taste the wares or enjoy the entertainment being staged at various named premises. For example, one read, 'Come to Roxs, the best cabaret in Limassol, dancing girls, wine and music'.

Limassol was a dead and alive sort of place; there was nothing to do except sit in the wine bars and drink. Needless to say the lads kept the proprietors of the wine bars in profit for many a month to come.

One evening when I was on duty, we brought the cutter inshore and there, swimming in full uniform, were a dozen of our own lads with some Americans off one of the merchant ships. We had a young midshipman with us who was acquiring experience, and here he was faced with getting these lads who were half cut – why else would they be swimming in full uniform? – onto the cutter and back to the ship with, of course, other liberty men who, though quite dry on the outside, were liberally lubricated on the inside.

The midshipman took the tiller and no sooner had we cast off when the lads started to sing.

"Quiet!" roared the Middy, but there was no response. He cut the engine and yelled out, "If you don't keep quiet I'll stop the boat until you do."

All was silent and the engine sprang to life. At the same time so did the passengers, rendering a mixture of sea shanties and other complimentary songs. The Middy stopped the boat and all was peaceful until we got under weigh again. The crew were getting fed up with this, for you don't control a body of drunken sailors like that.

Suddenly Geordie stood up and said in exasperation, "God knows what this bloody Navy's coming to. You get a short arsed little Middy, spent the war under his mother's wing and then comes out here and thinks he knows bleedin' everything. He knows bugger all."

This upset the Middy and, without further ado, the cutter returned to the ship with a party of happy singing sailors.

The following day the Middy said to Nobby, "I can't understand why the men were mad at me last night; after all, I have a duty to perform."

It was obvious that our Middy had learnt nothing from his experience. King's Rules and Regulations do not cater for a cutter full of drunken seamen, and if KRR doesn't provide an answer, then the problem doesn't exist. He will learn in time, but not today.

The following Monday we weighed anchor and steamed westward around the coast to Latzi in northwest Cyprus. There was nothing at Latzi, absolutely nothing. Well, that is not quite true. There was one house visible, and a stretch of golden sands that went right round the bay. As a background, there was a colourful array of shrubs and bushes. We went swimming off the ship until a hammerhead shark entered the bay. Now, I do or know not whether hammer headed sharks are dangerous or not, but anything that has shark as part of its name is enough to clear the waters of swimmers. Thereafter we dropped small charges in the water before we went swimming.

Fortunately the Skipper knew more about Latzi than we did, because unbeknown to us he had crates of beer brought aboard in Haifa. The off duty watch was ferried ashore using the cutter and the launches. A canteen was set up on the sands, and we were each given two bottles of beer and a packet of sandwiches and some buns. To keep the bottles cool we would bury them in the sands at the waterline with just the necks showing, and then we would spend the day swimming, walking and sunbathing. The atmosphere was so relaxing when compared with, say, Haifa or Trieste. We could have been a million miles away from the problems in the Mediterranean, and such was our enjoyment we wished that had been the case.

Within a couple of days we sailed back to Limassol. On our previous visit we had made friends with a young urchin of nine or ten. He was dressed in rags and had no shoes, but all day long he would wait for the cutter going to and fro. We would take him sweets and cigarettes and then later he would come armed with grapes and pomegranates for us. There were times when he gave us fruit when we had nothing to give in return. Obviously the lad enjoyed meeting us and the scale of bartering, especially with duty free cigarettes, increased. We had quite forgotten that this trading was taking place under the eyes of those who worked or dwelt in Custom House. We soon realised our mistake when the wife of the Custom House official heard Nobby ask the lad for some ouzo. She immediately informed her husband, who tried to apprehend the lad, but he was too quick and was last seen ducking and diving between and over the girders and timbers that supported the pier, but he was back the next day.

The only game of gambling which is permitted aboard one of His Majesty's ships for money is Tombola, and I was singularly lucky at the game, for in the space of one month I had won £3/6/3, £1/12/-, £2/-/-, 18/-, £1/18/-, plus numerous prizes under a pound. Normally we only played the game when we were not at sea, but with my duties on the cutter I could not participate right through a session, so it was a question of playing one or two games, pick up my winnings and then off on another trip. Some of the lads who had sat there all night without winning used to get quite irate at my success, but as any matelot knows, it is just a game of luck.

We stayed in Limassol for five days, weighed the anchor and went back to Haifa. We were caught up with more trouble involving the immigrant ships, but the atmosphere pervading Haifa was sad and pathetic. It was a place without a soul. On the one hand you had the Arabs who didn't want any more Jewish people in the country. On the other hand you had the survivors from the ghettos and concentration camps of Europe, desperately trying to get into the Promised Land. Between them, you had the British forces endeavouring to keep the peace between both factions in accordance with the mandate and succeeding in pleasing no one or to put it more strongly alienating everybody. The countries of the world took the side of the faction they had sympathy for, but the British were held responsible for every injury, every death, yet we were truly the innocent party. The various parties would have tested the patience of a saint and a British serviceman is no saint, and sometimes allowed his frustration and anger to boil over. Who can blame them? Who, in fact, does blame them?

It was with some relief that after a few days we ploughed a furrow back to Malta. The times we had moaned about Malta, but all that was now forgotten. We were going back to regular runs ashore, all night leave, crates of Blues, and a haven of peace.

We arrived in Grand Harbour in the first dogwatch on Monday the 9th of September, 1946. It was Allan Wheeler's birthday and I had promised to take him ashore and act as policeman – in other words keep an eye on him and make sure he came to no harm.

Our first port of call was at one of the cinemas where in the foyer they sold Danish Tuborg beer. Now, this Tuborg was not only grand beer, but it was also very potent. We drank a bottle each but Allan wanted to move on to The Gut, so we left. We started at the top of The Gut where we had a good meal. This would give our stomachs a good lining for what was to follow. We slowly made our way down the narrow street until we came to the Lucky Wheel. On entering we saw Bobby in his usual attire of a pink frilly blouse open to the waist and long black satin bell-bottom slacks. His partner, who I assumed to be Sugar, had long blond wavy hair, with a deep voice and a pock-marked complexion. Appearances can be deceptive and I had heard that both these fellows knew how to look after themselves, and could, if the occasion warranted it, pack a mean bunch o' fives.

"Let's go someplace else," said Allan, so further down The Gut we went.

We found a quiet little place and slowly the table started to fill up with empty bottles of Blues. There is one thing sailors object to, and that is someone clearing the table before their evening drinking has been accomplished. Somehow a table full of bottles and glasses is like a medal – it reflects what you have achieved.

Allan and I had been in there for some time when we noticed two ladies sitting at our table. One was between thirty five and forty, and the other well over sixty.

"Where the hell did they come from?" I said.

"I dunno," said Allan, his eyes looking very glazed.

"Did you see them arrive?"

"No," said Allan.

"How long have they been there?"

"I've no idea."

The old wrinkled lady with a shawl pulled tightly around shoulders bent with age said, "Please buy us a drink."

Now Jack ashore will buy anybody a drink, but he certainly doesn't like dipping into his pockets and paying for wines or spirits, when he knows the landlord only gives aniseed water and they split the profit between them.

"Buzz off," I said.

"Why for you not buy me a drink?"

"Because I don't want to – now scram."

There was silence for a while and then more futile demands for drinks, but then when they realised they were on to a loser, they left us in peace.

As Allan's birthday came to a close, I took him back to the ship. He was a little unsteady on his feet, but not too bad. Back aboard, the lads had already slung our hammocks for us. The spirit among one's shipmates is beyond expectation. Not only do they sling your mick, but they'd help you turn in, and would even keep some food back in case you may need it.

For some time I had been turning over in my mind thoughts of getting married to Anne. It is true to say that our letters never specifically dwelt on the subject and though I did not know Anne's thoughts, as far as I was concerned it was a foregone conclusion. In retrospect, there were many things I should be thinking about, namely work and housing prospects, whether to live in Scotland or England, and then difficulties that could arise with Anne being Catholic and my being Protestant. To me these were trivialities when compared to the depth and strength of my love.

My parents were not aware just how strong this relationship was, so I thought I had better let them know. I think it came as a shock to them, because within a week I received a typewritten letter from the old man saying,

'My Dear Son,
I know the sun has many effects upon one's mind, but I didn't know it went this far'.

I then tried to recall exactly what I had written in my letter, but alas, nothing came to mind. I suppose I must have conveyed the impression that I was going home, then straight to Scotland, getting married, and then coming home and saying, "Hi folks, meet the wife." I had not, of course, intended to get married immediately I was demobilised so I replied, giving what I hoped was a saner view of my expectations.

When I left UK waters, I thought it would be a matter of weeks before I was sent back for demob, but the weeks turned into months and there were still no prospects of my returning.

Such was my optimism, and with the knowledge that clothes were still rationed at home, I set out to buy the basics of my future wardrobe, as well as presents for the family and items of a more delicate nature for Anne.

On Monday the 16th of September, Captain Stanfield left his command to go back home. He had been Skipper of the *Mauritius* since October 1944, and had seen action with her off Norway and guided her through a refit and recommissioning. He was a good Captain, who the crew liked and respected and would most certainly miss. Already aboard was our new Skipper, Captain F.J. Wylie. I must confess that my first impression of this short, stocky and ruddy complexioned man was that he was going to be a real disciplinarian a modern Captain Bligh.

A Fleet exercise had been in the offing for some time, and orders had been posted that we were to sail on the Wednesday. On the Tuesday we were given a briefing by the Navigating Officer and he spoke these words which I would remember at a later date and words which could be construed as offensive and a threat to Albania.

"The first part of our exercise," he said, "is to take a convoy to Nauplia in Greece. We shall be leaving Malta in company with the *Leander* and two destroyers. We will meet the convoy at sea and it will comprise of *HMS Ranpura*, a depot ship, the *Maine* , a hospital ship, *Fort Charlotte*, a supply vessel *Blue Ranger*, a naval oil tanker and two landing craft. These will be escorted by aircraft carrier *Ocean,* and nine destroyers. We shall be known as *Red Force*. The attacking fleet comprising the cruisers *HMS Liverpool* and *Phoebe,* and some destroyers, and will be known as the *Blue Force*."

He then outlined the necessity of being alert and briefed us on the technical side of working guns, predictors and radar sets in conjunction with one another. He then spoke of the second part of the exercise using those memorable words, which if conveyed outside the confines of the *Mauritius* could be construed as being inflammatory.

"I want you to imagine," he said, "that a hostile country has been firing on our ships – for example, Albania."

It is as well to remember that in the previous May Albanian shore batteries fired on the *Orion* and the *Superb*.

"We are going to suppose that Cape Arnauti in Cyprus is this particular country. The fleet under cover of aircraft are going to sail pass the Cape, using our guns as a cover to the troops in the landing craft, who will go in and blow up the gun emplacements. They will then withdraw when their task has been completed."

We left Malta late in the forenoon on the Wednesday and duly joined up with the convoy and at the same time prepared the ship for anticipated 'trouble'. We did not expect contact with Blue Force during the hours of daylight, but rather suspected they would try something during the hours of darkness, but again all was quiet. I kept the middle watch on Thursday and, with the lights in the convoy all blacked out, it was a grim reminder of the Russian convoys except this wasn't cold. About 02:00 in the middle watch, we sighted a ship on the horizon in a blaze of light from stem to stern. She could, of course, be a passenger ship, but as soon as it became practicable, contact was made with her by flashlight. By all accounts she was a Greek merchant ship making for one of the Greek ports. Slowly the merchant ship and convoy converged and we thought she was going to sail astern of us, but this was not so, because as soon as we were in gun range of one another, she doused all her lights and all hell was let loose on the convoy. This so-called merchant ship was a destroyer which dashed through the middle of the convoy like a greyhound. She claimed the *Ocean* as being sunk, and numerous other vessels being damaged. There were a few red faces among the senior officers responsible. "Not cricket, old boy, not cricket." They were the subject of many a wardroom joke after this event.

On the Friday, both forces joined together and we all sailed in formation.

On the Saturday, we entered the Gulf of Nauplia and, with high rugged mountains as background and a beautiful blue sea below, the Fleet presented a picture the like of which I had never seen before. The cruisers *Liverpool, Mauritius, Leander* and *Phoebe* sailed in line, abreast with the carrier *Ocean* a little aft. The convoy was in formation astern, and the destroyers lined the flanks and the rear.

The entire fleet covered a few square miles, but with the bright morning sun and the calm sea, this magnificent sight exuded power and strength and might. With all our yearnings for home and demob, we were proud to be part of this great navy.

Just before we reached the Gulf, one of the sailors on the *Leander* fell overboard so the fleet set about making a search. He was eventually picked up none the worse for his adventure, but the Admiral, learning of this, sent a message to *Leander* to clap the man in cells – after all, we couldn't have one careless matelot screwing up the Fleet's manoeuvres.

At 08:00 on the Saturday, we arrived in Nauplia. Nauplia jutted out into the water. On one side was a bay with a small castle, which was being used as a hotel. I had heard that over two hundred soldiers were killed trying to capture it from the enemy. On the other side of the peninsular was, of course, the Gulf of Nauplia. The headland was about two hundred feet high and sloped down to sea level. The town had a number of low built whitewashed wine bars, but the nearer you got to the centre so the buildings got higher and more attractive looking. Behind the town was the hill of Palamidhi, which rose almost vertically, the top of which was capped by some old ruins. To reach them you had to climb a series of zigzag steps, the majority of which were broken and in need of repair. On my first day ashore three of us, including Nobby and Allan, climbed those steps, arriving at the top quite short of breath. The view was magnificent and all round us was a rugged mountainous countryside. The sun shone down on the white-topped roofs of the buildings below, while in the bay the fleet looked like toy models on a lake, the water of which was so calm it seemed like a polished mirror.

The ship had declared an open day, so the following afternoon when I was on duty, we spent the time ferrying visitors to and fro. Our first boatload was full of Girl Guides, so I soon had them singing some songs I knew from my scouting days. They certainly knew the tunes, but with their Greek and my English words it must have sounded rather strange. We also took some Scouts aboard, and one of them who spoke English well told me that they had, during the German occupation, carried on their troop meetings by going into the hills. On another trip we had in the boat three young girls, one of whom told us that as there was a shortage of men in Greece they could not be seen out with foreign servicemen in case it spoiled their marriage chances; however, they emphasised the fact that it was alright after dark. One did not need to be an idiot to understand the drift of the conversation. I made no attempt to avail myself of the opportunities being offered, but I told my messmates. I was called for everything for not acquainting them earlier of the offers being made.

We all longed to go swimming but we were denied the pleasure, due to the bay being full of jellyfish. There was hardly a square yard of seawater that was not full of huge brown jellyfish, and even as the cutter ploughed its way, so you could see the propeller slicing them to bits.

The time came for the fleet to depart, and indeed to split up. Some were going to Crete, others to Cyprus, and some to Malta. As far as *Mauritius* was concerned, we sailed for nine hours and anchored off a place called Monemuasia. We were in this large bay, but the only sign of civilisation was four squat fisherman's houses. The surrounding country was scrubland, a mixture of sandy soils, huge boulders strewn all over the place and interspersed with a variety of wild shrubs all struggling to survive. You couldn't call it mountainous country though one could see mountains in the distance standing out against a grey misty sky. A few of the lads did go ashore and they found a village over the hills and a few miles inland.

One day when the cutter was inshore we were hailed by some people in a boat. On investigation we found there were two boats, one towing the other and over both vessels there were about fifteen people, one of whom was an old lady wrapped in blankets and lying on the deck. They asked us for water, a commodity we did not carry in the cutter and which we couldn't take from the ship without the permission of the Officer of the Watch.

A young girl stood up and said, "I'll come with you."

One of the crew with a glint in his eye said smilingly, "By all means."

Seeing this, a young man in one of the boats said, "And so will I."

Nobby could not take them back to the ship without some authority, so when we arrived at the gangway the Duty Officer was informed, but he just dismissed the episode as being of no consequence. This response caused us considerable unease as it looked as though we had abandoned them, but on the other hand they were only fifty yards offshore, so why not get water there? There was also another troublesome feature. We believed they were Jewish immigrants making for the Promised Land. If we had pressed the Officer of the Watch he may have reached the same opinion that we held and arrested them. On the other hand, it would have looked strange and could have been embarrassing if it were discovered that the Royal Navy had provisioned an immigrant ship lying off Greece, only for another to arrest it as it approached Palestine.

Storms and rough weather were a common occurrence in the bay. Normally this would not have mattered, except that our mail was brought to us by seaplane, and if it was rough she couldn't land. The plane, an old Walrus, came from *HMS Ocean*, and after numerous abortive attempts, she did on the fourth day finally make a landing. We went out to meet her while she motored inshore to calmer waters. We allowed the Walrus to come close to our stern and to transfer the mail and then, when the mission had been accomplished, she took off in very choppy seas.

It was those same rough seas that carried a whaler away which we had to rescue. We were not sorry to leave Monemuasia, but Poro Bay – where the hell was that? We soon found out that it was in the Mirabella Gulf on the eastern side of Crete. We arrived there the following day, but once again there was very little to do ashore. The village itself was some miles inland on the shores of a large lake. A narrow canal joined the lake to the bay in which we were anchored. The canal was just wide enough to take the motor cutter and near to it were some small windmills. Each of them had twelve sails, and each sail was made of cloth, which could be furled in high winds, similar to reefing a ship's sails. I went inside one and found that, apart from the millstone, all the machinery was made of wood. An old lady could be seen sitting outside spinning cotton, while in the adjoining field you would see her husband, an old bearded man with black baggy trousers who was guiding a plough pulled by a mule.

No one could fail to appreciate the quiet calm and dignified pace these people enjoyed in such tranquil surroundings, but in sailors, any appreciation of this nature is short lived. A decent shore leave was missing. We had been to Nauplia and Monemuasia, and now to Poro. They were alright in their way, but there was no noise, no music, no drinks, no females, and no singing. A man cooped up in a mess deck with his shipmates was in order for a short time, but not all the time. One sensed a frustration fermenting below the surface, but who was going to crack first? We soon found out. The last liberty boat from shore was 18:00. This in itself was indicative of the fact that there was nothing to do ashore. I was on duty at the time but with the prospects of an early night I decided to turn in. I had just slung my hammock when at 21:00 we were called away.

"What the hell?" we echoed in unison as over the side we went, along the boom, down the Jacob's ladder and into the boat. We made our way to the gangway. On the quarterdeck a body of Officers, well liquored up, endeavoured unsuccessfully to stand up straight. Guns stepped forwarded and in a slurred voice gave the command, "Man the boat." Suddenly, this motley collection staggered down the gangway. Some had rifles, some had swords and some had tin hats.

On arrival in the cutter, Guns gave further orders: "Commander Engineer take charge of the engine room, Paymaster, starboard lookout, Radar Officer, port lookout. Jimmy, where's 'Jimmy the One'... ah, there you are – you take charge of the armaments and I will be coxswain." As he uttered the last few words, he stepped towards the tiller and said, "Alright, Leading Seaman Clark, I'll take the wheel."

Now there is one rule in the Navy that says that a coxswain is Captain of his boat and all that is in it. What would happen if an Admiral tried to take over, I shudder to think.

I saw Nobby bristle and he responded thus, "I," he said with a strong emphasis on the I, "I'm the coxswain of this boat, and I repeat I keep the wheel."

I've never seen Guns so deflated or lost for words, but all he said was "Oh."

The Officer of the Watch had instructed Nobby to take this party to the *Leander*. The night was dark, warm and sultry and surprisingly apart from a few muffled giggles all was quiet in the boat.

As we neared the *Leander,* Guns suddenly yelled out, "Stand by to board." Now the bowman and the sternsheets man each have a boat hook and before going alongside you swing those boat hooks around in a prearranged drill. It's all very swanky and impressive but if you are very careful, it is possible to overdo the drill and crack a few heads that happen to be in way. We both managed to do this very effectively and it would of course add to the following mornings' hangover, which some of them were guaranteed to experience. They had of course erupted into a cacophony of yells, screams and oaths, but suddenly all went quiet.

Guns had noticed that *Leander* had a film being screened on the quarterdeck and very soberly he said, "Well, boys, we can't very well bust up their show, and we've all cooled down a bit, so let's return."

It was a bit of an anti-climax, though on return to the ship the boat drill antics claimed a few more victims, and a boat hook between the legs as they were ascending did not exactly improve their progress.

On the Wednesday night we left Poro in company with the *Leander*, four frigates and two landing craft and exercised with the rest of the fleet. These exercises went on for three days when the second phase of the manoeuvres previously mentioned took place, namely the bombarding of Cape Anauti.

When a warship is firing its big guns, the noise between decks is almost intolerable and that's how it was with us, as salvo after salvo was discharged. The mess decks took on the appearance of a London fog as the vibrations disturbed dust and asbestos fibres and flecks of paint and broken crockery. Fortunately it was all over by 11:30, so we sailed away to Famagusta, the principal port in Cyprus, where we anchored in the early hours of the following morning.

Famagusta gave us, and indeed the other naval vessels, the opportunity to indulge in some sailing. We carried some 14 foot sailing dinghies which were of a standard design. There were just two of us in the crew, with about twenty six boats participating over a three mile course. In two races we achieved a second and a third place, so that was quite satisfying. A sailing dinghy in wartime is not part of a ship's inventory. so it was refreshing to enjoy one of the luxuries of peace.

The dockside at Famagusta used to be a hive of characters. One night we tied up the cutter between two merchant ships and then went ashore to await the liberty men. There were loads of stores stacked around with two soldiers to guard them. The two that spoke to us were huge fat fellows.

"D'you want any pillowslips or blankets? There's tons of 'em along 'ere. We're guarding 'em."

As tempting as the offer was, we replied that time did not allow us to take advantage. When they heard this, they both unbuttoned their tunics and handed over to us a dozen or more pillowslips.

The soldiers and the matelots used to get on very well together. One evening, as we arrived at the dockside, we found a party of soldiers had met up with some of our lads and had accompanied them back. When we caught up with them they were all huddled together as though they were in a rugby scrum, singing a song which went on forever, but the first two lines went,

"Julieta, Julieta she's lovely, the girl who's never been kissed.

Julieta, Julieta she's lovely, the girl who's never been pissed."

While this was going on, Geordie was having his usual swim in full uniform.

One evening whilst waiting for the lads, Dennis, our stoker and myself were sitting having a smoke on this upturned water tank. Now I've already mentioned Dennis' rather high voice, which gave some people the wrong idea. Well, a Petty Officer off the *Leander* came and sat next to Dennis. The next thing is he puts an arm round his shoulders and a hand on Dennis' knee.

Looking into the stoker's face, he said, "My, you're bloody nice."

Dennis' reaction was immediate. He leapt off the tank yelling, "Why does this always happen to me?"

He then sat the other side of me which, of course, put me next to the amorous PO, but I was ready for him.

He sidled alongside and said, "You're not so bad either."

He had hardly finished his sentence before I whipped round, grabbed him by the knot of his tie and twisted it, at the same time laying him flat on his back. As I did so, I was conscious of commissioned Officers and the other ranks watching what was going on. I could have cheerfully knocked him for six, but he was now bright red and choking.

I released my grip slowly and he said, "Sorry, are you one of those big sailors who don't like that sort of thing?"

I said, "You come behind these bloody tanks and I'll show you whether I like it or not."

He declined my offer, meanwhile the onlookers, including Dennis, enjoyed the confrontation.

Famagusta was an odd sort of place, being split into two parts, the old and the new. The old city was surrounded by a wall and was out of bounds to the forces. The new city boasted a NAAFI canteen and that was a large marquee set in the middle of a field. It also had a beautiful sandy beach. Small buggy cabs were the commonest form of transport, but I never used them, for they had a nasty habit of taking you where you didn't want to go. I'm sure the expression 'being taken for a ride' originated with these cabs. They were popular with the local prostitutes, who would pick up their clients and take them to more congenial surroundings where they could practice their calling.

The lads would come back to the ship with all sorts of tales of enticement and propositions, but you could never quite sift the truth between fact and fiction.

One story was told of a sailor who went into the old city purely out of interest. As he was going along, looking at all the old buildings, a mother, father and daughter spoke to him. Before long they invited him back to their home for tea, and in all innocence he accepted their kind offer. On their arrival they went into the lounge and invited their daughter to entertain Jack while they prepared tea. Up to this moment the young lady had never said a word, but as soon as the door closed behind her parents she was on him like a sex-starved tigress. Jack, however, was embarrassed by her attentions, and had no wish to abuse the hospitality of the parents by seducing their daughter, so he repulsed her advances. An hour elapsed before the door slowly and quietly opened and the father's head appeared. He was apparently checking on his daughter's progress or, as in this case, lack of progress. He went over to his offspring and whispered a few words in her ear and then again withdrew from the room. Regrettably I did not hear the end of the story and will forever wonder, 'Did he or didn't he?'

When I got back to the ship I bumped into Turnip 'Ead, and could immediately see he was not at ease. It did not take long for him to pour out his heart. Turnip 'Ead had been with a black girl. He was full of praise for this 'lush bit of goods', as he called her, but he was ashamed of what he had done. He would be ashamed to look his mother in the face again, he was disgusted with himself, and ashamed to think he had been unfaithful to his girl in Trieste.

"I will be true," he wailed.

I suppose the baring of his soul was done with the object of gaining some sympathy, but he didn't get it, because I exploded.

"For God's sake, Turnip, don't be such a bloody fool. Do you think that girl in Trieste is being true to you? She'll be having a helluva time with guys off the other ships. Be true to yourself and stop being so bloody stupid."

Turnip's mood changed to wrath, "You be careful what you're saying, Joey."

"Alright, alright, we say no more, but for your sake I hope the ship goes back to Trieste again."

Taking liquor aboard is against King's Rules and Regulations; nevertheless, even His Majesty's most loyal and patriotic subjects sometimes believe the rule doesn't exist, and carry alcoholic beverages aboard. Now, liberty men coming off shore leave are inspected by the Officer of the Watch on the quarterdeck, and if he finds any of the crew disregarding this order, they soon find themselves in trouble.

Collectively, alcoholic drinks were called 'Ooch', but more than likely it was the local brew of 'Ouzo' or 'Cherry Heering'.

There was of course a back door, to the ship and that was via the cutter's crew. We would be given bottles which we would bring in board late at night. Our chief client was Petty Officer Bower. He was short, fat and elderly and when I say elderly, I mean he was over thirty. He was a likeable character and always treated the lads decently.

Quite often on that last liberty boat, he would come up to me and say, "Lofty, stow these in your anchor locker." He would then discreetly hand over four or five bottles.

He would, with the other lads, go aboard by the gangway; in the meantime we would tie up to the boom, and then with a bucket full of bottles I would climb along the boom and make my way to the PO's mess. In recompense he might give me a bottle or a bag of fruit, or even eggs.

A Courts Martial was held while we were in Famagusta. Apparently a shore based Naval Officer had been caught working quite a racket with Naval stores. He was found guilty, sentenced to six months, dismissed from the service and lost his pension.

Chapter 29

Corfu

We eventually left Famagusta after a stay of about nine days and headed for the Adriatic, in particular Corfu. It took us three days to get there, but I'm sure we didn't take the most direct route and meandered around for some time.

The hook had hardly touched the bottom before a fleet of small boats surrounded us. They were selling almost anything. There were live turkeys, chickens, rabbits and tortoises. There was a variety of fish, and also sponges, apples and oranges. They would sell, they would buy and they would barter. One of the lads bought a puppy, and another bought two tortoises. In return sweets, cigarettes, soap and clothes were sold or bartered. This market and the trading took place out of the portholes, with goods on the end of a line being brought inboard and others being lowered.

The Master at Arms standing on the forecastle of a night time could and did indeed observe what was going on, but he discreetly turned a blind eye – until, that is, he saw bottles of liquor coming inboard and pussers', clothing going outboard. Immediately he called out the cutters crew and joined us in giving chase to these small boats. Now, these bum boats were quite fragile, being constructed of soap boxes and any other material the owner could get hold of. Having caught one, the Master would lean over the side and go through all the goods the boat owner had acquired. Although most of it was pussers' issue, he was only attracted to those articles of clothing bearing the last owner's name. He would take them away from the protesting boatman and drop the offending items just behind him in the cutter. The object of the exercise was so that when we returned to the ship, he would muster all those men whose names he had found stamped on the clothing and would then put them on a charge. There was of course a heated discussion taking place between the Master and the bum boat owners, which allowed the cutter's crew to pilfer from the Master some of the goods retrieved. This benefitted the shipmate whose name was blazoned all over it, and it benefited us when at a later date we resold it. Some of the Greeks would hang onto our gunwales, swearing and cursing, some even weeping. They refused to let go as we gathered speed to chase the other boats, so at times it was necessary to give them a crack across the knuckles with a boat hook.

Every time we went ashore, we were stopped with requests for anything we wanted to sell. One night I took two pairs of pyjamas ashore – they cost me seven and sixpence each pair, and I wanted 50,000 drachma all told, which was about two pounds ten shillings in sterling.

The first Greek who came up to me said, "What you got to sell, Jack?"

I showed him the pyjamas.

"How much?" he asked.

"Fifty thousand," I replied.

"Ten," he said.

"No fifty."

"Alright," he responded, and promptly stowed them in a sack. Now I should have learnt a lesson from Venice in not allowing a prospective purchaser to have the goods before he had paid for them, but no harm was done except when he came to pay me. Using five thousand drachma notes, he started to count, "Five, ten, fifteen, okay."

I was getting a bit agitated by now and snarled at him, "Fifty thousand."

I grabbed him with one hand and his sack with the other,

"Fifty thousand bloody drachma. Get it? Fifty thousand."

"Alright Jack," he said.

Using his five thousand notes he started to count out the money. "Five, ten, fifteen, twenty five, thirty five, forty..."

I stopped him in full flight. "You bloody scapegoat," I yelled.

"Sorry, Jack, sorry. I count it again."

"Not bloody likely," I replied. "I'll count it."

Eventually I got 47,500 drachmas out of him, which wasn't a bad deal.

I think Nobby struck the worst bargain when he sold a raincoat for 25,000 drachmas.

The Mediterranean fleet were due to hold a regatta off the west coast of Greece in a few weeks' time, so the bay in Corfu was full of whalers, their owners straining at the oars as many an hour was put into training the crews for the big day.

One of the destroyers, namely *HMS Saumarez,* had only one set of rowlocks which someone dropped overboard. Our Commander thought it would be good practice for the divers to go down and look for them. The cutter was used as the diving boat but although they searched the seabed all morning, they had no success. This meant that without the rowlocks they could not participate in the regatta. Little did we know then that this small insignificant episode would appear later with hindsight as a very meaningful omen.

At the first opportunity I went ashore to explore. I climbed to the lighthouse which stood on a peninsular with the town a little nearer the mainland. I then walked south through some beautiful countryside until I came to a small cliff which looked out over the magnificent bay. In the bay were two islands. One was called Pontekonisi, or Mouse Island. Greek legend tells us it was the Phoenician ship that brought Ulysses to Ithaca. The angry Poseidon turned it into stone. The other island was very small, much nearer and joined to the mainland by a narrow causeway about a yard wide. On the island was a small church, so I decided to go down and have a look. A couple of Marines off the ship must have had the same idea, because we met halfway down and went over to the island together. A wrinkled old lady met us, and though she did not understand our language, she conveyed with her hands signs of welcome and took us into the small church. She apparently lived on the island and was the caretaker. She then took us into her kitchen, a large whitewashed room with a cobble stone floor, where she made us some coffee. One of the Marines had brought with him some sandwiches and cakes which he shared among the four of us. There was however a considerable amount left over, which he gave to the old lady. She was so happy and showed her pleasure by nodding her brown wrinkled face, which was wreathed in a broad smile.

When we eventually made our farewells, she waved to us until we reached the mainland.

The three of us climbed to higher ground overlooking the bay, and came across two Naval Officers, a Naval Padre and three young ladies, all of whom were enjoying the scenery. The Officers were in civilian clothes, but I remembered their faces, having seen them come ashore in the forenoon.

We were making our way toward the town when a horse and carriage containing the Officers and their companions overtook us. A few yards further on they stopped and, to our amazement they suggested that we should join them. We availed ourselves of this very nice gesture, but somehow we got the feeling that the initiative for this kindly act came from the young ladies, and not the Officers.

The day following this run ashore, the ship prepared to depart for Argostoli on the island of Cephalonia in western Greece and south of Corfu.

Chapter 30

Minefield

Before we embark on the following sequence of events, it would be as well to go back to the time when the countries occupying the shores of the Adriatic Sea were liberated. Although those countries were now free, access to them by sea was a highly dangerous occupation. The enemy had mined the Adriatic so effectively that it presented the Allies with a mammoth task. To make this task somewhat easier, they decided that a channel should be cleared through the minefield, and that this channel should be available to all shipping. Part of the route was between the island of Corfu and the countries of Albania and Greece on the mainland, and was declared to be an international channel. By this means, the minesweepers could at their leisure sweep the rest of the Adriatic.

We now move forward to May 1946. The Adriatic is now clear of mines, but the decision to make the Corfu Channel an international route had not been rescinded, so *HMS Orion* and *HMS Superb* cruised through those waters. They did not however expect the type of reception they received, for the gun batteries on the coast of Albania opened fire on them. Neither the *Orion* nor the *Superb* responded to the firing, and any protests that became necessary were handled diplomatically by the Foreign Office.

We now move on to the recent fleet manoeuvres in September, and in particular our Navigating Officer's briefing. To recall his words, "I want you to imagine," he said, "that a hostile country has been firing on our ships, for example,

Albania. We are going to suppose that Cape Arnauti in Cyprus is that country."

We recall the recent exercises where, under cover of a fleet bombardment, a landing was made and imaginary gun emplacements destroyed.

The Government were not happy with the Albanian response to our protests regarding the shooting that took place against our men of war. The Royal Navy had been irritated by the event and yearned to redress the injustice that had been inflicted on them. The opportunity to do just that was now upon us. The agreement to make the Corfu Channel international had never been revoked, and while the merchant ships were now able to use the wider expanse west of Corfu, the British Government to make a point of principle decided to send some warships through the channel.

And so at 13:15 on October the 22nd, 1946 *HMS Mauritius* led the destroyers *HMS Saumarez*, the light cruiser *HMS Leander* and another destroyer, *HMS Volage,* all in line ahead. The crews were all closed up at action stations. The guns were ready to respond immediately to any hostile threat from the mainland. Behind the island of Corfu, a fleet waited in readiness to support any action the four ships may find themselves involved in.

It was a glorious day with the calm sea shimmering a thousand flashes of light in the bright sunshine.

Steaming down the middle of the channel, we saw the gun barrels of the shore batteries being elevated. Our own projectiles were ready for an immediate response. At 16:30 I was standing on the quarterdeck, when suddenly an almighty explosion astern of us shattered the peaceful surroundings. A pall of smoke rose into the sky from the starboard side of the *Saumarez*'s bridge. We did not know what had caused it. Certainly no shore-based guns had fired and Albania had no submarines or minelayers, so it could not be a torpedo or a mine. The *Saumarez* slowly came to a halt as her crew fought to get the fire under control. We likewise stopped engines to give cover and indeed assistance to this stricken vessel. Within minutes she was down by the bows. The *Leander* was instructed to go full speed around Corfu and give cover a little further south. It was apparent that if *Saumarez* could be saved she would have to return to Corfu. Meanwhile, the *Volage* had come to her assistance by getting a line to *Saumarez*'s stern, with the object of towing her back to Corfu. Our cutter and the motorboats had already departed with medical assistance, engineers, signallers, the photographer and a Chief Gunners' Mate to take care of the ammunition. Smoke and flames continued to rise from the *Saumarez* as she veered uncontrollably to port. Her forecastle was probably less than half a fathom above the waterline, but the damage control had effectively sealed the damaged part from the rest of the ship so the danger of flooding had been eliminated. *Volage* had, by now, got under weigh and slowly the haul back to the island began. Time had ceased to have any meaning as this drama slowly unfolded, and so it was when another explosion occurred. *Volage*'s bow was blown off, right back to the 'A' gun turret. It was as though a gigantic knife had sliced through the hull. *Volage* appeared to take this latest episode in her stride. Without hesitation she cast off her stern towing lines, performed a 180 degree turn and proceeded to reconnect the tow line to any available bollard bearing in mind the forecastle no longer existed. She then went stern first, towing *Saumarez* by the stern.

There was, of course, a lot of speculation as to what had caused this, and the conclusion was that we were in a minefield, but the big question was who had laid them. The Albanians had no minelayers and none of the Eastern Bloc countries had minelayers in the Mediterranean, but then, of course, they could have been laid from the air. The Albanians did not have the capabilities to do it, but could it have been one of their allies? Could it have been the action of the USSR?

Signals had been transmitted to the hospital ship *Maine*, and also the aircraft carrier *Ocean* to be prepared to accept casualties. While we were still in the middle of what we suspected was a minefield, the *Ocean* went round the south of Corfu and our boats were able to ferry the casualties to her. Casualties varied between the stricken vessels. Horrific burns were inflicted on many of the *Saumarez* crew, while the *Volage*, which did not catch fire, suffered serious injuries with the loss of limbs, including some lads who were still unconscious. Some of the injured just passed away as they were being ferried over. The *Maine* then arrived, and also the *Leander*, which had now completed her circuit of the island. She took both the *Volage* and the *Saumarez* in tow and steamed slowly back to Corfu. We maintained station to offer protection until they were in Corfu, after which we too sailed round Corfu, arriving in the early hours of Wednesday morning.

At first light, the cutter's crew were instructed to go over to *Saumarez* and take the dead ashore. The events of the last twenty four hours had a profound effect on the fleet. There was a definite atmosphere. It was not like the war where you knew your enemy and all you wanted was to avenge the death of your shipmates – this was different, because there was nobody, no country on whom we could vent our anger. Without a doubt it was a minefield, but who laid them, or was capable of laying them? Who indeed would want to lay them? There were so many questions to which at this stage no one knew the answers, and all we could do was to brood and mourn the wicked and tragic deaths of our shipmates, knowing in our hearts that whoever was responsible for this cowardly, wicked and evil deed was most certainly a country that either had been liberated by the very same men they now sought to kill, or a country that was once our ally, a country where thousands of our men had died in cruel, cold and merciless seas as they took lifesaving equipment, food and military materials to the north Russian ports.

As we approached *Saumarez,* we saw sitting on a bollard the Admiral of the Fleet, also Rear Admiral Kinahan and the injured Captain of *Saumarez*. All three looked despondent as they sat in a silent, contemplative mood.

We could on closer inspection see that the mine had exploded just aft of the bridge, killing the men in the transmitting station – reputed to be the safest place on the ship – and also killing most of the men in No 1 engine room. The hole in the side was quite large, with jagged pieces of metal pointing out at all angles. Part of her super structure was twisted into grotesque shapes, and all her paintwork was burnt or blistered to a dark brown. The decks were littered with the remnants of charred rope, wood and clothing. The acrid smell of burning equipment hung over the deck as steam rose out of the ruins.

The dead men were brought out onto the upper deck and passed down into the cutter. We could only take four at a time. Two aft in the cockpit and one either side of the engine. Their burnt and torn uniforms exposed red raw limbs, some burnt to the bone, scalps devoid of hair and deformed hands, fixed as though they were trying to clutch at life. Some watery looking blood seeped from open wounds and fell in small pools upon the deck.

A body wrapped in a blanket was passed into the boat. I took the head and shoulders, while Nobby and Scouse took a leg each. The wash of a passing motorboat caused the cutter to roll and with it, I fell backwards. The jolt caused the blanket to open and exposed a charred head with a wide gaping mouth, from which a set of dentures shot out. Scouse bent down and picked them up, looked at the dried blood between the teeth and, without further thought, prepared to restore them to their owner's mouth. Nobby watched all this without apparent effect. It was, in fact, like watching a slow motion silent film, but Scouse's action was too much, for Nobby just snapped, "Scouse." Scouse looked round, his hand still hovering over the dead man's mouth. Nobby just nodded toward the water, trying to suggest without actually saying it, to throw them overboard.

Scouse hunched his shoulders in a manner which suggested that someone was crazy, but nevertheless casually flicked them with a deft movement of the thumb so scribing an arc, and they flew through the air. As they hit the water, three pairs of eyes watched the crystal clear water splash and accept within its bosom the false teeth. They quickly disappeared from view, leaving nothing but a few bubbles in their wake.

I was still pinned down under the corpse, and when I did manage to extricate myself, I found that the wounds of our departed shipmate had weeped over the benches, the engine cover and myself.

It seemed that all of Corfu had come down to the harbour. They stood in their hundreds in a silent vigil as we lifted the inert bodies onto the quay side. The silence was almost uncanny, though now and again you could hear the sobbing of some young maiden.

Some nuns in their black habits approached us, their cheeks wet with tears. They begged us to tell them the names of the men who had been killed, but we couldn't help them. We did not know these men, but they were part of the Royal Navy, and just as much a shipmate as if they were off our own ship. Apparently the lads off both vessels had given a party aboard for children from the convent only the day before they sailed. We scrubbed the cutter after every trip but we could not erase all the stains, so they were left as a permanent memorial to the departed.

The next day, ten of those who were killed were buried in the military cemetery on Corfu. The marines and detachments from numerous ships paraded through the streets. Sailors from the *Mauritius* were pallbearers. Once again the town turned out and watched in silence as the victims of a tragic voyage passed by.

The next day, two more were buried, but even as they were being interred, bodies were still being extracted from the forecastle of *HMS Saumarez*.

I wanted to get away from the stench of death, but while physically you are able, mentally it stays with you. There was a film being shown aboard that night so I went to see it. It was called 'A Quiet Weekend'.

The whys and wherefores of this incident would undoubtedly be argued and debated for years to come, but who really was to blame? Both sides have reasoned arguments. We originally swept the straits clear of mines. It had been declared to be an International Channel and the edict had never been cancelled. Albania, on the other hand, took the view that once the Adriatic had been cleared of mines, then the Corfu Straits automatically came within the province of Corfu and Albania, and as such no vessel should use it without their joint approval.

Albania may have been right, but that in no way excuses her or the country backing her for the dastardly deed of laying mines to trap and kill unwary sea farers, but then my mind goes back to the words of the Navigating Officer. Did those words get back to Albania and if they did, did they the Albanians believe that we were going to land men with the object of blowing up gun emplacements? Is there a possibility they sought the assistance of Russian planes to lay those mines as a form of defence? If only we knew the answers to these questions.

Chapter 31

Fleet Regatta

On the Saturday we left Corfu and sailed for Argostoli, which is on the island of Cephalonia in western Greece, and where we arrived the same day. The anchorage was a huge natural bay, surrounded by land apart from a narrow entrance. It was big enough to accommodate a number of fleets; however, we anchored in such a manner that an area was left free for the boats taking part in the races, and which would allow the ships on the perimeter of this area to get a view of the proceedings.

The problems in the Corfu Channel had delayed the regatta, and the fact that *Saumarez* and *Volage* were not there did somewhat dampen the atmosphere. On the Sunday, a sailing race was held. The course was roughly twice around the bay. All the sailing dinghies bar one hugged the marker buoys, but that one dinghy made for the west side of the bay, then steered north. Normally being so close to the land would have been the kiss of death, but not this time. The wind seemed to fall down the hills and fill her sails. She just took off, and after the first circuit she was at least a mile ahead. Meanwhile, the lads on her parent ship *HMS Magpie* cheered and cheered until their throats were hoarse, but then on the second circuit she too hugged the marker buoys and again took off. The rest of the fleet, having seen *Magpie*'s successful route on the first circuit, decided to do likewise when they came to the second circuit but it didn't work for them, and the *Magpie*'s boat seemed to pass the winning post hours before the second boat came in. A truly magnificent victory, but her skipper must have been either a very lucky man or, as I prefer to believe, a good sailor who knew how to read the terrain and the weather conditions. Rumour did fly around that the clinker built dinghy had had her hull planed and sandpapered to such an extent that she looked as though she were carvel built. Frankly I didn't believe it, because she would have won in any case. If sails are full while others are becalmed, then you know which ones are being skippered by real yachtsmen.

On the Sunday, *HMS Surprise* entered the bay, carrying the wives of the Admiral and his staff, the idea being that Lady Willis would present the prizes at the end of the regatta. However, that same night a terrific storm broke out, causing the *Surprise* to drag her anchors, and then the cable just snapped under the strain. Before she could get up steam, she drifted toward the flagship *HMS Liverpool* with Admiral Willis aboard. Fortunately she missed *Liverpool* by a few yards.

The next day we noticed she was missing, but the Admiral informed us he had dispatched her to Malta to catch the better weather and expressed his apologies that his wife Lady Willis would not be able to present the prizes.

To me, *HMS Surprise* was always a mystery. What was she? I didn't notice her taking part in the fleet exercises. Was she just a glorified yacht used to transport wives around the Mediterranean and to hold cocktail parties aboard her? I never knew the answers.

On the Monday, the destroyers held their regatta. It was a miserable day weather wise, with constant rain, high winds and a choppy sea. It did not however mar the spirits of the participants.

Leave on Argostoli was only allowed up to 18:00. There was nothing much to do ashore, and it took the cutter half an hour to get there. There was a market ashore for anything and everything. Bits of old rope and canvas were swapped for packets of figs and boxes of Turkish Delight.

It was the night of the destroyers' regatta that a terrible storm was unleashed. With the shortened period for leave, there was no possibility of the cutter being called out after 20:00, so at 21:00 I turned in. The cutter was of course tied up to the boom on the port side, and was made fast with three ropes. There was a half-inch lazy painter, plus an inch-and-a-half working painter, plus a boat rope which was probably a four inches. The boat rope acted like a spring. It was attached to a bollard on the ships forecastle, fed through a huge block attached to the boom and then the end, which is a wire strop, goes through a ring on the cutter's bow and slipped round a cleat. Now, this is the traditional way for making fast, and the weight of the ropes between the ship and the block hangs down, thereby counteracting the movement of the waves. In other words, the pitch and toss of the boat would jar both boat and boom if it wasn't for the boat rope

At about midnight I was deep in the Land of Nod, when I was awakened by the vigorous shaking of my hammock. I was about to let fly with a string of oaths when I recognised the Bosun's Mate.

"Get to your boat at the double," he yelled.

I hastily donned my clothes and oilskins and made my way to the upper deck.

Already there was Nobby, Allan and Stokes. They told me that because of the storm we had to get the boat inboard. However, what did surprise me was that they hadn't got into the boat. Usually the stern sheetsman gets in first and pulls the boat under the boom, so that Nobby the coxswain, Dennis the stoker and myself as bowman could also get in, in that order. Looking over the ship's side, we could see the waters were boiling. The boat rope, instead of acting as a spring, was taut all the way from the inboard bollard to the block and to the cutter's forecastle cleat. Alan went down the rope ladder first, but try as he might, he couldn't pull her one inch. Normally this would have been a simple job, but conditions were certainly not normal. I then decided to go down the other side of the ladder, and together we would both pull her towards us, but again our efforts were wasted. The wind and rain lashed our faces, and the mountainous seas soaked our legs.

Over the noise of the storm I yelled to Allan, "I'll go down the boat rope". Whether Allan heard me or not I don't know, but with both legs around the boat rope and hanging on for dear life I made my way down until both my feet were crossed on the cutter's forecastle. Only now did I experience trouble. How on earth could I get my body, or indeed my hands, onto something solid by which I could haul myself aboard? All the time this was happening, her bows would dig deep into the raging sea, taking me with it. When she rose, her stem hit me up the backside and as the waves sent her backward so the boat rope went taut, shuddered and bit into my hands. This scenario was repeated over and over again, while above me all I could see was the blue arc light and a myriad of faces, including the Commander's, all yelling at me. I know I swore at them, though I know not what I said. My mind could only think of my beloved Anne and my parents, all safely tucked up in bed and not one of them knowing the drama that I was involved in. My body was being shaken like a dog shakes a rat. In and out of the water I went; my hands were sore and burning, my back hurt and with every wave so I was being weakened, and then, amidst all this, my grip finally went. My hands left the boat rope, but my crossed legs were jammed on the cutter. My body's upper half was now bent against the cutters' stem, my head was banged against it, and then upside down it was immersed in the turbulent waters. Alternately I was being knocked dizzy, only for the cold water to arouse me from a state of semi-consciousness, and then one of those miracles happened. I was going under for the umpteenth time when my left hand found a piece of rope hanging over the cutter's bow. I didn't know it then, but the lazy painter had broken. I pulled with what little strength I had left and managed to get aboard. I was gasping for a rest, but I had to deny myself this luxury. I went aft and started the engine, and then took the wheel and put her full ahead so that once she was under the boom, the rest of the crew could drop in.

To get the boat inboard necessitated our preparing the slings for hoisting, then the lads on the ship would let out the boat rope until we were under the crane which would hoist us inboard, but what happened was, being first into the boat I was doing Allan's job, and he stayed in the bows doing mine, but then for some mysterious reason Alan cast off the painter and the boat rope. The umbilical cord had been broken; we were now on our own and at the mercy of the elements. There was no time for recriminations.

"Put your life jackets on," yelled Nobby.

But before we had a chance to comply, a wave picked us up and slammed the cutter against the ship's side splitting our gunwale from stem to stern. Nobby tried to get us away from the ship, but each time we were knocked back. Eventually we reached the ship's bow and now had to face the storm in all its fury without the danger of the ships close proximity. To get back to the ship would necessitate a 360 degree turn, and that meant we would be broadside on twice. It was not a happy thought.

"Hang on," yelled Nobby, "I'm turning."

The seas lifted us up, they knocked us down, they broke over the top of us, they knocked us off course and for good measure they spilled their contents inboard.

All the time the ship had us in the beam of a blue search light, observing, watching but powerless to do anything. They saw our bows digging into huge black waves, they saw the boat sliding backwards into the troughs, and they saw us perched precariously on the crest of a wave and then momentarily disappear.

We made the second turn and headed for the boom. It was vital to get the boat rope reattached. It took us over half an hour and even then all we could manage was to get a rope through the wire strop and back to the cleat. With slings in place and attached to the crane we ascended out of that terrifying sea. I say terrifying, but at the time you were too busy to be afraid.

It was only later when I thought about it, I came to the conclusion, "What a bloody fool I am. Never again would I risk my life for a boat."

When I climbed out of the boat, the Commander walked over to me and said very quietly, "Good work."

It was very decent of him, and he didn't have to do it, but I think a good stiff tot of rum would have been more acceptable because I was shivering with cold and exhaustion.

The crew of the Admiral's barge which was tied up to the stern boom, and therefore in the lee of the ship refused to bring her inboard, but after our little episode they were given no alternative but to obey orders.

The following morning I went to the upper deck. The sky was blue, and the sea was calm and placid.

Looking down into the scene of last night's adventure I said aloud, "You bloody hypocrite."

The regatta continued and the cutter was used as the start boat. With loudspeakers and megaphones, we lined up the race participants and started them off.

The boats coming from the cruisers had been training for months and the odds on favourites were the crews from the *Liverpool* and *Mauritius*. To add spice to the rivalry between the two boats was the fact the Admiral of the Fleet, Sir Algeron Willis, flew his flag on *HMS Liverpool*, while Rear Admiral Kinaham, commanding the 15th Cruiser Squadron, flew his flag on *Mauritius*.

Two whalers from each ship entered the race, and following on behind were launches and cutters, filled to capacity with the occupants singing, yelling and screaming support. They blew bugles and swung rattles, they banged drums and tin buckets in a deafening crescendo of noise. This was indeed an all-male show and there was no doubt that the participants and the onlookers were all having a wonderful time. There was however one boat which stood out above all others, and that was the whaler crewed by the maintop division from *HMS Mauritius*. The superb stroke was none other than Dudley Light. Pre-war sailors who had experienced other regattas all extolled the ability of Dudley and his crew. To give you an idea of their superiority, they had as part of their training practised the possibility of breaking an oar, and how they would cope with it. At the beginning of the race, Dudley's crew did in fact break an oar, and as a result were over a length down. They immediately brought into use the spare oar, and proceeded to give the onlookers an exhibition of rowing as you were ever likely to see. The sweeps went through the water cleanly and smoothly. The boat looked as though it were gliding as it made up the distance between them and the boats ahead, and in a manner which looked effortless, they went into the lead and won the race by more than a length. No one could begrudge them such a remarkable victory.

It was the same day that the cutter's crew fell out with Nobby the coxswain. Following the previous day's atrocious weather, we all wore our oilskins, but underneath we had on our uniforms, except Nobby for he wore a boiler suit. We warned him that if we took off the wet gear he would be the odd man out, and the rules decree that all the crew must have the same attire. Nobby ignored our advice, and as the day got warmer we naturally wanted to remove our oilskins, but Nobby was adamant for the reason already stated. We then picked up the Navigating Officer who, of course, was unaware of the problem existing between crew and coxswain.

One of us, I know not whom, said in a light-hearted manner to the Navigator, "Is it alright if we remove our oilskins, Sir?"

In the heat of the day, he probably thought we were mad to be so attired; anyway, he immediately responded to our enquiry by saying, "Of course."

Nobby was fuming. He stood at the wheel biting his lip and looking at his mutinous crew with venom. We all carried sickly grins but we knew that as soon as our passenger had disembarked Nobby would let loose, and sure enough he did.

"You won't get away with this," he threatened. "I'll have you all on the quarterdeck."

When his tirade finished, Stokes said, "I too am a Leading Seaman and you have no authority in the engine room."

The ground had been effectively cut below his feet, and nothing more was said on the subject.

At 12:30 we were relieved by the other watch and were able to watch the races from the ship. A tote had been fixed up, and soon it was doing a thriving trade. The betting lads however were not very astute for they merely placed money on a boat to win, whereas the Commander Engineer backed *Mauritius* in every race for a place. In view of the fact that *Mauritius* had to be in one of the first three places, the Commander made himself a small fortune.

Dudley's whaler was in another race that day which they also won quite handsomely and when they came alongside, the

Royal Marine Band played the Eton Boating Song. It is, of course, the custom for the stroke to pitch the coxswain over the side. The coxswain of the Officer's boat happened to be the son of Admiral Mansfield, and by coincidence as he rose to the surface from his immersion it was to find that someone had ditched some gash over the side, comprised of bits of potato, cabbage, tealeaves and all the other sickly components you find in a gash bucket. With vegetables sticking out of his ears and matted into his hair, he seemed somewhat displeased.

When the regatta finally came to an end everyone was in good spirits, though most of us were hoarse from cheering. We in the *Mauritius* won it with 215 points, *Liverpool* came second with 200, and *Ocean* third with 196. The boats from *Mauritius* entered seventeen races. We won seven and had seven seconds, two thirds and one fourth. Now we knew why the Commander Engineer was a rich man.

The first prize was a shield, on which a carved cockerel had been mounted and brightly painted. Sir Algernon Willis, on presenting the shield to the *Mauritius,* said, "Today I have seen a boat crew race twice. In all my years in the Royal Navy, I have never seen a boat raced as fast and as well. I congratulate them."

It is hardly necessary for me to add that they were the maintop division crew from *HMS Mauritius.*

That night, all the winning crews were invited to the wardroom, where they were treated to all the drinks they could hold, after which all the boats were called away and a mass exodus from the wardroom headed in the direction of the gangways and the powerboats. Spread over the various boats were the Royal Marine Band and all the recent well-oiled occupants of the wardroom. The shipwright had made a large cut out model of a cockerel and mounted it on the bows of the cutter.

When all the boats were full, the Buffer yelled out, "Alright lads show the cock to the fleet." Suddenly the air was filled with the merriment of singing and yelling. We were not just showing the cock, we were showing off. The *Liverpool* was our first target. With the Admiral of the Fleet aboard. *Mauritius* had blue searchlights trained on us, and the band struck up 'Cock of the North'. The *Liverpool* had not been idle and had obviously expected something of this nature to the extent that as we drew near hosepipes were exposed to view and pointed in our direction, but someone on *Liverpool* forgot to put the power on, so amidst much good natured cheering and jeering we went on our way. The next target was the *Ocean*, but she had already been alerted by the noise and had opened up the spud locker and armed her crew accordingly. With potatoes flying all over the place, we sped out of range. When every ship in the fleet had been visited, we returned with our passengers a little more sober than when we started out.

The cutter's crew were inclined to be a little mischievous at times, and even Nobby would sometimes join in. One day coming back from shore, Allan had joined me up forward, leaving Stokes and Nobby aft. Then Stokes took over the wheel and Nobby came forward, brandishing the boat hook. Allan and I got on the forecastle to avoid this whirling dervish, and then when he got near we rushed him, took away the boat hook, trussed him up hand and foot with rope and jammed him under one of the benches. Nobby was yelling and cussing and threatening while we gave him a running commentary as to how near the ship we were, which of course we made out to be nearer than it actually was. Nobby's face was purple as he imagined the indignity of being seen by the Officer of the Watch to be not in control of his boat. He did extricate himself in time, but he wouldn't speak to us for a week.

Every evening, the water in the bay turned rough and became most unpleasant. It was one such night that we went inshore to pick up the Commander Engineer. The further we got from land the rougher it became, with seawater pouring over the bows and into the boat. Our clothes were already wet, having changed them twice that day, so we all had a cavalier attitude to this further soaking. The water in the boat was above the boards, but the crew just sat there with the water over their shoes, as though this were an everyday occurrence. We could see that the Commander was getting edgy. He couldn't understand why we were so complacent, and yet there was on his part a reluctance to express his fears. He kept looking over each side of the boat and his knuckles stood out white as he clutched the gunwale.

Eventually he spoke. "Coxswain," he said, "do you think we should go back?"

"No," said Nobby casually. "It's okay, Sir."

The Commander started to fidget and then said, "Coxswain, don't you think we should start baling the water out?"

Nobby looked at the water lapping over the Commander's polished shoes. "Don't worry, Sir. We'll do it when we get alongside."

This did not satisfy the Commander, and grabbing a bucket, he started to furiously bale out while with complete unconcern we watched him.

"Coxswain," he piped up again, "if I get aboard, I'm going to have you hoisted out of the water."

But when we got back to the ship, the Officer of the Watch sent us to look for an overdue missing whaler. Out of the whole of the fleet there were only two boats active on the water. We were one of them and both of us were looking for the whaler. The other boat found it upside down and floating just below the surface. The mast and the sails had been carried away, but there was no sign of the crew. We did find a drifting lifebelt, but that was all.

As the days passed the fleet slowly dispersed in ones and twos to carry out their duties the length and breadth of the Mediterranean. With a couple of other vessels we were left, and the reason for that was that they wanted minesweepers to be brought in to sweep the Corfu Channel and we were to be there to protect them.

There was in Rome a Mine Sweeping Control Board who monitored the clearing of mines over the entire Mediterranean. The matter had been referred to them, but the only minesweepers in the Med were British, and the Albanians objected to them being used. They preferred minesweepers from any other nation than Britain. This was of course out of the question, so while they argued among themselves in Rome, we stayed in Cephalonia. The days passed slowly and the lads were becoming restless. There was very little to do ashore, and even then leave was short. After the regatta the only excitement we had was when the hospital ship *Maine* went aground on a sandbank just outside the entrance to the bay. A destroyer tried all ways to tow her off, but without success. The following day we thought we would try, so hawsers and wire ropes were all laid out ready and, with steam up, we exited the bay, but at that precise moment a favourable wind and tide, with some help from the destroyer, brought her into deeper water. Apart from a few buckled plates, she was seaworthy; nevertheless, she was sent back to Malta to have her hull looked at in dry dock. We went back into the bay.

At long last, the powers that be came to a decision. It was of course the usual compromise. Albania agreed that British minesweepers could carry out the task, but insisted that Naval Officers of other countries should accompany the force. How childishly tedious people can be when ships are in danger and lives have already been lost. On the 11th of November, we finally weighed anchor and headed for the Corfu Channel. The following day we provided cover for the minesweepers while they carried on with the sweep. We were of course closed up at action stations, and this lasted from 13:15 on the 12th of November until 19:00 on the 13th of November. The minesweepers came across twenty-two mines. Twenty they exploded, and the remaining two were taken to the depot ship *Ranpura,* which was tied up in Corfu. It was vital that we should know where those mines came from. One of our motorboats had followed the minesweepers, with the object of retrieving the two mines. Aboard she carried a warrant gunner, a somewhat older man than the rest of us. It was he who courageously dived overboard and tied ropes to the mines so that they could be towed back to Corfu.

Considering nothing was known about the type of mine that had been laid, he was a very brave man.

Chapter 32

Twenty-First Birthday

With our task completed, we headed back to Malta. The crew were looking forward to a run ashore, and those men who had not lost money at Tombola, the tote or the canteen had a nice little sum with which to go on the spree. One did not have to be a prophet to know that for the next few evenings there would be a number of riotous shore leaves.

One of our Chiefs was a mean and nasty individual, and many a sailor has cast doubts upon his parentage. Discipline is a necessary requirement aboard a ship and especially is that so regarding a man of war. The men accepted it; they could live with it and even respect it. There are, however, some people in positions of authority who do not know how to apply discipline, and this Chief was one of those. The men had no respect for him, and certainly no liking. One night, one of the lads came aboard seven sheets to the wind. Two Marines were detailed to escort him forward to the capstan flat. This was the customary place for drunken seamen to spend the night, and if they became violent then they were put into a straitjacket.

It was while our drunken sailor was being escorted that, as they neared the cabin of the unpopular Chief, they saw him standing in the doorway, dressed in a shirt and underpants and well liquored up.

"Hold that man while I sock 'im," he yelled to the Marines, and before they could do anything the Chief's fist sank into the sailor's stomach.

The blow must have had a very sobering effect, because the two Marines let go of his arms and the sailor then waded into the Chief. The Chief took a battering, and it was only after he lay prostrate that the Marines intervened and then took both parties back to the quarterdeck. Within twenty-four hours, the Chief was reduced to a Petty Officer and was drafted off the ship the same day. No charges were brought against the sailor.

It was while we were in Malta that notices had reached the ship that my particular demobilisation group would be released between the 25th of November 1946 and the 30th of March 1947. I was elated at this news and thought that I would not be going on any more trips, but would be sent home, maybe even in time for Christmas. Draft chits for twenty lads in my group arrived, but my name was not among them. The *Ranpura* was going back to Blighty in a few days and these lads would be going with her, but I was optimistic that there was still time for me also to join her. Four days later, I saw the *Ranpura* sail out of Grand Harbour without me. I felt depressed, or as a sailor would say 'two blocks', but there was the overland route. They called it 'MEDLOC', though I never did discover what it stood for. There was a MEDLOC vessel called the *City of Tunis*. She would take you to Toulon in France, then you went by train to Calais and subsequently the ferry to Dover. In all, it would take five days, and I'd beat the old *Ranpura* home. Imagine – in a week's time I could be home, and be with Anne and my family. The thought just filled me with excitement, I was riding on a cloud but I had made no provision for these events not taking place. I had not allowed for the Navy's unpredictable ways, so when the *City of Tunis* also left without me, I wallowed in a pit of despair and frustration. This black mood manifested itself in many ways, but whatever way you viewed it, it still unreasonably came back to the conclusion that the Royal Navy had a vendetta against me. In this unbalanced state of mind, I viewed that within Kings Rules and Regulations, I was going to make a nuisance of myself. I would endeavour to avoid any form of muster or parade. I would escape duties and do as little as possible. The ship had a labyrinth of cubbyholes where a man could sleep all day without being found. One such caboose was just aft of the bridge, and below the signal deck on the port side. Inside were lifebelts, lifebuoys, lengths of rope and canvas covers for the sailing dinghies. I pulled all the gear toward the entrance and climbed over behind it. In some twisted way, this helped me to come to grips with my disappointment.

Three days after the *Ranpura* sailed, I celebrated my twenty-first birthday. As soon as 'Up Spirits' was piped, I was down among my fellow shipmates. This was a time to call in favours I had done them, or favours they expected from me in the future. As soon as they had their tot in hand, I was offered sippers or gulpers depending on the size of the favour. A tot of rum is unofficially split into lighters, sippers, gulpers or a grounder. With a 'lighter' you are merely allowed to touch the golden liquid with your lips. A 'sipper' is just a sip, like one might have of the communion wine. A 'gulper' is literally a gulp, such as the Padre gets when he offers the wine, and a 'grounder' is when you get the whole lot, and to earn that you must have done one hell of a favour. I was granted a generous mixture of sippers and gulpers. The end result meant that I could not perform my duties in the afternoon. The duty Petty Officers were most obliging by turning a blind eye. As for me – well, who in their right mind would want to be on that old rust bucket *Ranpura*? Not me.

I was not watch ashore. Nevertheless, one of the lads did a sub for me, so at 15:30 I was dressed in my number ones and standing in the ranks of the liberty men. I suddenly felt very downcast – where was I going, and what was I going to do? My usual shore-going shipmates would all be on duty, and aboard the ship I was on my own.

I ambled across town and caught the ferry to Sliema. Why I don't know, and nor did I know what I was going to do there. I saw a building with the windows open and from which I could hear music coming from the first floor. Fascinated, I watched in silence, and then occasionally I caught sight of a matelot. This, I decided, was the place for me. I climbed up a wide staircase devoid of carpet and went in the direction of the music. I pushed open the door and found myself in a fairly large room, the walls of which were painted blue. The lighting was dull, and the couples on the dance floor were locked in tight embraces, moving slowly and dreamily round the floor. I ordered a beer, and as my eyes slowly became accustomed to the light so I could see the occupants more clearly. The Royal Navy was well represented – in fact, the only men there were all matelots and then the women, as I looked, so it slowly dawned on me, they were all bloody prostitutes. Their jet black hair shone in the dim light, and their clothing was of bright coloured blouses with deep cleavages, short black skirts and high heels. Their suntanned skin looked swarthy, and those who were sitting the dance out with a potential client, wrapped their long limbs around their partners' legs in a provocative and suggestive manner.

I was absorbed in what was happening, but I hadn't realised that my face was portraying my innermost feelings. I was decidedly two blocks. I noticed another sailor come through the door and come up to my table.

"What's the matter Lofty?" he said. "You look bloody cheesed off."

"I am," I replied. "Today's my twenty first birthday."

"What?" he shouted. "Waiter, bring on the drinks, because tonight we celebrate."

His cheerful disposition snapped me out of the doldrums, and so bottles of Blues began to appear again and again and again. I don't know the lad's name – he may have told me, but if he did the events of the evening would surely remove from my brain anything to do with retaining knowledge. I do know he was off the *Ocean*, and that is about all I do know. I never saw him again, and even if I did I wouldn't recognise him – but to continue the story. The room appeared to become hazy and then the walls started moving in and out, so we decided it was time to move on. It was now dark, but with our arms round each other's shoulders, we meandered down the narrow streets toward the waterfront. Some neon lights drew our attention, so we headed in that direction, only taking a zigzagged course. On closer inspection, the lights said 'Empire Cabaret' and the sound of more music tickled our ears. We pushed our way through the swinging doors and then blinked with the bright lights which confronted us. This place was entirely different. Tables ran down either side of the hall, and at the far end a small orchestra played well-known wartime melodies.

There were plenty of young lady hostesses whose job it was to keep you drinking, but they were a nice bunch of girls, not like some you would see down The Gut. One young lady was from Australia and had fallen in love with an English sailor. When his ship left Australia to return home, she followed him and they met at every port of call. She had a temporary job in the Empire Cabaret and sitting alongside her was her young sailor.

As the evening progressed then so did the noise and then I saw some lads off the *Mauritius*, and they, knowing it was my birthday, lashed me up with more of the Blues. Never, never, never will you meet in a bar anybody more generous than a sailor, and the lads were most generous to me.

There was a blonde singer attired in a long white dress. I can recall being on stage with her and singing a duet. I can remember being on the dance floor by myself and dancing some unheard of jig, and at the same time singing a variety of sea shanties. I can remember thinking, what the hell am I doing here? I can remember thinking my life long pal from the *Ocean* was looking a bit cross-eyed and bow-legged, and I can remember the Red Caps coming in and chucking us out.

We sat on the kerb, struggling to think what next we were going to do.

"The ferry has closed," I said. "The last one went ages ago."

"Lofty," he said, "I don't give a bugger. I'm sleeping here." He lay down in the road so I had to pull him back to the pavement.

"The last bus has gone too," I said.

"Sod the last bus," he replied.

"We're going to walk to Valetta," I told him.

"Walk? Walk? I'm not bloody walking."

I don't know how far it is to walk to Valetta from Sliema, but I managed to get my companion to his feet and, with arms around each other's shoulders, we staggered off very slowly into the night and singing very quietly in somewhat slurred voices.

Constantly I had to keep him awake and half carry him, and though we thought we were being quiet, the deserted streets seemed to magnify every noise. We saw an empty, ramshackle old bus standing outside a house.

"Lofty," said my mate. "I'm going to drive that thing back to Valetta."

"You're bloody not," I responded.

"Well, if I don't drive it, we can sleep in it."

Like a slow moving film, thoughts of my demob and the prejudicial effect such actions would have on it passed through my mind.

I pulled him away and said firmly, "We're walking."

As we approached the Florencia Hotel, a dhjasa cab drew abreast.

"You like a ride, Johnny?" said the driver.

"How much?" we asked.

"Six shillings," he replied.

"What?" we echoed in unison. "You can stuff that."

Whether he did or not we'll never know, but he soon departed.

It was well past 01:00 when we finally reached the locked doors of the Vernon Club. We both of us were dead on our feet and yearned to get to bed. We knocked and knocked and swore and knocked until eventually an old boy came to the door, grumbling like hell. He finally agreed we could stay the night, but if I had thoughts of a good night's sleep, they were soon dispelled, because as soon as I shut my eyes, everything in the room started to revolve. I opened them, but no luck. I stuffed my clothes under the pillow, thinking that if the pillow were higher, it would help me to sleep. It didn't. I shut one eye and kept the other open, and that didn't help. I did go to sleep – I don't know what time or what caused sleep to come but it was probably just utter exhaustion.

The following morning, my companion of the previous night woke with a splitting headache, double vision and a mouth that was as foul as the heads on a slave ship. I had sobered up pretty well with few after-effects.

We went down to the jetty together and I thanked him for making my birthday the memorable occasion it was. We shook hands, never to meet again. I still did not know his name, nor he mine.

In the days that followed, my whole being was consumed with the desire to be demobbed. I think that this long parting from Anne had in some way clouded rational thinking. Every delay became an exaggerated obstacle intentionally put in my way by authority. I tried to counteract this by telling myself it was only a matter of days before we would be drafted and, in any case, there were others aboard in the same group as myself, but the days passed and we were still part of the crew when we sailed out of Grand Harbour.

Foolishly I adopted a devil may care attitude that bordered on the insolent. I was given a severe reprimand for being late on gun drill, but it was water off a duck's back. The following day, which was Thursday the 5th of December, I kept the morning watch on the bridge. Also on the bridge was Sub-Lieutenant Mansfield. We were on route to Trieste, and were at that time steaming along the coast of the heel of Italy. Anyone who has sailed in that area knows that the place is a mass of lights. I was rather irked that as port lookout I was expected to give a continuous dialogue of lights seen. This seemed crazy to me, so I slowly relaxed my reporting and confined it to other vessels in the area, or such things as lighthouses and buoys.

Suddenly the Subby called out, "Port lookout, there's a white light bearing red two zero. I've seen it there for twenty minutes. Why didn't you report it?"

"Don't worry, Sir," I replied in a cavalier fashion. "I've seen it for half an hour and thought it of no significance."

The episode passed, but I could see I had niggled him.

Later on in the watch, one of the lads brought me up a mug of Kye. I engaged my pal in conversation while drinking the hot chocolate and knew it was annoying our Sub-Lieutenant especially as I was not keeping a lookout.

"Port lookout," he snapped. "I will not have this skylarking on the bridge."

He was right, of course, and I was just being stroppy. I continued to sweep the horizon and caught in my binoculars a moving vessel approaching, but I could not determine what it was. I duly reported it and in reply, the Officer of the Watch asked me what sort of vessel it was. I told him I had no idea, for I had never seen one with that shape before. It did have what looked like three tall slim vertical funnels, but what on earth could it be?

The Subby then said, "It's pretty obvious to me. It is two landing craft side by side".

Although I didn't know what it was, I certainly knew it wasn't two landing craft. Dawn had broken, as also had the smug expression on our Sub-Lieutenant's face, for the unknown vessel turned out to be a tug towing a small floating dock.

On the Friday we arrived in Trieste, but what an atrocious day it was. The weather had, as we steamed north, got progressively colder and that was to be expected, but what we hadn't bargained for was just how cold it turned out to be. Snow covered everything and the decks were like ice. Had we been out in the stream we could have just dropped the anchor, but when you tie up alongside the mole as we did then, you have to handle the bow and stern lines, the springs and breast ropes. Working with wire hawsers in that type of weather is a cold, chilling and thankless task. To add to it, there is this strong wind they call a Bora. It sweeps through the mountains and valleys, and then passes through Trieste. Its strength and intensity needs to be respected. Meanwhile, the deck crew were being whipped by the spray. It felt as though one's flesh was being cut open and all you could do was to hold onto something solid. Poor old Jock didn't. He was literally lifted off his feet, carried a good five yards, and dropped on his face. He had a grazed face and a bashed in nose, but these after-effects were similar to those he suffered from a good run ashore, and these were free of charge.

Chapter 33

Cortina D'ampezzo

Trieste was a lovely city in which to have a run ashore, and between my duties, I took full advantage in order to enjoy the amenities available.

The ship would provide men to assist in making up a patrol ashore in order to help out the permanent Naval Police. The riots we experienced during our last visit were something in the past, and the only trouble we anticipated having to handle would come not from the local population, but rather from a seaman with too much liquor aboard. I was instructed to join one such patrol with three other lads, plus a Petty Officer in charge. The first thing he did was to take us to a Forces canteen where he treated us to a meal. In the canteen were a number of sailors off the ship, who kindly gave us a few cans of beer.

In retrospect, I think the PO had an ulterior motive in being as generous, because in a confidential manner he said, "If by chance I should disappear, just carry on patrolling the route I've given you and I'll catch you up."

It seemed to us that our PO knew more about the seamy side of Trieste than one would suppose, but although we had a good idea of what he was up to, the opportunity did not present itself, and our randy PO had to remain unfulfilled.

Another duty which I quite enjoyed was that of Bosun's Mate. This entailed standing by the forward gangway and logging details of anybody who came on board or left the ship. During the middle watch, it gave me a chance to sneak out to the sentries on the mole with a supply of duty free cigarettes that I had been collecting for such an occasion. The Officer of the Watch would retire to the wardroom and get his head down. As soon as the Quartermaster gave me the all clear, then I would quickly run down the gangway with two packets of cigarettes hidden under my overcoat. The object was to give them to the sentry, who in turn sold them to dealers through the night, but on this particular night I had a shock for, as I neared the sentry box, I saw a lorry from the Provost Marshal's headquarters no more than three yards from the sentry. There was no way I could blatantly leave these cartons, so I beat a hasty retreat and tried my best to conceal the guilty looking bulges in my coat.

Normally when the ship is alongside the mole, the motorboats are kept inboard, but by some quirk of fate the cutter was tied up alongside. I quickly jumped aboard and hid the cartons under the benches.

The next morning, I told one of the cutter's crew what I had done, and he promised to await an opportune moment when he would give them to the sentry. For two days no aspiring buyer came near the sentry, and that included Tickler Lil. I knew it would not be long before we sailed, so other measures became necessary. On my next run ashore, I waited until it was dark and visited the sentry box. I could hardly believe my eyes because that box was like a tobacconist's shop. It was piled high with every make of cigarette, and took up so much space there was barely room for the sentry. I took one of my cartons with the object of negotiating my own sale. I was going to say I was guilt ridden at what I was embarking on, but that would not be true, I did not feel guilty, but I did feel self-conscious and thought the whole of Trieste was a witness to my nefarious deed. In reality the citizens of Trieste were indifferent, but the children weren't. They had seen me and watched the action of concealing the carton. They knew what it was and immediately surrounded me, all yelling, "ceegarette, ceegarette." I was trying to act in a nonchalant manner and here were these little buggers telling the world.

Through my teeth I hissed at them, "Sod off, get to hell out of it." After a hundred yards or so they got the message and disappeared, leaving me to turn off the main street and into the darkened side streets. Almost immediately I was approached by a rough, greasy looking man, asking for cigarettes. I showed him what I had and he beckoned me to follow him. I felt a sense of unease about the man, but as long as it was just him and me, I was not concerned about danger. After a short while he stopped outside some huge doors which were the entrance to a row of terraced apartments. As he pushed one of the doors open and motioned me to follow, I became very suspicious, and was alert to any false move he may have made. In the split second that I had to view the interior, I saw an office with glass partitions, and sitting at a desk was a man wearing an Army great coat. I had walked into a trap and immediately backed out and sprinted up the road, with the greasy looking man following me. For some inexplicable reason I stopped and let him catch me up. Neither of us spoke the other's language, and yet somehow I sensed I could trust him. I returned to the open door, entered and found to my relief that the man in the Army great coat was in fact a civilian. We haggled over the price, but eventually he paid me out. The process was very slow and all the time I had this feeling that at any moment I would have the hand of authority on my shoulder. With a sense of relief I returned to the sentry box and picked up the other carton. This time I brazenly put it under my arm, and found that it drew less attention than my previous efforts.

On the mole was a large hall which the ship hired in order to hold a dance to which the locals were being invited. I went along more out of curiosity than anything else. The sailors had been given tickets which entitled the holder to two free meals. If you went up on your own you only got one meal, so rather than waste it, I suggested to a young lady that she may like to participate in this meal.

To my surprise she spoke perfect English and said, "If you give the ticket to me, I will get them."

I duly obliged and then watched her go to the head of the queue, flash her eyes at the sailor being served and returned with the food. As I watched her performance, I could not help thinking what a bunch of suckers the British are. I have no doubt all the Italians present had laughed and fraternised with the German Army of occupation, and would be prepared to do so with any power that occupied their land. I could not escape from my inbred feelings that they lacked courage, they lacked the courage of their convictions, they bent with the wind and, like a barnacle, they clung to the winning side. The young Italian girl returned with the food which we ate together.

There was no dialogue and when she finished, she just said, "Thank you. I must go and find my friend."

As she turned to depart I merely said, "I hope you find her."

I was relieved she had gone, but it left me with a feeling that I too had debased myself.

On the Sunday night, I was given the duty of Jetty Sentry from 22:00 to midnight. I suddenly realised the importance attached to my task. I was now in charge of the tobacconist shop, and I would meet and trade with the local dealers. It was time to restock the kiosk, so with arms full of duty frees, I went on watch. The snow lay thick on the ground and the icy wind came down the hills with a venom. We had a brazier which we kept alight all the time and on which we would roast chestnuts. It helped to thaw us out, and the lads coming off shore leave always stopped for a warm, and to relate their various amorous experiences.

No dealers came that night – maybe it was too cold, maybe they were observing the Sabbath, but I did not sell any cigarettes and had to take them all inboard.

One day I was detailed to take half a dozen ordinary seamen and get them to take some old lockers ashore. The lockers were constructed of aluminium and about six feet tall, so they were very light. By coincidence a Bora was blowing which meant that if the lads were carrying a locker down the gangway they were in danger of being blown overboard. They say that power and authority goes to one's head.

Now, I do not know who 'they' are but it is true I had the power and the authority so, as a fully-fledged Able Seaman, I said to these wet behind the ears Ordinary Seamen, "Right lads. It's too dangerous to take them down the gangway, so we will do it with a bale sling strop."

I can still see those boys silently mouthing 'bale sling strop' while their eyes betrayed the fact that they didn't know what the hell a bale sling strop was. I knew – it was as easy as falling off a log, it was almost like doing up a parcel. I acquired a heaving line, put a bale sling strop on the locker, got two lads to go ashore and pull the locker toward them, while two more lads lowered it over the ship's side. Halfway down, the Bora caught the locker, lifted it up, smashed it against the ship's side and then it fell out of the strop, landed on the water and slowly sank. I couldn't believe it. Here for the first time in my seagoing life I had been given the opportunity to use a bale sling strop and I screwed it up, but not only had I screwed it up, but I had also been instrumental in giving half a dozen wet behind the ears bloody ordinary seamen something to laugh at.

I was soon hauled down to the quarterdeck with my cap off. The Officer of the Watch said I would be referred to the Commander as a defaulter, and so it came about that the very next day a much-deflated Able Seaman was marched before the Commander. He deferred punishment, as the Officer of the Watch was not available.

In the meantime, I was seconded as a cell sentry. They had no need for bale sling strops down there.

In Trieste were two large Royal Navy landing craft. Apart from the crew, the vessels also carried a number of German prisoners of war. It was their task to load the ship with all the ex-enemy bombs and ammunition that had been acquired, and then dump it somewhere in the Adriatic.

These boats were tied up to the other side of the mole. Two of her crew while on duty thought it was time to have a run ashore. The fact they were leaving their post and deserting their ship had not occurred to them. The additional bags of duty frees that adorned their persons were treated by them as being of no consequence.

Whatever Kings Rules they broke when leaving the ship, they doubled their misdemeanours on return. They came back drunk and with pockets full of liquor. They disobeyed orders and they broke open the canteen. They threatened a Petty Officer and also the skipper, and one of them allegedly tried to commit suicide. There are, of course, no cells on a Landing Craft, but there were some on the *Mauritius*, so they came to us and that is how I became cell sentry. The duty of a cell sentry tends to be boring, for the reason that the cells are located in an isolated part of the ship, in our case right up in the bow and just above the cable locker. We however were fortunate because next door to the cells was the paint locker and it is a well-known fact that it makes no difference as to whether you are an ordinary seaman or an Admiral, everybody who has ever worn a Naval uniform visits the paint locker. In fact, in some of the old boats, they say that they've had so many coats of paint it had became thicker than armour plating. The close proximity of the paint locker meant that there was a continuous stream of shipmates with whom one could discuss pleasantries. Pleasantries is not quite the correct word to use but any discerning reader will know what I mean.

Of an evening, the sentry could also slip out to the mess deck and acquire something to eat, and also mugs of char for the prisoners. The cells were about eight foot high and four foot wide. A porthole high up gave the only natural light. The bed was a wooden board hinged to the metal walls, and there was also a small wooden flap, which was the table. They were cold and miserable places in which to be incarcerated so when the coast was clear we would let them out into the capstan flat. Although the prisoners were not *Mauritius* men, they were treated as you would any other shipmate. They were never short of food, cigarettes or rum. It is doubtful if the Master at Arms knew what was happening, but on the other hand, the ability to see with Nelson's eye has long been a Naval tradition.

The next day following these duties, a notice went up offering the lads a free trip to Cortina in the Alps as guests of the army. Now volunteering for anything in the Navy is alien to a seaman's nature, and yet the thought of getting away for a week had a certain appeal to it, so I volunteered. My decision was partly influenced by the failure to repatriate me and this strong desire to do as little as possible.

I packed a steaming bag on the eve of our departure, for the reason that I kept the middle watch, and as we had to be on the mole by 08:30, it would leave me very little time to pack.

On the Friday morning, the party of aspiring winter sports seamen stood at the foot of the gangway where we were inspected by the Officer of the Watch. Snow lay a foot thick, and a keen wind lashed our faces in below freezing conditions. Three lorries came through the gates to transport us to our destination. Two of them looked alright, but the one to which I had been directed was an eight wheel articulate with a torn canvas cover. Behind the driver's cabin there was no protection at all. The Chiefs and Petty Officers had noticed this and quickly made for the better-protected vehicles, leaving us to travel in this wreck. It was so cold on the jetty that we thought anything with a semblance of cover would be an improvement. The other two lorries departed, but for some reason or other, we did not leave until half an hour later. The wind came through the front of the lorry like a wind tunnel, while we huddled together for warmth. A mile up the road, we were flagged down by the Chiefs and POs. Their lorry had broken down and they wanted a lift in ours; well, the irony of the occasion did not go by unnoticed, as we all erupted in a crescendo of cheering. They climbed aboard and all had to sit in the only available space, namely the opening behind the cabin, where they provided a very effective windshield for the rest of us.

We made a number of stops and took the opportunity to fill up with rum punches and other warm and sustaining beverages.

The snow was quite fresh, having fallen in the last twenty four hours. It did however get thicker as we started to ascend the mountain range. The higher we got the colder it got, and seemingly the hairpin bends became more acute. This was not so bad, except that there were no chains on the tyres and frequently we heard them spinning as they failed to grip the road.

On several occasions, the driver could not get round the bend in one go and had to resort to backing and accelerating. Now, one did not expect this on an articulate, but the most frightening part was when he reversed and braked; the lorry went on sliding, and then stopped with the tail board hanging over a sheer drop with us looking out with fear in our eyes. The passengers became strangely quiet, conversation ceased, but one suspected that an awful lot of praying was taking place.

By the time we arrived in Cortina, it was dusk. The lorry stopped outside the Albergo Cortina, and as we clambered out stiff and frozen, the first thing we noticed was the difference in the air. It was fresh and sweet, but stung our nostrils and made our eyes moist with tears. To avoid the pain in our noses, we were forced to breathe through the mouth.

We looked around us and were smitten by this quaint mountain village bathed in the light of a bright moon. The beauty of the place was stunning. There was so much to take in. The mountains stood out against a purple background, their snow-capped peaks glistening in a moon drenched sky. Through the pine and fir trees we saw the twinkling lights from the Hotel Savoy. We picked up our gear and trudged ankle deep in snow to the Cortina Hotel. The warmth hit our frozen cheeks as we entered, and there inside was an Army Captain offering us a welcome. The hotel had only just been refurbished and all was expensively laid out. The deep piled carpets, the ever open bar; the sheer luxury of the place had to be seen to be appreciated.

We were shown to our rooms. There were two men to each room, but as the door swung open, we were taken aback by the opulence of the furnishings. Wardrobes, bedside tables, and wash hand bowls with hot running water. There were pictures on the walls and table lamps, easy chairs and the mattresses I swear were a foot thick. The windows were double-glazed. If only the lads on the ship could see this – what a contrast, what a difference. It seemed so long ago since experiencing such civilised surroundings that one had almost forgotten they had existed.

After stowing our gear, we went downstairs and reported to the ski store. Here we were fitted out with all the necessary equipment which would allow us to benefit from the skiing tuition we were about to get the following day. We were given a khaki vertical ribbed jersey, silk trousers and a top complete with hood. We had caps with large peaks and red goggles, gloves and thick woollen stockings, mountaineering boots, skis and sticks. The novelty of having all this gear was too much to resist the temptation of getting into your room, dressing up, and preening yourself in front of the mirror.

Dinner was sharp at 20:00 and the order of the day was No. 1 uniform. As I went downstairs so the strains of beautiful music could be heard, and though I appreciated what was being played, it did not have my full attention merely because it was just one other item in a day of pleasant surprises. The dining room doors opened automatically, and there inside was a small Italian gentleman in winged collar and a tail suit. He bowed graciously and said, "Good evening Sir." This was like a dream – I mean, I am Able Seaman Geoff Shelton and who on earth would bow to me and call me 'sir'? Instinctively I looked behind me thinking that the remarks were being addressed to a high-ranking personage bringing up the rear, but no, there was no one following – this courtesy was directed to me. I felt ten feet tall. I was ushered to a table and noticed that my guide bowed his head to the other lads who had preceded me. The starched linen tablecloths almost sparkled and the cutlery that was laid out before me was three times as much as one would get aboard ship. The silver plated condiments were uniformly placed around a small cut glass vase of flowers.

The music I had heard coming down the stairs came from a small string orchestra, and as they started to play 'Sorrento', my thoughts turned to my beloved Anne, and wished she could have enjoyed this experience with me.

'Sorrento' was the most popular piece of music being played at that time in Italy, but in this beautiful setting I had never heard it played so well.

While I was absorbed with the music and my thoughts, a waitress had put before me a bowl of boiling hot soup. Conversations from the other tables could be heard.

"Just call me Baron Rothschild," said one, or "Geordie, look at that cracking looking blonde bird – we'll sit over there tomorrow," and yet another could be heard praising the management's ingenuity at placing so much cutlery against each place setting, thereby saving time for the second sitting.

Course after course came and went smoothly, silently and efficiently. We soon found out that we were not only the only occupants of the hotel, but were indeed the first since its opening after the end of the war. They had in fact opened it earlier just for our benefit. There is no doubt that if this place was a pointer to Army life – we were in the wrong service. Following dinner, we adjourned to the bar and made the most of the vast display of alcoholic beverages available.

Crawling into bed between crisp white sheets seemed all a dream; everything was out of perspective. Twenty-four hours earlier I had been lying in an old well-worn hammock, swinging above the heads of my messmates as they played cards on the table below. There were no white tablecloths on the ship, no Chief to call you 'sir' and show you to your table. There was no orchestra. I think we all fell asleep feeling a little like Cinderella at the ball, and awaiting the hour of midnight after which all would revert back, and we would find that it all was just a dream.

The following morning I awoke to a room bathed in bright sunshine. There was a knock on the door and a young lady came in with tea and biscuits. I felt like a lord, but the dream continued.

We donned our ski gear and went down for breakfast. Once again we were welcomed by a smiling gentleman.

"Good morning, Sir." The breakfast was magnificent and the service excellent. On returning to the room we found the beds had already been made, the room cleaned and even our clothes had been folded and placed in orderly fashion. There is no doubt a man could quite easily become accustomed to this life.

At 09:00 we mustered outside the ski store where we were met by a fully qualified instructor. He led us along the main street which gave me an opportunity of studying Cortina in daylight. On either side, the most noticeable features were the large eaves that protruded from the buildings. On the right hand side the structures were perched on steppes until they gave way to the slopes of huge towering mountains. On the left hand side behind the buildings the ground fell away on a fairly steep slope to a rocky mountain stream in a valley below. The cold clear waters rushed and danced over the rocks with amazing speed and meandered between banks of high snow. The terrain then rose the other side of the stream until it met a forest of huge pine and fir trees. The trees on the higher slopes slowly thinned out until they became non-existent. Above them the mountain tops capped with snow looked gaunt and forbidding. All of this majestic beauty had as a backdrop a clear blue sky.

Our instructor took us to the nursery slopes, ground with a slight incline and covered in a thick layer of virgin snow. All morning we endeavoured to get to grips with the art of skiing as we slowly went down the hill and even more slowly came back up. By the time lunch had arrived, we had all worked up a pretty big appetite and though the meal was excellent, all of us were eager to test our new-found skills on the steeper slopes.

There were no ski lifts to transport you up the mountain, it had to be done the hard way, and so we set off by foot. It took at least two hours before we reached a spot that was high enough to cope with our limited experience. By then we were hot and sweaty, but we put our skis on and started the descent. Now the excess of forty sailors with three hours of tuition and a few lunchtime bevvies swilling around their scuppers is not a pretty sight on a ski slope. I felt my own performance had improved considerably, except for one important aspect. I did not know how to stop. That is not quite true – I knew how to stop, but I could not master the art of pointing the skis together and putting them at an angle to the ground. They called the movement a 'snow plough'. My only means of stopping short of hitting a tree was to throw myself backwards and hope the deep snow would slow me down. It certainly had the desired effect, but it was most ungainly, very bad on the ankles and not to be recommended.

One day my pal and I skied off the usual run, when we soon found ourselves gathering speed and heading for the edge of something. We didn't know whether it was the edge of a sheer drop, an incline, or even something considerably more treacherous. Two yards from the edge, we still couldn't see the other side, so I thought it prudent to fall backwards. Momentarily I was airborne then this useless bundle of maritime inefficiency, dropped into deep snow with skis and sticks in all directions. Below the steep slope in which I now lay was a cold mountain stream, threading its way through a mountain ravine.

As we became more proficient, so we climbed to the higher slopes, forsaking the slight inclines for something higher and steeper. It would take us three hours to reach the point of descent, and this allowed us just one ski run in the morning and one in the afternoon. Below us, Cortina looked like a model village, while above us red cable cars went to even greater heights. Our instructors still accompanied us, and usually one led while the other brought up the rear. We would all set off in Indian file, zigzagging down the slopes in a carefree manner. The bottoms of the fir trees were badly scarred where previous exponents of the art had come to grief. My roommate nearly had a nasty accident – somehow or other he got off track and couldn't get back on. Suddenly he was confronted by a fence with horizontal, parallel bars. Like me he lacked the ability to stop, so threw himself over backwards and gaily skiied under the bottom bar, his knees and nose missing it by inches. When we reached the bottom we looked back and marvelled how in a few minutes we had come down a mountainside that had taken us three hours to climb. We had however worked up an appetite and a thirst, which the Albergo Cortina was more than capable of satisfying.

There was a high ski jump slope where we would watch the skill and bravery of men launching their bodies into space. The height and the distance were fearsome.

Apart from smoking and drinking in pleasant little taverns, there was not much to do in the evenings. I did hear that one of the hotels held a dance, but there was only one woman there. There was also an open skating rink where, for some ridiculously low price, you could hire skates and spend as long as you liked making an ass of yourself. I must confess I surpassed anything I had ever achieved in civvy street, namely staying on my feet for over twenty yards.

One evening I walked through the main street of the village. It was dark and exceedingly cold, with fresh snow falling and building up small ridges on the window frames of the shops and houses. It was very quiet, except when our feet compressed the virgin snow with a distinctive crunch. It stuck to the soles of your shoes and made you walk awkwardly so that you shuffled and kicked in an endeavour to dislodge it. I pulled my collar high and dug my hands into the pockets of my great coat. I went down a side turning and there I found a small beer bar. Pushing open the doors, I felt the heat come upon my face in waves. Not only was it pleasing to the nose, but it brought with it the smell of beer and freshly ground coffee.

Most of the drinking places in Cortina were like American bars, glitzy, bright and loud. This one was different. The tables were separated from one another by high partitions. The lights hung low over the tables, the shades being made of parchment. In one corner of the room, red crepe paper had been pinned to some trellis work. Slats shaped like crescents were the dividing lines between walls and ceiling. The slats had been varnished, and attached to them were various suits of playing cards arranged in patterns. The seating facilities hovered between covered benches and solid looking off white chairs. The place was similar to what I imagine an Austrian beer house would be.

I stayed late, enjoying the beer and the quaint atmosphere of the place.

At length I stepped out into the even colder night air. It had stopped snowing, but the thick carpet of the fresh snow in the glare of the shop windows glistened and took on a pale peach colour.

Arriving back at the hotel, I looked behind and marvelled at the beauty of nature marred only by my oversized footprints.

We were, to our regret, due to leave the hotel on the 23rd of December, but the Captain responsible for the hotel requested and was granted a twenty four hour extension to our leave. That very night, he kept the bar open until 03:00. It was the birthday of one of the lads, so the time was spent profitably in toasting his health. On the eve of our departure they laid on a Christmas dinner in our honour. The hotel was decorated in festive manner, and the meal was served by waitresses dressed in smart green uniforms. The dinner could not have been surpassed, and everyone was so kind and thoughtful. We were so overcome that words became an inadequate medium with which to fully express our appreciation to the management and staff.

The following day, we went round the shops with the object of buying some souvenirs. Woodcarving was a popular type of gift, ranging from cigarette boxes, corks and book ends. Many of them were made to work, such as mouths being opened with levers, or moving eyes and dogs standing up. One shop had some beautiful filigree displayed in the window. One piece took my eye which I thought Anne would like, but regrettably the shop was closed.

The time came to pack our bags. We had a collection between the lads that we could give to the staff ,and we all left our names in a book. Suddenly we found ourselves indulging in a last look. A last look at our rooms, a last look at the hotel itself, and the main street. It became very important to etch on our minds memories of a wonderful leave in beautiful civilised surroundings, and in an area of awe inspiring grandeur and beauty.

Instead of going back by road, we went to a nearby village and caught a train to Trieste. It was far more comfortable than our previous transport and we were once again privileged to see this wonderful scenery as the train meandered round the mountainside. We had to change trains as this was but a local one. We all were directed across the lines to a waiting room on the other platform. Here we were told that the train had been held up and would be a few hours late. There was no point in staying in the overcrowded room, so a party of us headed into the small town. I had very little money left, but at least I found a bar where I was able to purchase some vermouth and biscuits. The locals viewed us with a mixture of odd amusement, but this soon changed to looks of resentment as soldiers and sailors slowly came in and drank the landlord's supply of liquor.

Back at the station, we forced our way into the waiting room. It was already overcrowded, hot, smoky and fuggy, but the alternative was to stand outside in the freezing, rarefied atmosphere.

A number of lads were seven sheets to the wind, and there was a lot of jostling and shoving, but it was all in good humour. Every now and again a sailor passed by calling out "Mind my dog, mind my dog, come on Fido, this way." Automatically a space appeared for the master and his dog to pass, but we never did see Fido. I'd like to know where he had been drinking.

Just after midnight the train arrived, so there was a mad rush for seats. To our surprise we found that the Officers were already aboard and had arranged two Officers in each compartment, with their luggage discreetly scattered over the empty seats. None of us had any desire to stand all the way to Trieste, so we invaded the Officers' occupied compartments. They protested that this accommodation was restricted to the Officers. We however, without blushing, told them that a special carriage had been attached to the rear of the train and that other ranks were forbidden to ride in it. They must have thought us honest men, for without a protest they left the compartment. We obliged them further by putting their luggage in the corridor.

We arrived onboard *HMS Mauritius* at 04:30 on Christmas Day.

In our absence, our shipmates had put up decorations in the mess and the table had a bowl of fruit and various types of nuts in it. Each mess had been given a printed menu showing what we could expect that special day, but the phraseology used to describe the courses bore no resemblance to reality. We all eagerly awaited 'Up Spirits' at midday, but Jock had no need of it. The contents of his locker had already been transferred to his stomach, and his unsteady legs advertised the fact. The Captain, Commander and a long retinue of Officers visited the mess deck to wish us all a Merry Christmas. We all stood to attention, making sure that two of the bigger men concealed Jock by standing in front of him.

As Lieutenant Ryan expressed his greetings, so Jock poked his head between the men in front of him and offering his hand he said, "Happy Christmas, Sir, Happy Christmas. I don't bear any malice. We're all pals at Christmas. God Bless and a Merry Christmas, Sir."

Just when we thought this touching scene was over, Jock repeated it all again and again, pumping Lieutenant Ryan's hand all the time. Jock's first declaration of seasonal friendship had obviously impressed our Divisional Officer as his broad grin revealed, but the continued repetition of these sentiments removed the broad grin, only to be replaced by a look of embarrassment, and then followed a look associated with someone suddenly coming to the conclusion that a certain Scottish seaman was drunk. While he must have wondered how the aforesaid seaman had acquired the means for being in this condition, Christmas Day was not a time to find out.

It was only fitting that after such a wonderful time in Cortina I should resume my duty as cell sentry, so on the afternoon of Christmas Day, I went forward with a collection of nuts and fruit and even some of my rum. When I got to the cells, I found the prisoners slurring their speech, smoking cigars and being unable to sit on their bunks because of all the sweets and biscuits and cakes that many of the messes had contributed. They had probably consumed more liquor than anyone else on board except, of course, Jock.

Once again this little episode was a clear example of the shipmate spirit. I don't know why it should surprise me, but it does every time. The crew of the ship from which they came would have looked after them, but they knew we would be honoured to do it for them. I was going to say a shipmate is like a brother, but that is not so, it is more than that. It is a bond created by many things. It could be the weather, the enemy, the cramped living conditions, no one really knows, but the outcome is always the same – you look after each other.

The prisoners fell asleep on the deck of their cells, but toward the end of my watch they woke up, and both joined me in the capstan flat, where all three of us had a glass of liquor and a cigar each.

On Boxing Day I was taken before the Commander again regarding the loss of the wretched locker, but he deferred sentence as he wanted to send the divers down to look for it. He didn't want the dammed locker – all this charade was to be an exercise for his divers. I think the last time they went down was when they were looking for the rowlocks that were lost overboard from the *HMS Saumarez*. I wonder who lost them and whether they were put on a charge – anyway, he was going to send two divers down with six men to manage the diving gear.

On December the 27th, a boxing match had been organised at the Dance Hall on the mole. It was a challenge match between the Army and the Royal Navy, and was comprised of eight bouts. One of our boy seamen went into the ring and fought a Sergeant. The Sergeant didn't last very long. Then Paddy Slavin stepped into the ring. He had trained constantly and had a fine physique. I know from experience he had a devastating right hand, but I had until now never seen him in a bout. Heavyweights always attract attention, and this was no exception. Both were big men, but Paddy was the more muscular. The bell went, and within ten seconds the Army lad was out cold. I've never seen such a vicious punch. It was the only punch. Paddy didn't even smile as the referee counted the other man out.

There was a feeling that our stay in Trieste was coming to an end. We thought our departure would be in the early days of the new year, which was no bad thing seeing we would get a whole months' money on the 31st of December, and with that in our pockets, New Year's Eve was going to be one helluva time. Sailors are ever the optimist. We did get paid on the 31st, but we sailed after one hour into the forenoon watch. The oaths and curses that accompanied this would fill another chapter.

That very same morning, I was once again called before the Commander, for the divers had recovered the locker.

"Off caps," ordered the Jaunty. "Two paces forward. MARCH."

This brought me before the Commander at his green baize topped table. "Shelton, PJX 629972, dropped a locker over the side on the 18th of December last, and which has since been found by the divers, Sir," read the Jaunty from his defaulters' book.

The Commander looked at me for a second and asked how the locker happened to fall over the side. I told him the facts and my desire to show the younger seamen how the bale sling strop could be of assistance.

He then said, "Do you wish to became a Leading Seaman?"
"No, Sir," I replied.

He raised his eyebrows and snapped half in anger. "Why not?"

"Well Sir, I hope soon to be demobbed."

He then went on. "Do you know what you have cost me?"

Then, before I had a chance to reply, he carried on, "You've cost me six hands working three hours apiece in the forenoon, that's eighteen hours' work you've cost me, and by damn you are going to pay for it. Unfortunately this is a matter of carelessness, and on that charge, the maximum I can give you is three days number sixteens."

The Jaunty then said, "On cap, about turn, double march."

The punishment was light, entailing two hours of additional work each day for three days, but I was incensed at what I considered to be the injustice of it. If I had allowed those lads to take the locker down the gangway, the Bora would have picked them all up and deposited them either on the jetty or in the drink. I prided myself on my knowledge of knots and splices, and even though I had correctly tied the bale sling strop, and it was the appropriate knot to use I had not foreseen the effects that a Bora could have when smashing a locker against the ship's side.

I resolved I would not on a point of principle respond to this punishment. On the first night when I should have done two hours' work, I was duty watch, so that was out. On the second day the time to report for punishment coincided with the times one visits the sick bay. I visited the sick bay for a non-existent cold. On the third night, we arrived in Malta in the dogwatches. Everyone had to turn out for entering harbour, so again I avoided doing any duties over and above my normal ones. As far as I was concerned, honour had been satisfied.

I had for a long time cherished the thought that one day I would take Anne as my wife. My letters did not convey my thoughts in that direction, for the reason that I felt any proposal should be undertaken when we were together. It is true to say that a refusal had never entered my mind. This was not due to over confidence on my part, but merely because my heart was so full of love for her that I could not envisage a life without her. Without Anne there was no future, there was no hope, and there would be no life. No one could doubt the depth of my feelings. I really had it bad.

It was logical for my next step to be the purchase of a ring in anticipation of this momentous occasion, and if I acquired it in Malta it would be free of purchase tax. At the first opportunity, I went ashore and paid a call on a jewellers shop in Main Street Valetta. I was shown a variety of rings but the one that appealed to me and which I hoped would appeal to my intended was a five stone diamond ring set in an old fashioned Italian rose setting.

I was delighted with my purchase and was conscious of the little yellow box holding the ring lying in the depth of my overcoat pocket. I kept away from The Gut and all other places, thinking I was carrying jewels beyond price upon my person, and was therefore open to attack by any cutthroat who happened to be around. I booked a room in the NAAFI and when I went to bed I put, for security's sake, the ring on my little finger. I could not sleep, thinking and pondering where and when the proposal would take place. In my mind's eye I could picture her beautiful face, and this ring would be a sign, a symbol of what she meant to me. It would link us together in a bond of love and affection. With my head stuffed with romantic notions, I fell asleep.

The following day I was sitting at the mess table, when news came that a draft had arrived on board to replace those due to go home for demob. I jumped up quickly and as each relief came into the mess deck I stopped him and enquired as to which mess they were going and who they had come to replace. When the last man came in I knew that once again I was going to be disappointed. The previous evening my spirits were high, but tonight I wallowed in a pit of misery.

The next day others joined the ship and, to my surprise, one of them was my relief. I was so elated that when the grog came round I presented it to him. My excitement was not shared by my messmates. We had all been together for some time and rubbed along pretty well, but now it seemed the family was breaking up. I must confess that selfishly I was only thinking of my own hopes and aspirations.

I spoke to some of the other lads who had reliefs on board, but no one had any idea when we would be leaving the ship. With our replacements on board, all we now needed was another boat homeward bound, one that took us to Toulon and then we would go overland to Calais. Nothing was said to us which meant we all had a fear that when next the *Mauritius* left Malta, we would still be aboard. The very idea was unthinkable. I then bought a copy of *The Malta Times* and found that the MEDLOC vessel *Citta di'Tunisa* was due in Valetta on the Thursday, so I took it upon myself to act as spokesman for the other lads and pay a call on the office of the Captain's Secretary.

"Excuse me, Sir," I said. "I am one of the men whose relief is on board. Do you know when we leave the ship?"

"I've no idea," he replied. "There has been no notification of ships due or leaving for the UK"

"What about the *Citta di'Tunisa*, which arrives on Thursday and leaves on Friday evening at 18:00?"

"I know nothing about that," said the secretary. I then showed him a copy of *The Malta Times,* whereupon he promised to set the wheels in motion.

On Wednesday morning, the Master at Arms sent for us and gave instructions that we were to undertake drafting routine. This necessitated visiting the Medical Office and other sections of the ship including the Paymaster, from whom we collected a war gratuity paid into the Post Office Saving Bank. That night I packed up all my gear and filled a steaming bag with sufficient clothes to satisfy my requirements until I reached the UK.

At 07:40 on the 9th of January 1947, I entered the launch for the last time, having already said cheerio to my shipmates. In a sense, it was sad going down the gangway. The *Mauritius* had been a good ship, a happy ship. She had provided me with adventurous experiences and allowed me to mix with some of the finest men anyone could wish for. For a fleeting moment I forgot my strong desire to go home, and felt a degree of regret, but it didn't last long because something stronger was pulling me.

Chapter 34

Homeward Bound

The launch deposited us all at Bakery Wharf. From there lorries took us to HMS Euroclydon, the shore-based Naval barracks.

The parade ground was quite small and was flanked on two sides by the living quarters. The messes were also small, with merely one window and a door facing the square. A table and benches stood in the middle of each mess, while overhead, hammock bars spanned the length of the distempered room. Had we not been going home then these premises could have been a most depressing place to stay.

One of our draft was also a late member of the cutter's crew, and he had brought with him some oilskin clothing which he should have returned to the store. He freely admitted he had no intention of doing that, hence his overloaded kit bag. The *Mauritius,* however, was aware at what had taken place so they sent a signal which said in essence, "Return the gear, or we'll stop your draft." The gear was duly returned.

That very same night, our names headed a list of those going on draft the following morning. Once again we went through the drafting routine, but this time it included changing our money into sterling a most enjoyable feeling.

We anticipated leaving in good time to join the MEDLOC vessel, but she had a breakdown, so very frustratingly we were kept for another night.

Saturday morning came round, and with kit bags and hammocks, we were transported from Euroclydon to an embarkation spot in the Grand Harbour. We were then split into different parties. Our gear was loaded onto a barge and then transferred to a lighter. When this was full, our lines were cast off and we headed across the busy harbour. We shook the soil of Malta from our shoes for the very last time.

The *Citta di'Tunisa* turned out to be a passenger ship that had been converted to a troop ship. She was very smart and clean, having recently been painted. She was somewhat overcrowded, having embarked a large number of soldiers and sailors from the Eastern Mediterranean.

We should have slipped our moorings at midday, but more technical problems delayed us until 18:00. At last we got away, but we had to pass *HMS Mauritius*, and all those lads who had served on her lined the upper deck and cheered until their voices were hoarse. It was dark so you could not identify individuals; nevertheless, we made so much noise it wasn't long before we saw portholes opening with faces peering out, wondering what the hell was going on. Never has such a party of sailors left harbour in such an undignified manner.

Travelling by troop ship was to be a novel experience – there would be no duties, there would be nothing to do except sit, sleep and laze. How foolish one's imagination can be. Being sailors, we were instructed to take over all watches on board. We had to take over all lookout positions, all fire picket duties, and in fact all duties – and what did the soldiers and the airmen do? – why, they sat and slept and lazed.

We had an old sailor in the mess who was so steeped in the Navy it was as though he had been brainwashed. Whenever he spoke, his sentences contained naval slang. He would never ask anyone to pass the salt, it was always, "Lot's wife." If he wanted the butter, it was, "Pass the slide," or "Where's the bubble and squeak?" was where is the soup. There is no doubt that Naval slang is a very colourful and expressive way of making a comment. The Cockney language is good, but I do not believe it is in the same league as Naval slang. To call a stoker a 'clinkerknocker' has such a wonderful descriptive sound to it. It just rolls off the tongue, but nevertheless contains a certain logic that attentive landlubbers can understand.

Our journey took us through the Straits of Messina, and then we passed Elba and Sardinia, arriving in Toulon late on the Monday night. We couldn't get alongside the wall until

Tuesday, but there awaiting our arrival was a Petty Officer from the Transit Camp we were going to. For some unknown reason my name was in the first twelve to disembark, and as we did so the Petty Officer approached us.

"Now lads," he said, "if you give me a hand to clear some of this cargo, I will see that you are free of all duties for the rest of the time you are in the camp."

What a very thoughtful PO he was. This was an opportunity too good to be missed, but had we learnt nothing after all this time. Did not the unwritten word say 'volunteer for nothing'? This was different. Here was a man we could trust. This was a good bargain in any ones book. What blind, blithering, blasted idiots we were. It was only when we arrived in the camp that we found out that there were no duties anyway.

Being in ignorance of this confidence trick, we set to removing iron beds and blankets from the ship's hold and stacking them on lorries. At midday our Petty Officer took us to a first class dining hall for lunch. Apart from our holiday in Cortina, we were not used to this service. Sailors become very suspicious when they are treated well.

After lunch we clambered aboard the lorries which took us through the streets of Toulon and in the direction of Hyeres. I could not see much of the countryside from my position in the lorry, but from what little I could see I formed the opinion that it was a flat and dusty terrain.

The lorries swung through the gates of the Transit Camp. Buildings constructed of brick and wood stretched as far as the eye could see. There were also large Nissan huts, and all were joined together by a maze of concrete roads.

The lorry dropped us off at a small hut and then we found that our PO and the PO in the hut constituted the entire Naval personnel in the camp. They looked after the drafts and it was they who distributed cards to each of us entitling us to breakfast, lunch, tiffin, suppers, sweets, cigarettes and beer. The fact that these cards contained the word tiffin, an Army term, suggested that the camp was militarily orientated.

We were sent to a large Nissan hut that looked more like an aircraft hangar. Double-tiered iron beds went down either side, but as we were the last of the shipment to arrive, we had no choice but to take what beds had been left.

Three or four bare electric light bulbs were suspended from the ceiling, and these in turn were festooned with cobwebs.

Having acquired a bed, I then asked the other occupants about duties around the base. I was not looking for work, but thought it would be nice to know what we had avoided as a result of the labour we had invested at the dockside. When we found out that there were no duties, and that we should have known better than to be a sucker for the yarn the PO pitched to us, then it became necessary to be rather personal about his parentage.

Washing facilities were very primitive, being carried out in small aluminium bowls in the open air. Being January, it was freezing cold with bitter winds. Even the puddles on the site were frozen over.

The German prisoners of war were taken care of, for they had an ample supply of hot water, which they would bring round each morning and swop for a few cigarettes.

The camp did boast a very big and exceedingly good NAAFI, where every night an orchestra made up of prisoners of war would play for us.

The YMCA had set out in some gardens brightly coloured chairs and tables. I am sure that in good weather it would have been most pleasant to have taken advantage of this facility, but our minds were not focused on the amenities being offered, but rather on the lack of news regarding our departure. Every time we approached one of the resident Petty Officers, they would hedge and beat a hasty retreat. Something was wrong – they knew what it was, and we didn't – so one day, we surrounded them and forced the truth out of them. I say force, but that is overdoing it – they were coerced by sheer weight of numbers to impart the knowledge.

"Well," said one, as he began to open up his heart, "it's like this. The Commander in Chief of the Mediterranean Fleet, Admiral Sir Algernon Willis, is paying us a visit, and we've got to have someone for him to inspect. You lot are the only ones we've got, and if we let you go there's only we two left."

With open mouthed amazement we were speechless, but he continued.

"When your ship was delayed coming into Toulon another troop ship from Port Said beat you to it and the order in the camp is, as you came in then so you go out in the same order, and that means umpteen thousand soldiers will have to go before you leave."

Apart from a few murmurs there was nothing we could do but accept the situation, but then he said, "By the way, if you have any sterling on you, change it into francs as having English money in France is a criminal offence."

Can you believe it? Can you really believe that after liberating their bloody country they had the audacity to ban the presence of English currency? Needless to say, the lads reaction was quite simply to say, "Stuff you, stuff your francs – we're keeping our English currency, and you can go to hell."

Morale was up and down like a yo-yo. You were either riding on the crest of a wave, or deep in a trough of depression. Home was almost in our grasp, but never quite there.

Tuesday, Wednesday, Thursday came and went, but without news of the homeward trek. On Friday, a great event, we were all issued with mattresses. Why? Well, the Commander in Chief was due to visit us on the Saturday, and then there was a flurry of activity because all roads and grass verges had to be cleaned up.

Saturday morning, the Admiral carried out his inspection, and great news because we were all leaving that very afternoon. The Petty Officers split us up into parties of ten and assigned to each party various duties, they had to be responsible for in the train journey across France. They did however honour the pledge they made to us on the dockside at Toulon, so maybe we were a little hasty in casting doubts on their parentage.

It was dark when we left Hyeres for the railway station in Toulon. Our kitbags and hammocks were chucked into wagons, while we with our hand luggage were checked into the carriages. There was plenty of room but certainly no comfort. There were no upholstered seats or backs, just plain wooden benches. There were no windows, having been blown out some time during the war. In their place wooden slats had been nailed up which allowed the ice-cold wind to whistle and blow down our necks. We were given a blanket for the journey, and though it was filthy and alive with fleas we were forced to wrap it round us. During the evening the train stopped at Dijon where we had a meal and also the opportunity to wash in the open, but in piping hot water. Prisoners of war served the meals. They appeared a nice, courteous bunch of men.

Half an hour into the middle watch, we arrived in Calais. Our limbs were stiff with cold and our bleary eyes advertised our lack of sleep. We were directed to a mess hut where a large plate of steaming hot porridge was put before us. On finishing our meal we were told to find a bunk in any of the huts scattered around the camp. It had once been a prisoner of war camp, so conditions were quite primitive. Inside the huts were two and three tiered wooden bunks. Straw palliasses lay on top of wooden slats, except they had no straw. We did succeed in promoting a cross fertilisation between the fleas we had inherited from the train, and the army of monsters that dwelt in these bunks. We couldn't sleep – we could only rest and lie awake all night vigorously scratching, but consoling ourselves that Blighty was just twenty odd miles away.

On the Sunday morning we were sent for to change our francs into sterling. They must have thought we were all poverty stricken when no one took advantage of the offer.

We then had to fill in a customs declaration form, and given a stern warning about undeclared goods. I had no money to pay duty on Anne's ring, so I sewed it into the small finger of my woollen gloves and vowed not to blush when going through the customs.

After final instructions, we were marched to the quay where the 'Golden Arrow' was already being loaded with our kitbags and hammocks. We filed aboard and for many of the sailors this was to be their last seagoing trip. For the many hundreds of soldiers and airmen, this was the beginning of their leave, but for us it was the gateway to a life in civvy street.

The Channel crossing was calm but very cold, and visibility was not very good – in fact, we saw little of the French coast, and the white cliffs of Dover were covered in a veil of mist.

The thought in all our minds was, "Will we get leave tonight?" They had already told us that the other services would disembark first. Why this was so I do not know, but it seemed pointless for people to refer to you as the senior service and then to stop you leaving the bloody ship.

At long last, we went down the gangway and into the huge customs shed. Long horseshoe-shaped counters took up most of the space. A Customs Officer told us to put our cases and bags on the counters and to open them up. A quick glance at my shipmates told me that they were feeling as apprehensive as I was. I only hoped that the Customs men did not notice the expressions of guilt. I opened mine, and then one of the Customs men called out, "Don't worry lads, do your cases up. It's the Air Force and the Army we are after, for they are on leave every three or four months."

"Thank God for that," whispered one of the lads. "I've got five thousand fags in mine."

A train was waiting to take us to Victoria, and as we entered so the contrast between these carriages and the French ones became most noticeable. First of all the warmth hit us with welcome waves, then the luxury of the padded seats and the comfort. Things we used to take for granted now assumed airs of great importance – they were signs that we were truly back in the old country.

As the train pulled out, so the English countryside flashed by. It was like an intoxicating drink, a drink that made one light headed and happy. This was England, the finest country in the world. The trees stripped of their leaves looked good and solid. Everything that came into view was as though it were a symbol, a sign which, while we were away, had meant something to us. It was as though our absence had bred in us a greater appreciation, a greater awareness of all the things we held dear.

For a fleeting moment I took my eyes away from the passing countryside and looked at the other occupants of the compartment. No one was speaking and each of them gazed out of the windows, silently revelling in the moving picture before them. They sat as though hypnotised, lighted cigarettes smouldering unsmoked between fingers, their eyes transfixed, and yet even as I observed all this, I knew that their thoughts were also my thoughts.

Getting near to London so the scenery changed. The green fields and rolling hills gave way to row after row of little cramped terrace houses. Each had a small back yard cluttered with old tin baths, boxes and all the junk imaginable. Many of them still had the Anderson Air Raid Shelters, and here and there a gap in the terrace was a grim reminder of the suffering a little family had experienced at the hands of an enemy aircraft. The walls of these small dwellings were still grimy, and the woodwork had not seen a paintbrush since before the war. The fences were falling into decay, but far from feeling sad I felt happy for them. One had to look further than dirty walls and peeling paintwork. You had to imagine that each of these dwellings was a little castle and that the wives and children had held the fort against air attacks, rockets, buzz bombs and the shortage of food and clothing while husbands were away in the forces. Those box-like little places took on a new dimension, waiting to welcome the menfolk back into a cocoon of love and warmth and happiness. Yes, the old saying that you cannot judge a book by its cover applies to so many things, but none more than the brave hearted inhabitants, who refused to give in.

Why the train went via London instead of direct to Portsmouth I don't know, but it did, and we were warm and comfortable and happy with our private thoughts.

Arriving at Portsmouth, we still retained an air of optimism that tonight we would be on leave, so to expedite that happy moment we all set too to unload the gear. The Chiefs and Petty Officers were happy to sit back and watch us also moving their gear, but we did not mind if by so doing it assisted us to go on leave.

Would we never learn? Had we not been in the Navy long enough to know that our hopes and aspirations would not be fulfilled? The Chiefs and the POs knew, which is why they sat back with smug complacent grins on their faces, while we did all the work. In the twilight of our Naval service, we were still naïve, simple idiots.

Had we given the matter a little more thought, we would have realised that they would not have granted leave on a Sunday night, and certainly not without seeing the Commander of the barracks first.

We were sent to HMS Victory barracks at Portsmouth, and were being housed in a double floored wooden hut situated behind the huge Victorian brick edifices. To our surprise, there were a number of men lounging about in civilian clothes. On enquiry it transpired that they had returned to the Navy after sampling civilian life.

"It's a swine," they said. "No jobs, low pay, can't keep pace with it."

There is no doubt that especially to full-time sailors, civvy street can be hard. In the Andrew all your needs are catered for – food, clothing, accommodation. You don't have to worry about a house or rates or lighting or heating, and I can see that suddenly acquiring this type of responsibility can be too much for some men.

Our experience of the outside world was limited to the information contained in the newspapers, and from them we gleaned a world of plenty of jobs, high wages and security. Somehow the two sides did not add up, so we reserved our judgement.

That evening we spent our time in the wet canteen and had a sing-song.

On the following morning, Monday, we had all written out requests for leave, and promptly presented them to the appropriate office. By midday we were informed that our requests had been granted and that we could have eight days leave. There was now a flurry of activity, kitbags and hammocks had to be stowed in a kit store. Ration tickets, a rail warrant and money were also needed.

Once again we were on a train speeding towards London. By the time I got to Waterloo it was dark, but I soon found the connection for Staines, and then I had a surprise – it was the lights. London was lit up. This was something I had not thought about. I stared with child-like fascination. My mind turned back the years. This was 1947 and I was twenty one and had lived within sixteen miles of London nearly all my life, yet I could not remember having seen the lights before. It is true the blackout came into operation when I was thirteen, but I had no prior recollection of these millions of lights. There were so many things I had lived with for years, but seeing them now for the first time with the eyes of a child, I welcomed each discovery with enthusiasm.

At long last, as I stood before my home, I noticed the lights shining through the stained glass in the front door. I rang the bell and as its ring echoed inside so I could see additional lights as the kitchen door opened. I was pent up with excitement as I heard the sound of feet rushing along the hall. Ma was first, then little John, now not so small with his tousled hair. My father's huge frame appeared and blocked the passage, while Brian struggled to look over his shoulder. A warm homely aroma filled my nostrils. The next few minutes were filled with the usual embraces and welcomes that take place when a family comes together.

Very soon I opened my case and handed gifts to Ma and Pa and my brothers, Brian and John. This was accompanied with stories of my travels and adventures.

I had been very conscious that in this last two days the train had passed very near to where my beloved Anne was now staying. For while I was away she had moved down to a village near Guildford, but she had made me promise that I would devote the first three days of my homecoming to my family, and this I did, but my heart just yearned to see her again.

The third day arrived and, with a thumping heart and weak legs, I made my way to the bus that would take me to Woking. There I changed and caught a local bus to the beautiful little village of West Clandon near Guildford. As I got off the bus I looked around me for the name of the house, but it wasn't necessary, for running across the road came the loveliest, most beautiful and sweetest girl you ever did see.

When you have been away for some time from the one you hold most dear, there is always the fear – have either of you changed in affection or feeling for the other? I knew that as I took her into my arms and held her tight, my love was as sure as ever.

Anne had met my parents while I was away; nevertheless I wanted to take her home with me. She was, in fact, the very first young lady I had ever taken home.

The family went to bed while Anne and I sat by the fire. We didn't talk about the past but the present and vowed our love a thousand times.

I was indeed a very happy man.

Chapter 35

Demobilisation

On returning from our leave, we were transferred to Victoria Barracks at Southsea. This was far more pleasing than Pompey, and the discipline was not so strict.

I decided that as I was so near to my demob I was worthy of a more relaxed life than that experienced so far. Had my superiors known about this, they would have no doubt formed a very harsh and contrary point of view. To achieve my object, it was necessary to use the system. One can achieve much more by using the system than bucking it, so at this late stage I was learning fast.

Courses had been introduced for Educational and Vocational Training (EVT). The idea was to make our passage into civilian life smoother. The courses were held in Pompey Barracks, so I duly applied.

These courses opened up all sorts of possibilities not connected with the course, for example. The winter of 1947 was bitter. Snow lay thick on the ground, and there was no heating at Southsea, whereas the classrooms where the courses were held were warm and dry. Further, free bus tickets to the value of three pence a day were granted. We signed into Barracks and we signed out, but no one checked.

I found the course interesting and educational, and the roaring coal fire in the grate engendered a degree of sympathy for those men that could be seen sweeping the snow off the parade ground.

During the morning break we had priority passes for the canteen, and at lunchtime if I didn't fancy going back to Southsea, I would frequent the magnificent new NAAFI canteen in town. They had papers and books to read in a beautiful lounge, plus a wireless to listen to.

There were similar procedures at teatime, and in the mornings there were opportunities to lie in bed longer. One also had the choice of having breakfast either in the Barracks or one of the small shops along the waterfront. The only limitation to all this was the size of one's pocket.

We were allowed a long weekend leave occasionally and again the course had advantages, for the reason I could leave from Pompey rather than Southsea, which was nearer the station. Further, I could check out on the course early on the pretence of going back to Southsea, but in fact going straight to the railway station. It is true I only gained three to four hours, but every minute was important on a weekend leave.

Back in Southsea, our barrack room was at the top of a large block of buildings. Most of the lads were off the *Mauritius,* including some who had left the ship before we went up to Trieste, so all my fears of being last were, in the end, of no consequence. We in the main were a cheerful gathering, though a condition called 'demob happy' was prevalent among the lads. Demob Happy was a mental condition that allowed the affiliated person to adopt a cavalier and could not care less attitude toward officialdom while maintaining a degree of anxiety regarding the delay and time it took to become demobilised.

By coincidence, the sailor who fell overboard from *HMS Leander* while she, with ourselves and the rest of the fleet, were undertaking manoeuvres off the Greek coast, told us his side of the story.

Apparently he had been working outside on the guardrails, had a blackout and fell over the side. He was picked up and taken immediately to the Medical Officer, who confirmed he was none the worse for his adventure. He was then clapped in the cells. Eventually they sent him back to the Naval hospital in Malta, where several neurological tests were carried out.

Nothing amiss was found, but they still sent him home. I must confess that if I had been the Medical Officer, I would have had second thoughts about my diagnosis.

The general level of conversation concerned our occupation in civvy street. Some favoured the Fire Service, others the Police, and one lad wanted to express his artistic flare – though from what I saw of it at E.V.T. centre it was pretty lousy. Others had an easy and foolproof guaranteed system to win on the horses, but whatever our preferences we were all united in one thing, none of us were going to re-join the Royal Navy.

One lunchtime, we were sitting in the mess when suddenly one of the lads burst in.

"The lists are up," he yelled.

We all made a hurried exodus, knocking tables and benches over in the rush to see if our name was shown. There was a huge crowd gathered around the noticeboard, but I gathered the notice advised that we would be demobilised in alphabetical order. Just my bloody luck – why did I have to be at the end of the alphabet?

On the third day, the third list went up and they hadn't even reached C. It was as if I was going to be there forever. I didn't even bother to go and look and then, "Quick, quick they've changed their minds," yelled someone.

I leapt off the bench with optimistic enthusiasm and ran downstairs. The notice read that demobilisation in alphabetical order had proved to be impractical, so names were now being taken at random. I then looked at the list and oh glorious, happy days there it was. The clouds had lifted, and with them my spirits.

The following day, those on the list were sent to Portsmouth Barracks. We joined a new mess and told that we would be demobbed the very next day on Friday. Part of the leaving routine would be carried out on Thursday and part on Friday, and the sooner we did it, the sooner we would leave. I needed no second bidding and literally ran from place to place. Each of us had been given a card which had a grid printed on it. Each box stood for something and needed to be initialled – for example, there was the Medical Officer, the Dental Officer, the gas mask centre, the lifebelt centre, the X-Ray room. When I went for the medical inspection I was looked over very quickly and asked if I felt alright, and then told to sign a paper saying I had been passed A1. Many of the lads, in a hurry to get out, were happy to sign it, but I refused for the reason that I wanted it on record regarding the problem with my legs.

The Medical Officer said, "I will offer you an operation and you can stay in the service a little longer."

This sort of talk usually encouraged men to sign, but I said, "No, Sir, I've already had one operation and that didn't do any good, so I will sign the papers, but add a rider to say I have varicose veins and that I have refused an operation because the previous one was a failure."

He agreed to this, and I was satisfied that it was now on record.

By Thursday night I had completed my routine faster than anybody, but that was nearly the cause of my undoing.

We had been split up into four parties, and I was in the first, but officialdom found out from my form that instead of putting my forenames in full, I had just put the initials. For my error the Chief took me out of the first party and put me at the end of the fourth one, telling me at the same time that I was lucky not to be kept in barracks for my sins. Internally I seethed at such pettiness, but with the gate to freedom so near I held my peace.

We collected our pay and were allowed to sell our biscuits (mattresses) to a private concern. The mattresses were less than five foot in length and were apparently used for children's cots. It does not sound very hygienic, but in times of shortages, beliefs and principles tend to get a little distorted. We boarded a lorry to take us to Cosham, and as we passed through the huge gates of Portsmouth Naval Barracks, there was an audible sigh of relief. All of us were tempted to utter a few chosen words of farewell, but a wise voice from the back said, "Don't say what you are thinking. They can still take us back."

When we arrived at Cosham, our measurements were taken – head, chest, height, feet, shoulders, legs. We then went from one counter to another collecting a suit, hat, shirts, shoes, etc. We were fully kilted out with civilian clothes, which was a wonderful feeling. In retrospect it would today take longer to purchase a shirt than it took us to be equipped with everything, but the system worked almost like a conveyor belt – plus the fact that all we wanted to do was to get away with a seventy day leave pass in our pocket, at the end of which we would be free men.

For a long time I had dreamed of this moment, and at the back of my mind I had always felt that when this day arrived I wanted to have with me everything that I had gained since first I left home. I stood on Portsmouth Station with these thoughts going through my mind, but I felt incomplete; my most precious and cherished possession was missing, my beloved Anne, the young lady to whom I was now engaged. I rang her up and she promised to meet me on Guildford Station. She arrived soon after I had left the train and no one, not even Anne, will ever know the happiness I experienced having her by my side.

Arriving home it was as though the wheel had completed its circuit, and so as one phase in life closes another starts.

Although my story really ends here, I could not close it without reflecting on this period in my life. It would be very easy to assume that because I was so anxious to get out it means that I was unhappy in the Navy. This is not so. I have packed into my short period of service more excitement and adventure than most men have in a lifetime. I have no regrets; indeed, I am pleased and proud to have served my country, and to have met men from all walks of life, from different social backgrounds, different educations, different nationalities and different religions, but they all had one thing in common – they were all bound together by threads of gold that collectively made them shipmates. It is very hard for anyone who has never been part of a ship's crew to understand this bond. It is like a brotherhood that is difficult to believe exists anywhere except among men of the sea.

My experiences have broadened my outlook. It has helped me to understand without having to agree the thoughts of others. It has helped me to tolerate men who believe themselves to be men of principle, but whose actions suggest to the contrary. It has helped me in so many ways, but the greatest of these is the indebtedness I owe to the Royal Navy for allowing my old ship *HMS Vindex* to call in at Lam Lash in the Isle of Arran, and thereby giving me the opportunity of meeting such a wonderful young lady. Yes, I am glad I am out, but I was happy to be in.